Eve's Monsters

- Book 1 of the Abomination Series -

By Felicity Thorne

This is a work of fiction. Names (excluding historical figures), characters, businesses, places, events and incidents are either the products of the author's imagination or used in a fictitious manner. Any resemblance to actual persons, living or dead, or actual events is purely coincidental.

Any trivial references made to real people, places, or media is done so without malice or endorsement.

Enjoy!

The Abomination Series:
Eve's Monsters
Eve's Curse
Eve's Sins
Eve's Revelations

Check out the accompanying Spotify playlist:

The Abomination Series by Felicity Thorne
https://open.spotify.com/playlist/6rVzdKXwm0lk5Bsz1G3SqZ?si=
HgeRqP-KSnyqk7RcltflDg&pi=9X79qnTQQcS8F

"He who fights with monsters might take care lest he thereby become a monster. And if you gaze for long into an abyss, the abyss gazes also into you."

-Nietzsche

1
Are You Going to Play Nice?

Eve slowly blinked her eyes open, her lids heavy and drooping. Through dry, blurry eyes and the pastel pink hair hanging in her face, she tried to scan her surroundings, but she could only make out basic shapes and colors. The comfortable temperature and scent of wood and stone and plaster told her that she was indoors. She shifted her weight in the hard, straight-backed chair in which she was seated, and it creaked. Wood. She tried to reach up to rub her eyes to clear her vision, but quickly discovered her wrists were bound to the arms of the chair with rough cloth.

Movement caught her attention, and she fought to focus on the tall, black mass that passed in front of her. She clenched her eyes shut, then blinked repeatedly. Her sight was beginning to restore, but it was taking longer than she would've liked.

"I'm sorry about the theatrics," a smooth, confident male voice spoke. She watched the black mass shrink down to her level, and she heard the creak of a chair. She could now make out the shape of a man with an odd shock of platinum white hair. His fuzzy outline leaned forward in his chair, resting his elbows on his knees, his hands folded under his chin. "I'm sure we'll get along just fine, but until I know for sure, I don't want you hurting yourself."

Eve coughed to clear her dry throat. She croaked, "What is this?"

"This is your interview. Don't worry, you're doing splendidly so far," he said cheerfully.

"Interview or interrogation?" Eve asked spitefully as she tried to move her feet, only to find her ankles were bound to the legs of the chair.

"I don't know that there's much of a difference, really. I guess an interview is more polite, maybe? So, I suppose, it's up to you whether this is an interview or interrogation. Are you going to play nice?"

"I don't play."

He laughed. "Oh, but you do. You're playing tough guy right now. It's cute. But I'm going to level with you: it won't help. I'm not interested in how tough you think you are. Just be straight with me and you'll be out of those bindings in no time."

"And what happens then?"

"That remains to be determined. Are you ready to begin?"

"Do I have a choice?"

"Do you not know how an interview works? I'm supposed to ask the questions, and you're supposed to answer. You're not very good at this. I know I said you were doing splendidly a minute ago, but now you're kind of floundering."

Eve could see him clearly now. He was seated, but she could tell he was tall and well-built, with long legs and broad shoulders. He wore a black, long-sleeved shirt and black slacks, and when he moved, she could see that his body filled those clothes quite nicely. His eyes were obscured by odd little round-framed sunglasses, but his face was symmetrical, smooth, and handsome. And younger than she expected. He looked to be in his late twenties or early thirties, but that platinum white hair was unusual. It was just long enough on top that it might hang over his forehead and into his eyes if it weren't so impeccably styled. His calm, arrogant, but intrigued expression did nothing to put her at ease. Psychopaths were great at making that face.

She set her jaw and fought the urge to ask more questions as she glanced around at the room she was in. It seemed to be a rather elaborate library, the likes of which one might find in an old English abbey. Or a Disney movie with singing beasts.

"Well, I can't say you're *floundering*," he amended. "You're remarkably calm, so, kudos for that. Some people wake up in that chair and utterly lose their shit. But it does make me wonder *why* you aren't utterly losing your shit."

Eve just stared at him, and he stared back – or at least, she assumed he did. Was he blind? Is that what the sunglasses were hiding? She twisted her wrist under the bindings and flipped him off.

He raised his eyebrows, which Eve noticed were just as white as the hair on his head. "Well, maybe later, if you're offering. But first I'd like to know if I have to kill you or not."

Those words shot like ice through Eve's veins. Her calm façade threatened to crack.

The man leaned back in his chair and rested his arm on the back of it, crossing one long leg over the other. Eve noticed the flash of red on the bottom of his shoes. Louboutins? Who the hell was this guy?

"You're Evrys Alarie," he stated. "But you go by Eve. Twenty-six. You're single and you live alone. Estranged from your family. You're a hobby painter, but you make the majority of your income by entering and generally dominating amateur MMA tournaments. Your hands, and therefore your art, must suffer for it, but for some reason, you persist. Why?"

"I see you've read my Tinder profile."

"Sarcasm as a defensive tactic. Cliché. Don't be boring and predictable, Eve. Predictable gets you killed. Just answer the question."

Ok, ouch. "Why do I keep painting, or why do I keep fighting?"

"Yes."

Eve furrowed her brow at him. "I suppose I like it. All of it. It's not one or the other for me. And it never affects my art. My hands heal quickly."

"Hm. Have you ever killed anything?"

Eve hesitated. "Like, people? Or animals?"

"Or anything in between."

"Uh…I guess I've run over animals with my car…"

"On purpose?"

"No. I'm not a psychopath."

He smiled pleasantly at her. "You say that like you're sure of it. And proud of it."

"I am…I guess?"

"Oh, now you sound like you're not sure of it. *Are* you a psychopath?"

"No!"

"How do you know?"

"I just do!"

"You're awfully defensive. Methinks the lady doth protest too much."

"I'm not crazy, ok?"

"I didn't say you were crazy. Why would you say that?"

"You're trying to make me sound crazy," Eve argued.

"*You're* making you sound crazy. Do you even know you?"

"Yes! And you don't know me, so quit acting like you do!"

He suddenly slid his chair right up to Eve's, the knee of one long, lean leg bumping up against the edge of her chair between her legs. He rested his elbow on that knee and propped his chin on his fist, his face close to hers. With one finger, he tapped the side of his sunglasses, causing them to slide half an inch down his nose. He tilted his head down and looked over the top of his sunglasses at her with the most startlingly aqua-blue eyes Eve had ever seen. They were mesmerizing.

"I would like to know you," he purred. His beautiful eyes searched hers. "And I sincerely hope that there's a crazy little psychopath in there somewhere."

"You smell expensive," Eve replied. It was neither here nor there, but it was the first appropriate thought in a long string of thoughts that popped into her head in that moment.

He grinned, then pushed his sunglasses back up his nose to hide his eyes. "Oh, I come cheap." With a flash of silver, Eve felt the binding on her right hand loosen and fall away. She watched him quickly slice his knife through the rest of her bindings, wondering where he'd been hiding it and when he'd unsheathed it.

"You're letting me go?"

"I didn't say that."

"So, what, you don't think I'm a threat to you anymore?"

He laughed again. He had such an easy laugh. "I never did."

"So why tie me up?!"

"So you wouldn't do anything foolish and make me hurt you. But I think we're beyond that." He stood up and pulled his chair away from hers, then sheathed his knife under his sleeve.

This guy was kind of terrifying. "Who are you, and why am I here?" Eve asked.

"Oh, wow, I didn't introduce myself, did I?" He held his hand out to her. "I'm Lucius Fagerberg, but everyone calls me Luc. And you're here because you're special."

Eve scoffed. "And now I know you're full of shit."

Luc shook head and stuck his hands in his pockets. "Oh, come now. Self-deprecation? Boring. Disappointing. Don't bore me, Eve."

"It's not my job to entertain you."

He shrugged his shoulders. "It would be in your best interest, though."

"I've kept my cool. I haven't screamed or 'lost my shit,' as you said. That must count for something."

"Oh, it does. Points. Gold star. And that's how I know you're an excellent candidate."

"What do you want from me?"

Luc smiled mischievously. "I want to know if you'll kill for me."

Eve was taken aback. "Kill who?"

Luc turned his back on her and started fingering the books on the shelf behind him. "More like kill *what*, but I do love that you immediately assume it's a *who*. I mean, I suppose sometimes it's a *who*."

She folded her arms over her chest and crossed her legs. "I'm beginning to think you actually enjoy the theatrics you apologized for earlier."

He chuckled. "Oh, I absolutely do. Never trust an easy apology." He pulled a book off the shelf and sauntered over to her. He held the book out to her.

Eve took the large, black, hardcover book from his hand and read the title. "*Grimm's Fairy Tales*?" she read aloud. "What's this for?"

"*Grimm's Fairy Tales* – fact or fiction?" he asked.

Eve looked at him skeptically. "I want to say fiction, but I have a feeling you're going to say fact."

"What? No. Of course it's fiction."

"...Ok..."

"But the creatures aren't."

"And there it is."

"There it is," he parroted.

"And now you're going to tell me you chose me to fight these evil creatures to save the world."

Luc narrowed his eyes at her – or, she assumed he did, but she couldn't see them behind his sunglasses. "Did you get a peek at my script?"

"This is ridiculous." Eve sighed in irritation and pushed up from her chair.

"Oh good, I was so hoping that would be your response."

"Why?"

"Because it makes this next part so much more fun." He pulled the knife back out of his sleeve and handed it to her, then took his sunglasses off and hung them from the collar of his shirt. He stood in front of her with his hands folded behind his back, piercing her with the gaze from those crystal-clear aquamarine eyes. "Stab me in the face," he requested.

Eve scoffed incredulously. "I am *not* doing that." It would be a shame to mess up that masterpiece, she thought.

"Fine, punch me in the face. Or gut. Or wherever." He raised his eyebrows and giddily proposed, "Ooh, surprise me."

"I'm not hitting you. This is nonsense."

He pouted. "Really? You're a lot less fun than I hoped you would be." He reached out and grabbed the front of Eve's shirt in his fist and pulled her body roughly against his. She clenched her eyes shut moments before his lips came crushing down against hers.

He tasted a little like expensive whiskey. When she felt his tongue invade past her lips, her eyes shot open and she pulled away, her fist reflexively striking out at his face.

Then the strangest thing happened. Right before her eyes, the shape of her fist warped and contoured itself through the air just millimeters around his face. Her hand didn't hurt or feel any differently, but she could *see* it happen, and her hand passed right across in front of him without resistance. Eve lost her balance, expecting an impact that didn't occur, and Luc tightened his grip on her shirt to steady her.

Now it was time to lose her shit. "What the fuck was that?!" she shrieked, trying to push him away. He held tight to her shirt for a moment longer, then released her. She jumped back two paces.

"Stupid, right?" he teased. He flashed a devastating smile. "I love the expression on your face right now."

She sort of loved the expression on his, too, but that was beside the point. "How did you do that?!"

He held up jazz hands and said, "Magic!"

"Really?!"

"No, not really. That's stupid." When she fixed him with an irritated stare, he laughed and put his sunglasses back on. "I just warped the space around my face that your hand was occupying."

"How is that not magic?!"

"Because it's physics."

"Not normal physics."

"Yes, normal physics. Abnormal physiology."

"But you can be touched. Your mouth touched mine. How did you make my hand go around you?"

"It's these eyes. They can warp space at my whim."

"But *how*?" she marveled.

He shrugged casually. "I don't know. I just can. I've heard the nerds at the Vatican call me the Black Hole, but that's not entirely accurate." He paused. "Though, now that I think about it, maybe they said I was 'the *ass*hole.' That's more accurate."

"The *Vatican*?"

There was a knock on the door that Eve didn't even realize was behind her.

"Come in," Luc called in a singsong tone.

In walked a man who bore a mild resemblance to Luc. He was tall and lean as well, but Luc had a few inches on him. But it was his hair that first caught her attention – it was silver-white, much like Luc's. His attire, however, was quite different. He wore all black like Luc, but his outfit looked more like military fatigues, and rather than Louboutin's, he wore old black combat boots. He had a mask pulled up over his nose and the lower half of his face and neck, like a tight-fitting gaiter.

His most striking feature, though, was his mismatched eyes. He had one charcoal gray eye, and one bright, aquamarine eye. So it came as little surprise when Luc introduced him as his older brother, Bo.

"Well, half-brother," Luc corrected. "My brother from another mother. His real name is Babhdán, but we call him Bo. He hates being called Babhdán, don't you, Babhdán?"

Bo couldn't have looked less impressed with Luc. But when he turned to Eve, those mismatched eyes looked at her with a surprisingly kindly expression that indicated he was smiling beneath the mask. She tried not to stare at the long, vertical scar over the darker eye as she shook his hand. Was it different from the other eye because he had injured it? It looked like a perfectly well-functioning eye.

"I apologize for him. He thinks he's charming," Bo said in a kind tone. He felt like someone who could be trusted...unlike his brother.

"I was just showing her my specialty," Luc said suggestively.

Bo raised one eyebrow. "I don't need to know about all that."

Luc laughed boisterously and clapped his hand on Bo's shoulder. "I showed her mine. Wanna show her yours?"

Bo's cheeks were suddenly tinged pink where they were visible above his mask. He pulled a folded-up paper out of his pocket and slapped it forcefully against Luc's chest. Luc took it from him and unfolded it as Bo explained, "Bear attack up at Sugarloaf. College student."

Luc scanned the paper before him, then folded it back up and stuck it in his pocket. "Anybody nearby?"

"I think Remi, Ruger, and Cassie are out that way investigating a wolf case."

"Ah, Team Flannel. Good. They blend in up there. They can handle that." Luc turned his attention back to Eve. "Remi and Ruger are two of our hunters. Brothers. Their specialty is rather unique: they don't stay dead. Cassie is Ruger's wife, and a real savant with a blade."

"And I take it they're hunting fairy tale creatures?" Eve surmised sarcastically.

"Who's afraid of the big, bad wolf?" Luc replied, imitating claws with his hands.

Eve looked at Bo. "Is this guy fucking with me?"

Bo looked at Luc. "As a general rule, yes, but in this case, no."

"So what the hell am I doing here? And while we're at it, where exactly is 'here'?"

Luc raised his arms wide. "Welcome to Knighco - Knights of the Holy Covenant!" When Eve gave him a strange look, Luc said, "I know, it's boring. We run it under cover of a religious monastery."

"Boring is good," Bo pointed out. "We're not trying to draw attention."

"Or pay taxes. But boring is *boring*," Luc complained.

"Great, so where do *I* fit into all of this?" Eve asked impatiently.

"Ideally..." Luc began, then grabbed Eve by the shoulders and moved her to stand next to Bo. He continued, "Right here."

"She's Shira's replacement?!" Bo was taken aback.

Luc smirked. "She has *das blut*, Bo."

They both looked at Eve, Luc with a smug, satisfied grin, and Bo with an expression of disbelief.

2

Only Monsters Can Kill Monsters

"*Das blut*? What the hell does that mean?" Eve demanded.

"'The blood.' It means you're special, Eve," Luc said simply.

"Yeah, you said that already. I need more than that."

"Eve, when was the last time you were sick?"

She was quiet for a long time. "I don't know…but I was really sick for a long time when I was a kid. I guess I almost died, but I don't remember much from it."

"When you turned thirteen?" Bo chimed in.

Eve was startled. "Yeah. Well, I got sick the day before my thirteenth birthday. It was Halloween. How did you know?"

"They couldn't figure out what was wrong with you, and then you miraculously got better two months later," Bo stated.

"…Yeah."

Bo turned to Luc. "How did you find her?" he asked.

"I didn't. Mira and Celeste did. They were searching hospital records for signs of previously untraced blood healers, since Shira's family tree was a dead end. Eve just kind of popped up out of nowhere. No family history of it on her mother's side, and no record of her father on the birth certificate. Must be from his side, whoever he is. Or was."

"Have they tested her yet?"

"Preliminarily. She looks to be the real deal. Would you like a taste?"

"I'm not injured."

"I can amend that for you," Luc offered darkly.

Eve took a step back from the two men. Their conversation was making her deeply uneasy. "Tell me what all of that means. Please. And if you say 'you're special' one more time, I'm going to…" Eve couldn't think of a threat that would work, so she just let it hang in the air, unfinished.

"Well, it's your *blood* that's special, to be precise," Luc said. He reached out and took Eve's arm gently in his hands, then moved closer to her as he ran his fingertips over her skin. He lifted her hand and brought the delicate underside of her wrist close to his lips. "Your blood, when ingested straight from your veins, can heal injury, disease, infection…" He ran his tongue lightly across her wrist. She gasped and pulled back, but his grip tightened, holding her firmly. "Basically, if the body is trying to fix it, your blood will make it so."

"Luc," Bo warned in a low voice.

Luc grinned and kissed Eve's wrist, then released it. She yanked it back and held it to her chest. "What do you mean 'ingested from my veins'?"

"I mean you can't just bottle it and sell it. It has to be straight from the tap."

"Why?"

"Because one of the healing properties is your own chakra - your energy field, or life force, if you will. If you separate the blood from your body, it just becomes regular, boring blood."

"So, for it to heal you, you'd have to suck it out of me like a vampire?"

"Yes."

"Ew."

Luc clicked his tongue. "No, not ew. It's actually quite erotic. You'll see."

"So, who is Shira?"

Luc replied, "Our late blood healer."

Bo said softly, "Shira was part of my team. She died last year."

"Died? Does our own blood not work on ourselves?"

Luc explained, "It has its limits, like any specialty. It can't stop an imminent death. But it makes you immune to illness, including the curses passed through the monsters we hunt, and it makes you heal faster than most. That's why you don't suffer the same long-term injuries seen in most MMA fighters."

"But I was so sick I almost died as a kid."

"That was your specialty's activation phase. Most people with your specialty don't survive activation."

"How many people have this kind of specialty?" Eve asked.

"It's incredibly rare." Luc took Eve's face in his hands. "You, my dear, are very valuable indeed."

"So you never intended to kill me, like you threatened earlier," she deduced flatly.

"Oh, god no. Idle threats are simply my love language." He stepped back and clapped his hands together. "All right! Shall we take the tour and meet your new family?"

"Wait, wait, wait," Eve protested. "I haven't agreed to anything! I don't even know how I got here! Or how much of this insanity I'm willing to believe! Or where this monastery is! And what about my apartment and my job? Do you expect me to just drop everything and join this...this...*cult*?"

"Yes," Luc replied simply. "Even if we brought you home and said, 'Oh, never mind,' do you think you would be satisfied with that?"

After a moment's contemplation, Eve realized he was right. She would forever be wondering.

He continued, "Oh, and as for how we got you here, I had to drug you. We have a talented young man here who has a rather…skilled tongue, but it didn't seem to work on you."

"Excuse me?"

Bo clarified, "His specialty is the power of persuasion. If he says 'sleep,' you sleep."

"Or if he says 'come'…" Luc said seductively.

"Luc," Bo chastised.

"…you come running," Luc finished. He looked at Bo innocently. "What were *you* thinking?"

Bo blushed hard and turned away from them. He grumbled, "Let's go." He shoved his hands in his pockets and exited out the same door he'd entered from.

Luc grinned with amusement and grabbed Eve's hand in his enormous mitt, strutting along behind Bo and dragging her along with him.

Eve was led along a long corridor before they reached a tall staircase that led up to a metal door with an industrial-grade locking mechanism. Bo entered a code that Eve didn't see, and they stepped out into a vast garage, but only a couple of cars were parked inside.

"You need a giant garage for a compact car and an SUV?" she asked.

"We have more, but they're out right now," Luc explained.

They walked through the garage and exited out into the daylight. Eve looked around at her unexpected surroundings. "This doesn't look like a monastery," she said. Aside from the garage they'd just exited, all she saw was what looked like a dorm or apartment complex.

"That's because it isn't, obviously. It's more like a compound. It's mostly underground," Luc replied. "Except for the apartments. Nobody wants to *live* underground."

"Where is everyone?" Eve asked. It seemed deserted.

"Summer is our busy season, so most teams are out on missions. But luckily for you, your team just got back the other day."

"My team, huh?"

"Well, Bo's team. Everyone is put into a team. Bo is your team leader. Your captain."

"And what are you?"

"I guess you could say I'm in charge of distribution. I assign teams to cases."

"Who's in charge, then?"

"That would be Sister Fiona. You won't see much of her. She prefers to run things from behind the scenes."

"Wait, are you guys actually a religious organization?" Eve asked.

"Not exactly, but Sister Fiona is a nun. Legit. She has connections to the Vatican, and you wouldn't believe the kind of information and resources the Catholic church has amassed regarding monsters. *Unholy things*," he added sarcastically. "The Vatican keeps an eye on us, though, because some of us also fall into the realm of *unholy things*. While we aren't fully under their direction, we do try to keep them happy so they don't give us trouble."

They walked across the paved path from the garage to the apartment building, and Bo entered another access code at the door. When they entered, Eve was underwhelmed. It opened into a large main room that looked like a lobby, and there were hallways on either side. There was a staircase to her left.

Eve could hear male voices coming from above her. There were two men talking as they descended the stairs.

The first voice was energetic and excited. "I call dibs if she's pretty. God, I hope she's pretty. We don't have enough pretty hunters."

"Who cares," an annoyed, deeper voice replied. "I just hope she doesn't drag us down."

Bo cleared his throat loudly and called out, "Zeke! Eoduun!"

"Oh, shit," the first voice whispered. "I think they heard us."

One set of footsteps raced down the stairs, and a young man in his early to mid-twenties rounded the corner and jumped down the entire last flight of stairs. He was wearing gray sweatpants with white high tops and a baggy orange hoodie. He smiled brightly at Eve, his caramel-brown eyes sparkling. His eager face was quite pleasing to the eyes. He ran one hand through his medium-length, sandy-brown hair and held his other hand out to Eve.

"I'm Zeke! Zeke Gagliardi. Nice to meet you!" he greeted.

She shook his hand. "Eve," she said.

The other man rounded the corner on the stairs at a much more leisurely pace than Zeke, and Eve looked up at him. He was dressed more formally than his friend, with dark jeans, a lavender long-sleeved shirt, and a gray vest. He stopped on the stairs and stared down at her for a moment, his onyx eyes appraising her critically from behind the long, dark hair hanging over his face. He looked to be similar in age to Zeke. He then looked at Bo. "Is she staying?"

Bo nodded. Then to Eve, Bo said, "This is Eoduun Kwon. Eoduun lacks manners, but I'm working on it."

Eoduun scoffed, but said nothing more. He leaned against the rail and remained on the stairs.

Zeke never took his eyes off of Eve. "Welcome to the team!" he said. "Do you have a specialty? I used to only have one – crazy strength – but now I guess I can kind of do other stuff because a witch trapped Dagon inside of me. And Eoduun is an eraser."

Eve just stared at him, not knowing what to say.

"She has no idea what the fuck you're talking about, Z," Eoduun said.

"There's a lot yet to explain," Bo said. "We'll get there."

Luc placed his hand on her shoulder. "I'll leave you for now so you can all get acquainted. But I'll check in on you later." He looked at Bo as he turned to leave. "I'm counting on you, Bo. Show her to her apartment and give her the rundown."

"Oh! You're across the hall from me!" Zeke exclaimed. "I can show you!"

This guy's energy was infectious. She followed him up the stairs as Bo brought up the rear. She was shown to her apartment, which was a surprisingly comfortable one-bedroom with a sizeable living room and a nice kitchen. They then brought her to the gym, which had weights, cardio equipment, heavy bags, sparring mats and pads, and a boxing ring.

"Do you do training for your specialties?" she asked.

"Oh, there are training grounds outside and there are reinforced rooms in the underground bunker," Zeke explained. "I used to have a room they set aside for me whenever Dagon would act up. But I have him under control now. For the most part. I mean, it's easy to control him right now, but when I get worked up, he still gets out sometimes. But he's not allowed to kill anyone who isn't a monster."

Eve gave him a sideways glance. They talked about fighting monsters, but to her, *he* sounded like a monster.

"I'm sure you'll meet Dagon soon enough," he continued. "I have a contract with him. He trades power to me when I need it as, like, rent, so he can keep living inside me. In exchange, we don't destroy him."

"How are you so nonchalant about something like that?" she wondered.

Eoduun chimed in. "You don't seem particularly frightened yourself."

Eve looked at Zeke. "Well, he doesn't seem particularly scary."

"Right now," Eoduun said ominously.

As Eve was about to turn her eyes away from Zeke, his bright, brown eyes suddenly flashed a deep, vermilion red, and his expression changed as though a shadow of dark intent had just passed over him. She gasped and blinked, and in that fraction of a second, Bo had thrown himself in front of her protectively, facing Zeke in a fighting stance.

Zeke suddenly scowled. "Hey! Stop that!" he yelled at himself. He looked past Bo at Eve with his normal, innocent eyes. "I'm sorry, Dagon's such a dick. It's ok. Don't be scared."

Eoduun looked at her face. "Too late," he observed.

"That's some real Jekyll and Hyde shit," Eve remarked shakily as Bo relaxed and stood down.

Eoduun leaned against the wall and crossed his arms. "Not even close. Dagon makes Hyde look like a schoolgirl."

"Guys. Enough," Bo said firmly.

"Do you want to spar?" Zeke asked Eve eagerly as though nothing unusual had just transpired.

"Not today, Z," Bo said. "We have a lot we need to go over before we head out tomorrow."

"You're leaving, too?" Eve inquired, feeling a mild panic. There didn't seem to be anyone else around in this place aside from the four of them and Luc. Luc made her uneasy in all kinds of ways. Zeke was kind of adorable, but his Dagon deal freaked her out. Eoduun acted like he couldn't stand the sight of her. The only one she felt comfortable around was Bo. She didn't want to be separated from him.

"*We* are. You as well," Bo clarified.

"I'm not interested in a babysitting mission," Eoduun complained.

"Don't worry, you'll get to kill something," Bo promised. "We have a lead on a supposed chupacabra case in northern Texas. It's reportedly acquired a taste for kids."

Eoduun frowned. "That's not their typical MO."

"I know. I think we may be dealing with two different critters altogether."

"Kids, huh? And a chupacabra…El Coco, maybe? But why would it hunt in the same territory as the chupi?" Eoduun wondered.

"They could be traveling together," Bo said. "But they're not usually stupid enough to draw this much attention to themselves. I don't know. We'll find out more when we get there."

Eoduun sighed. "All right. Well, I'll be outside training if anyone needs me. Come on, Zeke." The two young men left Bo and Eve on their own, and she was somewhat relieved.

Bo took Eve down into the bunker beneath the apartment building, accessing it through a secret door in the gym locker room. He showed her a room full of weapons. Some of them were strange, vintage looking contraptions. He pointed out which items were good against which cryptids.

"There's no way I'll remember all of this," she said. She still wasn't entirely sure she believed all of this, but after what she'd seen from Luc and Zeke, she wasn't disbelieving, either.

"It'll come with time. It's overwhelming at first, I know. But you're doing better than most." He glanced at her with those mismatched eyes. "Why is that, if you don't mind me asking? Have you seen things, or do you just have nerves of steel?"

She shrugged her shoulders. "I don't know. I haven't seen the things you've been talking about, but I have seen monsters, walking around wearing human faces without an ounce of humanity underneath."

Bo's masked face was hard to read, but his eyes were understanding.

"Can I ask you a personal question?" Eve asked. Bo nodded. "Why don't your eyes match?"

A brief flash of discomfort crossed his features. "Oh." He stuck his hands in his pockets and looked away from her. "Well, they used to both be like Luc's, but uh…I was injured during a fight, and it didn't heal properly."

"Does it affect your specialty?"

"A little, but I was never able to master the warping technique the way Lucius did, even with both eyes. He's on a different level from the rest of us." Bo gave her a sideways glance. "Be glad he's on our side."

"He kind of scares me. No offense."

"Why would I be offended? He's terrifying."

Eve was surprised by his reply. If his older brother thought he was terrifying, how truly powerful was Luc?

"Speaking of terrifying, what the hell is Dagon?" she asked.

Bo sighed. "Dagon is a huge pain in my ass." He leaned back against the utility shelves they were standing between and rested the back of his head on it, looking up at the ceiling. "Last year we had an incident with a witch, as Zeke said, and she was going to sacrifice a little boy to bring back a powerful, ancient entity that had been sealed away for millennia. Dagon. Zeke sacrificed himself to save the boy, and he became Dagon's vessel instead. But there was fallout. There's been fallout ever since," Bo said bitterly.

"Oh."

"It isn't Zeke's fault. He's a good kid. He has a good heart. But he's so naïve and trusting and he only sees things as he wants them to be, not as they are."

"Is that necessarily a bad thing?"

"In this line of work, it's a liability. I know we're supposed to be the good guys taking out the monsters, but once you've been in this life for a while, you'll understand that only monsters can kill monsters."

3
Maybe You Could Tell Me Why This Was All So Easy

Bo left Eve at her apartment with a stack of literature to go through. She had a lot to learn. As she curled up on the couch surrounded by dusty old books, she wondered when Luc was going to give her her phone back. There was probably a lot she could do with a Google or YouTube search right about now.

She picked up the book that Bo had put at the top of the stack. It was about ancient deities and demons, and it didn't take her long to find Dagon amongst its pages. When she learned he was such a well-known, widely worshipped and/or feared deity of fertility, agriculture, and fishing throughout ancient Middle Eastern civilization, she marveled at the fact that she'd never heard of him until now. He was an old one. He was even mentioned in the Bible and referenced regularly in pop culture. H.P. Lovecraft had a story about him. How the hell had he ended up possessing some guy in the middle of Nebraska?

And, furthermore, *he was real?*

It was clear from the way Bo spoke of him that Bo hated him. And though he claimed it wasn't Zeke's fault, Eve got the distinct impression that Bo did resent him in some way for taking in Dagon.

But Zeke himself seemed so sweet and innocent. The kind of sweetness and innocence that one like Dagon might enjoy corrupting. Eve thought about Zeke's pleasing face and athletic build and couldn't help but muse, *Hell, sweetness and innocence I would enjoy corrupting.*

Her research was interrupted by a knock at the door. She couldn't explain how she knew it, but she could *feel* Luc outside her door. She'd always been like that, though. Sometimes she just had these feelings about things, like just knowing what song was going to play on the radio next, or that a rock was going to fly up and hit her windshield when the next car passed her. She had a little saying she stole from a movie that she took very seriously: "Don't Think It, Don't Say It." Because it often seemed like as soon as she thought about something happening, it would. Did it happen because she thought it? Or did she think it because it was going to happen?

She reluctantly went to the door and looked out the peephole. Just as she feared. She opened the door a crack and peeked her head out.

Luc smiled charmingly. "How are we settling in?" he asked conversationally.

"Fine. But I have to ask: who collected all my clothes from my old apartment? I see my entire wardrobe is here already." She hoped to hell it was a woman, because all of her underwear was neatly folded and tucked away with care, and she was embarrassed to think of one of them standing in her room, rummaging through her unmentionables.

"You're welcome," Luc said. She felt the edges of her ears burning with embarrassment. He placed his hand on the door and leaned toward her. "May I come in?"

"Oh, I'm right in the middle of going through all the books Bo gave me…"

Luc pushed the door open and stepped inside. "Perfect, I can help you study up."

Just as Eve began to protest, Zeke's apartment door opened directly across the hall. He saw her standing in her doorway and Luc walking inside, and he left his apartment and followed along behind Luc into hers.

"Hey! Are we having a welcome party?" he asked cheerfully.

"Sure," Luc said.

"No!" Eve said simultaneously.

"Oh, don't be a stick in the mud," Luc said. He went to her fridge and opened the door. "I trust this is all suitable for you? I just got you things I thought you would eat based on what was in your fridge and cupboards at your old apartment. I did include some healthier and more refined options, too, because your diet sucks. Just because you can't get heart disease, it doesn't mean you should to eat like a teenage gamer."

She had looked in the fridge earlier, and it was filled with foreign looking items. "I don't recognize most of the foods in there," she countered. "That looks nothing like my fridge at home."

"Well, I did what I could with what I was given. I refuse to purchase frozen chicken nuggets."

"Oh, I love chicken nuggets," Zeke confessed. "I have some in my freezer if you want them," he offered as he reached around Luc and grabbed a beer from the shelf in the door of the fridge. He popped the top with his bare hands and took a swig, then made a disgusted face. He looked at the bottle, then at Luc. "What the hell is this?"

Eve snatched the beer from his hand. "*That* is the one thing I do recognize," she said as she took a drink.

"That's like the shit the Smith brothers drink. Ugh."

Eve looked down at the cheap, domestic beer in her hand. "Are those the guys from Team Flannel I heard mentioned earlier?" she asked.

Luc replied, "That would be them, yes."

"I think I'll get along well with them."

"Are you insinuating you *aren't* getting along well with us?" Luc gave her a wounded expression from behind his sunglasses.

"No, it's just that…well, you're a *lot*. Sorry."

Luc hummed, the smile returning to his handsome face. "You have no idea."

Eve didn't know exactly what that was supposed to mean, but she had her suspicions. The first response she thought of saying was, "*Nor do I want to*," but she didn't say that - because she didn't really know if it was true or not. Maybe someday she did want to.

Instead, she said, "Guys, it was lovely of you to check in on me, but I really need to get back to it." She indicated the books scattered over the couch.

Luc withdrew an apple from the fridge and closed the door. He took a bite as he walked past her out to the living room. He picked up one of the books and sat down on the couch. "Well, let's see what you have here."

While Luc was looking down at the book, Zeke started to walk past Eve to join him in the living room. As he passed, however, he suddenly stopped and turned to her. His hand reached out and grabbed her jaw, and he pressed himself up against her, pushing her back against the fridge. When he tilted her face up toward his, she looked up into vermilion eyes and a lecherous sneer.

"I like you." A voice that wasn't Zeke's came from those sneering lips. Eve tried to push him back, but he didn't budge. He released her jaw and intercepted her hands by the wrists, holding them up against the fridge door with a strength she had no hope of overcoming. He leaned his face in close to her and inhaled deeply along her neck, making her skin erupt in goosebumps. He tilted his head slightly, and she could see lines behind his ears, down the sides of his neck. They looked like gill slits or a tattoo of gill slits. She was sure that those weren't visible when Zeke was Zeke. "I like you a *lot*," Dagon murmured.

Eve was frozen in place while her heart tried to escape up through her throat.

"Zeke, put a muzzle on him, would you?" Luc implored in bland annoyance from the living room while he browsed the book in his hands.

"Don't worry, you'll come to like me, too, princess," Dagon asserted confidently. Then Zeke dropped her wrists and clapped his hands over his mouth, the red eyes shifting quickly back to brown. He took a big step back and clumsily ran into the kitchen island behind him.

"I'm sorry! I'm so sorry!" Zeke apologized. His face was beet red, and he pulled at the bottom of his sweatshirt. He averted his eyes and announced, "I gotta go." He rushed from the apartment, and Eve heard his door slam across the hall.

"He normally has a much better grip on Dagon," Luc mused. "He must really like you."

"Who, Zeke or Dagon?" Eve wondered, still leaning against the fridge, trying to gather her wits.

"Take your pick." Luc set down the book he was holding and crossed his arms on top of the back of the couch. He rested his chin on his arms and looked at her over the top of his sunglasses with those dangerous eyes. "But they'll have to get in line."

An uncomfortable laugh erupted from Eve's throat. "Are there just no other women here or what?"

Luc's sultry expression didn't change. "You know you're attractive. You don't go through life looking like that and not know it. You don't have to pretend. We don't stand on ceremony here." He took another bite of his apple, then a mischievous grin spread across his face. He whispered, "You know what he's doing next door right now, don't you?"

"We don't need to talk about it," Eve snipped, turning her back to Luc as she reached for the bottle of beer that she'd left on the counter. Yes, she knew what Zeke was probably doing. She'd felt it when he was pressed up against her.

"He's thinking about you, no doubt. I'm sure Dagon is giving him all kinds of ideas and imaginings to help him along."

"I said we don't need to talk about it. Is there any reason you're still here?" Eve rejoined in irritation.

"I was hoping to talk monsters with you and answer any questions you might have about your new team members, and maybe you could tell me why this was all so easy."

The way his sentence just ran on made her almost miss that last part. She turned toward him again as she took a long drink from the bottle. "Why does everyone keep asking me that?"

"Because, frankly, it's baffling. For those brought into the know this late in the game, there's always wild disbelief, maybe some crying, a little existential crisis, and a bit of a transition period and indecision. Nobody just accepts this. Nobody just leaves everything behind unless there's shit they want to leave behind. So what I'm wondering is, what is it you're so eager to run from that you're willing to dive into this without an ounce of hesitation?"

Eve sat on the other end of the couch and set her beer down on the coffee table. "Nothing. I'm not running from anything. I'm not leaving anything behind. That's the entire point. I don't *have* anything worth staying for. My job is shit, my boyfriend left me months ago, I'm a month behind on my rent, the only friend I had ran off with the aforementioned boyfriend, and I haven't talked to my family in years. I own nothing of value and have no one who will even notice I'm gone. So, when I suddenly find out I'm 'special' and am given a free apartment with a fully-stocked fridge and handed some ready-made friends, and told that my only job is fighting things…yeah, I'm jumping on that train and riding it all the way to the goddamn station. Easiest decision I've ever made."

Luc leaned back into the corner of the couch and crossed his ankle over his knee, tilting his head in contemplation as he looked at Eve from behind his sunglasses. "I worry you may not grasp the gravity of the new life you've chosen, Eve. It isn't all free food and fast friends."

"I've gathered that. And I still think it beats the alternative."

"You couldn't even stab me when I asked. Are you sure you're going to be able to kill when it's required? Because it will be required."

"I know how to fight. I know how to shoot a gun. It shouldn't be a problem to use those skills to kill a monster."

"And if that monster looks like a five-year-old boy?"

"What?"

"The reason most people aren't aware of our monster problem is because they don't always look like they're described in the myths. They look like us most of the time. You've likely known a few in your life and not even realized what they were. And yes, they can look like five-year-old boys."

"I'll do what needs to be done. I'm sure I'll be able to tell when it comes down to it now that I know these things exist."

"If Dagon didn't take a shine to you and show himself, would you have ever known there was something like that in Zeke? Did you know Bo is part werewolf?"

Eve choked and sputtered on the sip of beer she'd just started to swallow. "Wait...does that mean *you*...?"

"Oh, no. His mom's side, not our father's. My mother is a witch. But the point remains: you had no idea."

"I don't understand...I thought we were supposed to be killing things like werewolves and witches."

"Do you want to kill Bo?"

"God, no. I like Bo," Eve blurted.

"But if he lost control and came after you, could you kill him? Or Zeke? Could you kill your friends if they became a threat to you or others?"

Eve furrowed her brow and didn't answer.

"These are the kinds of decisions you'll have to make as a member of Knighco. I mean, not the Bo thing – that was just a hypothetical. It's in his blood, yes, but he doesn't transform. He gets some of the perks without the body hair. He *does* have the obnoxious, uh," Luc bared his teeth and pointed at his canines, "and a heightened sense of smell, which is why he always has that mask over his face, but he's not going to lose control and come after you."

"Well, that's a relief, I guess," Eve muttered.

"Me, on the other hand…" Luc took off his sunglasses and hung them from his collar. He graced her with a dazzling grin and winked at her. "I can't make any promises."

She felt the color rising to her cheeks, and her clothes suddenly felt too heavy and constricting. She swallowed hard. She was annoyed with the way her body responded to him. She was even more annoyed with the way her thoughts were drawing up images of what his body looked like under those clothes and how much she wanted those soft lips to be on hers again. And that tongue…

"Are you thinking about it?" he asked perceptively.

"No!"

Luc laughed. "So, if I tried it right now, you'd send me packing?" he challenged.

"I barely know you!"

"That's not a no."

"It's not a yes, either."

He bit his lip and smiled seductively at her. "Hm. Ok." He leaned forward and put his sunglasses back on. "But you will be mine."

"What the fuck, seriously, am I the only woman around here or something?!"

Luc stood up and laughed. "No. I mean, there aren't a *lot* of women who choose this life, but that's not why you've captured my attention. You intrigue me."

"Nobody ever tells you no, do they?" she asked flatly.

"To be fair, you didn't either." When she narrowed her eyes at him, he added, "But that's not why you're intriguing." He turned and sauntered to the door. "I'll see you before you head out tomorrow." He raised his hand and said, "*Ja ne*," before closing the door behind him.

Eve got up and locked the door. Her legs felt weak after her exchange with Luc. Why was he so obsessed with her? Was it just because she was the new, shiny thing at the compound, and his interest would naturally wane after a while? Or was it because of the special blood she supposedly had – blood that no one had bothered to test yet? What if it wasn't actually special when it was put to the test? Would she be cast out just as quickly as she'd been brought in? Would Luc's interest evaporate?

The thought of going back now was unbearable. She meant it when she said she hadn't left anything behind. She had nothing to go back to. If her blood wasn't actually special…if *she* wasn't actually special…she would be utterly devastated. It would be like clawing her way out of purgatory only to be drop-kicked back in by an angry Spartan.

As Eve paged through the different books Bo had sent her home with, hoping to make herself useful and thereby reducing her chances of being cast out, she thought about her new teammates. Zeke had a monster in him. Bo was part monster, apparently. But what about Eoduun? Bo told her that his specialty was a kind of telepathic one. Zeke had called him an eraser, and that was because one of his most valuable skills was making people forget things. Like Luc, that power seemed to originate in his eyes. Eve couldn't help but liken it to the kinds of powers often attributed to vampires. Was he a vampire? How many other monsters were there at the compound?

And how worried should she be that Dagon had decided he liked her? Everything she'd read about him earlier was conflicting. The accounts of him ran the gamut from benevolent god to downright horrifying demon. The way he looked at her with those red eyes felt anything but benevolent. It was like he wanted to devour her, but when that expression came through Zeke's cute face, it was more exciting than it should have been. If it had been purely Zeke looking at her like that, Luc would have a formidable rival for her attention. But Dagon?

Just…what the hell was she supposed to do with that?

She suddenly remembered the way Bo had reacted when Dagon made his first appearance to her. Just a flash of his eyes, and Bo had jumped in front of her to shield her from him. But tonight, Dagon had put hands on her and pushed her up against the fridge, and Luc hadn't lifted a finger. He was hardly concerned at all. Mild annoyance, maybe. Why had they reacted so differently?

And then came the real question of the night: did Zeke truly go home and alleviate that rock-hard erection she'd felt swelling in his sweatpants when Dagon had pushed her against the fridge? A shameful tingle zinged through her belly when she thought about it.

She was starting to doze off with a book in her lap when she was startled awake by a sound at the door. She sat up, alert. She could see a small piece of paper on the floor in front of the door. She got up and retrieved it, then looked out the peephole. No one. She returned to the couch and opened the little ripped piece of notepad paper. There was a messily handwritten message inside.

I'm so sorry. Please don't be afraid of me. I won't let him out again, I promise. -Zeke

P.S. I swear I'm not a pervert.

P.P.S. Your pretty.

Eve smiled. Ok, that was kind of adorable, even with the misspelling.

4
What Do You Wear for Hunting Monsters?

Eve woke up in her bed in her old apartment. As she lay there in the dark, listening to the familiar din of city traffic and staring at the glow of the clock on the nightstand without really looking at the time, it dawned on her that she wasn't supposed to be here. Panic welled up in her chest. Had everything about the compound, Luc, her team, and the monsters all been a dream? A hallucination? Or, worse, had it been real, and they just decided they didn't want her?

"No, no, no," she fretted, bolting upright.

"Yes, yes, yes," a deep, taunting voice in the dark replied. Two crimson eyes set in a dark shadow arose from the chair in the corner and moved across the room toward the bed. When the shadow reached the side of the bed and stepped into the dim light coming in through the window, she saw Zeke's face. He smiled darkly and lifted off his shirt, tossing it to the floor. She was surprised to see his toned pectorals and bulky shoulders were covered in tribal-like tattoos. Zeke was too cute and innocent to look this dangerous with his shirt off.

"What are you doing here?" she asked.

He stood there, looking down at her with Dagon's eyes, and a ravenous expression overtook his features. "You called to me."

"No, I'm pretty sure I didn't. How did you get in here?"

"You let me in." Dagon snatched up the comforter and yanked it off of her.

"I want to talk to Zeke," Eve demanded, but the conviction in her voice was weak as she sat there in her underwear and a tank top. She wrapped her arms around herself to hide from his roving gaze.

"He can hear you, if I let him." Dagon put a knee onto the bed and reached out, running a finger down her arm, leaving a trail of heat in its wake. "He can feel you and see you, too, if I want him to." Dagon came closer and leaned over her, his muscles moving and flexing deliciously beneath those black tattoos, and he brought his mouth next to her ear. Hot breath lightly caressed her ear as he whispered, "Do you want me to let him watch?"

Fear and excitement stirred in her belly, but it felt wrong. This was the wrong response. She was messed up for enjoying any bit of this, wasn't she? She needed to put a stop to it before she gave in to something she knew she shouldn't.

She wasn't supposed to like this.

Eve suddenly threw an elbow into Dagon's – Zeke's – handsome face, knowing she couldn't overpower him, but hoping to catch him by surprise. She dived from the bed and ran to the bedroom door, but as she turned the knob and began to wrench it open, a large hand flew past her head and slammed against the door, shoving it closed again. The heat from Dagon's body behind her radiated through the inch or two of space between them and melted into her skin, making her heart race. She could feel him looming over her. His other hand came up and pressed into the door on the other side of her, trapping her between his strong arms. He leaned closer, and his lips touched the side of her neck. Her breath caught in her throat.

She wasn't supposed to like this.

She whirled around to face him and backed herself against the door to put distance between their bodies. Dagon grinned at her, his tongue slowly running along his injured lower lip, licking up the blood she'd drawn with her elbow. He closed the distance between them, pressing his hips against her as his mouth descended upon hers. His tongue pushed past her lips, the metallic flavor of his bloody lip spreading over her tastebuds as he massaged her tongue with his. His hands moved to the sides of her face and tilted her chin upward to give him better access to her mouth. She was mortified when a soft moan emanated from her throat.

She wasn't supposed to like this.

She placed her hands on his chest, intending to push him away. The hot, bare skin beneath her fingers was so damn inviting, though. Firm, yet supple. She lightly dragged her palms down his pectorals, exploring the muscular transitions between the pectorals and his ribcage, obliques, and lats. Her fingertips traced over the hard ridges and bumps of his abdominals. She wanted to feel those muscles and bare flesh against hers.

No, she wasn't supposed to like this.

His fingers slid behind her ear and into her hairline, eliciting soft tingles throughout her scalp. Dagon whispered against her lips, "Keep going. Touch me."

Her hand continued south, moving through the light trail of hair below his belly button before her fingers slipped under the waistband of his sweatpants. She ran her palm down the underside of his hard shaft, then gripped his impressive girth firmly. A pleased groan rumbled in his throat as she slowly worked her hand up and down.

Dagon licked his fingers on one hand and plunged them down the front of her underwear. She inhaled sharply as his warm, wet fingers slipped between her legs. She rocked her pelvis against his hand as she felt her pleasure quickly rising with his skilled ministrations.

Oh, God, she wasn't supposed to like this.

Eve's eyes shot open as her body spasmed in ecstasy, her knee knocking a book off the couch onto the floor. She bit her lip and pressed her hand between her thighs as she rode out the aftershocks of her pleasure.

She sat up and looked around the living room of her new apartment, relieved that she hadn't been rejected and expelled from the compound after all. She tried to ignore the tiny pang of disappointment, as well. She'd never had a dream quite like that before, and she wished she would've slept just a *little* longer.

She stood up and stretched out her cramped neck muscles. She must've fallen asleep on the couch while reading about monsters last night. She looked at the clock on the wall. A little after 9AM. She had no idea what time they were supposed be leaving today, but she wanted to be ready. She headed off and took a shower.

She stood in her bedroom with a towel wrapped tightly around her, her damp hair hanging down her back, and stared at the clothes in her closet. There were outfits in here that weren't hers. New, with tags. Had Luc taken liberties with her wardrobe like he had when picking out food for her fridge? She found a suitcase on the floor in the closet, but she didn't know what to put in it. What do you pack for a monster hunting trip?

She heard a knock on the front door. Shit. She quickly dropped the towel and threw on the bathrobe hanging on the back of her bedroom door. She hurried to the door and looked through the peephole.

Bo was standing in the hallway, holding two stacked Starbucks cups in one hand and looking down at his phone in the other.

She was relieved to see it was just him. She didn't know if she could handle Zeke or Luc just yet. She opened the door. Bo looked up from his phone, and the corners of his eyes crinkled in a smile, the curve of his lips hidden behind his mask.

"*Ohayou*," he greeted. He stuck his phone in his pocket and held one of the coffee cups out to Eve. "Black."

She wasn't going to bother asking how he knew she drank it black. Instead, she asked, "Ohio? Is that where we're going?"

He chuckled. "No, O-H-A-Y-O-U. It means 'good morning.' *Bonjour. Buongiorno. Buen dia. Zaoshang hao.*"

"A simple 'good morning' will do," Eve said, then stepped back and gestured for him to come in. "Thanks for the coffee, Bo." As he walked past her, she could smell the sweet aroma wafting from his cup. "Is that a pumpkin spice latte? How did you get one of those this time of year?"

"Hm? Oh, no. I just put creamer from home in it."

"Pumpkin spice, huh? I didn't peg you for a basic bitch," she teased.

"Shows what you know," he deadpanned as he walked into the kitchen and pulled up a stool at the kitchen island. He sat down and pulled his mask down to take a drink of his coffee, then slipped it right back into place.

Good lord, he was just as handsome as his brother beneath that mask.

"I need your help," Eve said.

He glanced at her. "Maybe you should get dressed first."

"Well, that's part of my problem."

"You want fashion advice from a basic bitch?"

Eve laughed. "I don't know what I'm supposed to pack. What do you even wear for hunting monsters? Is there some kind of dress code?"

"Just wear something comfortable and unrestricting. The boys wear the same kind of stuff you saw them wearing yesterday. I wear stuff like this," he indicated his outfit, which consisted of black cargo pants and a white t-shirt. "Just don't show up in an evening gown and high heels, and you'll be fine. Oh, but do pack at least one business outfit. Slacks and a nice shirt and blazer. I'm sure Luc has something for you in there." He looked up at the door. "You should go get dressed. I think Zeke is coming."

"Oh, did you stop and see him before you came here?"

"No, but I can hear him putting his shoes on and I can smell the coffee in his travel mug. He's getting ready to head out, and this is the most likely place for him to stop first."

She stopped and listened. She couldn't hear anything. Then, a few seconds later, she heard the door across the hall open and close. Steps toward her door. *Knock-knock-knock.*

Bo stood up and waved her toward her room, then walked to the door. She did as he indicated and went to her room to change. She could hear Bo and Zeke's voices conversing out in the other room as she shimmied into her favorite pair of stretchy blue flared jeans and threw on a cropped graphic tee. She decided to toss some clothes into the suitcase while she was in there, too. She was looking for any excuse to delay going out into the other room and having to face Zeke. Not only would he be awkward because of what happened yesterday, but she would be awkward because of the dream she had this morning. She desperately hoped that he had a better handle on Dagon now, because she especially didn't want to have to face *him.*

She ran out of things to do in her bedroom entirely too quickly. Zeke turned to look at her as soon as he heard her bedroom door open. He smiled brightly at her.

"Good morning! Are you excited for your first hunting trip?!" he bubbled. No awkwardness at all. Just cheerful Zeke.

"I think I'm more nervous than excited," she admitted as she joined him and Bo in the kitchen.

Zeke jumped up from the other stool at the island. "You can sit here," he offered. She sat down, and he walked around to the other side of the island and leaned his elbows on it, facing her and Bo. He took a drink from the travel mug in his hand.

She had a hard time looking at that cute face without seeing Dagon's lustful expressions from her dream interposed over top of it. She felt a blush beginning to burn in her cheeks as she looked across the countertop at him.

"Are you feeling ok? Do you have a fever?" Zeke asked. He reached across and put his hand on her forehead.

That hand. Her eyes widened and she inhaled sharply at his touch. Instant arousal. Goddammit.

Bo gave her a surprised sideways glance and Zeke yanked his hand back, regret washing away his cheerful expression.

"I feel fine. No fever," Eve said as her cheeks burned embarrassingly. "I'm just nervous, like I said."

"Oh. Ok. Sorry, I shouldn't have just touched you like that," Zeke apologized. He rubbed the back of his neck and looked off to the side. "Did you, uh, get my note?"

"I did. Don't worry about what happened yesterday," she said softly, also looking away from him. She looked over at Bo and discovered that he was watching them keenly. He must not have heard what happened yet.

"It won't happen again," Zeke avowed.

Bo looked down at his watch. "Are you packed, Z?"

"Oh, shit. I'll go do it now." He pointed at Eve. "Do you play Cards Against Humanity?"

"I do, yes."

"Sweet, I'm packing it! Bo and Eoduun don't like to play it with me, but I bet they'll play if you and I both want to." And then he ran off back to his apartment, leaving his travel mug sitting on her countertop.

"He's like a whirlwind of chaos," Eve mused.

"What happened between the two of you?" Bo asked.

She shook her head and looked down at her coffee cup. "It's nothing, really. Luc was there, and he didn't seem overly concerned about it."

"What happened?" he repeated.

Eve sighed and waved her hand dismissively. "Nothing, just some Dagon stuff."

"Dagon is not nothing," Bo said, suddenly agitated. "What happened?"

She exhaled. "He got a little handsy. Told me he liked me. But Zeke put him back, and Luc was right there," Eve said nonchalantly as she gestured toward the couch.

Fury filled Bo's eyes, and then Eve saw something strange. His scarred eye suddenly flared from charcoal gray to an intense yellow-gold. With his bright blue left eye and yellow-gold right eye, he looked like a wolf with heterochromia. She slid off of her barstool and took a step away from Bo.

He instantly knew why she was retreating. He clapped one hand over his eye, then held one hand out in front of him placatingly. "It's ok, don't be afraid. It doesn't mean anything when that happens. I'm still me. I'm always me," he insisted. "I don't change. I'm not like Zeke and Dagon."

"Why did your eye do that?" Eve asked suspiciously.

"It's just an artifact of my curse, that's all. High emotions bring it out. It isn't me changing."

"Because you're part werewolf," Eve said.

"Luc told you."

"He mentioned it in passing."

"Did he bother to let you know that I don't actually turn into a wolf?"

"He did."

"You have nothing to fear from me, Eve. I promise you that," Bo pledged, gazing at Eve earnestly. "You can sit next to me. I'm safe." He removed his hand from his eye, and it had returned to its usual charcoal gray again.

Eve came back and sat on the stool next to him. "Most men who feel the need to declare that they're 'safe' usually aren't. But for some reason, I believe it when you say it."

"I didn't mean to get upset, but Dagon scares the hell out of me," Bo confessed. "I was just starting to trust Zeke again until all of this. I really thought he had Dagon under control."

"Why doesn't Luc seem scared of him?"

"Because Luc could destroy him if he really wanted to. And before you ask why he hasn't done it yet, it's because it would kill Zeke in the process, and probably cause as much damage as setting off a nuclear bomb. Dagon and Luc have a mutual understanding, and that was why Dagon agreed to enter into a contract with Zeke. He's not supposed to kill anyone who isn't a monster, but that leaves a lot of gray area. I'm a monster, technically." Bo pulled his mask down to drink his coffee, and Eve caught a glimpse of the sharp canine teeth Luc had been talking about. Honestly, though, she didn't think they were *that* noticeable. They were longer and sharper than a normal man's canines, but they weren't as long as a typical wolf's fangs.

"You seem the least monstrous of any of them," Eve remarked.

He pulled his mask back up. "Hm. Well, we all have our moments." He leaned back on his stool and looked over into Eve's bedroom at the suitcase sitting on her bed. "All packed?" he asked conversationally.

Luc showed up at Eve's apartment while Bo was preparing to leave.

"Aren't I the popular one," she said as Luc stepped inside and handed her a plastic container. It was warm in her hands. "What's this?"

"Breakfast." He grinned at her. He was wearing the sunglasses again today. It must've been part of his usual attire, like Bo's mask. Were they simply a fashion choice or did they serve a purpose?

She opened the lid as she carried it to the kitchen. Inside the container was a display of eggs benedict that was worthy of its own exhibit at the Louvre. "Damn, where did you get this from?" she marveled.

"I made it," Luc replied.

She stopped and turned around to check his expression for sarcasm. "Bullshit."

"It's not bullshit," Bo confirmed. "The jerk can cook." He raised an eyebrow at Luc. "I don't suppose you brought anything for your dear old brother, did you?"

Luc clapped a hand on Bo's shoulder. "I didn't realize my dear old brother was going to be here when I arrived," he said, his voice tinged with annoyance. "My apologies."

"We were just talking about the trip ahead and catching up." Bo then crossed his arms, and his tone became slightly confrontational. "Speaking of, why didn't you tell me Dagon got out again?"

"I didn't want to needlessly worry you."

"Well, I'm worried. I'm heading out on the road with him. If he isn't stable, I need to know."

"He's stable. I've taken care of it."

"He'll burn through a seal in just a few days, Luc," Bo pointed out with dissatisfaction.

Luc patted Bo's back and walked away from him toward Eve. "Well, I guess you'd better wrap it up quickly, then, hadn't you?" he condescended.

Bo scowled at his brother's back and scathingly chastised, "You aren't taking this seriously enough."

Luc's typically nonchalant expression became suddenly vicious as he whirled around on Bo. "Do not purport to know my level of concern or my vested interests, brother," he seethed. "I take this *very* seriously!" Though he barely raised his voice, Eve felt as though the walls were shaking.

Bo's expression didn't change as he stared unflappably at Luc. "So long as we're on the same page, then," Bo said. "But if anything happens—"

"I will rain hellfire down on his pathetic existence, and he is fully aware of this, thank you," Luc spat quickly in agitation. He adjusted his sunglasses and ran his hand through his white locks before turning to Eve. In a flash, the rage was gone, and he smiled sweetly at her. "Enjoy your breakfast, love. We'll leave you to it."

Eve didn't realize she was holding her breath until she gasped for air the moment the brothers left the apartment. She still hadn't seen the full display of Luc's power, but just from that one little outburst, she *felt* the magnitude of it. The pressure in the room had made her eardrums feel like they would pop, and the air had been electrified, making the hairs rise on her arms and the back of her neck. The whole room had seemed to vibrate around him.

She now fully understood why even his own brother would call him terrifying. And yet, here she stood with a container of eggs benedict that he had so thoughtfully cooked just for her. She grabbed a fork and took a bite.

Welp. The jerk could cook.

5
It's Pretty Damn Hot in Texas

Eve lost the rock-paper-scissors competition for shotgun, so she ended up crammed in the backseat of the white Toyota Corolla next to Eoduun. She was pretty sure Bo couldn't have pushed his driver's seat any further back than it was, which was practically in her lap. This was going to be a very long eight hours.

It didn't help that Eoduun was doing everything he could to try not to catch her cooties, which was no small feat in that backseat. If her leg bumped against his, he jerked away from her. Zeke kept turning around and chatting away at them, but Eoduun wouldn't talk directly to her or even look at her, only to Bo and Zeke. She didn't definitively know why he loathed her so much, but she assumed he hated the fact that she was tagging along even though she was as green as green could possibly be. He was probably afraid she was going to get someone killed.

Hell, she was afraid of that. Why would Luc send her along?

When Zeke interrupted his incessant jibber jabbering to inquire about the case specifics, her ears perked. "So, are we expecting two cryptids or just one seriously fucked up chupacabra?" Zeke asked Bo.

"After hearing the details, I think Eoduun was right about possible El Coco involvement. It started three weeks ago with mutilated cattle, drained of blood. One or two killed every few nights from different farms, all within a ten-mile radius. Seems like a pretty straight-forward chupi case, right? Well, last week, a three-year-old kid went missing from the same general area. Two days later, a six-year-old went missing from a home four miles away from the first kid's home. Three days ago, they found the chewed-up remains of the first kid on a riverbank five miles from where he went missing, and that same day, *another* kid went missing from a home near where the remains were found."

Eve asked, "Have the cattle mutilations continued?"

"Yes, but they slowed down. Only two cows were killed since the kids started disappearing."

"And the other two kids haven't been found yet?" Eoduun asked.

"Not yet," Bo confirmed.

"So how are we playing this?" Zeke wondered.

"Wildlife Service," Bo replied.

"Aw, shit," Zeke said, biting his fist. He cringed at Bo.

"Goddammit, Z," Bo sighed.

"What?" Eve asked.

"He forgot his fucking IDs. Again," Eoduun answered in exasperation.

"Well, it's not like I do it on purpose!" Zeke defended.

"I didn't get any IDs," Eve mentioned.

Zeke's disappointment vanished. "You can hang back with me, then!" he exclaimed. "We can do some more research on El Chapo and do some non-official digging."

"El Coco, you idiot," Eoduun corrected, and if Eve wasn't mistaken, that was an amused smile playing at the corner of his lips.

"I don't remember reading anything about El Coco last night," Eve said.

"The El Coco line is an ancient one," Bo informed her. "There are different variations, and my guess is this one, if it is a Coco, is probably a cucuy, especially if it's coexisting with a chupacabra."

"What do they look like?"

"Chupacabras? They are super fugly," Zeke said. "You know those gross little hairless purse dogs? They look like a big version of that. But with spines and sharp teeth."

"Only when they phase. Otherwise, they look like normal people," Eoduun added while looking out the window.

"What does a cucuy look like?"

Bo answered, "It depends on its lineage, but usually around here we're talking red eyes, razor sharp teeth, hairy, and creepily childlike size in their phased form. They can hide anywhere – and unlike most cryptids, they can shape-shift. They don't have a definite humanoid form. They can look like anyone they want to."

"So it could pretend to be any one of us and the others wouldn't know?"

"Dagon can see their true form when he's at the helm," Zeke said. "But he's locked up right now, so he won't be any help."

"Luc sealed him? What if we need him?" Eoduun worried.

"It was necessary," Bo said. "He was misbehaving."

"It's because of *her*, isn't it?" Eoduun practically hissed.

"It's because Dagon is Dagon, Eoduun. He is the only one to blame," Bo countered.

"It's because I wasn't being careful enough," Zeke said. "If you want someone to blame, blame me for letting him take it too far."

"What?" Eoduun was confused. He suddenly reached over and grabbed Eve's face, turning it toward him. His eyes bored into hers, shifting from the darkest brown possible to deep purple. His irises began to spin, and her mind's eye began shuffling through her recent memories. The memory of Dagon shoving her against the fridge popped up, and quickly following it was her memory of the dirty dream she had this morning. Her brain was suddenly flooded with angry thoughts of jealous rage. Thoughts that didn't feel like hers.

Then it stopped as Zeke's hand clapped over her eyes. "Eoduun! What the fuck, man?!"

"How did you do that?!" Eoduun yelped in surprise at Eve.

"What's going on back there?!" Bo shouted.

"He was reading her without asking!" Zeke accused angrily.

"Eoduun!" Bo chastised. By his tone, it was apparent Eoduun had done something egregious.

"That rule is only for Knighco members!" Eoduun defended.

"She *is* a Knighco member!" Zeke growled.

"Hardly!"

"Jesus Christ, I will O'Doyle this car right off a cliff if everybody doesn't just calm the fuck down," Bo threatened, exasperated. He grabbed Zeke's shoulder and shoved him back down in his seat, then reached back and pointed at Eoduun, taking his eyes off the road momentarily. "Watch it, boy," he warned, fixing him with menacing yellow and blue eyes.

Everyone fell silent. Bo rubbed his forehead in agitation. Eve saw his eyes turn to her in the rearview mirror. His wolf eye hadn't changed back yet, but it was anything but threatening now. His expression was apologetic.

"Guys," he said calmly. "We are a team. We need to have each other's backs, no matter what, and the only way to achieve that is with trust. Using our specialties against each other only hurts us. Eoduun, you know what you did sucks. Don't even try to justify it. Apologize, or you'll be sitting the bench for this trip."

"Did you know about Dagon wanting to fuck her?" Eoduun rejoined.

"Bench it is, then," Bo shot back.

"You talk about building trust, but you don't want to be straight with me about what's really going on? It *is* her fault Luc had to seal Dagon."

"It is *not* her fault! And we don't need Dagon for a damn thing," Bo retorted. "Dagon isn't to be trusted. We've grown too complacent with him. We needed this wakeup call."

Eoduun glowered at Eve. Eve's blood was boiling. She wanted to hit him so badly. She wanted to throw him from the moving car. Instead, she sat back in her seat and crossed her arms and asked, "What is your problem with me? You haven't even given me half a chance."

He scoffed and looked out the window. "We don't need you. You've fucked everything up."

"I'm sorry you feel that way. I had no intention of getting in the way. I'm just trying to do what I've been asked. But I'm not going anywhere. I do plan to stay, and I hope, in time, you can learn to trust and accept me, and I hope I can do the same with you. But from here on out...stay the fuck out of my head."

"You couldn't *beg* me to go back into that wasteland," Eoduun informed her rudely.

"We shouldn't have a fucking problem, then," Eve said, calmly fuming.

"Hm."

Zeke's concerned eyes flitted from Eoduun, to Eve, to Bo, back to Eve, and back to Bo again. "Maybe Eve should sit shotgun for a while," he suggested.

"Please," Eoduun agreed sardonically.

Bo pulled the car over to the side of the road, and Eve stepped out and walked around the back of the car. She didn't see Zeke get out, but when she opened the passenger side door, she saw him clambering clumsily between the front seats into the backseat. She glanced at Eoduun as she waited for Zeke's feet to finish making the transition to the back, and the smug smirk on his face was puzzling.

...Until he rested his head on Zeke's shoulder when Zeke settled in.

So that's how it was. Eoduun was jealous of the attention Zeke and Dagon were giving her. But were Zeke and Eoduun in a relationship? It didn't seem that way. After all, Zeke had called "dibs" on her if she was pretty. That's not something he would say to a boyfriend. And it's not something he would say if he knew Eoduun was into *him*. She watched the two in the backseat through her peripheral vision, and Zeke's eyes were constantly drawn to her while Eoduun's eyes were closed, a content little grin on Eoduun's face. Zeke didn't seem even remotely bothered by Eoduun's head on his shoulder, but he also didn't seem to be reciprocating or leaning into it, either. She knew that if she were to lay her head on Zeke's shoulder like that, his response would be much different.

Eve could only conclude that Zeke either didn't know Eoduun was into him, or he didn't care.

What was this going to mean for her position on this team? She got the distinct feeling that Eoduun was going to play dirty as long as he viewed her as a threat. The fact that he would break the rules and use his specialty on her like that told her everything she needed to know. She needed to watch her back. Jealousy makes people do terrible things.

All's fair in love and war.

Zeke passed out in the backseat for a good chunk of the trip, so when they arrived in Texas that night, Zeke was ready and raring to go while everyone else was exhausted. Bo gave him the credit card and sent him in to secure two rooms at the one run-down motel in the small town they'd ended up in.

When he climbed back into the car and handed Bo the card back, he said, "They put us in Room Five."

"Five and what?" Bo asked.

"Just five. It was all they had left."

"You only got us one room?" Eoduun complained.

"It was all they had left!" Zeke repeated. "They told me there's some kind of convention in the next town over, so all the lodging around here is booked up."

"Great, a convention *and* a cucuy," Bo said. He was thoughtful for a moment. "I wonder how long the convention runs."

"I think they're typically just over the weekends," Eve said.

"You're wondering if the cucuy would go to the convention?" Eoduun asked.

"It was just a thought," Bo replied. "Zeke, did the desk clerk happen to mention what kind of convention it was?"

Zeke shook his head. "But we're going out tonight, right? Someone will know."

Bo parked the car in front of the door that had the number five on it. He stuck his keys in his pocket and yawned. "I don't know if I have it in me tonight, Z."

"Is this what happens in your thirties? You can't get it up past eight-thirty?" Zeke teased as they all stepped out of the car.

Bo gave him an impassive glance as walked around to the trunk. "Yep."

Zeke took Eve's suitcase from her as she started to lift it from the trunk. "You'll come out with me, right?" he asked hopefully. "You'll be able to get people to talk to you."

She was exhausted, but she wanted to be useful. She nodded. "Yeah, I guess."

Zeke grinned from ear to ear. "All right!"

"What about me?" Eoduun fussed as he threw his duffle bag over his shoulder. "You didn't ask if I would go."

"Why wouldn't you?" Zeke said as though it were a given.

They walked into the cramped room, and the first thing Eve noticed was the two tiny beds. Eoduun threw his duffle bag on the bed furthest from the door. "Zeke, we can share this one," he said.

"Oh, come on, you're going to make the old guy sleep on the floor?" Bo objected.

"Just sleep with me," Eve offered with a shrug, tossing her suitcase on the other bed. "I don't hog the blankets."

"Or Bo can sleep with Eoduun, and I'll sleep on the floor," Zeke suggested instead.

"Yes, let's do that," Bo said quickly, tossing his backpack on the bed next to Eoduun's things.

Eve was taken aback. "What, do I smell or something?"

"Or something," Eoduun mumbled snidely.

"No, nothing of the sort," Bo said, scowling at Eoduun. "It's just...I mean...you know."

Eve put her hands on her hips. "What, because you're a *boy* and I'm a *girl*?"

"Because I'm a man and you're a woman, yes. And because I get the feeling Luc might have his own opinions about it."

"What the fuck does Luc have to do with it?" Eve asked.

"Everything."

"Is there some kind of rule I don't know about?"

Eoduun chimed in, "Yeah, hands off anything that belongs to Luc."

"I don't belong to Luc!" Eve protested.

"Regardless," Bo said, holding a hand up to quiet Eoduun's reply, "I'm not looking to step on any toes. That's all."

"Whatever," Eve said as she opened her suitcase. "Have fun spooning Eoduun."

Eoduun suddenly sidled up next to her slyly. "Do I detect a hint of disappointment? Did you *want* Bo spooning you?"

"Are you disappointed it'll be Bo spooning you instead of Zeke?" Eve shot back. Eoduun's eyes widened, his sly grin falling slack. The color rose to his cheeks. "Yeah, I've figured you out," she whispered smugly. "And if you want me to keep it to myself, you'll play nice from now on."

He glanced over at Zeke, who was looking down at his phone, then turned back to Eve. "You say anything to him, I'll tell him about your Dagon fantasy," he hissed.

Eve feigned a scandalized look. "Oh, no, anything but that," she whispered sarcastically.

Eoduun flared his nostrils and scowled at her.

"That's enough," Bo said wearily from the other side of the room. He was sitting in a chair in the corner of the room with his eyes closed and his head resting back against the wall.

Eve clamped her mouth shut. Had he heard all of that?

"What?" Zeke looked up from his phone in confusion.

"Nothing. Z, order us something," Bo said.

"What do we want? I don't think they have room service here," Zeke replied.

They all agreed to get burgers from one of the few big-chain restaurants in the area, but Zeke had to go pick it up. By the time he came back, Eoduun had fallen asleep on top of the covers right in the middle of his and Bo's bed, and Bo had passed out in the chair. When Zeke tried to wake Eoduun, he wouldn't get up or move.

"Fuck off, man," he grumbled in his sleep.

"I'm going to eat your dinner if you don't get up," Zeke threatened.

"Fucking eat it, Zeke," Eoduun replied. He rolled over, and with his face in his pillow, he sleepily added, "Put it all in your mouth."

Zeke stood bolt upright, his eyes wide. He looked at Eve to see if she heard.

She just shrugged her shoulders. "Let's wake up Bo."

"I'm up," Bo said from the chair behind them. He got up and dug his dinner out of the bag. He slid his mask down and took a huge bite of his burger.

Eve couldn't take her eyes off of his face as he chewed with his mask down. She wondered if she would feel quite so comfortable around him if he didn't wear the mask. His features were handsome in the same way Luc's were, but at the same time, he had something...more. But she couldn't put her finger on what it was. Maturity? Ruggedness? Earnestness? Whatever it was, she liked it. She liked it a lot. Maybe she *was* a little disappointed that he didn't want to spoon her.

He caught her looking, and he self-consciously took another bite and pulled his mask back up while he masticated. She quickly looked away, embarrassed that she'd been staring like that. She'd even had her mouth hanging open like an idiot.

"Are you sure you don't want to go out with us?" Zeke asked Bo as he plopped his duffle bag on Eve's bed and began rummaging through it. "I asked at the restaurant, and they said the Laughing Horse Bar is the place to go around here. They even have karaoke on Saturdays, so we've got that to look forward to tomorrow." He pulled a pair of jeans and a shirt out of the bag and laid them on the bed.

"I guess I'd better stay here and rest up my singing voice for tomorrow," Bo said.

Zeke lifted his shirt off and started changing his clothes right there next to the bed. Eve watched from the middle of the room as his shirt came up over his shoulders and over his head, and her knees went weak.

Black tribal-like tattoos covered his chest, stomach, and upper arms. Just like in her dream. *Exactly* like in her dream. Flashbacks of how his muscles felt against her fingers, his – Dagon's – mouth on hers, his – Dagon's – tongue dancing sensually with hers, those big yet nimble fingers in her hair, down her pants, on her—

"Shouldn't you be doing that in the bathroom?" Bo's voice interrupted her thoughts.

"Why? I'm not getting naked," Zeke said as he dropped his sweatpants to his ankles. "I still have my boxers on, see?"

Eve quickly turned away, and her eyes happened to end up meeting Bo's. She could tell he'd noticed her noticing Zeke. He pulled his mask down and took another bite of his burger, then returned the mask. "Just know that I'm out of ones, Z, so I can't tip you," he deadpanned from around a mouthful of food.

"That's ok, just buy me a drink," Zeke jokingly replied, and Eve looked over at him just in time to see him wink at her as he pulled his jeans up over his toned hips. She couldn't keep her eyes on his face, and it wasn't only because his body was that alluring. It was because it was *too* familiar. How the hell did she know what he would look like without a shirt on? How did she know he had those tattoos? She was certain she hadn't seen them before her dream, so how did her subconscious know to display him that way?

Zeke threw on a tight-fitting black shirt and smiled at Eve. "Well? Ready to go? Or did you want to put on some shorts? It's pretty damn hot in Texas."

It sure fucking is.

6
You Aren't Going to Puke on Me, Are You?

When Zeke and Eve strolled into the Laughing Horse Bar, she felt like all eyes were on them. She'd decided to put on shorts after all, because Zeke was right, it was hot in Texas. But she was aware of the small-town eyes on her well-toned legs. Legs that should've been bruised all to hell from fighting, but never were. She'd almost forgotten about her "special blood." No one had mentioned it again since Luc and Bo had told her about it. Did Zeke and Eoduun even know about it?

Eve leaned close to Zeke and shouted over the loud country music blaring over the Bluetooth speakers, "Did Luc or Bo ever tell you if I had a specialty?" She took a drink of her cocktail and leaned her elbow against the bar.

Zeke leaned close to her to reply. She took the opportunity to inhale his crisp, clean scent. It was like citrus and pine and fresh clothes on the line. "Bo told us this morning that you had the same specialty that Shira had. Panacea Blood. That's super rare, you know."

"So I hear."

"Do you have any other specialties?"

"Not that I'm aware of," she said. *Not unless guessing what you look like naked counts.*

"I'm at a bit of a disadvantage right now, specialty-wise," Zeke confessed. "Usually, I would put Dagon in the driver's seat for a few minutes and have him take a look around the room to see if there were any cryptids, but I can't do that when he's in lockdown. I can't use his other powers, either. It feels weird to be back to just super strength."

"Are you upset that he's sealed away right now?"

"Not upset, but it's kind of lonely, you know? He's a real dickhead, but he's always here with me. I've gotten used to hearing him in my head. It's too quiet with him locked up." Zeke realized he was talking about the entity that had pushed Eve against the fridge last night, and backpedaled a little. "But I get that he's being a problem right now, so I'm not at all against putting him in timeout. I'm really sorry for the way he's behaved toward you. He hasn't done anything like that since the very beginning." He smiled warmly at her. "I'm just glad you're still willing to spend time with me."

"Do you suppose Eoduun is going to be pissed he didn't get to come along?"

"Oh, definitely, but it's his fault. We tried to wake him up. Although I do kind of wish he had come along, just because we could've used his eyes to read people. It's so much faster and easier than trying to get people to talk about what they know." Zeke chugged the rest of his beer and looked around the bar. "Well, time to put those legs to work, Eve. You've got about twelve pairs of eyes on you right now, and any one of them could have the information we need. I'm going to go mingle, because they're not going to talk to you if I'm hovering like a jealous boyfriend."

Eve had no trouble at all getting people to talk to her, and she had several drinks bought for her. She kept an eye on Zeke as they both worked the room, and she was aware that he was keeping an eye on her as well. She could easily defend herself against regular drunks, but now that she knew the world was full of *other* things that could be disguised as regular drunks, she was comforted by his eyes following her. He knew how to handle the *other* things.

She took a few moments through the night to simply observe Zeke around other people. His energy drew in the people around him like a magnet. He was so friendly and kind, and even though he was sometimes a little thick and clumsy, he did everything with a delightful sincerity and enthusiasm. His smile and laughter were so bright and effortless, it was hard not to smile back at him. His cheerful personality made people want to be his friend.

And there were a lot of women who wanted to be his friend tonight, Eve noticed, with perhaps just the tiniest tinge of jealousy.

By closing time, Eve was half in the bag. She hadn't meant to drink as much as she did, but she felt more comfortable having a drink to sip on while she was talking to strangers, and she'd done a lot of talking. She'd apparently gotten so careless in her current state that she'd lost track of Zeke, too. When all the lights came on, she didn't see him anywhere.

She followed the crowd out the door, then stood out front, looking around for Zeke. They had walked there together from the motel, and she wasn't sure she was in any condition to be making the walk back alone. He had to be around somewhere. He wouldn't have left her. Would he?

"Hey, darlin', you looking for someone to take you home?" a man asked Eve. She turned around and saw a rough-looking, hairy fellow standing there with his tall, lanky friend. She had talked to them both earlier in the night, but they hadn't had any good information for her, so she didn't chat long with them. He was more interested in telling her how good she looked and smelled than he was in having any kind of real conversation, and his scrawny friend kept staring at her creepily with his buggy eyes, like he was right now.

"No, I'm good, thanks," she replied confidently, trying to hide her level of inebriation. "My friend is coming for me."

"Is she as pretty as you?" the hairy man said in an oily tone, advancing toward her.

Eve suddenly felt a large presence behind her, and a strong, heavy arm slid over her shoulder and came down across the front of her torso protectively. She smelled the comforting and familiar scent of citrus and pine as Zeke's body loomed behind hers. He leaned forward over her other shoulder as he fixed the two creeps with a threatening glare.

"I don't know, am I as pretty?" Zeke asked. When the two guys just stared at him, he looked down at Eve and said in a low, but still clearly audible voice, "They don't think I'm pretty."

"That's ok, Zeke. I think you're pretty," Eve assured him, patting his hand. "Let's get back to the room." It didn't appear that Rico Suave and his sidekick were interested in pressing the issue, so Zeke and Eve began their stumble back to the motel.

"I think I drank too much," Eve said.

"You and me both, sis," he commiserated.

"Did you find out anything?"

Zeke pulled five or six napkins from his back pocket and handed them to Eve. She blinked repeatedly, trying to make sense of the blurry ink marks, but Zeke explained, "I got a bunch of phone numbers."

"Does that help us?"

"It's a real confidence booster." He grinned at Eve and pointed at the napkins in her hands. "*They* thought I was pretty."

"I'm sure they did. I got several propositions tonight, but no phone numbers. You win."

"Some lady kept offering to blow me in the bathroom."

Icy prickles of jealousy spread through Eve's belly. She wanted to ask him if he did it or not, but she also knew she had no right to these feelings or to that information. He wasn't *hers*. But she was certain none of the bitches at that bar deserved to have him.

"Oh, so you got numbers *and* propositions. I guess you really win."

Zeke hummed. "Hmm, what do I win?"

"I don't know. What do you want?"

Zeke stopped in the middle of the sidewalk, and since she was leaning on his arm for support, she stopped alongside him. She looked up at him, and he down at her. A satisfied grin spread across his face. "I got my prize."

"And what's that?"

He started walking with her again. "I get to walk home with the prettiest girl in all of Texas."

Eve giggled. It was corny, but it was damn cute, and it melted away even the iciest prickles of jealousy.

They arrived at the motel, and after dropping the key twice and suffering several fits of the giggles, they finally made it through the door. When they walked in, Zeke activated the flashlight on his phone and shone it around the dark motel room. They found Bo sleeping on the floor with a pillow and the comforter from Eoduun's bed. Eoduun was still sprawled out like a starfish in the middle of the bed he was supposed to be sharing with Bo.

"We should draw penises on their faces," Zeke whispered conspiratorially.

"We should get to bed, you menace. Go drink some water."

When Zeke took his phone with him into the bathroom, Eve stumbled through the dark to her suitcase by the bed, deciding to take the opportunity to quickly change into her pajama shorts and a baggy t-shirt. Even if Bo or Eoduun were awake, they wouldn't be able to see her in the dark anyway. She wasn't even sure Eoduun would care.

When she was done changing, she saw that Zeke had left the door to the bathroom open, and she could hear him running the water from the tap, so she joined him. She grabbed one of the little disposable cups from the counter, filled it, guzzled it, and repeated it two more times. She wanted no part of a hangover in the morning.

The room suddenly went dark as Zeke's phone entered low-power mode, killing the flashlight. They tripped over each other and snorted noisily with laughter as they tried to navigate their way through the room without stepping on Bo or tripping over luggage.

As Eve climbed into bed, Zeke asked, "Can I borrow one of your pillows and a blanket? I think there's space on the floor for me over there."

Eve sighed and found his hand in the dark. She tugged at it. "Just get in bed with me. I swear I won't bite."

Zeke hesitated. "Bo won't like it. Luc won't like it."

"Eoduun won't like it," Eve completed the sentiment. "But it's just sleeping." When Zeke still showed reluctance, Eve said, "If you don't get in this bed, I will sleep on the floor with you. So there. Now you have to get in the bed."

Eve could hear the shuffle of clothing, and she could see his blurry outline shucking off his jeans and t-shirt. "Fine, but if I get in trouble for this, I'm totally throwing you under the bus." The bed sank and creaked as his warm, muscular body slid under the covers next to her.

She rolled onto her side to face him, and her eyes had adjusted to the dark enough to see his face in profile as he lay on his back. "Is the room spinning?" she asked.

"More like swaying," he whispered. He turned his face toward her. "Is it spinning for you? You aren't going to puke on me, are you?" he worried.

She chuckled softly. "No, gross."

After a long silence, Eve was starting to fall asleep when Zeke whispered, "Are you still awake?"

Eve murmured, "Sort of."

"Can I tell you a secret?"

"Tell me a secret."

"I really wanted to kiss you tonight."

Eve's eyes shot open, and her heart took off like Secretariat out of the starting gate. Her pulse pounded so loudly in her ears that she barely heard her own reply. "Why didn't you?" she whispered.

"Would you have let me? I was worried after yesterday..." His voice trailed off.

Eve reached over to Zeke in the darkness, her fingers lightly tracing over his arm, across his bare chest, and up the side of his neck. She ran her hand along his jawline, then caressed her thumb over his soft lips. That was her guidepost so she didn't miss in the dark. She leaned in and touched her lips to his, gently at first, but he reciprocated enthusiastically, his fingers sliding into her hair. Her long, pink locks tangled around his fingers as his tongue tangled with hers, and he sighed softly against her mouth and kissed her more deeply.

She allowed her hands to explore the firm flesh of his chest and shoulders and was again surprised by how familiar he felt under her fingertips. He kissed differently than Dagon had, but the way his body looked and felt were exactly as she had imagined him in her dream. She reached down, dragging her nails lightly over his hard abdominals.

She just had to know.

She slid her hand into his boxers. His swollen manhood was hot and hard against her hand, and as she wrapped her hand around him and began to stroke him, she realized that his cock was also exactly as she had dreamt it. Maybe it was all the alcohol in her system, dulling her good sense and crushing her inhibitions, but at that moment, she wanted nothing more than to feel him inside of her.

And then Eoduun rolled over and snored loudly in his sleep, dragging both Eve and Zeke back to their senses and reminding them of their current surroundings. Zeke grabbed Eve's forearm to stop the movements of her hand on his shaft.

"We should stop," he whispered breathlessly. She felt him throb in her hand, and his hips flexed forward slightly.

"It doesn't feel like you want to stop," she whispered back.

"Of course I don't *want* to, but we need to. Bo told me I wasn't allowed to touch you." He throbbed again, and his hand tightened around her arm.

"But I'm touching *you*," she countered.

He groaned softly. "Please. It's taking everything I have right now to stop."

Eve reluctantly released her grip on him and withdrew her hand from his boxers. She knew in her head that he was right, but her desire was doing its best to muffle her voice of reason. As far as bad ideas went, having sex with him in the same room as their sleeping teammates after a night of drinking was right up there at the top of the list.

"You're not going to go sleep on the floor now, are you?" she asked.

"I probably should."

"Don't. Please," she begged.

He didn't respond right away, but when he did, he simply said, "Ok." He sought her hand out under the covers and intertwined his fingers with hers. "Goodnight, Eve," he said softly.

When Eve woke up to Bo shaking the bed, she still felt a little buzzed.

"I see we decided to throw sleeping arrangements out the window," Bo said disapprovingly.

"I made him do it," Eve replied groggily. "I didn't want to give up any of my blankets."

"Yes, I'm sure you really had to force his hand."

Zeke sat up, scratching his fingers through his disheveled hair. "She couldn't resist my boyish charms."

"You're still drunk, aren't you?" Bo asked flatly.

Zeke squinted one eye at Bo and crinkled his nose. "Maybe just a little."

Bo gave an exasperated sigh. "Did you at least get something from your escapades last night? Any leads?"

"Oh, yeah, I think I did," Zeke said. "I talked to some woman who told me the most recent kid taken was her neighbor. She said the day before he went missing, she saw him talking to a couple of teenagers out in front of his house after school. But they weren't kids she had ever seen before."

"Did you get her name? Maybe Eoduun and I can pay her a visit and see if we can get a description of the teenagers?"

"Um…" Zeke looked at his jeans on the floor next to the bed. Then he looked over at Eve. "I think I gave you the numbers I collected, didn't I?"

Eve remembered him handing her the pile of napkins. But what the hell had she done with them? She had no recollection of what had become of them after that. They were in her hand, and then they weren't. Shit.

Eve climbed out of bed and began digging through her suitcase. She checked the pockets of her shorts. She found a folded-up piece of scrap paper in her back pocket, but no napkins. "Shit."

"Great," Bo sighed again. "Well, we'll just have to pay a visit to all of the neighbors, then. Do you remember what she looked like?"

Zeke shrugged. "I think she had medium blonde hair. Or light brown. Or maybe it was red? But she was short! I do remember that. She barely came up to my nipple," Zeke said, holding his hand at chest height.

Bo looked to Eve with weary mismatched eyes. "Did you get anything?"

Eve looked down at the paper she'd taken from her shorts pocket and fidgeted with it as she replied, "Just some guy who said his friend's dog found the body of the first boy, but he didn't know anything else." As she spoke, she noticed writing on the inside of the folded paper in her hand. She unfolded it, and when she saw what was written on it, her eyes widened.

"What's that?" Bo asked.

Eoduun was just coming out of the bathroom in a fresh outfit and the same old gloomy expression on his face. He came over to see what had suddenly caught everyone's interest.

Eve handed the paper to Bo, and Eoduun looked over Bo's shoulder at it. "That was in my shorts," Eve said. "I think someone at the bar must've slipped it into my pocket last night."

"What is it?" Zeke asked.

Eoduun read aloud, "Tell Dagon hello for me. -R."

Everyone fell into an uncomfortable silence.

"Who is R?" Eve wanted to know.

"Ruthlys," Zeke answered somberly. "She's the one who resurrected Dagon."

7
Do I Detect Jealousy?

"What the hell is she doing *here*?" Eve wondered.

"This is bad," Bo said quietly, still looking down at the paper. "You have no memory of anyone giving you this?"

"No. It was pretty crowded in there, and my ass got touched more than I cared to take notice of, so anyone in that bar could've slipped that into my pocket."

"You don't remember anyone saying anything strange to you?"

"Not any stranger than the shit drunks normally say."

"This is going to be incredibly awkward, Eve, but I need to look you over. You too, Zeke."

Eve didn't see what was so awkward about that. She stood up and held her arms out. "Ok," she acquiesced.

"Undressed."

She immediately clamped her arms down in front of herself. "What?! Why?!"

"I need to check for hidden hexes. If Ruthie planted one on you, I'll be able to see it."

Ruthie?

"Just give me a mirror and I can check myself," Eve suggested desperately.

Bo pointed at his blue eye. "Only Luc and I can see our sister's hexes."

"Your *sister*?!"

Bo just gazed back at her apologetically.

"I'll go first," Zeke offered. "I mean, I'm already half-naked," he chuckled. He climbed out of bed and he and Bo went into the bathroom for the hex inspection.

As soon as they were alone, Eve felt Eoduun glowering at her. "You guys went without me last night. That was shitty."

"We tried to wake you up. We really did. And just FYI, Zeke heard you say something weird in your sleep." She told him about the "put it all in your mouth" mumblings, and Eoduun's face burned with embarrassment.

"What did he say?" he asked hesitantly.

"Nothing. But he was definitely startled by it. His eyes got all big."

"You didn't say anything to him, did you?" Eoduun asked suspiciously.

"Of course not. It's not my place to say anything." "Well, you didn't waste any time jumping into bed with him," he criticized jealously. "Disappointed it wasn't Dagon?"

Eve crossed her arms. "You know how shitty it is to hold something someone *dreamed* about over their head?"

"It's not just the dream. It was your thoughts and feelings, too."

"Wait, it all comes through, then?" Eve asked, her interest suddenly piqued. "When you read someone, you get the whole experience? The feelings they felt?"

Eoduun's perpetual scowl softened slightly when he realized that she was being sincere. "Yeah. Memories come to me with all the feelings that have been attached to them."

"That can't always be easy to take on," Eve empathized. "Especially in this line of work, I would imagine."

"It isn't. Especially when I have to read someone or something recently dead or dying."

"You've had to read a dead person? How does that even work?!"

"The brain can be accessed for a very brief window after death. We're talking minutes, though. And it isn't pleasant."

Eve was horrified. "You've experienced death."

"How it felt for the people who died, yes."

"Is it something that automatically comes through, or can you block certain memories or feelings?"

"What's with the twenty questions?" Eoduun said uncomfortably.

"I'm just fascinated. I've never known anyone who could do anything like what you do. I'm not trying to be annoying. It's just, when you were in my head, I felt like you were rifling through my memories the same way someone would flip through folders in a filing cabinet, so it seemed like you had a way to control what you were looking for."

"I know what I'm looking for, but I don't always know what I'm going to come across while I'm looking. Some memories push themselves onto me. Like your Dagon dream. And your traumas from Grant and Adam. And seriously, Adam and Eve? That should've been a red flag enough."

Eve didn't realize those memories had come up when Eoduun was in her head. He'd been flipping through them so quickly, she could hardly keep up.

"Oh," was all she could say.

"I'm sorry, by the way," Eoduun said in an uncharacteristically kind tone. "Some people are just more garbage than human."

"Monsters in their own right," she agreed.

Eoduun looked at her curiously, a crease forming between his brows as he chewed on the question he seemed to want to ask.

"What is it?" she asked.

He lowered his voice. "How did you reach back? When I was in your head."

She lowered her voice to match his. "Do *what*?"

Surprise colored his features. "You didn't mean to do it?"

"Do what?" she repeated.

"You reached back."

Eve shook her head. "Yeah, I'm not following."

"But I felt it. When I was reading you, you started reading me. How the hell did you do that?"

"I don't think I did that."

Eoduun was growing frustrated. "I *know* you did. I felt it. It was only for a split second, but it definitely happened. The only person I've ever come across who could reverse a reading was Ruth. So why can you do it? And why are you trying to lie about it?"

"I'm not!" Eve defended. "The whole thing happened so fast that I didn't even know what was going on! So how would I know how to do it back to you?!" Eoduun's ebony eyes searched hers for sincerity, and she boldly gazed back at them. "Read me, if you have to. I have nothing else to hide," she offered.

Eoduun seemed far from satisfied, but he grunted and turned his back to her as Bo and Zeke came out of the bathroom.

"I'm free and clear!" Zeke announced merrily, snapping the waistband of his boxers and then throwing his hands into the air in exaggerated celebration.

"Go put some clothes on, for fuck's sake," Bo said.

"Take it off, Z. Put it on, Z. Make up your mind, man," Zeke mocked.

Bo glanced apprehensively at Eve. "Ready?" he asked. Eve's stomach dropped. It was her turn to go stand naked in front of Bo's probing eyes. No, she wasn't ready. But that wasn't going to change anytime soon, so she might as well get it over with now.

She followed Bo into the bathroom and shut the door behind her. He stood in the far corner, arms crossed, with his back to her and the mirror.

"Let me know when you're undressed. I'll try to make it quick," he said nervously.

He's not doing this because he wants to. He's trying to make sure we aren't in danger. Pretend he's a dermatologist. Just a really attractive dermatologist.

Eve's fingers trembled as she pulled her shirt off and dropped her shorts. She looked down at her underwear. She had the most embarrassing question, but she had to ask it. "Do I have to take off my underwear if I'm wearing thongs?"

"Oh...uh...no, you can leave those on. I should be able to...uh...see enough." He was even more embarrassed than she was.

She faced the large mirror over the counter and looked at her mostly naked form. The lighting wasn't overly flattering, but thankfully it wasn't brutal, either. "Ok, then I guess I'm ready," she said quietly.

Eve watched in the mirror as Bo turned around, and they made brief eye-contact in the mirror. He quickly averted his eyes from hers.

"Arms out, legs slightly separated, please. Sorry," he apologized. He walked around her, looking her over carefully as he nervously chattered, "I know this is awkward, and I am sorry...My sister is a devious piece of shit, and I have no idea how she even knew to put that in *your* pocket...I really am sorry about all of this...aaaaand you are all done and you're clear so get dressed!" Bo practically sprinted from the room when he was done, leaving her standing alone in the room with her arms out like a scarecrow.

She was glad he didn't just gawk at her in creepy silence. She'd been afraid it was going to feel like an appraisal, but it didn't. She worried he was going to make her self-conscious of her body or that he was going to stare at her or touch her, but that didn't happen either. It was awkward, yes, but he did his best to break the tension without being creepy about it.

Now, if it was Luc doing the inspection…he probably would've made sure that Eve inspected him, too. Luc may look classy and refined, but Bo was definitely the more gentlemanly of the two.

Once everyone was dressed in their business professional attire and ready to tackle the day, they discussed the gameplan. First and foremost, what to do about the Ruth development. They had to assume that she must somehow be involved in what was going on with the cucuy/chupacabra case. But to what end, they didn't know. She'd been flying under the radar ever since Dagon had been resurrected into Zeke, so for her to pop up now was completely unexpected. They needed to be ready for anything. They couldn't just abandon the case, but they were in over their heads if Ruth came after them directly – not only were they teamed with a greenhorn, but they were essentially down a man with Dagon's power sealed away.

Bo called Luc to apprise him of the situation. Luc immediately recalled the other teams to return to the compound. They were going to need reinforcements. This was an all-hands-on-deck kind of situation, Eve learned. Luc had some other things to tie up at the compound before he could leave, but when he was able, he would meet them in Texas.

In the meantime, they were to work the cucuy/chupi case as planned, but keep their wits about them at all times. Since Bo and Eoduun were the only ones who brought their IDs, they would be meeting with officials. Zeke and Eve would have to act as their trainees or assistants. They planned to talk to the police and medical examiner and see if they could get a look at the body of the first victim. Bo hoped that if he could get a scent profile from the body, he could potentially use it to identify the cucuy and/or chupacabra if they came across them. They also wanted to interview the parents and neighbors of the most recently abducted child, and the man who found the body, using Eoduun's reading skills to search the interviewees memories for anything they may be reluctant to share. People are generally afraid to say anything out of the ordinary, like "I saw a hairy monster running from the scene."

Bo had wanted to post someone at the convention at the next town over – it was a comic book convention, and had the potential to have children in attendance that could draw the cucuy. Additionally, it happened to be right smack dab in the middle of the cucuy/chupi hunting grounds. But with Ruth somewhere out there, he didn't want to split the group up too much or put anyone in a big crowd. Until backup arrived, they would have to play it safe and stick together.

Bo dropped Eoduun and Zeke off at the house of the last boy who had gone missing.

"Make sure you find that neighbor you talked to last night, Zeke," Bo instructed as they exited the vehicle. "Call me when you guys are wrapping up interviews and we'll come get you."

Eve watched Zeke and Eoduun walk away from the vehicle in their business suits, and she had to admit, even if she didn't know them, she'd let them in. Eoduun had his hair tied back out of his face in a neat bun, showing his austere face for once, and Zeke had his hair slicked back and parted on the side. They looked *good*.

As they drove away, Eve looked over at Bo in his business suit, his hand casually perched atop the steering wheel, his elbow propped on the armrest between them, those heterochrome eyes fixed on the road in front of him, and she couldn't help but take a mental snapshot. If only she could ask him to take that mask down, just for a few minutes, the picture would be perfect.

But she'd also come to appreciate him in the mask. She'd seen his face behind the mask, and that somehow made her feel like part of some elite few. She was sure all the other hunters must have seen it, too, or anyone who ever ate or drank in public with him, but for the general public, his face was hidden. She rather enjoyed the idea that she didn't have to share that face with everyone.

Not that it was hers.

"Do I have something on my face?" Bo asked.

"What? No. I was looking out your window," she lied.

"Hm."

"So, Luc is coming today, huh?"

"It seems so. And until he gets here, you aren't to leave my side. Luc's orders."

"Why? It sounded like Ruthlys was more interested in Dagon."

"But it was *your* pocket she placed the note in."

"What does she look like? Maybe if you describe her to me, I'll remember seeing her."

"If she'd been there in her God-given form, Zeke would've recognized her instantly. She was likely disguised as someone else."

"Oh, I don't know if Zeke would've noticed. He was rather preoccupied with women offering to blow him in the bathroom," Eve said more bitterly than she intended.

Bo glanced sideways at her. "Do I detect jealousy?"

"No, it was just gross."

"Hm."

"I didn't fuck him, you know."

"I know."

The certainty with which he replied caught her off-guard. How did he *know*? But that also got her thinking about tonight's sleeping arrangements. "What are we going to do with Luc? And the other hunters that are supposed to be coming as reinforcements? We took the last available room for the weekend."

"Oh, Luc would never stay in that motel. He'll find something nicer."

"But the desk clerk told Zeke everything was booked up in the whole area."

"Luc doesn't know the meaning of 'no.' If he wants a room, he'll get a room."

"That does seem to be a defining trait of his personality," she said.

Bo chuckled. Eve liked the way the corners of his eyes crinkled when he smiled and laughed. He had a genuine kindness about him. He turned to her, his eyes still smiling, and said, "I think you'll be good for him. He needs someone to tell him to fuck off once in a while."

"I'm not with him."

"I didn't say you were. I only meant having you around will be good for him."

"Oh." Eve immediately felt foolish for jumping to conclusions. "Sorry. It's just that everyone seems to have this misconception that we're somehow already an item. Even him."

"Like I said, he's not used to not getting what he wants. He doesn't know what to do with it, so he pretends he *is* getting his way."

"I don't get why he's so obsessed anyway," she mumbled, looking out her window. She could see her reflection in the side mirror. She wasn't ugly, by any means, but she was Midwest pretty, while Luc was California pretty. They were on completely different levels.

She gave Bo a surreptitious sideways glance. He looked like Luc, but his mannerisms, scars, and strange eyes made his prettiness so much more approachable to her. And, in a sense, more appealing. Perfect is always applauded, but, as Luc might say, perfect is boring. Which was ironic.

"Are you sure I don't have something on my face?" he asked again.

"I wouldn't be able to tell even if you did," she retorted, gesturing to his mask.

"I keep feeling your eyes on me. If it's because of this morning, I'm sorry. I was just as uncomfortable as you, but I had to be sure. I can have Eoduun wipe the image from my mind if it makes you feel better."

"He can do that?"

"He can read and erase. When we've resolved a case, Eoduun usually erases all memory of us and the creature from the memories of anyone involved."

"Doesn't that leave people with huge blank spots? Don't they question that afterwards?"

"The human brain has a remarkable ability to fill in blanks with its own comfortable creations."

"So, if he erased one of my memories, including the memory of him erasing my memory, I would have no idea that something had happened? It would just be...gone?"

"Correct."

"That's a little scary. Can he put it back once it's gone?"

"He can tell you what the memory was, because *he* still has it in his own memory vault, but he can't just put it back. Once he extracts it, that's it."

"So, if you had a really traumatizing memory, he could remove it and you'd never have to relive it again?"

"He could, but he won't."

"Why not?"

"He has his reasons. He takes what he has to in order to keep our existence secret and to prevent panic, and he'll take something minor if he's asked, but he refuses to remove anything formative or significant."

"Even if it can help a person heal from a deep-seated psychological trauma? Why?"

"Where do you think that traumatic memory goes when he erases it?"

Eve remembered Eoduun telling her the way he experiences other people's memories when he's in their head, and she understood. That trauma wouldn't just disappear from the world. He would have to swallow it himself.

"I don't think I've given Eoduun enough credit," Eve conceded.

"I know you two got off on the wrong foot, but Eoduun is good to the people he cares about. He cares more deeply than he lets on." Bo guided the car into the parking lot of the local police station. He turned to Eve. "Let's go see what we can find out."

Bo and Eve looked at police reports under the guise of a Texas Parks and Wildlife official and his trainee. The main point of interest in the reports were the lack of animal prints around the boy's mutilated body, other than those of the dog that had stumbled across it. It was clear to Bo that, even though the photos of the body showed that he'd been exposed to the sharp teeth of a predator, the body had been dumped there by some*one*. One lone shoe print was found at the scene, but it wasn't a clear print. They couldn't be sure it wasn't from the dog's owner. The police had no real leads.

They moved on to the medical examiner's office next to get a look at the body. When the cadaver was rolled out for their inspection, Eve had to look away. She'd never seen a dead body before. Well, not one like *that*. She'd seen dead relatives at funerals, but that didn't prepare her for this. She was glad Bo didn't ask her to participate as he looked at the torn flesh and bite marks. The medical examiner pointed out one strange mark on the boy's wrist that hinted at contusions consistent with struggling against restraints, but since the body was so badly mangled, it was impossible to tell for certain.

The most prominent detail that stood out, however, was how much of the boy's flesh was missing. The medical examiner expressed to them that it wasn't from post-mortem scavenging. He had been consumed shortly after he was killed or as he was dying, and the tooth marks didn't match well to any specific scavenger or predator the medical examiner had ever seen before.

Eve felt sick. Maybe she wasn't as cut out for this as she had thought.

Back in the car, Bo said, "That body reeked of Ruthie. She definitely has something to do with this. There were two other scent signatures as well, but those were not the tooth marks of a chupi. The pictures of the mutilated cows were classic chupacabra. Undeniably so. But not this. So, we have Ruth, a chupi, and something else that I'm still convinced could be a cucuy. The question is: *why*?" Bo reflected on what they'd learned so far today and deliberated their next move. He looked down at his phone. "I want to go to the scene where the body was found. It hasn't been that long, so I may still be able to pick up and track a scent."

Eve suddenly got a bad feeling in the pit of her stomach. "I think we should wait for Zeke and Eoduun."

Bo raised an eyebrow at her. "Why?"

"I don't know. I just feel like we shouldn't go alone. It's a 'Don't Think It, Don't Say It' thing."

"A what?"

She explained her occasional intuitions and her nickname for them. "It's been eerily spot-on more times than not, so I don't like to disregard it when I think something bad is going to happen."

"Did you tell Luc about this?"

"How could I? It just happened."

"No, I mean the intuitions in general. You could be sitting on an incredibly useful latent specialty," Bo said with a hint of surprise.

"I don't know about all that," Eve dismissed. "It's not like I'm psychic or anything."

Bo dipped his head to the side. "Maybe you are, but you haven't fully awakened it yet."

"Psychics aren't real. ...Are they?"

"My brother and I can bend space with our eyes, Eoduun can read and erase people's memories, Zeke can rip a phonebook in half and has an ancient god living inside of him, and your blood cures everything. Is being able to see events outside of your local present-time really that much more difficult to fathom? It's just remembering in reverse. We have a clairvoyant at Knighco, and what you described sounds very similar to what he does."

"I wouldn't get too excited just yet," Eve downplayed. "It could also just be a coincidence."

"Coincidences don't just happen coincidentally. Incidentally."

8
I Get Shivers When You Boys Get Serious

Eve and Bo sat in the parked car on the curb, listening to the radio, waiting for Eoduun and Zeke to finish their interviews. Bo stared down at his phone while Eve watched out the window. She missed the option of staring down at her phone when she was bored or had nothing to say.

"Hey, when am I going to get my phone back?" she asked Bo.

"I don't know. Luc has it. I think he was having it transferred over to a new phone on our plan."

"He didn't ask me if he could do that."

"He doesn't ask. He just does."

"Somebody needs to put that guy in his place," Eve grumbled.

Bo laughed. "Oh, I'm sure you will."

"Me? No, not me."

"Yes, you," he said warmly. He regarded her with kind, heterochrome eyes. "Definitely you." He then returned his attention to his phone.

After a long silence, Eve asked, "So, are you going to do it?"

"Do what?" Bo asked indifferently.

"Have Eoduun erase the, uh…inspection."

"Oh, that. Would it make you feel better if I did? I could, but I will point out that *he* would have it then."

"Yeah, but I mean…it wouldn't really matter to him, would it?"

"Eoduun likes girls too, you know," Bo revealed, still looking down at his phone.

That caught Eve by surprise. "But…but I thought…"

"He likes men? He does. But he likes women, too. He drinks red wine *and* white wine."

"Oh! I didn't see that coming."

"So, is that a no on the erasure, then?" Bo asked casually. "Because, if it's all the same to you, I, uh, don't *mind* keeping it."

Eve glanced over at him, catching his wolfish, sideways glance before looking back down at his phone. Her stomach nearly burst with butterflies.

She gave a short, nervous laugh. "I guess you can keep it. It's not that big of a deal anyway." As she thought about erasing memories, she remembered what Eoduun had accused her of earlier this morning. "Hey, Bo."

"Hey," he replied, scrolling on his phone.

"Is it possible to reverse read someone?"

"You mean like look at their memories while they're looking at yours?" When she nodded, he answered, "It is possible, but rare. I know Eoduun thinks you did it, but that would be wildly unlikely. I wouldn't fret about it just yet."

"Wait, how did you know Eoduun said that to me?"

He tapped his ear and looked up from his phone. "I don't miss much." His eyes lingered a moment longer on hers, and for the briefest moment, she swore his charcoal eye flashed yellow as he said, "I hear a lot more than you might imagine." He returned his attention to his phone once more.

What did he mean by that? Was he insinuating that he *wasn't* asleep last night? Was he referring to something else? Or was it nothing at all, and she just had a guilty conscience? Eve wondered what all Bo knew that he wasn't letting on.

She glanced over at his phone, curious about what it was that was holding his attention so completely. He quickly angled his phone away from her prying eyes.

"What do you want?!" he demanded, overly defensively.

Eve laughed, intrigued. "What are you looking at?"

"None of your business."

"It must be something bad if you're being this weird about it."

"It's not bad. It's just none of your business," he huffed, blackening the screen on his phone.

"It wasn't porn, was it?"

"No!"

"I'm going to believe it was porn if you don't tell me what it really was."

"Why would I sit next to you and look at porn?!"

Eve shrugged her shoulders. "I don't know, why did you?"

"I didn't!"

"Then just tell me what it was. You're making it weird now."

"You're making it weird!" His cheeks were blazing red above his mask.

"Just show me," Eve implored.

"No."

"Please. My curiosity is killing me now."

"No."

"It's porn," she surmised.

"No."

"Worse than porn?"

"I will make you wait outside."

"Oh, come on! Give me a hint."

He sighed. "Here's a hint: it isn't porn."

She tapped her finger on her chin. "What's not porn, but equally embarrassing to be caught looking at?"

Eve saw Zeke and Eoduun strolling up the sidewalk toward the car. Bo started the car as the two climbed into the backseat, and she turned around, unable to leave it alone.

"Does Bo sit and look at porn on his phone when he's with you guys?"

"Hey!" Bo protested.

"Oh, you mean those girly manga he's always reading?" Zeke answered. "I don't think I would call it *porn*, but some of it is pretty spicy."

Bo rubbed his hand across his forehead. "Thanks, Zeke. Ok, happy? Let's fucking go," Bo grumbled, his ears as red as the bottoms of Luc's Louboutins.

On the way out to the location where the body was found, Zeke and Eoduun filled Bo and Eve in on what they found out from their interviews. A couple of the neighbors had mentioned having two teens, a boy and girl, come by offering lawn care and window cleaning services. They were described as looking like they could be homeless, but they had an old truck with lawncare equipment in the back. Eoduun had pulled an image of them from the neighbor's memories, and when he did a search on his phone for runaway and missing teens in the area, he found a picture of them in an article from a local newspaper. They'd gone missing over a month ago.

Bo asked about the truck, and when Eoduun described what he'd seen in the interviewees' memories, he confirmed that it matched the description in one of the police reports of an old farm truck that had gone missing from one of the farms that had reported an attack on their livestock.

"So, does that mean those two teens are the monsters?" Eve asked.

"Looks like," Bo sighed. "I fucking hate it when it's kids."

"Something seems really strange about all of this," Eoduun said. "Two friends from good families, according to the article, with different cryptid traits, run away from home and start attacking livestock first, then children...this isn't a normal hunt."

"Ruth definitely has something to do with this," Zeke said. "She has no qualms about using kids as pawns."

"What the hell do we have here?" Bo mumbled, looking in the rearview mirror.

Everyone else turned around and looked out the back window and saw a big red Dodge rapidly gaining on them. It flew up behind them and swerved out into the other lane to pass them, the exhaust system roaring loudly. A thick black diesel cloud enveloped the car as it abruptly lurched over into their lane before it had cleared the front of their vehicle. Bo slammed on the brakes, pulling the car off to the side of the road. The truck also came to a sudden stop, and then the reverse lights came on.

"Be ready," Bo instructed. "Evie, get the gun from the glovebox. Boys – grab something from the back."

Zeke and Eoduun pulled down one of the back seats to access the trunk, arming themselves with a couple of pistols, a rifle, and a shotgun. Zeke handed Bo a pistol.

Eve quickly grabbed the gun from the glovebox, her adrenaline surging so much she ignored the fact the Bo called her "Evie." What the hell was going on? Was this a monster? An idiot with road rage? A serial killer?

The truck backed closer to them, then stopped. The driver's side door of the truck opened, and out stepped a tall, leggy woman with long, platinum blonde hair. She was wearing designer clothing and her fingers sparkled with diamond rings as she reached up to remove her sunglasses from her face.

She was stunning.

Bo opened his door and stepped out of the car, leaving the door open as a shield between him and the woman.

"Ruthie," he said calmly. "It's been a while."

Zeke and Eoduun followed suit and stepped out of the vehicle, also leaving their doors open. Eve decided to join the gang.

"Babhdán, long time, no see. Is that Dagon's vessel back there?" Ruth asked casually.

"I have a name, you bitch," Zeke barked.

"Zeke," Bo warned in a low tone. Then, to Ruth, he asked, "To what do we owe the pleasure? I'm sure you didn't run me off the road just to say hello."

"Straight to the point. You never were quite as much fun as Lucius, but I always liked that about you. You are so much easier to read. So irrepressibly honest. You think the mask helps hide all those pesky emotions, but your eyes are your downfall." Ruth walked toward their car, and Eve saw that everyone readied their weapons, so she did the same.

"That's far enough, Ruthie."

"Pointing guns at your baby sister. Is that what we've come to, dear brother?"

"You didn't play so nice the last time we met."

"I see your eye didn't heal," she commented with a hint of amusement. She stopped her approach and put her hands on her hips. "Your girlfriend couldn't save it, huh? I hear she couldn't save herself, either."

"Don't even talk about her," Bo said threateningly.

Ruth's eyes turned toward Eve. "The new one is pretty, Babhdán. I do approve. I hope I don't have to kill her. That would be such a waste."

Eve's blood turned to ice under Ruth's scrutiny. Her eyes weren't the intense aquamarine blue like Bo and Luc's. They were a deep, emerald green.

"What are you doing here, Ruth?"

"Ooh, you must mean business now. I get shivers when you boys get serious." When she didn't get a rise out of him, she continued, "I want what you took from me. Give me Dagon back."

"Dagon isn't yours!" Zeke snarled.

"Zeke," Bo warned again. "Leave it to me. Don't let her rile you."

"He certainly isn't *yours*, boy. *I* tracked him down. *I* broke the seals. *I* resurrected him. He is mine, and you stole him. It's time to give him back. You've had him long enough."

"And if I say no?" Zeke said.

"Well, then we move on to Option B. B for bloodbath. I must admit, a small part of me was hoping you would go for Option B."

"We aren't playing your game," Bo informed her. "Luc is on his way. You should probably be gone when he gets here."

"But I haven't told you about my new trick yet! I'm really excited about it. I've been working on it for almost a year now, and I was so happy that it caught your attention."

"What are you talking about?"

Ruth squealed with delight. "Ok, ok," she grinned, holding well-manicured hands out in front of her. "So, get this: you know those monsters you've been investigating?" She chewed her ruby-red lower lip with anticipation.

"What about them?" Bo said slowly.

"I *made* them!" She jumped up and down, clapping like a child.

Bo lowered his gun slightly in shock. "That's not possible. Chupis and cucuys are born, not made."

"Not anymore! With the right ingredients, I can make almost anything that goes bump in the night. I have Lilith's grimoire," Ruth revealed. "You might know it better as *The Book of the Damned*."

Bo blinked in disbelief.

"I just wish Dagon hadn't killed your blood healer. You wouldn't believe how many of these spells call for Panacea Blood! She didn't happen to leave behind, like, a baby or something, did she?"

"Ruthie, please tell me you didn't turn innocent kids into monsters just to get our attention," Bo said.

"I thought you'd be flattered," Ruth replied. Then she laughed. "Oh, relax, it wasn't *all* for you. I wanted you to see what I could do, and to understand that I'm not playing around anymore. But ultimately, I did it so you would bring Dagon to me." She gestured toward Zeke and clapped her hands together. "And you have!"

"If you made those kids into monsters, you can change them back," Bo reasoned.

Ruthlys laughed. "What? No. That's like trying to unscramble an egg. Not happening."

"What do you even want with Dagon?" Eve asked before she could stop herself.

Ruth's and Bo's eyes both turned to her in surprise. "Back down, Evie," Bo advised.

Ruth took two steps toward Eve, a wild grin spread garishly across her face. Eve immediately regretted opening her mouth. The gun in her hands trembled.

"Uh oh, Bo. You got a mouthy one." She then narrowed her eyes at Bo. "Hmm…no. I was wrong, wasn't I?" She appraised Eve with curious eyes. "Luc would never let you have this one. He loves a sassy little piece of ass."

"All the more reason for you to leave her the fuck alone," Bo said.

"So, what makes you special?" Ruth asked Eve. "What makes you worthy of a place on the dream team?" Ruth advanced another two steps.

"She—" Bo began, but Ruth cut him off.

"—has a voice of her own, thank you very much." Ruth came even closer, and when she was close enough for Eve to smell her expensive perfume being carried on the air, Bo raised his gun over the hood of the car at Ruth's head.

"I'm not playing games, Ruthie. Back off." Eve glanced over at him fearfully, looking to him for some kind of guidance, but his focus was fixed firmly on Ruth. Eve saw that his eye had turned yellow.

They were definitely in danger.

An expression of sheer delight washed over Ruth's face as she looked back at Bo. "Whaaaat?! What is up with your eye?! Holy shit, that is *cool*! It didn't do that before! Did that happen after the injury?" She barely even noticed the gun pointed at her head.

"I'll tell you all about it. Just back the fuck away."

"That's your wolf showing through, isn't it? Well, I'll be damned. You want me to take out the other eye so you can have a matching pair? The yellow suits you," Ruth said, unmoving.

"Evie, get behind Eoduun," Bo instructed.

Eve felt Eoduun's hand grabbing her arm from behind her and pulling her backward. She was afraid to take her eyes off of Ruth, but she didn't want to run into the open car door behind her, either. She quickly glanced back as she moved toward Eoduun, and in that second, the sound of a gunshot exploded in front of her.

9
You Enjoy Crushing Me, Don't You?

Startled, Eve tripped over her own feet and fell on the ground, banging the back of her head against Eoduun's car door. Ruth held her bloody hand and shrieked, "Ow! You fucking *shot me,* you dick!" She turned glowing emerald eyes toward Bo as she snarled an incantation, then flicked her bloody hand as though throwing something invisible at him. He tried to dodge, but it wasn't the kind of attack that could be dodged. He was thrown like a ragdoll clear to the other side of the road.

Without missing a beat, Ruthlys turned her attention to Eve, another incantation rolling quickly from her tongue. Eve had only time to close her eyes and hold her arm up over her face before the attack commenced. She felt a woosh of air and heard the impact of several projectiles around her. But she didn't feel anything hit her.

Eve opened her eyes and lowered her arm, shocked to see Zeke's back in front of her. In a flash, he was standing facing Ruth, and he reached out and grabbed her by the throat, lifting her feet off the ground. Blood was dripping down his arms, and Eve could see several large splinters of wood sticking out of the backs of his arms. Then she saw the gill slits behind his ears.

Ruth choked out, "Dagon?"

"Die," Dagon seethed.

Ruth began to sputter and struggle as he squeezed her neck without mercy.

Suddenly, his hand passed right through her and she fell to the ground, landing hard on her ass. She scrambled to her feet and looked back at them with confusion and rage.

"Run away," Bo growled as he stumbled back to the car.

"Fuck you," Ruth hissed, then scurried to her truck and sped off, spitting gravel all over their car.

Dagon watched Ruth speed away, and to Bo, he warned ominously, "You'll regret saving her."

When Dagon turned Eve's way, she was horrified to see Zeke's body was riddled with large wooden splinters, blood streaming from his wounds. Dagon's red eyes met with hers, and he smiled wickedly. "Now, let me taste you."

Eoduun stepped in between Dagon and Eve just as Bo rushed to their side. "Zeke, come back now," Eoduun demanded.

"Zeke can't come back until this body is healed, Eodie," Dagon said defiantly.

"Don't fucking call me that," Eoduun snarled.

"If you want him to live, you need me." Dagon looked past Eoduun and Bo, fixing his eyes on Eve. He began pulling the wood splinters out of his arms, which only allowed the blood to pour more freely from the gaping holes left behind. "Better hurry up and heal me, princess."

Eve was desperate. She pushed through Bo and Eoduun and faced Dagon directly. "What do I need to do?"

Dagon licked his lips. "Offer up your blood."

Bo took her hand in his and said, "All he needs is a small cut on your hand or finger." He pulled out a sharp pocket knife. "I can do it for you, if you'd like."

"No," Dagon interrupted. "Not the hand." He reached out and caressed his finger slowly down the side of her neck. "I want it from there," he purred.

"Out of the question," Bo said firmly.

"I'm only going to keep moving south until you agree."

Eve pulled her hair away from the side of her neck. "Just do it, Bo. But don't let him bleed me dry."

Bo scowled, but did as Eve asked. He cupped her face gently with one hand and brought the knife to her neck on the opposite side. Mismatched eyes full of concern looked down into hers, and she nodded. She hissed between her teeth as he nicked the tender skin on her neck, being sure stay away from any major veins and arteries.

Dagon shoved Bo aside and took Eve up in his arms, his mouth descending ravenously over the cut Bo had made for him. Eve gasped as his teeth pressed into her skin and his tongue swirled over the bleeding wound. He gripped her hair and angled her head further to the side as he pulled her closer and suckled even harder at her neck.

The sensation was unlike anything she'd ever experienced. The flesh around the wound tingled decadently, sending sensual thrills from her neck to her core. Her toes curled as a warmth spread through her belly and awakened a need between her thighs. Her arms slipped around Dagon's neck and she pulled herself closer, pressing her body against him desirously.

The soft undulations of his tongue and the painful bite of his teeth as he fed on her healing life force made for a curiously delicious sensational pairing that was carrying Eve to the edge of ecstasy. He moaned against her neck.

She felt a hand around her arm, and she was suddenly yanked back, the growing pleasure from Dagon's mouth brought to an abrupt end.

"That's enough," Bo growled. Eve blinked her eyes open, not realizing she'd had them closed so tightly, and she looked up at Bo. His eye was yellow with fury and his breath was heavy as he held Eve away from Dagon with a firm grip. He pressed a cloth to the cut on Eve's neck.

Dagon smiled with satisfaction and licked the blood from his lips. To Eve's surprise, the wounds on his body had already stopped bleeding and were starting to close up.

"You almost came, didn't you?" Dagon said lewdly.

Eve blushed in embarrassment, realizing only then that Bo and Eoduun had been standing right there to bear witness to her shamelessness.

"You just wanted to finish her off yourself, didn't you, Bo?" Dagon said slyly. "Just dying for a taste, aren't you?"

Eve glanced over at Bo, realizing that he was scraped up and bleeding. He had been thrown across the road, after all.

"I'll live. Zeke, you can come back now. You're healed enough," Bo said.

There was a tense momentary struggle between Zeke and Dagon, and Zeke's eyes flashed strangely between vermilion red and caramel brown. Finally, however, they settled on brown again.

"Dagon, goddammit! What the fuck, man?" Zeke complained.

"Oh, thank god," Eve breathed, relieved. She pulled away from Bo and hugged Zeke around his neck, dragging him down to her level. "I'm sorry you got hurt," she said. "Thank you for protecting me."

Zeke gave an uncomfortable chuckle. "Well, I can't take the credit for that. I'm fast, but not that fast. That was Dagon."

"Not that I'm complaining, given the situation," Bo said, "but how the hell did he blow through Luc's seal? It's only been a day."

"I don't know," Zeke replied. "I was starting to dive through the car to get to Eve and Eoduun on the other side, and the next thing I knew, Dagon had taken over and we were taking a wood splinter shower. He just blasted out of his box like damn grenade."

"He's never worn through a seal that fast," Eoduun said warily. "I don't like that."

"Well, he did save our asses," Zeke pointed out. "So, I mean, I can't be too mad about it."

"He saved *Eve's* ass," Bo corrected. "Pretty sure he would've let the rest of us eat shit."

"Still not complaining about it," Zeke said, regarding Eve warmly.

"Well, no, obviously not," Bo backpedaled. "I was just saying…we can't treat him like he has our best interests at heart. Dagon only does what benefits Dagon. We just happened to be lucky that what benefited him also benefited us."

"How did it benefit him to get peppered with wooden stakes?" Eve wondered.

Bo shook his head. "I don't know, but he went to great lengths to protect you, which makes me incredibly suspicious. He never does anything for the sake of others."

Zeke shrugged. "I think…I think he just likes her."

"And I *really* don't like that," Bo frowned. He sighed. "Come on, back in the car. We still have shit to do."

"In this state?" Eve said, gesturing at him and Zeke. "Let's just call it a day. It's getting late anyway."

"She's right," Eoduun said. "I can drive us back to the motel."

Eve gave up the passenger seat to Bo, and instead sat behind him in the backseat, next to Zeke. As they took off back to the motel, Eve sat forward in her seat and hung her arm over Bo's shoulder. She held her forearm in front of his face.

"I see you wincing up there. I know you're injured. Just take some blood," she pressed.

He shooed her arm away from his face. "I don't need it. I'll be fine."

"Why don't you want it?"

"Because I don't need it."

"You were thrown across the damn road. I saw you limping," Eve retorted. "Is there a reason you won't take it? Is there something I don't know?" When he shook his head, she lowered her voice and asked, "Is it because of what happened when Dagon drank it?"

"No, it's fine. Stop worrying about me."

Eve saw his ears starting to flush, and she glanced at the side mirror to see his face. They caught eyes in the mirror, and he quickly looked away.

"Mr. Tough Guy," Zeke teased.

Eve dropped her arm across Bo's chest and rested her chin on the back of his seat next to the headrest. "Well, the offer stands if you change your mind, tough guy," she said softly. She patted his chest lightly and sat back in her seat again.

Was it pride? Was it embarrassment? Was it bashfulness? Why wouldn't he take her blood? Was he afraid of the way she would react to it? Or maybe he was afraid of the way he would react to it. It was an unquestionably intimate act, even if the cut was only on her hand. He probably just wasn't that comfortable with her yet.

She could understand that.

Bo's phone chimed. "Luc's in town," he informed them, looking down at his messages.

Without warning, an enormous body popped up between Zeke and Eve in the backseat, pressing each of them off to the side. Eve yelped and threw out a reactionary backhand.

Luc's strong hand caught her strike before it made contact. He then brought her fist to his lips and kissed the back of her fingers. "I missed you, too," he said smoothly.

"You can just *teleport*?!" Eve cried. She wondered how the hell he was even making himself fit in that tiny backseat with them. His head was ducked down and his knees were pressing into the seats in front of them.

Luc smiled at her and adjusted his sunglasses. "Well, not *exactly*, but you can call it that. I still have to move through space-time. I just change the shape of it so I can get through it faster." He looked around at the sorry shape Zeke and Bo were in. "Looks like I missed the fun."

"Ruthie caught up with us," Bo explained.

"And Dagon saved us," Zeke added.

Luc's typically calm expression pinched momentarily with confusion. "Dagon? What do you mean?"

"He broke through your seal," Bo said.

"In a day? Not possible," Luc said in disbelief.

"Apparently it is, because he did it," said Bo.

"Were you picking at it?" Luc accused Zeke.

"No! I didn't touch it. He just popped out! But he did it to save Eve, so it all worked out."

"So, he's not sealed right now," Luc said.

"No, not anymore."

"I want to talk to him," Luc said. He reached his hand over and placed the fingertips of his index and middle finger against Zeke's forehead, and from the side, Eve could see him close his eyes behind his sunglasses. They were both silent for a few minutes.

When Luc dropped his hand and opened his eyes again, he and Zeke both looked dissatisfied.

"Didn't go as planned?" Eve surmised.

Luc's dour expression was quickly replaced with a brilliant smile. He took his glasses off and hung them from his collar, and his arm slid across the back of the seat behind Eve's shoulders. "Nothing to concern yourself with, love," he said in a sugary tone. His eyes migrated down to the side of her neck where Dagon had taken her blood. Luc ran his finger lightly over the wound, sending a pleasant shiver down Eve's back. She noticed the cut and bite mark didn't even hurt anymore. "You'll start healing faster now. The more often you give, the better your own healing abilities will be." Luc frowned at the mark on her neck. "Still, Dagon didn't need to be so rough."

"It's ok, she didn't seem to mind," Eoduun blurted.

Luc gave her a devious look. "Didn't I tell you it was arousing?" He leaned closer to her, his face close to her neck and ear. "There's something else I didn't tell you. It's rather euphoric for the receiver, as well." He touched his lips to Dagon's faint bite mark, and Eve's heart beat a little faster. "I was so hoping I would be your first. I can't say I'm not a little devastated."

"You haven't been injured," Eve pointed out.

"Oh, but I am wounded."

"I don't think my blood fixes that," Eve said flatly.

Eve felt Luc's lips draw back in a smile against her neck. "Well, in that case, I guess you'll just have to hurt me first."

"I'll hurt you plenty, if that's what you're after," Bo grumbled from the front seat.

Luc sat up straight again and laughed, sliding his sunglasses back on. "It doesn't look like you're in any kind of shape to be attempting that, big brother." He leaned forward between the two front seats, propping an elbow on each seat. "Why aren't you healed, Bo?"

"I'm fine."

"He isn't fine," Eve interjected. "But he won't take any blood, either."

Luc knitted his brows. "Why won't you take the blood, Bo?"

"I don't need it."

"You've never turned down a good drink before."

"I said I'm fine."

Luc reached up and smacked Bo on the leg, and Bo flinched and groaned in pain. "Weird, that doesn't sound fine to me," Luc said. "What's your malfunction?"

"I don't have a malfunction. I just want to be left alone."

"Bo."

"Luc."

"You know, I'm a little offended. I want it, and she won't give it to me. She offers it to you, and you won't take it. It's a little insulting."

"It isn't insulting. I. Just. Don't. Need. It," Bo articulated.

When they arrived at the motel, Luc didn't climb out of the car like everyone else – he just appeared next to Eve after she had gotten out. "I have secured a suite at a hotel in the city," he informed her.

"After we get all caught up here, you can get your luggage and I can call an Uber."

"What? And stay with you?"

"Of course."

"Alone?"

"Ideally, yes," he purred.

"No."

"Why not?"

If she was honest, it was because she didn't trust herself to be alone with him. But she couldn't tell him that, because it would only encourage him. Instead, she gave him a different, but no less truthful answer. "Because I should be with my team right now."

"I am part of your team right now," he countered.

"But you'll be miles away. If anything happened to anyone, you'd be able to get here in a snap, but I can't. I'd be left behind at the hotel. I don't want to be left behind, so I'm staying here with everyone else."

"You enjoy crushing me, don't you?" Luc said with a wry smile.

"Not particularly. I think maybe you just crush too easily," Eve shrugged.

Luc clapped his hand over his heart. "Ouch, love."

Bo laughed and teasingly patted Luc's cheek as he limped by. "She's got your number, little bro."

10

You Don't Have Permission to Eat My Little Red Riding Hood

They all piled into the motel room, and Luc looked around at the tiny room and the two tiny beds. "Where is everyone sleeping in here?"

"Beds and floor, of course," Eve replied vaguely.

"We don't mind sharing," Zeke added.

"Nonsense, I'll find you another room," Luc said.

"They're booked up," Eve replied.

Luc waved his hand dismissively. "I can get you another room. It won't be a problem," he said confidently.

"But I kind of like sharing a room like this," Eve confessed. "It makes it easier to get to know everyone better."

Luc regarded her thoughtfully, then sighed and ran his hand through his white hair with a defeated smile. "Well, I do have an entire suite all to myself. There's really no reason we can't *all* utilize it."

Eoduun raised his hand. "Yes, please. I vote suite."

Zeke was conflicted, but ultimately voted to move to the suite as well, as long as everyone else went.

Bo was a little more reluctant, but he was aware that Zeke and Eve wouldn't go if he didn't, and he didn't want them to feel compelled to stay in that shitty motel. So, he also agreed.

Luc's suite made their room look like a coat closet.

"How did you get this room?" Zeke wondered as he began to explore.

"It was all they had left, so I took it."

"Is Knighco paying for this?" Eve asked.

"We spare no expense in spreading the good word," Luc replied.

"We have a jacuzzi!" Zeke shouted across the suite.

Eve raised an eyebrow at Luc, and Luc shrugged. "For our day of rest."

Eve laughed.

While Zeke, Eoduun, and Eve took turns showering and changing into more comfortable clothes, Luc ordered room service. The team convened in the dining room area for dinner and discussion. Luc was brought up to speed on what had transpired and what Ruthlys had told them about Lilith's grimoire and her new ability to create monsters. They also brought up her comment about needing Panacea Blood for many of her spells, but she didn't seem to know that Eve had it. The main thing she was after was Dagon.

Their unknowns, however, were problematic. They still knew very little about the teen monsters Ruth had created. Where were they staying? Did they understand what they were? Was Ruth keeping tabs on them, or had she just unleashed them onto the world and walked away? And was she currently working to make more? What kinds of monsters could she make without Panacea Blood?

"I'm going to have to call Sister Fiona," Luc said. "Her connections in the church will be able to track down Ruth's whereabouts and activity. In the meantime, though, we're going to have to watch our backs while we hunt the two monsters she made. I have Team Flannel on their way here to help out, and I've recalled the others to the compound with instructions to only handle cases nearby."

"Can I ask something?" Eve said. Luc nodded. "What does Ruth want with Dagon, anyway? I mean, isn't he just kind of a problem?"

"I don't know specifically what she plans to do with him, but it seems she has a spell to bind or enslave him to her. She basically wants to have him and his power at her beck and call. To what ends, I can only guess."

"She's your sister. How the hell did she end up on the side of the monsters?"

"She's not on anyone's side but her own," Luc said. "She uses monsters as a means to an end. Whatever it takes for her to get what she wants."

"And what is that? What does she want?"

"Who knows," Luc replied. "Power? Isn't that what everybody wants?"

"She wants to be noticed. Admired," Bo chimed in gloomily. "That's all she's ever wanted. To be acknowledged."

"Huh. Maybe," Luc said dismissively.

"You don't really care why, do you?" Bo challenged Luc. "She's just something else to conquer and defeat. That's all anything is to you. Something to dominate, crush, or control."

"Are you sympathizing with the enemy, Bo?" Luc asked in a threatening tone.

"She's our *sister*, Luc. She may be an evil bitch now, but she wasn't always that way. I just wish you'd show a little more compassion when talking about the little girl in pigtails who used to worship the very ground you walked on."

"That little girl in pigtails is long gone. She took your eye. She awakened Dagon and watched gleefully as he killed your partner. She turned two innocent teenagers into *monsters*, and is threatening to leave a trail of monsters in her wake. When she finds out Eve has the blood, she'll be after her, too. You want me to show compassion to someone like that? Not going to happen," Luc fumed. "Pigtails or no."

"I still have my eye. She could've killed me, but she didn't. I'm not saying she doesn't deserve punishment, because she absolutely does. I'm only asking that you at least try to understand why she's become what she has."

"'Why' doesn't matter," Luc said impassively.

"'Why' is the only thing that matters," Bo rejoined. "Knowing why can bring resolution."

The two stared at each other spitefully in a long silence before Luc said, "Eve, please heal my brother already. His bleeding heart is going to kill him."

Bo regarded Luc steadily. "At least I have one." He tossed his napkin onto his plate. "I'm going to take a shower." He stood up with some effort, then hobbled off to the bathroom.

Eve looked around at the solemn faces at the table. "Excuse me," she said as pushed away from the table and left the room.

She knocked on the bathroom door. "Bo?"

"I'm fine."

"I'm tired of hearing that."

"I'm tired of having to say it."

"Then stop saying it and admit that you aren't." There was a long silence. "Bo?"

He sighed heavily. "Can you help me for a minute?"

Eve opened the door and stepped into the bathroom, closing it behind her. Bo was standing in front of the sink with his shirt unbuttoned and one sleeve pulled partway off. He held his arms out to her pitifully. "Pull."

She grabbed one sleeve and pulled it off, then unbuttoned the cuff of the other and pulled it the rest of the way off. She looked down at his pants. "Do you need help with the rest of it, too?" she asked.

"No! No, I can do that," he quickly assured her.

She beheld his battered torso. "Oh, Bo," she said softly. It was a shame to see such a fit form looking so ragged. He wasn't as bulky as Zeke, but he was no less fit. His muscles were more defined, and his veins were more pronounced, but, at the moment, they were covered in scrapes, dried blood, and bruises. She also noticed several old battle scars beneath the current mess. His body had been through the wringer.

She looked up into those strikingly odd yet beautiful eyes and that long vertical scar. Aquamarine and charcoal. Like cold ocean waves crashing against dark, jagged rocks.

He looked exhausted and beaten down, and she wished more than anything that he would let her help him.

...Fuck it.

She perched on the edge of the bathroom counter and grabbed his hands. She pulled him closer to her, and when he was within reach, she wrapped her strong legs around him and used them to hold him close. No escape.

"Hey! What're you—"

She used her fingernail to gouge the scab from her neck, reopening the wound he had cut into her earlier. Then, with one hand, she yanked his mask down, and with the other, she tangled her fingers in his hair and pulled his face to her neck. "Just take it, Bo," she demanded.

His hands slammed down on the counter on either side of her hips, and he inhaled deeply along her neck. She felt all of his muscles tense. He whispered, "God, why do you smell so good?" His lips hovered over the blood on her neck. "Why would you do this to me?" He'd stopped fighting, but he still hadn't put his mouth on her yet. His breath was growing heavy.

"What are you so afraid of?" she asked.

He panted, his breath puffing softly against her tender skin. He inhaled again, and his whole body shuddered. "Losing control."

Those words thrilled her shamefully, and she gasped when he finally gave in. He sucked and licked at her neck, but the shallow wound had already mostly healed and gave out little blood. He slid his hand into her hair and brought his forehead to hers. He gazed at her with the dangerous eyes of a wolf.

"More," he growled hungrily.

She looked down at his parted lips and those sharp canines. She cupped his face and brought his mouth to hers, intentionally tearing her tongue across the point of his tooth. She tasted the blood spreading across her tongue and mouth, and he moaned and leaned into her while his tongue laved it up voraciously. She couldn't tell whether he was kissing her or trying to devour her.

His breath was ragged and heavy as she felt his hands on her bare thighs. He gripped them and pulled her to the edge of the counter, then spread her legs apart as he thrust his hips forward. She felt him swelling and hardening against her through the thin fabric of her shorts as another moan rumbled low in his throat.

"Fuck me," he begged against her lips. His hands slid up her sides, lifting her shirt and exploring the bare flesh beneath.

Knock knock.

"Bo?" Luc's voice called through the bathroom door. "Eve isn't in there with you, by chance, is she?" he asked knowingly.

Bo's hands paused, but he didn't drop them immediately. He looked down at her, panting, with agonizing indecision. He made a faint, almost imperceptible sound of disappointment.

"I'm sorry," he whispered. "I shouldn't be doing this." He looked ashamed of himself.

When Luc received no reply, he warned, "You don't have permission to eat my Little Red Riding Hood, Bo."

The door handle turned, and Bo jumped back, withdrawing his hands from Eve's shirt and shoving them into his pockets in an attempt to hide his visible arousal.

Luc walked into the bathroom and studied the two of them. Eve was still perched on the counter, but she was doing her best to try to look casual. Bo reached up and replaced his mask over his mouth and nose.

"I finally got him to take some blood," Eve said perkily. She hopped off the counter and started to walk by Luc. He caught her by the arm before she was clear, though.

"So I see," he said coolly. He pulled her back to him and looked down at her, but she avoided his gaze. He put a finger under her chin, angling her face up toward his. "Hm, but I see he missed some. Be a shame to waste it." He bent down to her and his lips pressed to hers, his soft tongue running lingeringly over her lower lip and tongue.

Eve's core pulsed, tendrils of hot need winding through her lower belly and inner thighs.

Luc stood up straight and grinned down at her. "Well goddamn," he praised. A devilish expression crossed his features. "I don't know if I can settle for just that tiny taste."

"Luc, don't be a bully," Bo chastised.

"Wouldn't dream of it," Luc replied, his eyes still on Eve. "And perhaps it would behoove you to follow your own advice, Bo."

"He wasn't being a bully," Eve said. "If anything, *I* was." She shrugged and walked out of the bathroom.

Eve heard the bathroom door click shut shortly behind her and Luc was right on her heels. He dragged her into the bedroom, which was next to the bathroom, and slammed the door behind them.

"What the hell?" Eve objected.

He backed her against the wall and rested his hand on the wall above her head. He leaned over her. "What did he do to you?" he demanded.

Though she tried to stop it, she could feel a deep blush rising in her cheeks and ears. "Nothing!"

Luc laughed humorlessly, and it was discomforting. He took off his sunglasses, gracing her with those gorgeous aqua-blue eyes. "I really like the face you're making right now. I just wish it was because of me, not Bo."

"I gave him blood. You know what it's like," Eve rationalized.

"I do. And I saw Bo's eyes. And your rumpled shirt. And his erection. And those handprints on your thighs. He took blood from your *mouth*, Eve. That's not the first place most would think of taking it from."

"We got carried away. It's really not a big deal."

"I don't like feeling like I'm competing for your time and affections. And I *really* don't like feeling like I'm losing."

"It's not a competition."

"Oh, but it is. And I intend to win."

"Why are you so obsessed with winning?"

His voice softened. "It's not the winning I'm obsessed with. It's the prize." His gaze dropped to Eve's lips and his hand came up to touch the side of her neck, his thumb stroking her cheek. "I've never wanted anything more in my whole life."

"It's the blood, isn't it?" she asked. "That's what you want so badly."

He shook his head. "No, it's you. The whole package. I want all of it. Your blood is just a perk."

It was Eve's turn to laugh cynically. "You barely know me. Once you get to know me, you'll change your mind. They always do. I'm kind of a bitch, I hear."

"That's my favorite part," Luc grinned. "You're the only one who isn't afraid to be a bitch to me, and I fucking love it."

"You don't think I'm afraid of you?"

"Are you?"

"I'd be an idiot not to be," Eve said.

"I'm not so scary. Not any scarier than Dagon, and you take him in stride."

"He scares me too."

"But he also kind of turns you on, right?"

Eve's eyes widened, giving herself away.

Luc brought his mouth close to her ear. "Just like I kind of turn you on," he purred. "Is it *despite* being afraid of me? Or is it *because* you're afraid of me, I wonder?"

"What makes you think you turn me on?" she countered.

"You wouldn't be letting me do this if I didn't. I've been watching you for months, and I've seen what you can do in the octagon. I know what you're capable of. You don't want to mess up this pretty face because *you like it*," he boasted.

Eve laughed, despite herself. "I think you've already proven I can't lay a hand on you, even if I wanted to."

Luc's fingers ran down her arm, and he took up her hand. He brought it to his chest and pressed it against his firm pectorals. "Oh, you can lay a hand on me if you want to. Are you telling me that you want to?"

Eve narrowed her eyes, then vindictively pinched his nipple through his shirt.

"Ouch! Eve!" Luc yelped in surprise, glancing down at her assaulting hand, and she released him. With his head still tilted downward, he looked at her deviously from under his brows. "I didn't say to stop."

Eve ignored his depravity and said, "Wait, did you just admit you've been stalking me?"

"Did you really think I would ask you to join Knighco without thoroughly researching you first? And I didn't 'stalk' you. I prefer the term 'scouting.'"

"So, you know all kinds of things about me, and I know hardly anything about you."

He looked down at her with hypnotic eyes and tilted his head slightly. "I'm an open book, love." He leaned down and touched his lips to hers, whispering, "I'll tell you anything you want to know," before kissing her softly. There was no urgency or impatience in his kiss, just a tenderness she didn't expect. His tongue was gentle and sweet, and his mouth tasted of the sweet red wine he'd had with dinner. When their lips parted, he said, "I want you to sleep in my bed tonight. I don't care if you build a pillow barricade between us. I just want you near me when I fall asleep."

This wasn't fair. Eve was completely blindsided by this strange tenderness from Luc, and she was defenseless against it. Was it a tactic just to get her in his bed so he could ravish her when everyone was asleep?

And what about Bo and Zeke? They both seemed to be of the mindset that she belonged to Luc, but even so, they'd expressed an undeniable interest. How would they feel if she slept in Luc's bed? And what about Dagon? He was no longer sealed. He could make an appearance at any moment if Zeke wasn't careful to keep him in check.

Eve's head was swimming. She wasn't used to all of this attention, and by God, was she to be blamed if she liked it? No one was asking her to be exclusive. She didn't have a boyfriend to speak of. Was it wrong of her to let it go on? If she was expected to provide blood to heal her teammates when they were injured, she wasn't sure she had the willpower to just stop herself beyond a certain point. It was an incredibly arousing act, and it swept her up in a lustful storm the likes of which she'd never experienced. It was like she'd been picked up and thrown into an entirely different world with different rules. She'd never been a prude, but she'd always been afraid of admitting that polyamory appealed to her. She'd grown up being taught that it was sinful. Disgraceful. Disgusting. Slutty. Whorish. Then she'd found Adam, who only instilled those feelings deeper. He'd made her afraid to *talk* to other men when she was "spoken for." Yet he had no qualms about sleeping around on her. The burden of monogamy fell strictly on *her* shoulders. If another man expressed any interest in her, it terrified her, because Adam would take it out on *her,* regardless of how she responded to it.

And now, she found herself the center of attention, and she had no idea what to do with it. The feelings of guilt and filth and shame felt out of place. They were a relic of a life she was no longer living. They were rules she no longer had to abide by. If these men were going to pursue her, knowing the others were pursuing as well, then who was she to say it was wrong? They were all adults here, and they all knew what was going on. Was it going to arouse feelings of jealousy? Was she going to become the Yoko Ono and break up the band? Was she going to eventually fall in love and want one in particular? Because right now, she had a lot of confusing feelings about her teammates, and it felt like trying to choose one was going to be an impossibility. But it filled her with so much regret to think of putting a stop to all of it completely.

Sometimes, a girl just wants to taste all the flavors behind the counter. Is that so wrong?

11
Don't Tell Me You've Gone and Fallen in Love

Zeke yelled through the entire suite, "Me and Eoduun are renting a movie! Come help us pick!"

Eve looked up at Luc. "Sounds important. We should probably assist."

"You and I *will* have uninterrupted time alone," Luc pledged. "As soon as this case is resolved, I'm having you for dinner at my apartment."

"You meant for it to sound that way, didn't you?" Eve asked flatly.

Luc straightened his back and flicked his sunglasses open. He grinned and slid them on his face, then left the room without answering her.

"Tease," she called after him.

Luc and Eve joined Zeke and Eoduun in the living room area. Zeke was sitting in the middle of the small couch in front of the television in gym shorts and a baggy orange t-shirt, while Eoduun was lying on his belly on the floor in front of Zeke with his lavender t-shirt bunched up around his armpits. Zeke had his bare feet on Eoduun, and he was lightly kneading them over Eoduun's bare back, like a cat making biscuits.

"Why are you doing that?" Eve asked them quizzically.

"I don't know, he just likes it," Zeke said with a shrug, staring at the television screen as he scrolled through the rental options and continuing to knead with his feet.

"It's relaxing," Eoduun said, his voice muffled by the pillow squishing against his cheek.

An impish grin curled Eve's lips as she plopped down on the couch and slid right up next to Zeke. She slowly touched her notoriously ice-cold feet right between Eoduun's shoulder blades.

He gasped and jerked his head up. "Eve! What the fuck?"

"What?" she asked innocently. "I thought you liked it." She matched Zeke's movements, and as Eoduun squirmed and whined under her cold toes, her foot bumped against Zeke's.

"Holy shit, your feet *are* fucking cold!" Zeke exclaimed. He reached over and grabbed her legs, swinging them around to bring her feet up into his lap. He lifted the bottom of his shirt and tucked her feet up under it, then wrapped his shirt and one arm around her feet, holding them against his bare stomach. "There. That'll warm you up." He continued browsing the rentals and kneading Eoduun's back with his feet. "See anything you want to watch?"

Eve leaned back with her head against the armrest of the couch, wiggling her cold toes against Zeke's hard stomach. "I don't care. Oh wait, scroll back up. I missed a bunch of them."

Meanwhile Luc sat in the nearby chair with one leg casually crossed over the other, hiding his mood behind his sunglasses and an impassive expression.

"Oh, that one!" Eoduun said, pointing at the screen as Zeke stopped on a recently-released horror film about a haunted house. "It's supposed to be a good one."

"Oh yeah, I heard that too," Eve concurred. "Let's watch it."

Zeke hesitated. "There isn't anything else you'd rather watch? What about that funny superhero one?"

"I already saw that one. It was good too, but I'm in the mood for scary," Eve said.

"Is this supposed to be really scary?" Zeke asked.

Eve looked at him curiously. "Do you not like scary movies?"

"They give me nightmares," he confessed bluntly.

Eve stifled a laugh. "Dude. You kill *monsters*. How can *movies* give you nightmares?"

"Think about it! Most people like scary movies because they can tell themselves that nothing like that could ever happen, that it's all pretend. Isn't it scarier to watch knowing that those kinds of things *do* exist? Those kinds of things *do* happen to people?"

Eve had to concede that his reasoning was sound. "Ok, I get it. But this is about a haunted house. Ghosts don't really exist, right?"

"Maybe not ghosts, per se," Eoduun replied, "but there are different kinds of powerful, malevolent entities that are often mistaken for ghosts. Like Dagon."

"So, like demons?"

"In a sense. That's what the church calls them," Eoduun said.

"Dagon's not a demon," Zeke said dismissively. "He isn't *evil*."

"Don't say that in front of Bo," Luc warned quietly from his chair.

"He'll come around someday," Zeke said.

"He will never forgive him for killing Shira," Luc disputed.

There was a long silence, then Eve asked Zeke, "Is Dagon listening to all of this?"

"He is now. He usually perks up when he hears his name. Especially when you say it, Eve."

"Does he feel what you feel?"

"Most of the time. If he's out of the box, that is. When he's sealed away, he doesn't feel or hear anything, as far as I know."

"And he isn't sealed anymore? He's just...hanging out, hearing what you hear, feeling what you feel?" Eve asked.

"Yep. And he said your feet are like those of a corpse," Zeke chuckled, patting Eve's feet, which were still under his shirt, pressed against his stomach.

Bo strolled into the room, and the conversation immediately died. He was comfortably dressed in black sweatpants and an olive-green shirt, but he still wore the mask. He had his phone in his hand, and he sat in the remaining chair, opposite Luc.

Bo silently surveyed the room, then looked up at the television screen. "Is this what you're watching?" he asked skeptically. "Zeke's going to have nightmares."

"We'll all be sleeping out here together," Eoduun pointed out. "I think he'll be fine. Won't you, Zeke?"

"I guess," Zeke said uncertainly. He started the movie and cast aside the remote.

"If anything comes after you," Bo said, "Evie can just threaten it with her corpse feet and scare it away."

Bo doesn't miss much, Eve noted. She wondered if he heard her conversation with Luc earlier, too. His heightened sense of hearing made keeping any kind of secrets from him damn near impossible. She was almost certain after talking to him in the car today that he wasn't sleeping when she and Zeke kissed last night.

"Unfortunately for Zeke, Eve's corpse feet will not be available to protect him tonight," Luc said coolly.

"Will they be protecting you?" Bo inferred.

"I will be warming them," Luc corrected.

"I didn't agree to anything of the sort," Eve refuted.

"And I'm already on it," Zeke said. He hugged both arms around Eve's feet with a mildly possessive scowl on his face.

"Don't turn it down until you've felt those sheets, love," Luc said smoothly. "I would hate for you to miss out on the experience."

"Well, damn, if she doesn't want the spot, I'll take it," Eoduun said. "I like fancy sheets."

"Me too," said Bo. He was looking down at his phone rather than watching the movie. "I like fancy sheets, Luc."

"You know, that bed could probably sleep three or four," Eve suggested. "You guys could *all* enjoy the fancy sheets and my corpse feet can hold down the fort from the couch."

Luc removed his sunglasses and hung them from his collar. His platinum white hair hung messily in his eyes as he gazed at her from his chair. He rested his chin in his hand and smirked. "You're small. I'm sure we could squeeze you in, too. Right next to me." He rose from his chair, and to Eve he said, "I'm going to go have a hot shower. Care to join me?"

"No thanks. I already got cleaned up," she said as he walked by.

He stopped. He placed his hands on the couch armrest on either side of her head. She looked up at him as he leaned over her. He brought his face down to her and whispered in her ear, "Then how about I get you dirty, first?" He graced her with a light kiss on the ridge of her ear. He stood up and looked down at her flushed cheeks, and a crooked, satisfied grin curled his lips. As he started to turn and walk away, Eve saw him glance smugly at Zeke.

Eve looked at Zeke, but Zeke had his eyes fixed on the television screen. Was he really paying attention to it, though? His focus seemed to be elsewhere, and his jaw was clenched.

Eve wiggled her toes against his stomach, and Zeke glanced over at her. He smiled at her, but the shadow remained. He removed her feet from his shirt, but he kept them in his lap and began to rub them.

"Zeeeke," Eoduun complained from the floor. "You stopped."

"Sorry," Zeke apologized, resuming the kneading on Eoduun's back.

Eve wasn't sure at what point in the movie she fell asleep, but when she woke up, someone had turned the lights out. She had a blanket over her and her feet were still in Zeke's lap. She looked over at him, and he was asleep with his head lolled back on the couch, his face turned away from her. The movie was over and the television had gone back to the movie details screen. She heard Bo and Luc whisper arguing near her, and realized that it was probably them who woke her up.

"I'm not going to do anything untoward, Bo. I'm not a goddamn criminal," Luc whispered defensively.

"She's fine where she is. She's already asleep."

"She can't sleep there all night," Luc argued. "I'm taking her to my bed."

"She doesn't want to sleep in your bed."

"She never explicitly said that she *didn't*."

"Luc, how is she going to feel waking up next to you, wondering how the hell she got there? Wondering if you did anything to her in her sleep?" Bo asked.

"She knows I would never do something like that."

"*I'm* not even sure I know that. You're completely obsessed with her."

"Says the guy who tried to fuck her in the bathroom. Don't act like you aren't just as guilty."

There was a long silence. "I got carried away, but it was just the blood. It won't happen again."

"Until she has to heal you again." Luc sighed. "I don't even care about all that. I just want her to love me."

"Wait. What?" Bo was taken aback.

"You heard me. I want her to *love me*. I *need* her to love me."

Another long silence, then Bo said in a low voice, "This is unlike you, Luc. Don't tell me you've gone and fallen in love. Is that an emotion you're even capable of?"

"She scares me, Bo."

"Now you're just being dramatic. You've never been afraid of anything."

"I've never doubted myself, either, yet she crumbles my confidence like she's kicking over a sandcastle. Nobody has ever made me feel like that. I hate it...but I love it." Eve could hear his smile in his voice.

"You know Zeke has grown rather attached to her as well, don't you?" Bo said softly. "And she seems to have taken to him, too. What if she chooses him, instead?"

"Zeke's not man enough for her. I don't think it's Zeke she's attracted to. It's the monster inside of him that's captured her attention."

"You think she's in love with Dagon?!"

"No, but she's drawn to him. Fascinated by him. I just need to get her to focus on me instead, and make sure Zeke keeps him under control."

"He broke through your seal, Luc. And Zeke struggled to regain control from him afterward. I think it's very possible that he's stronger than he's been letting on and could become a bigger problem than we anticipated."

"My seal is imbued with my will. When Eve's life was in danger, Dagon's will and mine aligned in his desire to protect her in that moment. That was how he broke it."

"It's unlike him to want to lift a finger for anyone. Why would he want to save her?"

"Because he wants the same thing I do."

"...her?"

"Her."

Eve's heart was pounding so loudly she wondered if Bo could hear it. She wondered if he knew she was awake. She was trying to keep her breath slow and even, as though she were sleeping, but it was difficult to maintain when her heart was running a race.

How disappointed Luc and Dagon would be when they found out how unexceptional she was. The only special thing about her was the blood she'd apparently been born with. That alone did not make her interesting or captivating or worth their love and admiration. They would bore of her quickly. Luc had assured her that the blood wasn't why he was fascinated with her, but that had to be a lie. Was it like a drug to them? And here she was, a convenient supplier. It wasn't *her* they wanted so badly. Why would they?

So, what was she to do? Let it play out? Stop it before it hurt? Let them love her until they didn't? Stop overthinking it and just roll the damn dice? What did *she* want?

The wrong thing, usually.

12
You're Playing with Me

She moved and stretched on the couch, trying to alert Bo and Luc to the fact that she was 'waking up.' She sat up and scratched her head, looking around.

Luc was at her side instantly. He held his hand out to her, "Time for bed, love. I was just coming to retrieve you."

She ignored his hand and looked over at Zeke. He looked so uncomfortable sleeping in that upright position. She guided him into a lying position and covered him with her blanket. He groaned quietly in his sleep, but he didn't wake up. She stepped over Eoduun, who had fallen asleep on the floor.

Eve went to Luc's side. "Ok, let's go to bed."

His bright eyes nearly glowed in the dimly lit room as they widened in surprise. "Just like that? No argument? You must be tired."

As Eve shuffled toward the bedroom, she saw Bo standing off to the side. "Where are you sleeping?" she asked him.

"Recliner." He gestured toward the chair he'd occupied earlier.

"That doesn't sound very comfortable."

"It's better than the floor," he replied. "Granted, it doesn't have fancy sheets...but it'll do."

"Goodnight, Bo," Luc said pointedly, putting his hand on Eve's back to guide her along.

"Don't do anything I wouldn't do," Bo teased.

"Full blessings, then?"

Bo gave a short, humorless laugh.

Eve didn't realize how much differently it would feel to climb into bed with Luc than it had with Zeke. Albeit, climbing into bed with Zeke probably would've felt differently if Dagon hadn't been sealed. Zeke himself was safe. He didn't even take advantage of her inebriated state and forwardness last night.

Luc wasn't Zeke. And from what she'd secretly overheard, he was pursuing her with even more vigor than she had realized. She'd seen his teasing and propositions as just a game to him, but she now knew that he was playing for keeps. To what lengths would he go to get what he wanted? Should she be afraid? She already was afraid of him, but now she had all new reasons to fear him. A man who covets your love will either drag himself through the dirt to earn it, or he'll drag you through the dirt until you relent. What kind of man was he?

She liked him. He was intriguing, handsome, intelligent, and the jerk could cook. And those eyes...when he looked at her with those goddamn eyes...they were spellbinding. It was hard for her to deny that the idea of someone like *him* ever wanting someone like *her* was rather thrilling. She never attracted the popular boys. It was never the ten who approached her at the bar – it was his friend, the five or six. So, why did this *eleven* desire her so? It had to be the blood, right? She kept coming back to that. There was no other explanation. She loved the idea that maybe she was just that attractive, just that extraordinary, but experience told her better.

If she needed any other proof that her blood was the driving force behind all this attention, it was Dagon. If Dagon had designs for her, like Luc suspected, then it *had* to be because of the Panacea Blood.

Luc said something from the other side of the bed in the dark, but the air conditioner running on full blast drowned out his words.

"I can't hear you," Eve replied.

She felt him moving closer to her, and she wondered just how close he was going to get. "No pillow barricade?" he commented. He'd stopped about two feet away from her. She was within his reach now.

"Not enough pillows," Eve replied.

"Hm. Flimsy."

"You're right. There are plenty of pillows. I'm just too lazy."

"Are your feet warm enough?"

Eve rolled over to face him, then stretched her leg out toward him under the covers. Her cold toes touched his bare shin.

"Jesus Christ!" he exclaimed, jerking his leg away from her.

A delighted, wicked laugh bubbled up Eve's throat. She couldn't help it. "You asked."

"Do you want some socks or something? God…"

"Socks? In bed? Ew, are you a sock sleeper?!" Eve extended her foot out further, seeking out the leg he'd jerked away. Her toe touched his bare ankle, but he pulled away again.

"What are you doing?!"

"I was checking for socks."

"No, I'm not wearing socks," he declared.

She reached out her hand this time. "You are wearing *something* though, right?" Her fingers touched the bare flesh of his torso, and when he didn't answer, she repeated, "*Right?*"

He silently grabbed her hand and ran it down his hard, bumpy abdominals.

"What're you—?"

Her fingers encountered the silky fabric of the waistband of his shorts, and he released her hand when she yanked it away.

"Pervert," she chided.

"You asked," he replied.

After a long silence, Luc remarked, "So, it seems like you've gotten close with Zeke rather quickly. I hear you slept with him last night."

"So?"

"Did you fuck him?"

"Why?"

"Passing curiosity."

"Sounds like jealousy."

"I don't do jealousy."

Eve scoffed in disbelief. "Then sure, I fucked him. And it was so damn good. The things that boy can do with his tongue, you wouldn't believe."

"You didn't," Luc said flatly.

"No, I didn't. Not sure why you care either way, though."

"Bullshit." Luc propped his elbow on his pillow, then rested his cheek in his hand. "You know I want you, and you find it amusing to see how I'll react to news that someone else is getting what I want. You want me thinking about it. Picturing it. Getting upset about it. You're playing with me."

Eve paused. "No. I mean, you're right, I did say that just to see how you'd react. But I'm not playing with you. I'm just feeling you out."

"There's nothing to feel out. Like I told you, Eve, I'm an open book."

Eve gave a short laugh. "Open book? In what language, Greek? I don't think I've ever met anyone harder to read than you. I can't tell what's genuine and what isn't."

Luc's large hand sought hers out under the covers, and he gently intertwined his thick fingers with hers. "Maybe you're just not trying hard enough, because I don't know how to be any clearer." He came closer, his body leaning over hers and his hand pressing hers into the mattress next to her. He slid his knee between her legs, and the touch of his thigh against her womanhood sent a thrill through her core. His lips touched a kiss to her forehead, then between her eyebrows, then to the tip of her nose. She closed her eyes and tilted her chin up ever so slightly in anticipation for the kiss that would land on her lips. She felt the warmth of his mouth hovering near hers, but there was a long, frustrating delay. She opened her eyes.

"See?" he mumbled thickly, his lips inches from hers. "You can read me just fine."

The room was fairly dark, but she could see his eyes clearly with his face this close to hers. They were both soft and wild at the same time, like he was just as likely to watch her burn as he was to douse the flames. She waited in agony to see if he would light her on fire or leave her smoldering.

When he made no move, she whined, "What are you waiting for?"

"You."

"I'm right here. I thought you wanted me," she said, mildly irritated.

"I do. But I need to know you want me, too."

"But you started it."

"And I'm not going to finish it if you're lukewarm about it."

Eve had been revved up and left unridden too many times over the past couple of days. She wasn't letting the opportunity pass again. Scary or not, Luc was sex on a stick, and her body was yearning for his. She reached up with her free hand and buried her fingers in his messy hair, pulling him down to close the distance between their lips. As her tongue sought his, she wrapped her legs around him and forced his hips down against hers.

She broke the kiss momentarily and looked up into his surprised eyes. "You better fucking finish it."

"Goddamn," he whispered with delight, then devoured another kiss as his hips rolled against hers, the rigid shaft in his shorts grinding against her. His fingers squeezed her hand, pushing it harder into the mattress as his other hand slid up her shirt. She felt the warmth of his hand enclose around her breast, and she realized just how small she felt in his hands. She'd never been with someone so *big*. The whole team was tall, but Luc towered even over them at around 6'5". He was over a foot taller than her. That was a lot of man.

She ran her hand down the side of his neck, feeling all of the cabled muscles and tendons moving beneath the skin as his jaw worked against hers. She dragged her fingers down over his clavicle to his firm pectoral, and she ran her thumb lightly over his hardened nipple. He moaned against her tongue and squeezed her breast. As her hand traveled further down, he pulled his hand from her shirt and intercepted hers.

He sat back and grabbed the bottom of her shirt, lifting it off over her head. He then shoved his thumbs under the waistband of her shorts and underwear and slid them down over her thighs.

As she lay bare before him, the room began to fill with a soft, ethereal glow, like a dimmer switch was slowly being turned up. She quickly folded her arms over herself and looked around for the source of the light. It was as though the room was illuminated by a mysterious predawn radiance.

Luc took her hands and uncovered her, his bright eyes roving her flesh. "Don't hide from me. I want it all."

"How are the lights on when none of the lights are on?" she whispered.

"Is it too bright?" The light dimmed a little.

She widened her eyes in awe at him. "It's you?"

He smiled grandly at her. "It's me."

My, but what a sight he was. His platinum white locks fell in mild disarray around his intense eyes, and his gleaming teeth shone dangerously in a confident grin. His shoulders were wide and strong, and his torso tapered to a narrow, well-defined waist. She could clearly see the individual muscles of his obliques, abs, and hips disappearing into the waistband of his shorts. She longed to see them flexing and moving against her thighs, and to have that impressive mast buried deep inside of her.

Her legs were splayed open in front of him, her thighs draped over his. A rapacious expression overtook him as he beheld her. He leaned his much larger body over hers and grabbed her jaw with his huge hand. It occurred to her that she was completely powerless under him. He could easily crush her face with that hand if he wanted to. He devoured her kiss, dominating her tongue with his. If she changed her mind, there was absolutely nothing she'd be able to do stop him if he didn't want to.

She threw her arms around his neck and rolled her pelvis against his hard cock. Good thing she didn't want him to stop.

His mouth moved to her neck, and when he reached the spot where both Dagon and Bo had taken blood from her, he stopped. His tongue ran over the now almost healed wound, and she felt his teeth against her skin.

"No, Luc," she whispered. She didn't want him to have her blood. Not right now. She wanted to know that this pleasure wasn't blood-driven. "I want it to be real."

He paused with his teeth pressed into her flesh, not enough to draw blood, but enough to make her wonder if he would obey. His manhood swelled against her.

After a tense moment, he smiled against her neck. His lips continued down her neck, and he kissed her collarbone. As his mouth moved further and further down her body, her anticipation grew into a warm ache that demanded to be relieved. When his lips touched the dip between her leg and hip bone, she rolled her hips forward and whimpered, signaling her desires to him.

She felt his hot breath between her legs, and a tingle of pleasure spread through her thighs and belly. His mouth covered her intimate folds and his warm, wet tongue laved her ravenously. She couldn't stop the soft moans his tongue elicited from her. She plunged her fingers into his hair and she gyrated herself against his mouth as her pleasure bloomed. Her legs quivered and clenched as his tongue brought her to that sweet breaking point. He moaned as he feasted on her pleasure, the sound vibrating against her spasming folds when she cried out, and her body was rocked by a powerful orgasm.

As she writhed and trembled with the aftershocks, Luc slid out of his shorts. He climbed over her and whispered huskily, "That was beautiful." He kissed her, and she could taste her release on his tongue. He reached down and aligned himself with her center, and she felt his deliciously hot, hard flesh pressing against her. "Tell me you want me," he urged.

"Fuck me, Luc," she begged. "Make me come again." She wrapped her legs around him and wiggled her hips, drawing his girth into her slick readiness.

He groaned appreciatively. "Goddamn, Eve. You're going to kill me." He flexed his hips forward, thrusting his swollen desire deeper and deeper inside of her until he had filled her with his entire length.

He sat back and looked at her body laid out in front of him, his manhood buried deeply inside of her, her legs open around his hips. She saw the desire and satisfaction burning in his eyes at the sight before him, and it only fanned her own flames. His hands gripped her hips and he slowly pumped himself into her, watching his cock sliding in and out. He took her by the hand and pulled her into an upright position so she was chest to chest with him, sitting on his lap. He cupped her face with one hand and crushed his lips against hers, while his other hand gripped her bottom and guided her pace.

She ran her fingers through his hair and kissed him back as she worked her hips, moaning softly. His mouth again moved to her neck, his tongue savoring her flesh as his breath came in heavy puffs over her skin. She felt him swell inside of her.

"I don't know how much longer I can hold back," he panted with his face buried in her neck.

He put her onto her back once more and melded his huge body against hers. His hard torso flexed and slid against her as he rolled his hips against hers, his pelvis creating a pleasing friction against her clit. She clung to him and allowed her body to move as it pleased, chasing another fiery release. As she panted and moaned, her pleasure crested again, and she bit down on his shoulder to muffle her cries as her body squeezed around him.

Luc groaned and jerked his hips forcefully into hers, emptying every bit of energy he had left into her, and the faint glow in the room suddenly dissipated, bathing the room in darkness. He fisted his hand into her hair and brought her face to his, devouring the last of her moans as they finished together.

13

Tell Me Again How Much You Hated That

Luc lay next to Eve, his breath finally beginning to slow to a regular rate. "Goddamn," he marveled.

"You know, you say 'goddamn' an awful lot for someone supposedly from a religious organization."

"My apologies. Praise be."

Eve giggled, and Luc rolled onto his side and pulled her close to him, his arm draped over her and her head under his cheek. She felt like a child's teddy bear in his arms.

"I'm going to have to get up to get a drink and use the bathroom, you know," she said.

"Just let me have this," he begged softly. "Just for a few minutes."

"I didn't peg you for a cuddler."

"You make me want to do weird shit."

"Well, I guess as long as it's weird shit like cuddling and not weird shit like wearing socks to bed."

"There's nothing wrong with wearing socks to bed," he said with a low chuckle.

"You only feel that way because you have the AC cranked to the 'freeze hell over' setting and probably *need* to wear socks to bed."

"I like it cold when I sleep. And I'm not wearing socks. We already established that."

"Ok, but next time you complain about my corpse feet touching you under the covers, I'll kindly remind you that you said you like it cold when you sleep."

"Next time, huh?" he said hopefully.

Eve felt a jolt of panic. She hadn't meant to make it sound like she was already making plans for this to happen again. She didn't want to sound like she was expecting anything or reading too much into this.

"No, I just meant when I come back to bed. I'm going to the bathroom," she announced. She started to pull away from him, but he held on to her.

"If you don't come back, I'll go looking for you."

"I will. Let go."

He released her. She wasn't going to lie – it frightened her just a little at how completely effortless it was for him to hold her there. He meant nothing by it, but it was just another one of those jarring reminders of just exactly who she was fucking with.

She threw her clothes on before opening the door and stepping out into the hall. When she turned into the bathroom and pushed the door shut behind her, she didn't hear it latch. She saw a flash of movement out of the corner of her eye as she started to turn around, and she threw a defensive elbow up at face height as she swung around.

"Feisty," a familiar, deep voice teased. Dagon had his hand against her elbow, blocking her strike. He casually kicked the door shut behind him.

"L—" Eve began to call for Luc, but Dagon threw a hand over her mouth before she could even raise her voice.

"Shhh," he shushed her quietly, bringing his face inches from hers. He grinned wickedly, his vermilion eyes sparkling with mischief. He kissed the back of his hand over her mouth. "Easy, princess. We don't need Luc. I just wanted to spend some time with you. I'm feeling left out."

When he lifted his hand off her mouth, Eve asked, "Why isn't Zeke in control?"

"He's sleeping. I have free reign when he's asleep." He held his finger up to his lips and added, "but don't tell anyone. No one knows that. It'll be our little secret."

"Luc is expecting me back," she warned.

"I know, I heard the whole thing. You make the most appealing sounds, Eve. I wonder what kind of sounds you'll make for me." Dagon leered at her in her shorts and tank top. "Mmm. How the hell Zeke was able to stop is beyond me."

"What the hell are you talking about?"

"When you came on to him last night, and he chickened out."

"You were supposed to be locked away. How do you know about that?!"

"I didn't see it happen at the time, but he just can't stop thinking about it, and I see those thoughts. He wishes he had done it, you know. He keeps imagining all the different ways it could've gone. All the different ways he could've fucked you. I may have given him some ideas as well. Sorry, I enjoy fanning the flames."

"Is there a point to this?" Eve asked, trying to hide her fear with irritation.

"I think you touched Zeke because you were thinking of me." Dagon leaned closer, and she put her hand up against his chest to stop him. He simply brushed her hand aside and blocked the other hand as she tried to keep him at a distance. He grabbed her by the neck, but his touch was surprisingly gentle. He stood over her, looking down at her, and his hand slid from her throat to her hair. He closed his fist in the roots of her hair and pulled it back, forcing her face upward.

"You like the fight," Dagon observed. "You like it when it hurts, don't you? There's something inherently violent in sex. Inherently sexy in violence. I know you understand. When animals are fucking, sometimes it's hard to tell at first if it's a fuck or a fight. Sometimes it's both. It's an intimate struggle."

"Again, is there a point to this?" Eve wondered flatly.

"I just wanted to see your reaction, to see if you agree. And also to let you know that I would gladly help you explore that dark side of yourself. It's nothing to be ashamed of. Everyone has it, but most are too afraid of it to indulge. I see it in your eyes, Eve. You are curious. You don't want to be treated like a porcelain doll. You like the way I push your boundaries, even though you know you shouldn't."

"I think you're full of shit, Dagon."

"Am I?" He suddenly shoved her up against the wall. She gasped as he tightened his grip in her hair and dominated her mouth with his, stealing her breath away. When their lips separated, her chest was heaving. He kissed down the side of her neck and grazed his teeth over her skin. "Tell me again how much you hated that."

"Get out," Eve panted.

"Oh, look at that. Luc left his mark on you," Dagon said in a disappointed tone, touching his finger to her neck. "Well, that's not fair. You know, I'm the one who saved you, not Luc. Where's *my* reward?"

"Why *did* you save me?" she asked, ignoring his question.

"Because you're mine," he said as though it were obvious. "I wouldn't let that bitch take you from me."

"I'm not yours."

"You are. You just don't realize it yet. But you *feel* it, don't you?"

"I don't—"

"Fuck, Zeke's having a nightmare. He's going to wake up soon. I wanted to tell you something, but I thought I'd have more time to play first. The monsters you're chasing will be at the convention tomorrow. And so will Ruth. But don't tell anyone I told you."

"Why can't you tell them yourself?"

"Because they'll want to know how I know, and I don't want to tell them that."

"How *do* you know?"

"Never mind that. Just get them there if you want to stop Ruth. Now, Zeke's going to wake up. He'll think he's been sleepwalking. Don't tell him our secret, got it? If you tell, I'll hurt him."

"You're not allowed to hurt anyone who isn't a monster. Zeke isn't a monster."

"Then I'll hurt Bo. Or Luc. There are plenty of monsters for me to choose from. Just keep our secret, or someone dies, got it?" he threatened.

Eve didn't want to agree to keep that secret, but she also didn't want to find out if Dagon was bluffing or not. And if he'd been doing it all this time without anything bad coming of it, then maybe it wasn't something that she needed to worry about at the moment. Plus, it might benefit her in the long run if she had Dagon's confidence. She sighed.

"Fine. But only if you behave yourself during your free reign. The second I find out—"

Dagon's eyes suddenly turned brown, and Zeke blinked blankly at her. "Eve? What…" He looked around the bathroom. "What the hell am I doing in here?"

"I don't know, you just walked in here when I was getting a drink of water and started mumbling something. You were completely out of it. I think you were sleepwalking. Is that something you do?"

"Sometimes, yeah. Jeez, I'm sorry! God, that's embarrassing," he fretted, scratching the back of his head and smiling apologetically.

"It's ok. It was probably that scary movie we watched, making you sleep restlessly. You should head back to the couch and go back to sleep."

"Did I fall asleep during the movie? I don't remember the end of it or going to bed."

"We both did. Eoduun fell asleep on the floor, and Bo is sleeping in the recliner."

"Where are you sleeping?"

Eve felt a pang of guilt in her chest. "I was promised fancy sheets, so I took advantage."

Zeke nodded and averted his eyes. "Ah, yeah, I don't blame you. Well, I'll leave you to it. I'm so sorry I just barged in on you like that."

"It's ok. I was just getting a drink of water when you did. Goodnight, Zeke."

When Eve had finished in the bathroom, she glanced at herself in the mirror. Dagon was right. Luc had left a small mark on her neck. The sight of it made her feel strangely. It was a little embarrassing knowing that everyone was going to see it and know exactly what it meant, but…it was also kind of hot, for the same reason.

Maybe Dagon was right about more than she wished to admit.

When Eve climbed back into bed with Luc, he was fast asleep. When she settled under the covers, though, he groaned and his hands sought her out, pulling her to him. His big body curled up around hers, and his arm and leg both wrapped around her. He nestled his face into the back of her neck, and he mumbled her name in his sleep.

This wasn't casual for him the way that it was for her. She knew that. He knew that. But she also didn't trust his feelings the way he did. She'd known enough men who were "so in love" right away, then turned into complete shitheads a month down the road. This was likely no different – once she loved them back, they lost interest. They wanted to chase her and consume her while it was still fun, but when it turned to work, she was always too much effort to make them want to stay.

In the morning, Eve woke up to the gentle sensation of her hair being moved from her face. She opened her eyes and looked up. Luc was propped up on his elbow, looking down at her with a lazy smile on his face. Jesus, he was pretty.

"Good morning, beautiful."

She rolled back over and buried her face in her pillow. "Mphf," she grumbled.

"Sorry. I know. How cliché, right? But it is true," he said, his finger trailing lightly over her shoulder and arm. "You are beautiful, and it is a good morning."

"I should get in the shower," she mumbled.

He threw his arm over her. "Just stay a few more minutes."

"We need to get ready for the day," she said. "I really think we should put all our efforts into monitoring the convention today. I have a bad feeling that something is going to happen there."

"I think you're probably right, but five minutes lying in bed with me isn't going to change anything. I doubt Zeke is even awake yet. I've only heard Bo moving about out there."

Eve lay there, tucked tightly against that big man, feeling like his most prized possession, and wishing she didn't enjoy it. She shouldn't get attached. That would be stupid.

"Besides," he continued. "I don't know when you'll let me do this again, so I have to get my fill of it now." He nuzzled his face into her neck and inhaled the scent of her hair. "What I wouldn't give to just keep you," he sighed.

Pretty words from a pretty mouth. The kind that seep right through the cracks in your walls and into your heart. The most dangerous kind.

"You left a mark," she said.

"Hm?"

"You left a mark on my neck. Everyone is going to know." She turned her head to see his face.

He glanced down at her neck, and if she wasn't mistaken, pride filled his bright eyes. She noticed they looked more blue than aquamarine in the morning light.

A pleased grin lit his face. "Sorry."

"You don't sound sorry."

"I'm not," he admitted. She felt him growing hard under the covers.

"Ok, I'm getting out of bed before you get any ideas," she announced. She brushed his arm off of her and pulled away from him.

"I could join you in the shower. I'm all about water conservation. A real environmentalist," he offered slyly.

"I'm good, thanks." She didn't look back at him to see the puppy-dog eyes he was undoubtedly giving her before heading to the bathroom.

After her shower, while she worked on her makeup in the mirror, she fought with herself over whether to cover the love bite on her neck. In the end, she dabbed concealer over it. Her business didn't need to be everyone's.

She went out into the living room and found Zeke still passed out on the couch. He had one leg up over the back of the couch and one arm hanging off the side. She sat down on the edge of the couch in front of him and patted his chest. "Hey, Zeke. Time to wake up."

He furrowed his brows and grumbled, but didn't rouse.

Luc walked into the room. He leaned down and propped his forearms on the back of the couch, looking down at Zeke from behind his sunglasses. He reached over and roughly patted his cheek. "Rise and shine, ponyboy. Places to go, monsters to kill," he declared loudly. As Zeke opened his eyes and complained, Luc looked at Eve. "Oh, you got a little something there." He licked his thumb and reached over, swiping the makeup off of the hickey on her neck. "Much better," he smiled shamelessly.

"Thanks," she said sarcastically.

"Anytime, love."

Zeke looked up at her, and his eyes dropped immediately to the mark. "Did you...did you bite her?" Zeke scowled at Luc.

"Love bite," Luc corrected proudly. He saw Zeke's disapproving scowl, and said defensively, "Don't look at me like that. She had no complaints, did you, Eve?" Luc smiled at her.

Eve ignored Luc and said to Zeke, "Get dressed. We have shit to do."

Zeke sat up and ran his hand through his hair. "What's on the agenda for today?"

Luc answered, "We need to get to the convention. I think that's our best shot at catching the chupi and cucuy. Eve agreed."

Eve added, "It's Sunday, so there shouldn't be as many people there, but it'll still probably be a long wait getting in. We should leave as soon as we can."

"Have you been to a comic con?" Zeke asked.

"No, but I've been to HorrorHound conventions. I imagine this is much the same."

"Are we dressing up?" Zeke asked excitedly.

Eoduun and Bo walked into the room from the dining area. They both had disposable coffee cups from the nearby gas station. Bo had two in his hand.

"I doubt we have time to go costume shopping, Z," Eoduun pointed out.

"And I'm sure the local shops are all out of Wonder Woman outfits. Sorry, Zeke," Bo added.

"You got the last one, didn't you?" Luc asked Bo jokingly.

"So what if I did?" Bo said, raising an eyebrow at Luc as he walked by. He handed Eve one of the coffee cups in his hand.

"Oh! Thanks, Bo." Eve accepted the drink graciously.

Bo nodded and smiled with his eyes at her. Then his gaze traveled down her neck to Luc's mark, and the smile faded. He turned his attention to the cup in his hand.

As Eve stood next to Bo, feeling annoyed with Luc for rubbing off her concealer, she noticed the height difference between him and Luc in comparison to herself. Bo was tall, but he wasn't abnormally tall. She looked up at him and tried to guess how tall he was. He was a little taller than Zeke, but shorter than Eoduun. A little over six feet, maybe? Six-one?

"Do I have something in my teeth?"

It took Eve a moment to realize Bo was talking to her, because he wasn't looking at her. But she was staring at him, she realized with embarrassment. Why did he always catch her staring at him? Why *was* she always staring at him?

"Oh my god, no, I'm sorry," she apologized. Then she furrowed her brow at him. "Like I would know if you had anything in your teeth anyway," she laughed.

He raised an eyebrow at her and gave her an amused sideways glance.

"I was just wondering how tall you were. Sorry, it's stupid, I know."

"You're sizing me up?"

"No, I was just compar...ing you to me." Did she really almost tell him she was comparing him to Luc? Idiot.

As if on cue, Luc walked over and stood next to him. "My little big brother," Luc teased. He then ruffled Bo's hair and sauntered off to the shower. Bo's eyebrow twitched in mild irritation.

"I'm six-one...and a half."

"And a half?" Eve questioned.

"And a half," Bo confirmed. "I'm not short. Luc just likes to make it seem that way."

"By standing next to you?" Eve teased.

"You should see what you look like next to him."

"Probably like an Oompa Loompa," Eve remarked.

Eoduun choked on his coffee from across the room, and Eve wasn't sure if it was so funny to him because it was so absurd, or so true.

14
Trust is for Fools

When they finally got through the doors into the convention center, the sheer number of people gathered in colorful, wild costumes was visually overwhelming. There weren't a lot of children there, but there were enough that a cucuy could have a field day.

They were supposed to rendezvous with another team at the convention: Team Flannel, as Luc called them. From there, they would split into three teams. They needed to first *find* the chupacabra and cucuy and, if Dagon was right, Ruth. But it wasn't going to be easy to recognize even familiar faces in this crowd of costumes. Not to mention, the cucuy can change its appearance, so it might not look like either of the teenagers, and they already knew that Ruth was a master of disguise as well. Therefore, they needed to spread out the team members best suited for identifying tricky targets.

Dagon would be needed, as he could see the monsters through their human faces. Whether it worked with physical masks, Eve didn't know. But wherever Dagon went, Luc would need to accompany him to keep him in check.

Eoduun would also be able to see through any tricks. Masks wouldn't be an issue for him as long as the other person looked at his eyes. He didn't even need to be able to see their eyes clearly to flip through their memories and thoughts. If he read either of our monsters, he would know immediately who they were.

Bo, while unable to visually see through a disguise, would be able to identify any of their targets by scent. He had gathered a scent profile from the monsters yesterday, and he already knew his sister's. If anyone was going to track down the culprits in this massive crowd, Bo would probably have the best chance of all of them.

Eve and her team met with Team Flannel (should she call them that? Was that really their name?), and Eve was surprised to see that they came in costume.

Zeke was delighted. "Holy shit! Michonne, Rick, and Daryl! You guys look just like them!" he gushed.

"Honestly, it wasn't too far off of what we normally wear," Cassie laughed. "Remi just needed to put a little grease in his hair, Ruger skipped his morning shave, and I put a headband on. Too easy. Besides, it seemed the easiest way to carry our weapons in here."

"They didn't check them at the door?" Eve asked. She'd had to be careful how she wore the knife she'd been given so it wasn't confiscated on their way in.

Bo explained, "Cassie can manipulate the way people see things. She can make them see what they might expect to see, rather than what they are really seeing."

"The guys at the door saw a plastic katana and crossbow and toy guns," Cassie said.

"Pretty fucking awesome, babe," Ruger said, smiling at Cassie admiringly. Ruger was dressed as Rick, and he was quite convincing, aside from having a midwestern accent rather than a southern one.

"I am pretty fucking awesome, I know," Cassie boasted, tossing her long braids over her shoulder, and Eve couldn't help but notice her biceps. Eve was quite muscular herself, but she looked at Cassie's arms with envy. She would likely make a formidable opponent in the octagon.

"So what's the plan?" Remi asked. He was dressed as Daryl, and while he had the long hair and outfit down, he didn't fit the role as well as the other two. He was way too tall for Daryl, and he looked too tame. And clean.

Luc filled them in, then separated the teams. Zeke/Dagon would be with Luc; Eoduun would be teamed with Cassie and Ruger; and Bo would take Eve and Remi. Luc gave Eoduun and Bo earpieces so the teams could keep in contact as they scoured their designated areas.

Before they went off in separate directions, Luc slapped Bo on the back and said, "I'm trusting you to keep her safe. No fuck ups."

Bo just nodded, glancing at Eve. What, *her*? She was supposed to be part of the team, fighting alongside them. It irked her a little to think they saw her as something that needed to be shielded.

As Bo, Eve, and Remi made their way through throngs of costumed attendees, Eve looked up at Remi. "Your costume doesn't have quite the same effect after being separated from your team."

"I didn't really want to dress up anyway. That was all Ruger's idea. And if you ask me, he was way too excited about it."

"Sounds like Zeke. He would've dressed up in a heartbeat if we'd had time to prepare. I wonder what he would've gone as," Eve said, looking to Bo for input.

Bo just shrugged.

"Bo was going to dress as Wonder Woman," Eve teased.

"What do you mean 'was'? I have the costume on under my clothes," Bo deadpanned. Eve laughed.

Eve asked Remi about the hunt his team had to leave to come assist them, and he told her about the wendigo they were closing in on.

"Not a werewolf, then?" Bo inquired.

"Definitely not. But it was trying to make it look that way to throw us off of its trail."

"I still need to get used to the idea that we're hunting things that are that clever," Eve commented. "It's like hunting people, but worse."

"It takes a special constitution to hunt things that hunt you back, I suppose."

"Is it true that you can't die?" Eve blurted. It was the question she'd been wanting to ask since she saw Remi and Ruger, but hadn't found a good opening for it. So she made one.

"No. My brother and I can die. We have died. It just hasn't stuck...yet."

"So, does that make *you* the walking dead?"

Remi smirked. "Have you been talking to Ruger? That's why he thought these costumes would be funny."

Eve was pretty sure she already liked Ruger.

Remi asked her and Bo some questions about the chupacabra and cucuy they were hunting and they discussed the new developments regarding Ruth.

"What is she thinking?" Remi asked rhetorically. "I mean, this is bad, even for her. This obsession with Dagon is absurd. She can't possibly be so delusional to think she'll be able to turn him into her own personal henchman. We've had him, what, a year? And he still pulls the rug out from under us on occasion."

Eve ventured, "Maybe it's more than just wanting to use his power. Maybe it's just *him* she's obsessed with."

"Are you suggesting she's a fangirl?"

Eve shrugged. "I don't know. Just throwing it out there. He does have a certain appeal to him. I could see it, that's all I'm saying."

Bo gave Eve a concerned sideways glance, but said nothing.

"He's a monster," Remi argued. "He shouldn't be out here walking around with the rest of us. I still think there must be a way to extract him from Zeke. I don't know why Luc hasn't tried harder to get rid of him. As long as he's topside, we're all in danger."

"Luc has his reasons," Bo responded. "And we've been indebted to Dagon's power more than once. It is a risk to have him around, but the benefits so far have outweighed them. Ruth probably thinks she'll be able to have the same kind of relationship with him. What she doesn't understand is that it's all Zeke and Luc that make it work. Anyone other than Zeke wouldn't be able to handle Dagon's immense presence, and anyone other than Luc wouldn't be able to rival his power enough to keep him in line."

"What's this talk of him breaking through Luc's seal and throwing himself in front of Ruth's wooden stakes?" Remi asked. "Did that really happen?"

Bo nodded.

"Why?"

"To protect a teammate," Bo said simply.

"Dagon doesn't see you as teammates," Remi scoffed.

"Maybe he's starting to. Who knows. Dagon does what Dagon does, and there isn't always rhyme or reason behind it," Bo said.

"Or maybe he's in cahoots with Ruth, and it was part of some elaborate scheme to gain your trust," Remi suggested cynically.

"Possible."

"Probable," Remi corrected. "He got blood for his efforts, didn't he? That's how Zeke is walking around alive and well right now, isn't it?"

"We didn't have a choice," Bo replied.

"You hadn't tested it before that, had you?"

"...Not in such a capacity, no."

Remi looked at Bo knowingly. Eve didn't like the insinuation he was making, but she had no reason to not like it. It wasn't her job to defend Dagon. He was a monster. She had no reason to cling to the deluded idea that he only did it to save her as some selfless act of sacrifice.

"I don't know if he could've broken through the seal if he had ulterior motives," Bo countered.

"What, you think he couldn't break through a seal with ill-will in his heart? He's done it before."

"Not that quickly."

"You can't possibly be suggesting that *you*, of all people, believe Dagon did a good deed."

"I'm not naïve. But I'm also not one to look a gift horse in the mouth. He did what he did, and I am grateful that he did it, regardless of his reasons. If he hadn't, Eve might've died."

Remi glanced down at Eve walking between them, and his tone softened. "I wasn't implying I'm not glad of the outcome. I am. And it's great to know we have Panacea Blood in our corner again. I'm glad you decided to join us, Eve." Then he added, "I just don't trust Dagon or his motives."

Bo suddenly stopped and lowered his mask below his nose. He was sniffing the air. His eyes scoured the surroundings.

"You got something?" Remi asked.

Bo put his finger to the earpiece and said, "They're here." He waited for a reply, then said, "Roger," in confirmation of whatever Luc said on the other end.

Eve tugged at his sleeve. "What's the plan?"

"Stick to me like glue, got it? This is your first hunt, so hang back, don't get involved if you don't have to. You'll be responsible for healing us when it's done, so don't get yourself killed."

"We're just going to kill them here in the convention center? Right in the middle of all these people?" Eve sputtered.

"No. Separate and extract." He touched his finger to his earpiece again. "They're close."

As Eve scanned the people milling about around them, her attention was drawn to one particular Spider-Man who seemed to be staring right at them. She tugged Bo's sleeve again and whispered, "Spider-Man, ten o'clock."

He nodded, having apparently already made him.

Bo, Remi, and Eve tailed Spider-Man at a wide distance until the two other teams joined them.

"Where are Eoduun and Cassie?" Eve asked when only Ruger showed up, but moments later, her question was answered. The overhead lights flicked off and switched to the emergency lighting around the doors as the fire alarm blared.

"Go! Go!" Bo commanded urgently, and they all ran after the fleeing Spider-Man.

As he ran, Spider-Man's form began to change, and he dropped down to all fours.

"Fuck! Luc!" Bo shouted.

"On it," Luc replied. He suddenly disappeared from their side and reappeared in front of the creature, grabbing it right off its feet by the neck and slamming it to the ground. People were still hurrying and panicking all around them, and Eve wondered if anyone had seen what just happened or if the chaos had effectively concealed the action.

The team looked around at the swirling mass of panic, trying to ascertain which person was the cucuy.

"Bo! Where's the other one?" Ruger growled.

Bo searched frantically. "I…I don't know! The scent is fading!"

"Fuck!" Ruger cursed in frustration.

"There." Dagon pointed across the room, not an ounce of urgency in his actions or tone. "The one dressed as a…Zeke says Gamora …the green one in the cheap pleather."

"Go fucking get her!" Bo shouted angrily.

"You heard him, Z," Dagon said lazily, then his eyes turned brown and Zeke took off like a bat out of hell toward the exit Gamora was running for.

A sudden flash of blinding light filled the room, and everyone shrieked in panic. When it evaporated, the room was blanketed with a thick smoke.

"Goddamn it, I can't smell anything but smoke," Bo said.

Luc instructed Ruger to take control of the chupacabra, then he took off his sunglasses. He focused his eyes on the smoke near the exit, then he disappeared.

Bo put his finger to his earpiece. "Say again?" He then looked up toward the exit. "Are you fucking kidding me?" He sighed. "Ruger, Remi, go load the cargo in the trunk. We're going to bring him home with us. We're done here."

Remi injected the chupacabra with a sedative, then Ruger tossed it over his shoulder. It just looked like someone in a really strange crossover costume, so there shouldn't be too many questioning looks. As they made their way through the smoke toward the exit, Bo's hand found Eve's, and he slipped his thick fingers through hers and kept her close to his side. When they stepped outside into the fresh air, he surveyed the area quickly before letting go of her hand. The building had been evacuated at this point, but there were people standing all around and sirens could be heard in the distance.

They found Luc and Dagon standing off to the side away from the crowd, and as they joined up with them, Luc led Bo and Eve around to a more secluded area of the grounds while Remi and Ruger took the creature to the car.

They met up with Cassie and Eoduun in the secluded area, and when they stopped, Eve saw two bodies on the ground, and one of them was Gamora.

Eve felt a presence looming over her, and she looked over her shoulder. Dagon was standing there, crimson eyes gleaming. He grinned at her and plucked a small needle-like projectile from the back of his neck.

"Care to assist, princess?" He turned around and there were little needles scattered all over his back, like a giant porcupine.

Eve started picking the needles from his back. "Why are you at the helm again?"

"Z's getting some z's."

"Why?"

"These are poisoned. You'll have to heal me again," he said, turning his head to grin slyly at her.

"They are not," Eoduun said, stepping up to them and helping to pull out needles. "They're just tranquilizers. Zeke will be fine in an hour or so. He doesn't require healing."

"Eodie, must you be such a cock block?" Dagon complained.

"You better watch it, or you're going to end up in the box again," Eoduun warned.

"Oh, no, not the *box*," Dagon whinged mockingly. "Come on, I was just messing around. No harm done. At least I didn't try to get her to suck the poison out, hm?"

"This is why no one trusts you, Dagon," Eve said.

"No, they don't trust me because I killed their last blood healer and have zero loyalty to them. I wouldn't trust me if I were them, either. Trust is for fools."

"Must be lonely," Eve remarked. That was rich, coming from her.

He scoffed and turned away from her, so Eve turned her attention to Luc, Bo, and Cassie while she plucked needles from Dagon's back.

"What the fuck happened?" Bo wanted to know as he looked down at the dead girl and the body of a plump, middle-aged man.

"I was watching from the security cameras," Cassie said. "The girl ran out the door, and Zeke caught up to her and grabbed her. Then Ruth showed up and blasted him with some serious acupuncture, and he dropped like a sack of potatoes. The girl put her hand on Zeke and started to morph – I think she was trying to change to look like him. Meanwhile, Ruth looked like she was chanting some kind of spell over Zeke."

"And then I showed up," Luc chimed in. "Just in time to see Dagon reach out, grab the girl by the throat, and crush her windpipe and snap her neck. I tried to stop Ruth, but as soon as I laid hands on her, she collapsed to the ground, and wasn't Ruth."

"What the hell is it, some kind of shapeshifter?" Cassie asked. "Did Ruthlys make another monster?"

"I don't think it's a shapeshifter." Luc squatted down next to the body and poked it. "This guy's been dead for a while. And no shedding."

"A puppet of some sort?" Bo said.

"Possibly. Likely. I don't know what else to call it."

"Maybe some kind of shapeshifter-zombie hybrid," Cassie suggested.

They all stared at the corpse. "But it died and changed back as soon as I touched it," Luc said. "I didn't even try to kill it. I just grabbed it."

"Did you try to get a read on the cucuy?" Bo asked Eoduun.

"Either Ruth messed around in her head, or I was too late. I didn't get anything but jumbled images of core memories. And that guy's been dead way too long to read."

"Does Ruth have your specialty?" Eve asked Eoduun.

"No, she's way worse. She's a witch. Under the right circumstances, she can use spells to get into your head and implant ideas or fake memories. She can use hexes to make you hallucinate things, or even coerce you to do her bidding, kind of like possession. It could be what happened to the shapeshifter-zombie, if that's truly what that is."

Luc lifted the dead man's shirt to look at the body and rummaged through the guy's pockets. He rolled him over and looked under his shirt at his back.

"What the fuck is that?"

Eve craned her neck to see what Luc was talking about, but all she saw was a pasty white, moley back. "What? What's wrong?" she asked.

Bo stepped around and looked from Luc's angle. "I've never seen a hex that elaborate before. I don't think I like these new-found skills of hers." Eve surmised that this was one of those hexes that only Bo and Luc's eyes could see.

"We need to get our hands on that grimoire," Luc said solemnly.

15
You Don't Squash an Ant with a Bomb

"What exactly was she trying to accomplish here?" Eve wondered. "What was the purpose of all of this? Why send a puppet-shapeshifter-zombie to sedate Zeke?"

"She didn't realize it wouldn't sedate *me*," Dagon answered. "I think she planned to kidnap me and use a teleportation spell to move me to another location while that cucuy pretended to be me to delay your pursuit. And the reason she sent the meat puppet should be obvious. Send the pawn onto the frontlines, not the queen." He looked back at the dead man. "I must commend her, though. I haven't seen sorcery like that since the old days. Lilith was a force to be reckoned with."

"You knew *the* Lilith? Biblical Lilith?" Eve asked in astonishment.

"I'm mentioned in the Bible too, you know. I think you forget just how long I've been around, princess." As she was plucking a needle from his large trapezius muscle, he reached back and grabbed her hand and brought it over his shoulder. He turned his head and kissed the back of her hand. "And I've learned so many tricks that I can't wait to show you."

Luc was suddenly behind Eve. "I think she's seen enough of your tricks." He guided Eve away from Dagon. "Let me get the rest of those, shall I?" he offered as he started roughly yanking the remaining needles out of Dagon's back.

"Afraid I'm going to steal your new toy, Lucius?" Dagon taunted. "If you think a little love bite is going to deter me, you're sorely mistaken."

"Keep your hands off of her, Dagon," Luc warned.

"You know, it's funny. You keep making that threat, yet everybody keeps putting their hands on her. Is it strange to have your subordinates so blatantly disobeying you? I mean, I never listen to you, but they usually do."

"You're the only one I've said that to."

"Oh, that's right, it was *Bo* who told Zeke he couldn't touch her. I wonder why *he* would say that to Zeke. I was sealed away at the time, so it couldn't possibly have been because of me. Maybe Bo has his eye on her, too," Dagon provoked. "But which eye, I wonder? The human one, or the wolf one?"

"It's so sad and pathetic that you have nothing better to do than worry about my feelings. Pitiful. Maybe we should get you a plant to talk to."

"You're a big old bag of dicks, you know that, Lucius?" Dagon said with a cynical laugh.

Luc held his hand out, then yanked it back, and all the needles in Dagon's back flew out and fell to the ground as if they'd all been pulled out by a magnet attached to Luc's hand. Electromagnetism? Dagon hissed through his teeth.

"I am fully aware." Luc turned to the rest of the team, who had been standing over the bodies, talking amongst themselves. "Cass, did you take care of the security footage?"

"It's been scrubbed," she affirmed.

"Excellent. Let's scoot."

"What about the other missing kids?" Eoduun asked. "We aren't done here yet. I haven't even had a chance to try to read the chupi kid."

"You can read him later, and if you find something, we can let the police know. But we did our job. We took out the monsters. It's in the hands of the police to find the kids – we're killers, not cops," Luc reasoned.

"That's cold," Eve frowned.

Luc leveled a hardened gaze at her. "We can't save everyone. Better to accept that right now."

They were all walking back to their vehicles as Remi and Ruger were coming to join them. "What'd we miss?" Ruger asked.

"I'll fill you in on the ride back," Cassie said. She gave Ruger a peck on the lips and smacked is butt.

"Did you get the cargo secured?" Luc asked.

"All set for the trip home. Will you be following behind us?" Remi asked.

"We just need to grab our things from the hotel. Then they'll be right behind you," Luc assured him.

"What about you?" Eve asked Luc.

"I'll pack up and make sure Zeke wakes up, but then I'm going to take the shortcut home."

When they returned to the hotel, everyone packed up while Dagon lounged on the couch, insisting it wasn't his job to pack up Zeke's things.

"Fine, *I'll* fucking do it," Eve said in frustration. "How hard can it be? All the dude brought was a few clothes and a toothbrush. The suit he had went into the garbage."

"I can do it," Eoduun said. "I'm already done packing my things."

Eve was having a hard time getting a read on Eoduun now. She couldn't tell if this was him being nice, or him telling her to keep her hands off Zeke's things. He wasn't being as overtly bitchy as he had been, but the way he did things and said things could be interpreted either way. She thanked him, regardless, and continued packing her things.

When she went into Luc's room to make sure she hadn't left anything behind, she found him folding his clothes and aligning them carefully in his suitcase. When he saw her, he stopped what he was doing and bumped his sunglasses down his nose, eyeing her seductively.

Before he could say anything, she said, "I didn't come in here for that." But she couldn't deny the tingle that ran through her body when he looked at her like that.

He walked around the bed toward her, and her heart thumped with anticipation. Her body longed for his touch again, even if she thought better of it.

"We should have a quickie, for the road," Luc said, his eyes hungrily lingering on her lips as his body drew close to hers.

Eve's mind brought up the scene from last night when she was on his lap, his thick cock buried deep inside of her, and she felt a throb of need surge through her.

Bo called to them from the living room area. "We don't have time for that, you two. I want to get going."

Eve felt her cheeks flush. She looked at Luc with widened eyes. "Does he miss anything?" she whispered.

"No, I don't," Bo replied. "Especially when you leave the door wide open."

Luc grinned in amusement at Eve's embarrassed expression, then kissed her lips. "Hm, another time, then," he purred.

They heard Zeke groan from the couch, and Eve and Luc both joined the team in the living room to make sure he was all right.

"Ugh, I feel like I've been asleep for a month," Zeke grumbled. He sat up. "God, my back is *itchy!*" He started rubbing his back against the back of the couch.

"I imagine the combination of the sedative and the manner of administration are to blame for that," Eoduun conjectured.

Eve was standing behind him, and she lifted his shirt to look at his back. "Oh yeah, that's got to be irritating." His back was peppered with little red dots, the skin inflamed and red. "Dagon didn't say anything about it being this bad," she commented.

"I'm sure he thought he was too *cool* to complain about it." Zeke rolled his eyes.

"Will blood help?" she asked, looking to Bo and Luc.

"He doesn't need it," Bo said. "It's just a little irritation."

"But if it'll help, I don't mind."

"He'll be fine," Bo doubled down firmly.

Bo was in the driver's seat again, with Eoduun riding shotgun. Bo had suggested maybe Eve should sit in the front, but she offered to sit in the back. Size-wise, it just made more sense for her to give one of the boys the front seat. Zeke practically dived into the backseat after that.

As they headed home, Zeke asked a question Eve had been wondering herself. "I know we got the chupi and killed the cucuy, but why are we leaving when Ruth is still on the loose?"

"Because we need to regroup and come up with a better plan to deal with her," Bo replied. "And I doubt she's going to stick around in Texas after today's debacle."

"I don't know about *debacle*. We got the monsters," Zeke said.

"It was messy. I don't like messy."

"I'm calling it a win," Eoduun said. "It could've been a lot worse with all those people around."

"Speak for yourself," Zeke complained, rubbing his back against the back of the seat.

"Suck it up. So you're a little itchy. You'll live," Eoduun said.

"Well, you don't have to be a bitch about it," Zeke shot back.

"Oh no, a lover's spat," Eve teased. "Better kiss and make up, you two."

"Enough," Bo scolded.

Without thinking, and only intending to be sarcastic, Eve replied, "Ok, Daddy." As the words left her mouth, she realized the way it sounded. Zeke and Eoduun both looked scandalized. "I meant Dad! Ok, Dad! Not Daddy! That wasn't...I didn't mean it like *that*! I was just making a joke!" Her face and ears were on fire, and she felt instantly sweaty. "Oh, for fuck's sake." She buried her face in her hands.

"Are we there yet, Daddy?" Zeke asked Bo.

"Can we stop for snacks at the next gas station, Daddy?" Eoduun chimed in.

Eoduun turned around in his seat and looked at Zeke. "I think Daddy's embarrassed," he whispered.

Eve was sitting behind Eoduun, so she could see the side of Bo's face. He was in a deep blush above his mask.

"I'm not in the mood for this," Bo replied in exasperation.

"What kind of mood *are* you in, Daddy?" Zeke asked.

"I think Daddy's going to spank us," Eoduun said.

"Good God, you two." Bo shook his head. "Keep it up and I will slap you both. With my fist."

"Daddy's going to *fist* us?!" Zeke made a disgusted face.

"Do you want to walk home?!" Bo cried. "...Fuck is wrong with you two..."

"I'm so sorry," Eve apologized to Bo.

"Yeah, *Eve*," Zeke teased. "Look what you started! Why would you do that?"

"Fucking troublemaker, that's why," Eoduun piled on jokingly. "Jeez, Eve. Read the room, would you? God."

"You guys are the fucking worst," Bo chided.

"Aw, Eve knows we're just fucking around," Zeke laughed. He reached over and patted Eve's leg. "I'm sorry. We're just playing," he apologized.

"Don't worry," Eve replied, looking out the window. "I'll get you back when you least expect it."

"You aren't actually mad, though, right?" Zeke worried.

Eve turned and looked at him with narrowed eyes. She then quickly averted her eyes to the floor between them. "What's that?" she asked, leaning down, pretending to look at something.

"What?" he asked and leaned forward.

She sat up and slapped him as hard as she could across his back.

He shot up and cursed between his teeth. "Ok, truce!" he cried.

Eoduun began to laugh, so Eve reached up and flicked him in the ear.

"Ouch! Fuck!" Eoduun complained.

Bo chuckled from the driver's seat, the corner of his eye crinkling with amusement.

Eve woke up to darkness inside the car, hair in her face, and slow, even breathing in her ear. Zeke was sleeping with his head on her shoulder, and his arm was over her lap, his hand resting on her hip. She'd been resting her cheek against his head. She lifted her head. Eoduun appeared to be asleep in the passenger seat. She glanced at Bo.

"I really didn't mean to call you Daddy earlier," she said sheepishly.

"Let's just forget about that, shall we?"

Eve was quiet for a few minutes. There was a question that had been nagging at her since they left the hotel, and now seemed like a good time to ask it, while she had Bo alone...ish. "Why wouldn't you let me give Zeke a little blood to heal his back?"

"What?"

"At the hotel. Why were you so dead set against it?"

"Because he didn't need it. You don't need to offer yourself up to us every time we have a minor discomfort, ache, or pain."

"I wouldn't have minded."

"That's not the point. The point is that you shouldn't have to."

"Luc said the more I use it, the faster I will heal. It seems like I should use it whenever I can."

"It can also be somewhat addictive, like a drug. That euphoric pleasure is like taking ecstasy without any side effects. I don't need Zeke or Dagon getting hooked and taking advantage. Haven't you noticed how badly Dagon wants it? Even Luc wants it, and he's rarely injured."

"This might sound strange, but I noticed Luc has hardly any scars. I'm assuming it's because of his specialty? But…you have the same specialty, don't you?"

"And I'm scarred to shit? Yeah, I know. I'm not as skilled at using it as Luc is, especially now that only one eye can control it. But I also see a lot more frontline action than he does. He's kind of a trump card. A nuclear missile, to be saved for when you really need it. You don't squash an ant with a bomb. You use your thumb. I'm the thumb."

"Damn, if you're a thumb, what the hell am I? A hangnail?"

"You give yourself too little credit. You saved Zeke's life."

"Which I wouldn't have had to do if he hadn't had to save mine first."

"That's what the team is for. That's what we do for each other. That's the only way we can be successful."

Zeke's hand on Eve's hip suddenly twitched, and she felt his finger run along the edge of the bottom of her shirt. She froze as his hand slipped up underneath it. He began to gently fondle her breasts.

"Zeke, are you awake?" she whispered.

No answer. His hand then slid down her belly to her shorts.

"Zeke." She grabbed his wrist with both hands, but it was no use. He plunged his hand down the front of her shorts, beneath her underwear. She inhaled sharply as his fingers touched her. His other hand reached over and grabbed her thigh, pulling on it to open her legs wider so he could slip his fingers inside of her.

Was it Zeke, or was it Dagon?

"Is there a problem back there, Eve?" Bo asked.

Zeke moved his head, and Eve felt his mouth on her neck, trailing silent kisses up toward her jaw.

"No," she said, turning her head toward the window. She hoped Bo couldn't see what was happening in the darkness of the backseat.

God, why did Zeke's touch feel so goddamn good? It was like his mouth on her neck and his fingers between her legs were working in unison to make her come undone. She should tell him to stop, but she couldn't bring herself to utter the words. He was getting her there so quickly it made her head spin. She squeezed his wrist and thrust her pelvis against his hand as that hot coil in her core wound tighter…tighter…tighter…until it sprung. She bit her lip and forced herself to choke down the moan that wanted to erupt from her throat. Her walls spasmed around his thick fingers as she ground herself against the palm of his hand, and she felt him smile against her neck.

Then he suddenly froze.

"Eve?" Zeke whispered almost fearfully.

She swallowed and cleared her throat as her hips jerked with the aftershocks. "What?" she whispered back. She released her grip on his wrist, knowing he likely had her handprints imprinted on his flesh.

"Um…I…" He put his lips right up against her ear and whispered as low as he possibly could, "That wasn't me." He slid his hand from her shorts.

She suspected. She turned and put her lips to his ear. "Is it something you didn't want to do to me?"

"I didn't say that, but I don't know if it was Dagon or if I was doing it in my sleep."

"I'm not complaining, Z."

"But what if you didn't want me to do that? And I did it anyway? You'd hate me. I'd hate myself."

"Relax. I wouldn't have let you do it if I didn't want you to. Besides, I'm the one who attacked you the other night, so it isn't like you didn't know I was willing."

"Willing two days ago when you were drunk doesn't mean willing today," Zeke pointed out.

That was true. That was a truth most men didn't understand. He really was a sweet guy, and she didn't want him to agonize about this. She hated the way Dagon was manipulating them both, and she hated the way she couldn't separate the two in her mind. To her, it wasn't Zeke: the sweet jock, and Dagon: the completely separate entity that was only living in and using Zeke's body. To her, it was Zeke: the sweet jock, and Dagon: the dark Zeke. It was unfair to Zeke for her to see it that way, but the truth was so much harder to swallow. She liked Zeke and thought he was handsome. Dagon terrified her, but also turned her on. So her brain had no problem mashing the two together to make him what she wanted him to be.

"Like I said, Z, I would've stopped it if I wasn't willing." She reached over and put her hand on his leg, sliding it up to the erection she knew would be jutting up under his pants. "I can return the favor, if you want, when we get home."

She really hoped they were whispering quietly enough and the radio was loud enough that Bo wasn't overhearing every word of this.

"I didn't earn that," he said nervously.

Eve couldn't help but laugh out loud, and she saw Bo turn his head to look at her. "Oh, you sweet summer child," Eve said. She leaned over and kissed Zeke on the cheek.

She was going to Hell.

16

One of the Many Crumpled Dollar Bills in a Stripper's G-String

By the time they arrived back at the compound, it was late at night. Ruger, Remi, and Cassie made it back over an hour ahead of them (Ruger was driving), and the chupacabra boy had been safely delivered to a holding cell. Bo's team and Team Flannel had both been dismissed for the day.

Eve and her team all went back to the apartment building, and as they walked the halls to their doors, Eve noticed the sounds of life filling the building. She'd forgotten that Luc had recalled the other teams to the compound, so everyone was home. It felt like a completely different place. It wasn't just her and her team anymore.

That made her feel anxious. She was happy with just her and her team.

They saw two men walking down the hall toward them. One was shorter, probably only a few inches taller than her, with rather boyish features and sandy blond hair, and the other was taller with a lean but fit build. He had dark hair and a short, neatly trimmed black beard. His eyes were unusually light for his darker skin tone, and tended toward a strange mix of copper and green. He was striking. His austere expression, however, made him rather intimidating. If it weren't for the innocent-looking man-boy next to him, she would've avoided him as she walked down the hall.

"Congrats on a successful hunt," the tall man said pleasantly to the team. His politeness surprised her. She was expecting another Eoduun. His eyes met with Eve's. "This must be the newest recruit. I'm Ramil. This is Veris." He extended his hand and shook Eve's.

"Eve," she replied. "Pleasure."

"Mira and Celeste are over in the bunker with Luc right now, but I'm sure you'll meet them tomorrow. They're the other two members of our team."

"And other than Cassie, they're the only other female hunters we have," Eoduun informed her.

The two men went on their way, and Bo and Eoduun went on ahead to their apartments. As Zeke and Eve walked to their doors, Eve asked, "How many more teams are there?"

"Let's see, besides us, Team Flannel, and Mira's team, there are two others. Roy's team and Zephlyn's team. I'm sure we'll have a powwow tomorrow and you'll get to meet everyone."

"Seems like there's so many different kinds of people in Knighco, just from the ones I've met so far."

"You have no idea. We have nerds, rednecks, jocks, spiritualists, narcissists…a little of everything."

"That Veris guy didn't say anything when we met in the hall just now. Is that normal?"

"He doesn't talk much. His specialty is the power of persuasion. I hear he grew up voluntarily mute because he didn't know how to control it, and I think maybe it's just hard for him to maintain a normal conversation now. He can talk, and he does, just not a real chatterbox. He often has Ramil with him to do his talking for him."

"Ramil is kind of scary-looking." In a tall, dark, and handsome kind of way.

"He is, I know. He wasn't always on our side, either. That was before my time here, but I guess he really gave Luc a run for his money a few years back. It seems weird, because now he's the nicest guy you'll ever meet."

When Eve got to her door, she turned to Zeke. "Hey, you want to come in for a while? I'm kind of curious to hear about the rest of the people I'm going to be meeting. I'd like to be prepared."

Zeke looked a little nervous. "Are you sure? You don't mind being alone with me? I mean, Dagon has been kind of a creep, and I don't want you to be uncomfortable. And after what I did in the car..."

"I'm not afraid of you, Zeke. Quite the opposite. Now get in my apartment. I have candy," Eve coaxed jokingly.

He threw his duffle bag into his apartment, then came over to Eve's. When Eve walked into her apartment with him, she immediately saw a phone on the counter. She dropped her suitcase and picked up the phone. There was a text on it already, from "Sexiest Man Alive."

"I wanted to come see you tonight, but I'm tied up with work. I'll stop by in the morning, love."

Luc.

"Hey, didn't Ramil say that Luc was with Mira and Celeste in the bunker?" she asked Zeke.

"Yeah. Why?"

"No reason." Eve didn't like the stupid sinking feeling in her gut. She grabbed the bottle of Johnnie Walker off the top of the fridge. She held the bottle up, and Zeke nodded. She got out two tumblers and poured them each a generous amount of scotch. She slid Zeke's drink across the kitchen island to him and sipped at her own. "Tell me about Mira and Celeste."

"Celeste is our techie. She's fairly new, probably been here a year and a half. She doesn't have any kind of physical specialty, but she can hack pretty much anything."

"Did Luc ever have a thing with her?"

"What? No. Celeste isn't into men."

"Oh."

"Mira, on the other hand…I guess you could say it's complicated with her and Luc."

"Hm. How so?" Eve took a big, burning gulp of her scotch.

"They've always been on-again, off-again. For as long as I've been here, anyway." He looked at Eve, and he registered her annoyed expression. He started backpedaling. "But they've been off-again for months. They aren't dating or anything."

"She was the one who found me," Eve remarked.

"Yeah, she's our cryptid and genealogy expert. She keeps track of the major monster bloodlines and specialty bloodlines."

"What's she look like?"

"Uh, she's tall and thin. Long black hair. Glasses. Librarian-type style." So, pretty much everything Eve wasn't. Eve was short and athletic with pink hair, perfect vision, and she preferred baggy sweatpants and a t-shirt to a skirt and cardigan.

"Pretty?"

Zeke paused. "Not as pretty as you," he said, smiling.

Eve smirked. "Good answer."

Eve had absolutely zero right to feel an ounce of jealousy toward Mira. Luc wasn't hers, and she wasn't committed to him, either. But we often don't control what feelings decide to pop up into our hearts, however hypocritical they may be. She wondered if she'd feel so annoyed if he hadn't made it seem to her like he was completely infatuated with her and her alone. Maybe she wouldn't feel so surprised about him spending the evening with Mira if he hadn't made her foolishly feel like she was somehow special to him. Maybe it wasn't so much that she was jealous of Mira as she was feeling like he'd intentionally mislead her. Maybe.

She shouldn't be surprised. She knew he was probably that kind of man. She just hadn't realized that she'd *hoped* he was different.

She, however, had made no declarations of any kind to him. She was as free as a bird to do whatever she wanted with whomever she wanted. She looked across the counter at what she wanted and ran her finger in a lazy circle around the rim of her tumbler.

She listened attentively as Zeke told her about another team, which consisted of the older, rough and rugged redneck named Roy who was another cryptid expert, specializing in traditional weaponry historically used against different monsters. He had no physical specialties other than being a general tough old cuss. His team was a three-man team, and the other two members were Kai and Levi. Kai was a young Native skinwalker whose monster curse made him able to transform into animals. He was born a skinwalker, and his tribe had passed down a special warrior strain of the curse from generation to generation that was used specifically as a weapon to protect the tribe. The other member of Roy's team, Levi, was a middle-aged introvert with the ability to view locations remotely by projecting his consciousness outside of his body. Roy's team sounded like an odd mix of characters to Eve.

The last team was Zephlyn's team. Zephlyn was, according to Zeke, a bonified genius. But he was also a clairvoyant. He must've been the clairvoyant Bo had talked about when she told him about her "Don't Think It, Don't Say It" premonitions. Zephlyn's team was also only a three-man operation, and the other two members were Mendal and Dizzy. Zeke sounded envious of Mendal and his witty comebacks and impressive martial arts mastery. Dizzy, however, seemed like a strange addition. Zeke described him as awkward, scrawny, and dorky. But then he revealed to Eve that Dizzy was a shapeshifter. Another monster among them, disguised as the least intimidating member of Knighco. But Zeke swore up and down that Dizzy was good people, and he had none of the monstrous impulses that other shapeshifters have.

This was her new family.

It was going to take some getting used to.

"That's an awful lot of men for not a lot of women," Eve commented. "It sure explains a lot. I guess when I kept asking if I was the only woman around here, I wasn't far off the mark." She sighed. "To the hungry, any bitter thing is sweet."

Zeke furrowed his brow at her. "Is that supposed to mean we only like you because we're starved?"

"That's exactly what it means."

"You think we don't indulge when we're out on the road? Like, all the time? Ain't nobody starving around here, sis," Zeke said with a laugh. He glanced at Eve then amended, "But not *me*, of course."

"Mm-hm…" she hummed knowingly, then took a drink of her scotch. "You act like I don't have eyes, or that you didn't give me a whole pile of phone numbers you'd acquired in just one night at the bar. Or that you didn't have women offering to blow you in the bathroom."

Zeke laughed uncomfortably and scratched the back of his head. "Ok, but I *didn't*, though."

"You would've if I wasn't there with you."

"…Well, I mean…"

"Exactly."

"What?!" he shrugged defensively.

"I don't want to know about it," she said.

"You brought it up!"

"I can't believe I was going to give you blood just to heal your itchy back today."

"Oh, come on, what did I do?! Why are you mad at me?!"

"I'm not. I'm just…a hypocrite. Forget it."

She'd gone from feeling like the most desirable jewel to now feeling like one of the many crumpled dollar bills in a stripper's G-string. Such a ridiculous, fragile ego she had. She finished her drink and poured another one.

"You should probably eat something if you're going to drink like that, don't you think?" Zeke suggested. "We didn't stop for dinner on the way home." Suddenly, a moment of enlightenment changed

Zeke's expression. "Oooh...I know what this is. You're hangry. Hold on." He got up and left the apartment.

He returned with a bag of frozen chicken nuggets and a big grin. "Hmm? This is what you want, isn't it?" He popped a pile of them into the air fryer as Eve watched him in amusement.

It was hard to stay mad at him, especially when she had no reason to be mad at him in the first place. It wasn't even *him* she was mad at, really. She was just angry in general. Angry at Luc for making her feel like a fool, angry at Mira for existing, and angry at herself for being so fickle and hypocritical. She was a shitty person. She already knew that, but she hated being reminded of it.

Zeke plated her chicken nuggets and set them in front of her. "Bon appétit." He opened the fridge. "And what kind of sauce does the lady require with her meal? Ketchup? Ranch? Barbecue? I don't see honey mustard. Or sweet and sour."

"Ranch. Please and thank you," Eve said, her tone softer than it had been.

They sat at the kitchen island and ate chicken nuggets on paper plates, and Eve felt like shit about herself. Why couldn't she be cute and sweet like Zeke? She was certain he didn't have a mean bone in his body. Naïve, definitely, but there was something wholesome and incorruptible about him that warmed her heart. He really was like sunshine, she thought, as he took her empty paper plate along with his and threw them away.

That was potential husband material, right there. If only it weren't for that one, tiny little problem that lived inside of him and liked to sexually harass her, drink her blood, and manipulate her. That little problem that she hated how much she liked it.

God, she hated herself.

Eve had already finished her second tumbler of scotch, and was reaching for the bottle to pour another one, when Zeke snatched the bottle away from her. "Maybe it's time for beer, hey?"

"But I was just starting to feel pretty good," she said.

"Yep, time for beer, then." He took a beer from the fridge and popped the top, then handed it to her.

They moved out to the living room and sat on the couch. He sat next to her and grabbed her legs, swinging them around to his lap. He tugged her socks off.

"Hey, you don't have corpse feet today," he teased as he started to rub her feet.

"Why are you doing that?" she asked.

"You don't like it?"

"I love it, but what the hell do you get out of it?"

"I like that you like it."

She groaned. "Why are you so nice? And why is Dagon so terrible?"

"I don't know about *terrible*. There's some good in everyone. Even him. And I guess the opposite is true, too. There's a little bad in everyone. I'm probably not as nice as you think I am. I mean, look what happened in the car." He looked ashamed.

"Oh, that's right, I was going to return the favor, wasn't I?" Eve said.

His eyes widened. "No, that's ok, you don't need to do that..."

Eve moved her foot up his leg and discovered he was already growing hard just from talking about it.

"Z."

"Sorry."

"Don't apologize. Just let me. If you'd be willing to let some stranger do it in a sleezy bar bathroom, why wouldn't you let me do it?" Eve then frowned. "Is there a reason you keep turning me down? Do you not like me like that?"

"I very much like you like that!" he blurted. "It's just that...I...I've been afraid of losing my control over Dagon when I'm, you know, *in the zone*. And...the way he is about you...he's going to be right there, watching the whole thing, feeling what I feel, telling me to do things and say things...I worry about what he'll try to do."

Eve set her beer on the coffee table next to the couch and sat up. She climbed over Zeke and kneeled on the floor in front of him between his legs, resting her hands on his thighs.

"Eve…" he protested weakly.

She unbuttoned and unzipped his jeans, then withdrew his hard cock from his boxers. It was so engorged that it twitched with every beat of his heart. She looked up at him, and he gazed down at her with anxious anticipation. He wanted this so badly, but he was nervous.

She maintained eye contact as she leaned forward and ran her wet tongue from the base of his shaft all the way to the tip, then took him into her mouth. He closed his eyes and moaned in pure bliss as her lips closed around him. He opened his eyes again, and this time, they were filled with desire. She watched his face the whole time, making sure his eyes didn't turn red. His breath began to quicken, and she felt him swelling even more inside her mouth as she wriggled and pressed her tongue along the divot at the base of his crown.

His hips began to thrust forward as he groaned, "I'm gonna come…"

He groaned and spasmed as her mouth filled with his hot seed, and she gagged on the quantity of it. She allowed it to run out of her mouth and down his shaft as he thrust one last time, then she sat back and wiped her mouth. She looked at his face, pleased to see that his eyes were still brown.

"Holy fuck," he panted. He gazed at her with admiration. "Call me disgusting, I don't give a shit. Come here." He leaned forward, cupped her face in his hands, and kissed her. He thrust his tongue past her lips, tasting himself there, then moaned against her mouth. He broke the kiss to murmur, "Oh my god, that's so fucking hot," before kissing her again. He ran his tongue over her lower lip, then looked her in the eye. "Fuck, I think I love you."

She laughed. "You act like no one has ever sucked your dick before."

"Not like that, they haven't," he praised breathlessly. "God, I want to fuck you."

"What?" she looked down at his lap, and he was already growing hard again.

"Fuck me," he begged. "Please."

17

Do With Me What You Will

Eve didn't need persuading. She was already slick with arousal. She stood up and pulled her shirt off and shimmied out of her shorts and underwear while Zeke pushed his jeans and boxers completely off. He ripped his shirt off and threw it aside, then reached for her, grabbing her by the hips and pulling her to him. She straddled his hips and lowered herself onto his awaiting hardness. His hands slid up her back and unhooked her bra, tossing it to the floor as his eyes drank in the view. He gazed at her as she slowly took him inside of her, lowering inch by inch, stretching to accommodate his girth, until she came down onto his lap, fully sheathing him.

"Oh, god," he moaned as she began to roll her hips in slow circles. He embraced her bare body against his tattooed chest, his mouth descending upon her flesh. His tongue tasted the dip at the top of her sternum, then trailed lightly up the side of her neck to the fading mark

Luc had placed on her. He paused over that spot, and then devoured it, making his own mark over top of it, claiming her for himself.

Eve buried her fingers in his hair and threw her head back, reveling in the sweet sensations his lips left upon her skin and the hot thickness of his cock deep inside of her, filling her. The heat in her core burned more intensely with every thrust of his hips and touch of his lips.

"He's watching," Zeke informed her. "I'm sorry." But he didn't stop.

Eve brought her mouth close to his ear. "Let him watch," she whispered. She kissed the tender spot behind his ear, making sure that there weren't any gill slits forming there. She trailed light kisses along his jawline, then touched her lips to his. "Let him be jealous that it's you I'm fucking and not him." She looked into his eyes, and for half a second, his eyes flashed red.

"Sorry," Zeke apologized as his eyebrows drew together. "Don't provoke him. He wants out really, really badly right now." He ran his hand up the side of her neck and cradled her face as he kissed her deeply. Then he said, "But I won't let him have you."

He rolled her onto her back on the couch and looked down at her bare, athletic body beneath him. "God, you're beautiful," he crooned as he caressed her skin with his fingertips. She wrapped her legs around his hips and pulled him deeper into her. He groaned and pumped himself into her with slow, deep strokes. She admired the way all the bulky muscles in his body moved and flexed and bunched beneath his black tribal-like tattoos with every rolling motion of his hips. She ran her fingers up his arms and over all the hard bulges of his biceps, triceps, and shoulders, then dug her nails into the thick flesh of his back.

He wrapped his arms around her and held her body against his as he fucked her harder. He cradled the back of her head in his hand and kissed her passionately. She was getting close.

"Harder, Zeke," she begged as she used her legs to urge him on, her breath coming in shallow pants. He thrust into her harder and faster, and he moaned deep in his throat.

"Come for me," he begged her, gazing into her eyes as he brought her over the edge. She cried out his name in ecstasy, jerking her hips and clenching around him, squeezing him with her powerful thighs.

"Oh, god," he gasped. He buried his cock as far as it would go as he emptied himself into her, a deep groan rumbling in her ear.

As they lay, panting and spent, she ran her fingers up over his neck behind his ear.

"Still me, don't worry," he whispered. So, he'd figured out what she was doing.

"Just making sure," she said softly as she caressed the smooth skin there.

He propped himself up on his elbow and looked down at her with a soft expression in his eyes, his hips still between her legs. He ran his finger along her jawline, then leaned forward and kissed her sweetly.

"Do you want me to get off you, now?" he asked. "I'm probably heavy, aren't I?"

"You're not that heavy."

"You feel so small under me, like I'm crushing you."

"Is that a good thing? You say it like you like it."

"I kinda do. It makes me feel big," he said with an amused grin.

"You *are* big," Eve laughed.

"Everybody else on our team is taller than me. It's annoying. And then *Luc* comes and stands next to me…it's enough to give a guy a complex."

"Our teammates are just really tall. You're tall, too. You were taller than most of the people at the bar. It made you easy to pick out of the crowd."

"You know, that night…it wasn't because I didn't want to. You know that, right?"

"I know."

"It just wasn't the right place, and we'd both had a little too much to drink...I didn't want to do something that you were going to regret later. And even though Dagon was sealed away, I still didn't fully trust myself."

"You don't have to explain. I get it. I agree. I'm glad you had better sense than I did that night."

"It's probably none of my business, and I know you aren't *with* him, exactly, but...are you going to tell Luc about this?" He glanced down at Eve's neck. "He's going to notice that," he said as he touched the mark he'd made his own. "Sorry. I shouldn't have done that."

"I don't plan to run and report it to him, but I'm not going to try to hide or deny it, either. We didn't do anything wrong here," Eve reasoned. "I don't belong to him."

"I'm not sure he feels the same way," Zeke said ominously.

"He already got what he wanted. He's moved on."

Zeke frowned. "I doubt that." His frown faded and he regarded her with adoration. "Anyone who could walk away from this is a fucking idiot." He kissed her forehead.

"Well, there are several idiots walking around out there in the world, then," Eve said cynically. She wriggled out from under him and grabbed his t-shirt shirt off the floor. "I'm borrowing this," she said as she slipped it on. She stood up, and the shirt hung down to the middle of her thighs

"Oh my god, why would you do that?" he asked in torment, biting his lower lip.

"What?" she asked, looking back at him. Then she saw what. He was getting hard. Again. "Really, Z?!"

"Well, come on! Look at you, standing there looking all sexy in *my* fucking shirt...It's not my fault!" he cried, his eyes roving her body desirously.

"No! Put it away," she scolded. "Go get a drink of water before you dehydrate yourself, you fucking animal."

"I'll show you a fucking animal," he teased as he sat up and put his boxers on, tucking his erection into the waistband. He grabbed her by the arm as she started to walk away, dragging her back to him. He wrapped his big, tattooed arms around her and rested his cheek on top of her head. "I don't care if Luc thinks you belong to him. *I* belong to *you*. Do with me what you will."

Eve was given pause. Had anyone ever said something like that to her before? It was always *you're mine,* or *there's no one else for me but you,* but never this. Never *I belong to you.* It was like he'd just handed her his heart wrapped in a pretty little bow.

She couldn't take it. She didn't deserve such a treasure. She tried to think of something witty to say to shrug it off, to deflect, but her mind had gone completely blank. Instead, she melted into him, snaking her arms around his tapered torso, and squeezed him, her cheek pressed against his hard chest. Her eyes were suddenly wet, her throat thick. Why would he say that to her? Did he really not understand what a shitty person she was? Did he know that if Luc hadn't sent her that text earlier, that she'd probably be in bed with Luc right now instead of wrapped in his arms?

She hated herself so much.

She sniffled, and he noticed. He lifted his head and tried to step back from her so he could see her face, but she clung to him, not knowing what else to do. She couldn't let him see her face. He would want to know why she was crying. He would want to fix it. He would feel bad for making her cry. He would think he'd done something wrong.

She needed to get it together.

"Eve?"

"Shhh," she shushed him.

"Are you crying?"

Fuck. The more concern she heard in his voice, the harder it was to stop the tears. *Stop it stop it stop it stop it.*

"Mnh-mnh," she mumbled a negative.

"Is something wrong?"

She took a deep breath, knowing if she really concentrated, she could get two words out before her voice cracked. She broke away from him and quickly turned her back to him, blurting, "Gotta pee!" as she beelined for the bathroom.

So smooth.

She looked at her reddened eyes in the mirror, then saw the big hickey Zeke had left on her. Yeah, Luc was going to notice that. Why did she care? *Did* she care? Yeah, she did. Because, despite her apprehensions, despite her misgivings, despite everything...she was undeniably finding herself drawn to Luc.

But she liked Zeke, too. Zeke was everything she'd never had in a man. Zeke was kind and loving, and he would make her feel loved and never make her wonder if he cared...but Zeke didn't come alone. He and Dagon were a packaged deal, and Dagon...she didn't know what to do about Dagon or how to feel about him. She didn't trust him. She was terrified of him, yet something in her *craved* him in a primal way. Why did she always like the scary ones? Hadn't she learned by now?

By the time she'd used the bathroom and taken a few minutes to herself, she'd found her composure. She came out of the bathroom and found Zeke standing in the kitchen in his jeans, shirtless, making a sandwich at the counter. He glanced over at her and smiled brightly. "Want me to make you one?" he asked.

She just wanted to hug him like a sweet little puppy. A very *sexy*, sweet little puppy. Oh, Zeke...why couldn't it be simple with him?

"I'm good, thanks," Eve said. She went to the living room and put her shorts back on. She saw her shirt sitting on the floor, and after staring at it for a few moments, she looked over at Zeke in the kitchen. He was behind the refrigerator door, putting away condiments and lunch meat. She quickly kicked her shirt under the couch. Oops. Where'd it go?

She came back out to the kitchen and slid onto the barstool.

Zeke turned around to face her and leaned his elbows on the counter across from her. "You didn't get dressed?"

"I have my shorts on. Couldn't find my shirt."

He grinned around a big bite of sandwich and looked her up and down. "Mmm. You keep running around in my shirt, I might not be able to control myself."

"I'm pretty sure sleep comes next. Sex, sandwich, sleep. That is the man code, isn't it?"

"Oh, I'm sure I could squeeze another 'sex' in there. There's always room for more sex."

There was a knock on the door.

Eve's heart leapt into her throat. Did Luc decide to show up, after all? What was he going to say?

Zeke started to walk to the door to answer it, but Eve pushed past him to get it herself. It was her apartment, after all. She opened the door a crack.

Dark eyes greeted her from behind silky black, hanging locks. "Eoduun?" she said, surprised.

"Is Zeke here? He's not in his apartment."

Zeke grabbed the door over Eve's head and pulled it wide open, standing there shirtless, while she stood in front of him, wearing his shirt. Eoduun looked between the two of them, and Eve swore she could see his eye twitching.

"Well, that was fast," he said in annoyance, pointing at the two of them as he brushed past her and walked into her apartment without invitation.

"Well, at least I know you aren't a vampire," she grumbled.

He ignored her comment. "What are we doing tonight?" he asked as he went to her fridge. She heard him rummaging around.

Why was everyone always eating her food? "What do you mean? It's almost midnight," Eve said.

"Yeah, and we haven't celebrated the successful hunt yet." He then looked over the fridge door at Zeke and Eve and added, "Well, *I* haven't celebrated yet."

"Oh! Let's get Bo and play Euchre!" Zeke suggested. "We have four now!"

Eoduun took a jar of pickles from the fridge and popped it open. He plucked one from the top with his fingers.

"Fork, man. Use a fork. Jeez," Eve complained.

"My hands are clean. Besides, it was on top. It's not like I was digging around in there." He snapped off a bite of the pickle. He then addressed Zeke, "Bo hates Euchre. He's probably holed up in his apartment reading girly smut manga. What about Ramil? Or Zephlyn? Or Kai?"

"What about Mendal? Dude's a riot," Zeke said.

Eoduun made a face. "Come on, he's *such* a douche. He thinks it's funny to call me Udon, and I don't think he's even capable of understanding just how offensive it is, on so many levels. I'm pretty sure Eve won't like him."

"What? No. You really think so?" Zeke seemed surprised.

"Guys, I hate to burst your bubble, but I think I'm going to opt for a quiet night, so if you're going to have a game night or party or something, you'll have to take it somewhere else."

Eoduun took another pickle from the jar with his fingers. When Eve raised her eyebrows at him, he defended, "This one was on top too!" He closed the lid and returned the jar to the fridge with a pickle hanging out of his mouth. "Fine," he said around the pickle. "We can just hang out then. We'll celebrate tomorrow night." He pulled up a barstool at the kitchen island. "What do you have to drink?"

Zeke pulled out a tumbler and the Johnnie Walker and poured Eoduun a glass.

"It's not like this is *my* apartment or anything," Eve grumbled to herself. She picked up her dirty glass from the counter by the sink and held it out to Zeke for him to fill it.

"Nuh-uh. You have a beer," he refused, holding the bottle away from her.

"But I had chicken nuggets! I'm fine now."

"Nope. You can't go liquor, beer, liquor. You'll puke."

"That's not true. I'm not even buzzed anymore. Pour it."

"No."

"It's *my* whiskey, Z. You can't tell me no."

"No. Drink your beer. You'll thank me later."

Eve scoffed at him, but also realized that she'd left three-quarters of a beer on the coffee table. She might as well not waste it.

The three sat around the kitchen and talked about their most recent case, and Zeke and Eoduun talked about some of their past cases. Eve watched the way Eoduun's eyes lingered on Zeke's lips when he wasn't looking, and the way he seemed completely enraptured when Zeke was speaking. She saw the quick, sideways glances he stole of Zeke's body. Eoduun was hopelessly enamored. She wondered how long he'd felt that way about Zeke, and she couldn't help but feel sorry for him. Something he wanted so badly was just out of his reach, yet she could just take it whenever she wanted it. She'd been in Eoduun's position many times before, so it was strange for *her* to be the Jolene for once. It didn't feel as good as she thought it would. It just made her feel shittier.

The more she got to know Eoduun, the more she liked him. She wasn't sure he would let her call him a 'friend' just yet, but it felt like they were getting there. He had high walls, and she wasn't a very skilled climber, truth be told. His jealousy of her relationship with Zeke was her greatest obstacle to true friendship with him, and she didn't know how to fix that. But she was trying. He was her teammate, and he was important to Zeke and Bo; therefore, he was important to her.

She was dog-tired by the time the boys left a couple hours later. She'd had a few more beers as she'd listened to their stories, so by the time she brushed her teeth and crawled into bed, her head was spinning from minor inebriation and major exhaustion. She went to bed in nothing but her underwear and Zeke's shirt, which he'd insisted she hold onto for the night because he liked the way she looked in it.

She pulled the shirt up over her nose and inhaled the scent that clung to the fabric. His scent. Citrus and pine. Sunshine and strength.

Sweetness and loyalty. Perfection with a singular, inescapable, fatal flaw.

As she started to doze off, she heard her apartment door open. Her eyes shot open. Didn't she lock the door? She thought so, but she wasn't sure. There couldn't be anyone dangerous here, right? Not in the compound. Was it Luc? She sat up in bed and listened to the footsteps approaching her bedroom door.

"Who's there?" she called out.

A familiar form stepped into view in the doorway. The glow from the clock illuminated Zeke's bare chest as he walked into the room, his hands casually tucked into the pockets of his gym shorts.

Wait. The saunter. The way he carried himself. This wasn't Zeke.

18

Funny of You to Assume that There is a Choice to Be Made

"Dagon. Get out," Eve demanded firmly.

"Well, that's rude," he pouted. He walked over to the bed and looked down at her. "You've given yourself to Luc, you've given yourself to Zeke...when are you going to realize that you're mine, princess?" He reached for her hand, but she yanked it away from him. He leaned closer, and she finally saw the red in his eyes and the slits behind his ears. A devious grin danced on his lips. "Did you want to fight, first?"

"Didn't you get enough earlier? Zeke told me you were watching. I know you can feel what he feels. Pervert."

"Pervert? Yes. Absolutely. Did I get enough? No. Not even close. I want to be the one driving. I want you moaning *my* name, not his."

"Not going to happen."

He extended his arms, displaying his body to her. "Don't these scars mean anything to you? I took a damn forest to the chest to protect you. The least you could do is thank me properly."

"Thanks."

"With your body."

"I did. With my blood. I already returned the favor."

"Is that so? Well, then let me thank *you*."

"No need. We're even."

"What about my generous intel? Do I get something for that? It's because of me that you knew that Ruth would be at the convention."

"Ruth wasn't there."

"Well, close enough."

"How did you know that, by the way?"

"I may have picked something up when we ran into Ruth on the road."

"How?" Eve wanted to know.

"I'm a god. I have a few tricks."

He put a knee onto the bed and threw the covers aside. She was reminded of that erotic dream she'd had about him her first night here, and it flustered her. She scooted away, but he grabbed her ankle and climbed onto the bed, pulling her back to him. She cocked back her free leg and delivered a powerful kick to his chest. She couldn't bring herself to kick Zeke's handsome face, even if it was Dagon behind it.

Dagon intercepted the kick with his free hand and used it to pull both of her legs. She slid over the sheets and ended up on her back beneath him. She thrust a fist up into his solar plexus, and he flinched, rounding his back.

"Fuck! Easy, princess," he chided with an amused grin. He used his legs to pin hers into the mattress, freeing his hands. He snatched up her wrists and slammed them down on the bed above her head.

"You can fight *so much* harder than this. You're putting on airs, but for whose benefit? Because you think you aren't supposed to want this? Aren't supposed to like it?" He leaned down, bringing his lips close to hers, and she trembled in anticipation. "You don't have to pretend; it's just the two of us. Nobody else ever has to know. I won't even leave a mark."

"Dagon…"

He hummed. "Mmm, my name sounds positively decadent on your lips." He touched his lips to hers, then trailed light kisses down her chin to her neck. "Say it again."

"No."

"You want me to earn it, hm?" He ran the tip of his tongue up the side of her neck to her ear, then took her earlobe between his teeth. "Have you ever been tied up?" he whispered. He kissed the shell of her ear, and her body responded, not caring who it was touching her.

"Why are you doing this?" she asked, ashamed of the breathlessness in her voice.

"I think that's fairly obvious, isn't it?"

"You like tormenting me."

"You torment *me*." He inhaled deeply along her neck. "You're like a soft little rabbit, and I just want to crush you between my teeth."

He opened his mouth and pressed his teeth against her throat. Her heart froze as fear gripped her. Every muscle in her body tensed.

His tongue swirled over her skin, and he lifted his teeth from her, kissing her neck softly. "Figuratively, of course," he whispered. "I wouldn't hurt you." He sat up and regarded her with devious red eyes. "Unless you wanted me to."

"Why the hell would I want that?!"

He gave a low, condescending chuckle. "Oh, princess…you aren't that naïve. There's no way you don't know what delectable pleasures can be gleaned from a little pain. A little torture."

"I'm not going to let you hurt me," she asserted.

"We could start with some light bondage."

"No! What's wrong with you?"

"You."

"I've done nothing to you."

"I know, and it's really starting to piss me off." He gripped both of her wrists in one hand over her head while he dragged the fingertips of his other hand down her arms, down the side of her face, and then grabbed her jaw. He leaned down and took her mouth brutally with his. She moaned in weak protest against his invading, forceful tongue, but her toes didn't get the memo that they weren't supposed to curl like that for him.

He broke the kiss and looked down at her with mischief. "Do you want to hurt me?" he offered.

"What? No."

"Of course you do. When I kiss you, you want to bite my tongue. When I press my body against yours, you want to gouge me with your nails. I can feel it seeping from your pores, that delicious mix of desire and rage and fear. You struggle against it, but you *want* me to crush you between my teeth. You're just as curious and horny as you are afraid."

"And you're just as crazy as you are arrogant," she shot back.

"Maybe."

"You're boring me now, Dagon."

He grinned. "Ooh, deflecting because I'm getting too close to the truth? Accept it: you have dark desires. Explore them with me," he tempted her. "I don't judge. Pleasure knows no rules. Tell me, is there a dangerous little tingle in your belly when you struggle against me? Is there a part of you that wishes I would just overpower you and have my way with you? You knew it was me when I shoved my hand down your pants in the back of that car and made you come all over my fingers. You're welcome, by the way. And for the record, I don't think it's fair that Zeke got my reward. He was right. He didn't do a fucking thing to earn it."

"I'm not going to reward you."

Dagon suddenly released Eve's hands and rolled over onto his side, facing her. "You're already rewarding me," he said with satisfaction.

She was baffled. She blinked at him, then lowered her arms down over her chest. "What are you doing?"

"What? Disappointed I didn't ravish you?"

"No, I just…I don't know what this is…"

"It's conversation, princess."

"Duh, but why?"

"Because that's what I want right now."

"I thought you wanted to crush me between your teeth," Eve said sarcastically.

"Oh, I do. But I'm savoring it. The first bite is so much more satisfying after a long, thrilling chase. I'm going to drag this out to let the flavors develop."

"You really think you're going to fuck me?"

"I don't *think*. I *know*," he said confidently. "You may be insecure about your depraved fetishes, but your body doesn't lie. I've been around long enough to know when I'm wanted."

"Depraved? Excuse me?"

He chuckled. "Funny how you focused on that, rather than trying to deny that you want me."

Eve turned her head away from him and said nothing.

"You should've invited Zeke to spend the night. Then I wouldn't have had to break in to come see you."

"I wasn't going to invite him to stay with Eoduun right there, now was I?"

"Why not?" Dagon shrugged. "You could've invited them both to stay. Oh, the possibilities…"

"*That* is never going to happen," Eve declared.

"Never say never, princess. Eoduun would do it in a heartbeat, and I'm fairly positive Zeke could be persuaded. Have you ever had two men at once?"

Eve couldn't stop her brain from picturing it, and she quietly slipped it into her fantasy files for later. *Damn it, Dagon.*

She returned to the original subject. "*You* are the other reason I didn't invite Zeke to spend the night. Because I knew you'd come out while he was sleeping and be a problem for me. I didn't anticipate that you'd break into my damn apartment to harass me."

"Oh, but you're right across the hall, and you were all alone. How could I resist?"

"Go home, Dagon. Let Zeke sleep."

"I can sleep right here."

"No! No you can't! If Luc comes in the morning..." Eve paused.

"So what? You keep insisting Luc doesn't own you, yet you seem to spend a lot of your time worrying about how he's going to react to the things you do."

It was true. She was noticing that too. "I just don't want to cause any unnecessary drama," she reasoned. "I have every right to let Zeke sleep over, but it doesn't mean I need to flaunt Zeke in Luc's face, or vice versa."

Dagon reached over and caressed Eve's pink locks cascading over the sheets. He lifted a tress to his face and inhaled her scent. "You know, if you just choose Zeke, you could stop worrying about Luc *and* you'd get a rather amazing two-for-one deal."

"Funny of you to assume that there is a choice to be made, and not that they are just sleeping with me casually."

"You worry too much about their feelings for it to be casual, princess."

"No, that's just a flaw in my own personality. I worry about everything."

"Hm. Well, it doesn't matter anyway. Because in the end, it'll be me. Not Zeke. Not Luc. Me."

"Go home, Dagon. Zeke is going to start asking questions if you keep doing this, you know," Eve pointed out.

Dagon considered her point, then relented. He sat up. "You haven't told our secret yet. About my free time. Why? Is it because you actually look forward to time with me?"

"No. I just didn't want you to hurt anyone."

"Liar." He climbed off the bed and sauntered to the bedroom door, then turned back to Eve. "I enjoyed our little rendezvous. Let's do it again soon. Goodnight, princess. Dream of me."

"Lock the door on your way out," she grumbled.

Eve woke up to the alarm on her new phone going off in the kitchen. She looked over at the bedside clock. It was 6AM.

"Why the fuck would the alarm be on?" she grumbled as she shuffled out to the kitchen to shut it off. When she dismissed the alarm, the text notifications popped up. She had a text from Luc at 5:40AM.

"Good morning, gorgeous. I missed you last night. I will be around to see you before morning training."

Morning training? No one warned her about that, or she would've kicked the boys out earlier last night. She was running on about three hours of sleep, maybe less. Whatever kind of training they were doing today, she was going to be utter shit.

There was a knock on the door. Always with the knock on the door. They just couldn't leave her alone.

"What?!" she called grumpily.

"*Ohayou*," Bo called back cheerfully through the door.

What did that mean again? Good morning?

"*Arrivederci!*" she responded in annoyance. She considered not answering the door, but then she thought of Bo standing there, waiting, and she felt bad. She had a soft spot for Bo.

She opened the door, and Bo thrust a cup of coffee toward her. His heterochrome eyes were smiling.

"I thought you might be needing this today," he said kindly. He glanced down at Zeke's shirt, and she realized she was still in her underwear beneath it. It was long enough that it didn't look any different from when she was wearing shorts under it, and there was no way Bo could know that she *wasn't* wearing any shorts under it, but…

She took the coffee from him and walked away from the door, leaving it open for him to come in. "Thanks. To what do I owe the pleasure?"

"We have training in half an hour." Bo walked in and went to the kitchen, taking up his perch on a barstool at the kitchen island.

"Who, everyone?"

"Generally, yes. We usually train with our teams and rotate schedules, but today you'll be with just me. Hunters who come home from a hunt usually get a day off to recoup, but Luc didn't want to waste any time getting you started."

"So Zeke and Eoduun get to sleep in today," Eve said jealously. She leaned on the counter across from Bo.

"Did you guys...uh...celebrate last night?" Bo asked, his eyes again glancing down to Zeke's shirt, then lingering momentarily on her neck.

"They were here late," she replied. "We may have broken into the Johnnie Walker." She turned and looked up at the bottle sitting on top of the fridge, and realized it was three-quarters of the way empty. Or a quarter full, depending on one's perspective.

"How are you getting on with Eoduun now?" Bo asked.

"Better. We're still not best buds, but I think maybe he doesn't hate me anymore. We got along well last night."

Bo's eyebrows raised briefly. "Oh?" He glanced at her neck again.

"How long has he been pining for Zeke?" Eve asked.

"A long time."

"I feel bad for him. Like it's my fault, even though I know it isn't."

"Eoduun has options. Zeke just isn't one of them. Such is life."

Eve took a long drink of the coffee Bo had brought for her. "I know how he feels. It's a shitty feeling."

"I know," Bo commiserated.

Eve eyed him curiously. "What about you, Bo? Do you have someone special?"

"I did. She died."

Eve swallowed hard. "Oh. I'm sorry."

"That's the life of a hunter. It's a risk we all take...a burden we all carry." He then looked up at her with a kind expression. "And that's why you're stuck with me today. To train not only in how to kill, but how to not *be* killed."

19
For You, I Grovel

There was another knock at the door. Eve gave an exasperated sigh and stood up. "Is there a big neon sign outside my door or something?" She opened the door, and was greeted with sunglasses and a dazzling smile.

A very brief, dazzling smile. As soon as he looked down, it vanished.

"That's not yours," Luc said with knitted brows, pointing at Zeke's shirt. Then his hand moved up to her chin and tilted her head to the side so he could get a good look at her neck. "And that's not mine," he seethed. There was a pulse of energy that surged through the room, like the vibration of thunder without the sound. He looked up and saw Bo sitting at the counter. "You?!"

Bo held his hands up defensively. "Whoa, not me. I just got here."

Eve brushed Luc's hand away and walked away from him. "Good morning to you too. I trust you had a fine night with Mira and Celeste," she said bitterly.

"Not as fine a night as you, evidently," he growled back as he followed her into the apartment and slammed the door behind him. The walls shook. "Who did that to you? Whose shirt is that?" He looked around the room for an answer.

"It's none of your business."

"It is very much my business," he countered. He looked to Bo. "Whose shirt is that?" he asked him. "I know you know."

Bo shrugged, not wanting to get into the middle of anything.

"It's Zeke's, isn't it?" Luc guessed. "He was wearing that yesterday, wasn't he?"

"I'm free to do as I wish and wear whoever's shirt I want, Luc," Eve snapped.

"And I am free to be pissed about it, Eve!" he fumed, standing over her. The air crackled with electricity, charged with Luc's fury. "God, like fucking vultures around here!" he grumbled to himself. He raised his hand to rake it through his hair, but Eve reflexively flinched, throwing her forearm in front of her face and taking a defensive stance.

Bo jumped up from his seat, startled, and Luc froze with his hand in his hair. Eve couldn't see his eyes behind those little round sunglasses, but she saw his brow lift in the middle of his forehead.

The charged atmosphere instantly dissipated. "Oh, Jesus, no, Eve...I would never..." he said softly. He reached for her slowly, "No, Eve...come here. Please." She allowed him to slide his arms around her, and he held her tightly against him while she let her arms hang at her sides. He could squeeze the life out of her so easily, she thought as she stood there, trembling, wrapped in his big arms, his large body folding around her much smaller one.

"You're not supposed to be scared of me anymore," he mumbled with his face against her hair. "I would never hit you. I would never hurt you."

"They all say that in the beginning," she replied coldly. She hated that she couldn't stop her body from shaking. She really thought for a moment that she was going to have to defend herself from an anger that could wreck a city block, and that terrified her.

"Please stop trembling," he begged, squeezing her tighter. "You're tearing my heart to shreds."

"Maybe she just needs a few minutes, hm?" Bo suggested softly. He was standing nearer to them than she'd realized.

Luc released her and looked at her expressionless face. She'd felt it go blank as soon as he'd put his arms around her. She'd gone into fawn mode, emotionally. Frozen.

"I'm so sorry," he apologized sincerely. "It doesn't matter what you do or how angry I am about something; I will never lay a hand on you. Ever. I'd sooner die."

"Ok." She said flatly, looking at anything but him. She felt stupid. She didn't know what to do or say or how to act now, so she fell blank. "I'm going to go get dressed," she announced in that same flat tone. She turned and walked to her bedroom.

When she shut the door behind her, she could hear Luc from the other room. "What the fuck is wrong with me?" he said deprecatingly. "I don't do jealousy. I don't fucking do *jealousy.*"

She quietly and quickly changed, listening to Bo assure Luc that it would be fine, and that Eve just needed a little time to cool off. Then she heard Luc leave. She was still shaking when she came back out of her room. She stepped out into the open area between the kitchen and living room in front of her bedroom door and just stood there, looking at Bo, who was standing with his back leaned against the kitchen island.

He tilted his head a little and held his arms out to either side, his mismatched eyes regarding her softly.

She plodded over and bumped straight into him, leaning her body against his, tucking her forehead against his neck, letting her arms hang loosely at her sides. He folded his arms around her and just held her quietly while she processed what an overreaction she had caused. She was the fucking worst.

"I didn't think he'd be that mad," she mumbled against his chest.

"He's a drama queen. That's all it is," Bo assured her. "He's not used to feeling jealous. He doesn't know what to do with it. But he will never hit you. That's not who he is. You're safe with Luc."

"I didn't feel safe."

"Do you feel safe with me?"

"Always."

"Well, I was right there. I wouldn't let anything happen to you. And if you're ever feeling unsafe, just call for me. I'll never be too far away to hear you. Ok? I got you."

"I feel like a fucking idiot," Eve said miserably.

"You aren't. Luc feels like a piece of shit. He isn't. You two will have to talk it over later, but for now, let's try to give those feelings some air and maybe some time to shrink."

Eve felt like she could fall asleep standing up while leaned against Bo's strong chest like that.

"Are we ok now?" he asked soothingly.

A grin tugged at the corners of her mouth. "Yes, Daddy," she teased. She stepped back from him and tried to stop her smile by chewing her lip.

He pointed at her and raised his eyebrows. "No. No. None of that. Not again."

She picked up her coffee cup from the counter and went to the door to slip her shoes on. "Sorry, Daddy."

He sighed heavily and shook his head. "Why?" he asked himself.

For training, Bo first took Eve to the indoor shooting range, where he gave her three guns and got her familiarized with them. She was given a semi-automatic pistol, a rifle, and a shotgun. They would now be her guns, and she was expected to clean them, care for them, and practice with them. Whenever she left the compound, she was to always take the pistol. She was also asked to name them. They became Harry, Ron, and Hermione, and Bo was getting annoyed at her for yelling *Avada Kedavra* every time she pulled the trigger.

Next, he took her to armed martial arts training, where she learned some basics about handling knives, swords, and polearms. She had been given a knife when they were on the hunt in Texas, but she was given a second, larger one today. Bo was pleased with how quickly she picked things up, thanks mostly due to her previous and extensive martial arts training and experience.

By the time they finished with armed martial arts, it was time to break for lunch. She invited Bo back to her flat for whatever was left in her fridge after it had been picked over by the boys, but before they made it back to the complex, Luc found them.

"Can I steal her from you for lunch?" he asked Bo.

Bo quickly read Eve's face before responding. When he saw that she seemed quite at ease now, his eyes smiled at Luc. "Of course." As he turned to leave, he said, "I won't be far."

Luc took off his sunglasses and bowed his head to Eve. "I am deeply sorry about earlier. I had no right to behave that way. Forgive me."

Eve shoved his shoulder. "Stop. That's weird from you."

He looked at her from under his brows. "What?"

"You don't grovel."

"For you, I grovel."

"Let's just forget it, ok? Pretend the whole thing didn't happen."

"I'm not going to pretend it didn't happen. But I will make sure it doesn't happen again," he avowed. He stood up straight and put his sunglasses back on. "Let me make you lunch."

Back at Luc's apartment, which was on the first floor of the complex, Eve sat at the kitchen island and watched him prepare a chicken fettuccine alfredo for the two of them. He looked sharp in his black slacks and white oxford shirt, the sleeves rolled up and the buttons opened down to middle of his chiseled chest. He moved about the kitchen with ease and experience, and it was possibly the sexiest he'd ever looked.

When he plated and handed her her lunch, he brought up the subject she was trying to avoid. "So, I can't not talk about it. I don't like to let things fester. Tell me about last night."

"I don't know what you want me to say. I think you get the gist of it."

"You slept with Zeke."

"Yes. But he didn't sleep over," she replied. It was impossible to tell what Luc was thinking. His face was like stone, and his eyes were hidden behind his sunglasses.

"I'm jealous."

"I gathered that."

"I don't like being jealous."

"Nobody does."

"So, what do I do about it?" he asked.

Eve furrowed her brow and shrugged. "Deal with it, I guess? I don't know." It came out sounding so harsh, but she hadn't meant it to be. She just didn't know what to say.

"Do you like Zeke?" he asked, looking down at his plate.

"Yes."

"Do you like me?"

"Yes."

He looked back up at her. "What do I do, then? Because I am completely under your spell. I need you to be mine. I need you to love me the way I love you."

"*Love*?" She almost choked on her pasta. She set her fork down. "Luc, you don't really love me the way you think you do. You just can't. You're infatuated with my blood. That's all this is. It has to be."

He took off his glasses and set them on the counter next to him. "Look me in the eyes and say that."

She stared into those aqua-blue orbs that gazed back at her with adoration and earnestness. He could hypnotize a gypsy. But she'd been fooled before by soulful blue eyes. "You. Don't. Love. Me," she articulated.

"Eve, do you forget that we used to have a member of Knighco with Panacea Blood? I would know if I was drawn to the blood like that. I'm not. This has nothing to do with your blood."

"Well, it isn't love."

"Maybe not for you. But I know what I feel. I've never been more sure of anything," he affirmed.

"How does Mira feel about that?"

"What does Mira have to do with anything?" he asked, perplexed.

"Instead of coming to see me last night, you spent the night with her. So, she must have something to do with something."

An amused smile danced on Luc's lips, and he covered his mouth with his large hand. "Oh, Eve," he said, his voice muffled under his hands. His eyes glinted with pure glee. "*You're* jealous!"

"Fuck you, I am not."

He dropped his hands and laughed uproariously. "Oh, you have no idea how happy that makes me," he smiled widely.

"Well, I'm so glad I amuse you," she scowled.

"Eve, I was in the lab all night studying the chupacabra Ruger and Remi brought back. We were trying to find any kind of hex or virus or DNA signature to help us understand how Ruth had turned a normal kid into a chupacabra. I was *working* all night. I'm running on about two hours of sleep, which may have played a part in my crankiness this morning. I wasn't doing anything like what *you* were doing, love."

Ouch. Ok.

"Oh," she said, chagrined.

Luc leaned forward with his elbows on the counter. "Did you sleep with Zeke *because* you thought I was sleeping with Mira?"

"No! I slept with Zeke because I wanted to sleep with Zeke. But…I also didn't know you'd be that upset about it. I thought you'd gotten what you wanted from me and that was that."

"So, if I asked you to come over tonight, would you? Or are you going to be otherwise engaged?" He studied her with anxious eyes.

"Oh. Uh, I don't know what the plan is for tonight, because Eoduun and Zeke were talking about celebrating properly, so we might be going out for a bit. But," she said awkwardly, looking down at her pasta and playing with a fettucine noodle with her fork, "I wouldn't be *opposed* to spending some time with you tonight." She glanced up at him, and he was smiling at her, his chin resting in his hand.

"Excellent. I'll join you. I didn't get a chance to celebrate, either."

"Do you think Bo will come with us?" she asked.

"Bo?" Luc seemed surprised. "Hard to say. He's not a fan of the club, but he likes to drink. Did you want him to go?"

"I think I would feel better if he went."

"Why?"

"I don't know. I just do."

"Well, I'm fairly certain he would go if you asked him nicely." Luc brought his plate to the sink, and as he was rinsing it, he turned his head to the side and asked, "So, does Bo bring you coffee every morning?"

"Huh? I don't know. He has a couple times. Why?"

"Just curious."

As they were getting ready to leave Luc's apartment so Eve could return to training with Bo, Luc stopped her at the door. He lifted her chin with his finger and looked down at her over the top of his sunglasses.

"Why do you wear those?" she asked suddenly.

He was given pause. "What, these?" he asked, pointing to his sunglasses. She nodded. "Well, if the majority of your power originated from your eyes, wouldn't you try to protect them, too?" he reasoned.

"Wouldn't goggles or safety glasses be better?"

Luc threw his head back and laughed. "Oh, love, can you imagine me walking around in goggles or safety glasses?" he asked as though it were the most absurd thing anyone could ever have suggested. "That's just adorable." He leaned down and kissed her softly.

As they walked down the hall together, they saw Bo coming toward them. Luc handed her off to Bo.

"Well, I'll see you at the afternoon meeting, love," Luc said to Eve.

"Wait, what afternoon meeting?"

"We need to discuss Ruth and brief everyone on what happened in Texas," Bo informed her.

"Have fun training," Luc said as he turned around. He then turned back momentarily and added, "Oh, and Eve, don't forget you're working with someone who tried to fuck you on a bathroom counter in a hotel room, ok? Ok, byyyyye..." he said cheerfully with a wave of his hand as he walked away.

Bo just stared after Luc in utter mortification. His ears and the part of his face that was visible above his mask flushed bright red.

"Well, glad to see he's back to his usual self again," Eve remarked coolly.

20
What's the Nice Way to Say 'Bastard'?

Eve's training for the second part of the day was in the library. This wasn't typical training for the seasoned hunters, but it was mandatory for all new recruits until they were familiar with the kinds of creatures they would be dealing with most often.

"Specialty training would ordinarily be included in your daily regimen, but Panacea Blood doesn't require any kind of training. Did you talk to Luc at all about your occasional premonitions?"

"'Don't Think It, Don't Say It'?" she said. "No. I kind of forgot about it. I didn't think it, so I didn't say it," she chuckled to herself.

"I'll talk to him," Bo said.

"I think Zeke and Eoduun want to go out to celebrate tonight since we didn't last night. Luc said he would join us if we went out. What about you?"

"I talked to Zeke at lunch today, and he mentioned going to The Gutter. I told him I might tag along and have a drink, keep an eye on my wards."

"What's The Gutter?"

"It's the club everyone seems to favor. Loud. Sweaty. Crowded. High-end drugs and one-offs in the bathrooms. Not really my scene, but I go on occasion just to make sure everyone makes it home in one piece."

"It's hard to imagine sweet little Zeke frequenting a place like that," Eve mused.

Bo looked down at her neck and nodded at her mark. "Is it, though?"

The hair along the back of her neck prickled. There was that ugly jealousy baring its teeth again. Did he get blowjobs in the bathroom at The Gutter, too? She was the worst kind of hypocrite.

And she would be there tonight with both Zeke and Luc. Was she supposed to be *with* one or the other tonight? She'd already tentatively agreed to come home with Luc afterward, so she was essentially *his* for the night, right? What was Zeke going to say? How was he going to feel about that? He seemed to already be aware that Luc held sway, but he had just as much right to her as Luc did. Just…not tonight.

Tonight, Luc had claimed her, as it were.

She dropped her forehead onto the book she was unsuccessfully trying to concentrate on.

"I know for a fact you can't actually absorb the information that way," Bo commented absently, looking down at his phone.

"It's worth a try," she replied, her head still down. "My eyes sure as hell aren't doing the trick."

"Something on your mind?"

"Love is stupid. Feelings are dumb."

"Granted. Did things not go well with Luc at lunch?" Bo asked, still looking down at his phone.

Eve turned her head to the side, smooshing her cheek against the book so she could look at Bo. "It went fine. But I just don't get him. He's not normal."

"Understatement."

"And then there's Zeke. Sweet, sunny Zeke."

"Um, ok..." Bo replied, finally looking down at Eve, wondering where she was going with this.

"And then there's me, like a squirrel in the machinery."

Bo snorted, completely catching Eve off guard.

"Sorry," he apologized with a laugh. "It's just...vivid."

"And accurate."

"So you've shaken things up a bit. They'll settle again," Bo said unconcernedly.

"When are you going to start charging me for these therapy sessions?" Eve jested.

"As soon as I know I'm not completely full of shit myself. Now, quit fretting and get back to studying. Things have a way of working out how they need to, whether we worry about them or not."

"Ok. Thanks, Daddy," Eve said sweetly.

Bo closed his eyes and exhaled loudly, then stood up and walked away.

Eve returned to her apartment later that afternoon and showered and put some makeup on. She was still in her bathrobe when there was a knock at the door.

"It's open!" she yelled. She peeked her head out of her bedroom to see who came in.

Zeke. He smiled at her like he hadn't seen her in months. Radiant. Then he opened his mouth. "Dude, if I knew you had training today, I wouldn't have kept you up so late last night with Eoduun."

Dude. "No worries," she replied. "I survived." She went back into her bedroom and Zeke followed along behind her. He flopped down on her unmade bed while she looked at the clothes in her closet.

"So, we're thinking about going to The Gutter tonight. Did Bo tell you?"

"He did. Luc wants to come, too."

"Well, he's welcome to. I mean, he does own the place."

Eve raised her eyebrows and turned to face Zeke. "What?"

"Luc owns The Gutter. His family owns a lot of night clubs and hotels. Dude has money."

"Does that mean Bo does, too? He didn't mention anything about this."

"No, Bo's not part of that. He's a...um...what's the nice way to say 'bastard'?"

"He's illegitimate?"

"Yeah, that. Luc and Ruth are full brother and sister, but Bo is only half. He was raised with Luc and Ruth after his mom died, but he didn't get any of the money once he grew up and moved out. That's what I've heard, anyway."

"What? That's not fair," Eve said, outraged for Bo.

"Nope," Zeke agreed. "But Bo doesn't seem all that bothered by it."

"I think he's just good at hiding behind that mask," Eve said.

After a long silence, Eve pulled a red dress from her closet and held it in front of her for Zeke to see. "Does this clash with my hair?" she asked.

He shrugged his shoulders. "I don't even know what that means. But I know you'll look smoking hot in it and I'm going to be dying of jealousy."

"Oh, whatever," she brushed it off.

"With Luc going, he's not going to let you out of his reach," Zeke complained. "Man, I kind of wish he would head out to Rome or one of his business trips already."

"What business trips?" Eve asked curiously as she set the red dress aside and continued her search.

"He's always gone. Well, not *always*, but a lot."

"I thought he was basically in charge around here."

"He is, but he's also running around putting out fires all over the country and in Rome for both Knighco and his family's business. He's always busy."

Well. This was news to Eve. She couldn't help but feel just a little bit crushed. Of course she would get herself involved with a man who's eventually going to abandon her. What was she supposed to do now? Enjoy her night on his arm and then cut it off clean?

Nope. She already knew she couldn't do that. She just...couldn't. Fuck.

She glanced at Zeke, leaned back on her bed, looking like an invitation to drop her robe and take him for a spin, and she wondered if she would feel the same way if he were the one who was always gone. Yeah, she probably would. What a hot mess.

Knock knock. Eve rolled her eyes. "It's open!" she yelled impatiently. When the door opened, she yelled, "And you might as well leave it open!"

"You aren't used to other people being all up in your space, are you?" Zeke observed.

"No. It's kind of a lot."

"Evie?" Bo called.

"In here."

Bo came through the bedroom door and nodded to Zeke, then regarded Eve. "You aren't dressed. The meeting starts in ten minutes."

"Oh, shit. I was busy thinking about club clothes."

"Come on, Zeke, let's let her get dressed," Bo urged.

"Are you guys in here?" Eoduun called through the apartment from the doorway.

Sigh.

When they all arrived together to the meeting, five minutes late, everyone was already there. The motley crew seated around that long conference table was even more diverse than she'd expected. Luc was at the head of the table, standing with his hands in his pockets and a pleasant smile on his face, but as soon as he saw her, his lips widened into a real smile.

"Eve! Come up here," Luc called to her, holding his hand out to her. "Everyone, this is our newest recruit, Eve Alarie," he introduced her as she approached the head of the long table. When she reached him, he took her hand in his and kissed the back of her fingers chivalrously, giving her a quick, devilish glance over his sunglasses while his head was tipped. "Eve is a blood healer, and I am certain she will prove to be an instrumental member of this organization."

He took her under his arm and pointed around the table giving introductions based on teams. First was Team Beta, (she learned only then that she was on Team Alpha) or, as Zeke had called it, Mira's team. Mira Tachibana was the first introduction, but she required no introduction. If Eve hadn't been so focused on Luc when she came into the room, she would've picked out Mira instantly. She was seated, but Eve could tell by her long, lithe limbs that she was tall and svelte. She coolly measured Eve with critical, dark eyes from behind thick-framed glasses. She wore her hair in a high, stylish ponytail, and she was dressed like a CEO. And, as Eve expected, she was quite pretty. She exuded an air of intimidation, and it was blatantly intentional.

Eve had a sudden fear of standing next to that woman in Luc's presence. Eve would be found severely wanting next to someone like that, and if Luc were to have that comparison thrust in his face, he'd snap out of whatever spell he was under with Eve. He'd realize that Eve was, on all accounts, the silver medal. B-grade. Unworthy. The thought made her chest feel hollow.

"Delighted to meet you," Mira said coldly.

Luc moved on to Ramil Reyes and Veris Valentius, which Eve had already met, and then came the final member of Team Beta, Celeste Bradley. Celeste had a very geeky vibe about her. She was wearing a Star Wars t-shirt and khaki cargo shorts, and she had her cinnamon-red hair in low, braided pigtails. She seemed outgoing and friendly.

Next around the table came the introductions for Team Gamma. Luc introduced the captain, Roy Edlund, and Eve knew from Zeke's descriptions that Roy was the old guy at the table with the trucker hat and thick, rusty beard. It was clear that he had other things he'd rather be doing than sitting in that meeting. He gave her a gruff hello.

Then came Levi Oscar. Levi looked like a black-haired, blue-eyed Ken doll that came to life, married Barbie at a young age, had three kids, got divorced, took out a bunch of loans to send his kids to college, and then bought a motorcycle that sits in his driveway unridden while he spends his weekdays sitting behind a desk in a photo-bare cubicle. Zeke had described him as having a rather blank affect, often taking things too literally and having difficulty understanding sarcasm and pop culture references. Eve could see it.

The final member of Team Gamma was Kai Adakai, the skinwalker. He was young and handsome with long, straight black hair pulled back into a messy ponytail at the nape of his neck. He had somewhat of a wild look to him. His eyes were an unusual gold-brown color that were reminiscent of the eyes of a fox. He had his foot up in his chair, resting his elbow on his knee, and Eve could see that he wasn't wearing any shoes. He smiled and said hello to her, and she noticed his canines looked rather sharp. Not as sharp as Bo's, but they were noticeable.

Team Delta was next, and Luc introduced Zephlyn Albrecht first as the team captain. The way he surveyed her with interest caught her attention. His narrow, dark eyes sparkled with a hint of excitement. "You're like me, aren't you?" he asked her.

"I, uh…I don't know what you mean," she replied, confused.

"You're a clairvoyant."

Luc looked down at her with surprise. "You are?"

"No? I don't know? I…can we talk about it later?" She hated being put on the spot. She felt her ears beginning to burn for no particular reason.

Zephlyn nodded knowingly, his black, slicked back man-bun bouncing slightly. "You are. Or at least, you have an affinity for it. But yes, we will talk later."

Luc glanced at her again, almost suspiciously, then continued with the next introduction, Mendal Brown. He wore his black hair shaved close up the sides, then in tight cornrow braids at the top. It was a hairstyle Eve had seen often in the ring because it was the best way to keep an opponent from using your hair against you. She didn't know Mendal, but she could tell just by looking at him and that confident way in which he held himself that he was their martial arts expert. He had that "I fear no man" air to him.

And finally, Team Delta's oddball, the shapeshifter, Dizzy Xavier. He was not at all what one would expect a monster to look like. He was of average height and incredibly thin, and he sat with his shoulders slumped forward in his chair. His face was gaunt with eyes like a loris and an oddly crooked nose. His mousy hair was dull and frizzy and hung down over his ears and into his eyes. When he said hello to Eve, he used a strange, cockney English accent, then laughed awkwardly and looked around the table for a reaction.

Eve laughed uncomfortably. Luc quickly moved on.

"The last team, Team Flannel, you've already met. Ruger, Remi, and Cass."

"Technically, we're Team Epsilon," Cassie clarified, "but somehow Team Flannel is what stuck. I blame them." She jutted her thumb toward Ruger and Remi, who were both sitting there in plaid flannel shirts.

"What? It's a legit style choice," Ruger said gruffly. "And just like us, it'll never die," he joked loudly, raising his hand to Remi for a high-five. Remi just looked at him like he was an idiot and he was embarrassed for him. Ruger turned and raised his other hand to Cassie.

"Honey…no," she shot him down.

He dropped his hand and nodded in concession.

Eve wanted to be friends with Cassie. She liked her.

"Go ahead and have a seat, Eve," Luc said, gesturing to the chair in front of him.

She didn't want to sit there. It was the chair at the head of the table. It was the seat that he should be sitting in. If she sat here, everyone would look at her.

"Isn't that your seat?" she whispered.

"What's mine is yours," he smiled. "Now, please, sit."

She sat. She stared down at the table in front of her, feeling the eyes of the whole room on her and not wanting to meet any of them.

Luc placed his huge hands on the back of her chair and leaned forward over her to address the table. "As you all know, I recalled you here because Ruthlys has finally come out of the woodwork." He described to them what they knew about her new skills and Lilith's grimoire, and that she seems to be after Dagon. He also mentioned that if Ruthlys ever found out that Eve possessed Panacea Blood, she would be after her as well, so they were all to keep Eve's specialty strictly confidential. It wasn't to be discussed outside of that conference room.

"Maybe we should just exorcise Dagon once and for all," Roy suggested. "He's been just as much trouble as he's been worth. I know we don't have a surefire method yet, but I found a lead in some ancient Sumerian lore that might be helpful."

"I second that," Levi said.

Luc nodded, then said, "I hear what you're saying, but I'm not risking Zeke. As far as I can tell, Dagon can't be extracted without doing irreparable damage to his vessel. It'd be like tugging at a thread and unraveling the whole damn sweater."

"Love that song," Ruger said. When Cassie side-eyed him, he said, "What? Who doesn't like Weezer?"

"Honey…no," Cassie repeated.

Luc continued, "As for her new skillset, whatever spell she's using is unlike anything we've seen. It's a complete transformation of the victim, down to the DNA. The creature she made is indiscernible from a born and bred chupacabra. Which means that whatever else is in that grimoire must be incredibly powerful, and incredibly ancient. So, we may end up needing Dagon."

"He's about as trustworthy as a Taco Bell fart," Mendal said. "You really want to risk shittin' the bed with him?"

"That is the horse my money is on, yes. Mostly because he doesn't want to be enslaved to her any more than we want her to have his power at her disposal. And before anyone asks, no, I don't think there is any reason to believe they are working *together.*

"But we have a plan, so everybody listen up," Luc announced. "We need to locate Ruth and the grimoire. Sister Fiona is working on tracking her with Vatican resources, but I would also like Celeste monitoring for credit cards, phone calls, security cameras – any digital imprint she might leave. Levi, I need you to use your viewing skills to check around anywhere she may have gone, assuming that she isn't going to run too far away from her target. Zephlyn, I'm going to need you to try your best to tune into whatever frequency you need to to see what she's going to be planning next. Roy, Mira, Remi – see what you can find about Lilith's grimoire. In the meantime, until we find her, I want everyone training as though you're getting ready for a war. Because you might be. And brush up on your lore. Who knows what kind of ancient creatures she's going to be cooking up with her new spell book."

He straightened and came around to stand next to Eve's seat, sticking his hands in his pockets. "Questions? Concerns?" he asked the group.

"What happens once we find her?" Mira wanted to know. "We aren't letting her go again, are we?"

"We'll discuss the rest of the plan once we've located her. For now, train."

"So, we have no plan," Mira surmised contemptuously.

Luc smiled reassuringly and held his hands wide. "Do I look like a man without a plan?"

21

He Can Wait Until I'm Done with You

After Luc dismissed everyone, Eve rose from her seat and started toward Bo, Zeke, and Eoduun, who seemed to be waiting for her. Luc caught her arm and stopped her.

"You boys go on ahead," Luc said to her team. "I need to discuss something with Eve. Privately."

"Well, don't take too long, Eve, if you want to ride to the club with us," Eoduun advised her.

"Don't worry about that, Eoduun," Luc said smoothly. "I'll give her a ride."

"Do you want me to wait outside for you, Evie?" Bo asked as he paused in the doorway.

"You can go, Bo," Luc answered. "And close the door behind you."

"I asked her, not you, Luc," Bo said. His words were sharp, but his tone and eyes were friendly.

Luc raised his eyebrows at Bo. "Well, excuse me, then."

"I'll catch up with you later, Bo," Eve assured him. He nodded, then walked out the door, leaving it wide open.

"Somebody's got their damn panties in a bunch," Luc complained, looking after Bo. "I hope he finds himself a pretty little friend at the club tonight who can unbunch them for him."

A petty pang of jealousy flared in Eve's chest. Again. Where it didn't belong. But she couldn't help it. This was *her* team. These were *her* boys. Those girls could have any of the other ones, but not these ones. It had become glaringly apparent to her that it didn't matter who she ended up with; she was going to be jealous of the attention any of them paid other girls. Or boys that weren't Zeke, in Eoduun's case. It didn't make sense, and it wasn't cool that she was being so selfish and shitty.

But they were *hers*, she was *theirs*, and they didn't need any outsiders.

"I think Bo's just being considerate of my feelings," Eve pointed out to Luc. "He's been very kind to me today. So be nice."

"Hm. Or maybe he's beginning to take his guard duty a little too far."

"Guard duty?"

"He's in charge of your safety."

"Since when?"

"Since Ruth reared her little blonde head."

"Nobody told me about this," Eve griped.

Luc took her hands in his and looked down at her through his sunglasses. "Eve, love, Bo is your protector whenever I'm not by your side. There, I just told you."

"So, he's not just being nice to me, then."

"*I'll* be nice to you," Luc said softly, drawing close to her. She raised her chin, anticipating an embrace and a kiss, but he kept moving and brushed past her, leaving her hanging awkwardly. "...As soon as I lock this damn door," he added. He strolled to the door, shut it and locked it, then turned back to Eve. He slipped off his sunglasses and tucked them into his front pocket, then smiled mischievously at her. "You look flustered," he said in a pleased tone.

She crossed her arms. "You could've just teleported to do that. You brushed past me on purpose."

Luc laughed. "Could've *just* teleported, hey? You make it sound so effortless."

"Isn't it?"

He approached her. "Not at all. If it were, I'd *just* teleport everywhere." He brushed her hair from her shoulder and looked down at her. "It takes a Herculean effort and enormous amount of energy to bend space around me. It isn't like snapping my fingers. It's like lifting a truck." He tilted her chin up to him. "And I wanted to save my energy for better things."

He ran his thumb slowly over her lips, his eyes watching keenly as she parted them slightly. Her tongue slid up between her open lips and lightly caressed the pad of his thumb, eliciting a pleased hum from Luc. He leaned into her and brought his mouth to hers, his tongue slipping between her lips into her mouth, massaging her tongue softly. He inhaled deeply as he kissed her, and she felt his big hands sliding down to grip her ass. With what felt like effortless strength, he hoisted her up onto his hips, and she threw her arms around his thick neck and wrapped her legs around his waist. His cock strained against his slacks like a steel rod between her legs, and she rolled her hips, feeling it through the thin fabric of her jogger pants against her core.

If she could've wished away their constraints, he would've been inside her already.

She squeezed his waist with her thighs, using his body as leverage as she raised herself a little higher so she was at eye-level with him. She twisted her fingers into the hair on the back of his head and devoured a kiss from him, then slowly blinked her eyes open, gazing into those beautiful orbs that she just couldn't get enough of. He beamed at her.

"God, you're beautiful," he gushed. "I just want to see that pretty face come undone, my name dripping like honey from that sweet tongue." His lips curled dangerously and he looked down at her mouth. He kept one hand on her ass to help support her, but he brought the other up to her face, his strong fingers gripping her jaw. "Actually, I'd like something else of mine dripping off that sweet tongue, too."

"You're nasty," she said with a breathy chuckle.

"Is that a no, then?"

"Well…I didn't say that."

She felt him throb against her. "Oh, love, you have no idea how much I'll be looking forward to that. But for now, I think I'm going to have to fuck you before someone interrupts us."

"What if Bo is waiting?" Eve fretted.

Luc turned and pressed her back against the wall, then started to unzip his pants while she clung to him. "Then he can wait until I'm done with you." Once he'd freed his cock from his pants, he tugged her joggers down to her thighs. A big thank-you to whoever invented elastic waistbands.

He slipped his forearms under her legs and pressed his hands against the wall, using the crook of his elbows as a support for her to hook her knees over. Her arms pressed into the bulging traps around his neck as she held onto him, one hand across the back of his shoulders, one hand in his hair.

He aligned his hips with hers and slowly pushed into her eager wetness. He exhaled a contented sigh against her neck as he began to fill her. "Mm, you feel so fucking good, Eve," he whispered.

She panted against his shoulder as he thrust deeper and deeper, until he was fully sheathed within her. Had he felt this *big* the last time? Or was it just this precarious position she was in? She was stretching to her limits to accommodate him like this, and it made her involuntarily mewl with every thrust. "…Luc…" she whimpered.

He moaned in her ear and whispered, "I love the sounds you make when I'm fucking you. Say my name again."

She moaned his name once more, then she tightened her grip on his hair and brought her lips to his neck. Her mouth craved his skin. She wanted to devour him. She sucked and kissed the sensitive flesh beneath his ear and jawline, his quick breaths tickling her hairline and neck as she moved her lips closer to his mouth.

She brought her lips against his and whispered, "Deeper and slower," then slipped her tongue into his mouth. The way his tongue moved with hers, the sensation of the soft, warm flesh wriggling and dancing against hers, sent aching tingles of pleasure throughout her chest and core. He obeyed her request and slowed his pace, pressing his hips harder into hers, his motion becoming a deep, slow grind.

"Oh God, Luc, that's it," Eve praised. "Don't stop. Just like that...Mmm..." She could feel him throbbing inside her, and she knew he was getting close. He tried to slow down to make it last longer, but she was *ready*, and she fought him, rocking her hips and forcing him to continue his pace by pulling on him with her heels in his lower back.

"Fuck, Eve, wait..." he protested, but it was cut short as he burst, gasping and groaning as he felt her body spasm around him. She crushed her mouth against his, devouring his moans and muffling her own against his tongue as she let the pleasure wash over her, wave after wave.

When she pulled away from the final kiss, panting and breathless, she looked up into Luc's face. He slowly opened his eyes, looking down into her eyes adoringly with half-closed lids. "I'm not going to annoy you by saying it, but know that I want to," he whispered lovingly, planting a little kiss on the end of her nose.

She didn't ask what he meant, because the unmistakable tenderness in his eyes, the small, earnest smile, and the upturned eyebrows all told her exactly what he wanted to say. *I love you.*

And her stupid ears wanted to hear it, but she wasn't going to tell him that. Instead, she laughed and kissed his sweet, full lips once more.

"We should probably get out of here," she whispered.

He carefully lowered her to her feet and they tidied themselves and each other up. He took his sunglasses out of his pocket and flicked them open, giving her one last appreciative glance before sliding them onto his face. He shoved his hands into his pockets, and Eve admired his relaxed expression and posture as she fixed her sneakers.

"Even if I didn't know you, I would know you just had sex," she mused. "It's written all over your face."

He smiled. "You look pretty satisfied yourself."

As they walked together back to the apartment complex, she asked Luc, "So, Zeke tells me you own the club we're going to tonight."

"Mm-hm."

"And that your family owns a lot of clubs and hotels."

"Mm-hm."

"And that you're gone a lot."

"Does he always have so much to say about me?" Luc asked in mild irritation.

"Is it true that you're usually not here?"

"I have responsibilities that take me away from the compound on a fairly regular basis."

"So, yes," she surmised.

Luc stopped as Eve walked on a few paces. "Tell me what you really want to say."

She looked at her feet, her back turned to him. "I'm just trying to get a feel for you. That's all."

"Trying to decide if I'm worth the trouble?"

"Kicking tires, maybe," Eve said. Then she laughed it off. "Forget I said anything. I was only curious." She took a few steps, but he didn't move.

"Is it a dealbreaker?" he asked.

"What?"

"My traveling. You wouldn't bring it up if it wasn't a concern. But is it a dealbreaker?"

"If there were a deal on the table, it might be. But there isn't, so we're fine," she said elusively.

"What if I offered one?"

"Don't," she blurted. *Don't ruin it. Let it be.* She started walking again.

He didn't take long to catch up to her with his long strides. He reached out and slipped his hand over hers, intertwining his big fingers with her more delicate ones.

"We don't have to talk about it today. But it's a conversation that will happen," he informed her. "In the meantime, though, I'm not going anywhere until Ruth is dealt with."

Eve didn't reply. She marveled at the fact that Luc wasn't afraid to say anything. How could he be so blunt and forward all the time? Wasn't he ever afraid that his feelings wouldn't be requited? Wasn't he ever afraid that he was wrong? That he would be made a fool? Did he even know what insecurity felt like? She looked over at him. No. Someone like that, they have no fucking clue. The golden boy.

As they approached the apartment complex, Remi, Ruger, and Cassie came out the front doors, and Eve quickly withdrew her hand from Luc's. From the corner of her eye, she saw him look down at her indignantly.

"Do I embarrass you?" he wanted to know.

"No," she answered simply. And honestly.

Cassie called out to Eve. "Hey, what are you doing right now? We're going to shoot some pool and get some burgers if you want to join us."

"Oh, man, if I didn't already have plans tonight, I would!" She told them that the team was going out to celebrate, then invited them to join, pointing out that they were on that case, too.

Remi laughed a little cynically. "Well, we would, except Ruger isn't allowed to go to The Gutter anymore. Not since last time…" He looked to Cassie and Ruger with an amused smirk.

Cassie rolled her eyes. "This motherfucker, I tell you what," she chastised, shaking her head at Ruger.

"I swear, someone put something in my drink!" Ruger defended. "I would not have picked a fight with those guys otherwise!"

"Yeah, sure," Remi replied sarcastically.

"Mmm-hmmm…" Cassie mumbled simultaneously.

"Sorry, Ruger," Luc said casually. "Club policy. But hey, you can try again in, what, five months is it?"

"Four," Ruger asserted, holding up four fingers. "But who's counting?"

Luc clapped him on the shoulder. "Have fun at the bar and stay out of trouble, hm? I don't want my night interrupted by a call from the Sheriff's office again."

"He'll behave," Cassie confirmed.

When Luc and Eve walked into the building, she asked Luc about Ruger's incident.

"He started a fight with a group of thugs because they didn't appreciate his sense of humor. I believe he asked when their little dance troupe was having their next recital. It closed the place down for the night," he explained. "It was bad."

Eve couldn't help but laugh. If she hadn't been assigned to Team Alpha, she would've liked to have been a part of Team Flannel. They were her kind of people.

"Hungry?" Luc asked as she started up the stairs to her apartment. "I can make us dinner."

"That's ok, I think Zeke left chicken nuggets in my freezer."

Luc shook his head. "I'll bring you something, how about that?"

"You don't have to. I'll be fine, really."

"I'll bring you something," he said with finality as he headed off toward his apartment.

"I'm still eating the chicken nuggets!" she called back. He just waved his hand at her.

She returned to her apartment, and as she was closing the door behind her, she thought better of it. What was the point? She left it wide open. She'd noticed that, now that people were around, most left their doors open like that. She'd never lived anywhere where that was a typical practice, but she did remember visiting a friend at college once, and the dorms were like that. Kids just left their doors wide open when they were in their rooms and everybody came and went as they pleased.

She was so used to being alone, though, she was going to have to constantly remind herself that people could see and hear her when she left the door open. No pop-n-locking through the apartment while rapping badly at the top of her lungs. That was a big ask, but she would try.

She glanced over into Zeke's apartment as she was kicking her shoes off by the door. He didn't appear to be home, but his door was open. She walked across the hall and stuck her head in.

"Zeke?" she called.

He stepped out into the living room area from the bathroom, a toothbrush hanging from his mouth, a towel around his waist, his damp hair sticking up all over.

"Hey!" he said with a mouth full of toothpaste, waving at her. He held a finger up for her to wait, then disappeared in the bathroom again.

Oh hell. She should've just gone home. He was entirely too tempting looking like that. She heard him spit and water running, then he reappeared, still in nothing but a towel. He walked up to her, and she saw his eyes scanning her neck for fresh marks.

"Well…that didn't take long," he said. "Is he still planning to take you to the club with him? Or are you riding with us?"

"Luc? I'm pretty sure he's taking me."

"Is he your boyfriend yet?"

Eve shook her head and knitted her brows. "No."

"Are you going home with him afterward?"

Eve confirmed with a look. Zeke nodded, then drew closer to her. He glanced up at the opened door. "Then I'm going to steal this now," he said, slipping his arm around her waist and pulling her body against his. He leaned down and kissed her, his tongue still tasting of mint toothpaste. "You better not ignore me tonight," he said with a sly grin.

22
Lipstick on a Pig

"Oh, I'm sure you'll find someone to entertain you," Eve said, trying her best to not sound sarcastic or bitter.

"But I want *you* to entertain me," Zeke said, then glanced up at the door again before stealing one more kiss.

They heard voices in the hallway, and Zeke dropped his arm from her waist.

"Oh, hey, Eve," Eoduun said as he walked into Zeke's apartment.

Eve turned around. "Holy shit, Eoduun, you clean up well," she said, giving him a once-over. He was dressed in well-fitted black slacks, a black vest, and a tight, long-sleeved pink oxford shirt. He had some of his hair pulled back in a half-ponytail, but left some still hanging in his face.

"Are you saying I look like shit the rest of the time?" he asked.

"Your words, not mine," she teased.

Then Bo walked in. Eve's knees suddenly felt a little weak. "I thought you were with Luc," he said. He stood there in a suit similar to Eoduun's, but his slacks and vest were light grey, and the vest had a deeper cut. The sleeves of his black shirt were rolled three-quarters of the way up his forearms, and he wore a black bowtie. His mask looked almost seamless from his shirt to his nose. His silver-white hair was still a little messy, but he'd put product in it and styled it that way.

He looked at her with blue and charcoal eyes, his hair hanging over the scar on his right eye.

Oh, wait. Did he ask her a question?

"What?" she said stupidly.

"Luc isn't with you?" he asked.

"Oh. Uh, he went to his apartment. He'll be by later." Eve had to peel her eyes away from him. She turned back to Zeke. "I'll let you get dressed. I need to get ready, too."

Eoduun and Bo stepped out of the doorway so she could get by, but when she walked into her apartment, Bo followed her.

"Need a basic bitch to tell you what to wear?" he joked, and Eve turned around. He was standing in her doorway, his shoulder leaned casually against the doorjamb, his hands in his pockets, his ankles crossed.

"Stop that," she blurted.

He raised his eyebrows questioningly. "Stop what?"

She gestured at him. "Looking all…like that." The heat was rising in her cheeks as he looked at her. It felt like she was having a hot flash. She tugged at the collar of her shirt, fanning herself with it. "Is it fucking hot in here? It's fucking hot in here. Excuse me. I need to shower and get dressed."

"Did you eat?" he called after her as she walked to the bathroom, trying to get away from him.

"I will!" she called back.

"Do you want me go get you something while you're in the shower?"

"Why does everybody keep trying to feed me? No, I'm fine!"

She closed the bathroom door and looked at herself in the mirror. Her cheeks were beet red. "Oh, Daddy, I am a bad, bad girl," she whispered to herself.

She hopped in the shower and quickly washed away her encounter with Luc, then fixed her makeup and curled her hair. When she came out of the bathroom in her towel, she found the boys lounging around in her apartment. Bo was sitting at the kitchen island, staring at his phone, and Zeke and Eoduun were sitting on the couch watching anime.

Because of course they were. Why wouldn't they be?

"I ought to start collecting a cover charge," she joked as she walked to her bedroom.

She looked through her closet again. She liked the red dress she had gotten out earlier, but she was second-guessing it after seeing everyone else dressed in so much black. Maybe she should go with a black dress. She'd seen one in there. She found it and pulled it from the rack. It was simple, short, and slinky. She slipped it on. It was perfect. She looked at her modest shoe assortment, and suddenly realized that there was an extra pair of black heels in there that she didn't recognize.

When she grabbed them and saw the red on the bottoms, she almost dropped them.

"Holy shit. No fucking way. He did not."

Oh, but he did. Cinderella was definitely wearing these glass slippers tonight.

She came out of the bedroom and beelined straight for the kitchen. She still hadn't gotten her chicken nuggets yet. As she turned on the air fryer and got the bag of nuggets out of the freezer, she caught Bo watching her from the corner of her eye. She turned to look at him, but his eyes flicked back down to his phone instantly.

Zeke leapt over the back of the couch and came into the kitchen. "Wow, Eve," he said, looking her up and down. "Damn."

"Zeke," Bo chastised.

"What?"

"Inappropriate." Bo then looked at Eve. "Evie, you look lovely," he complimented her.

Zeke spied the bag of chicken nuggets on the counter. "Ooh, can you throw some of those in for me, too?" he asked Eve.

"They're *your* chicken nuggets, Z," she reminded him. "I can't really say no." She looked at his baggy black slacks and tight-fitting black t-shirt. She could see the outline of his pectorals and hard abs through the fabric of his shirt and a little bit of his tattoo poking out from beneath his sleeves. As much as she would've liked to have seen him dressed like Bo and Eoduun, this outfit did seem more his style. And he looked damn good in it.

"Luc is bringing you dinner, Evie," Bo announced, his eyes back on his phone.

"How did you know that?" she asked.

"Because I can smell it. He's on his way."

"What did he make?" Eve asked jokingly.

"Chicken Marsala."

"Oh, damn, that sounds good," she said.

"Can I eat your chicken nuggets too, then?" Zeke asked.

"...Fine."

Luc walked in a few moments later. "Strange. I could have *sworn* I came to Eve's apartment," he said facetiously.

"I'm in here," she called from the kitchen.

Luc came around the corner carrying a fancy-looking bento. He set it on the counter in front of Eve. He kissed her on the cheek and said, "You look gorgeous." He then looked over at the air fryer with the sheet full of chicken nuggets in it. "And I see I caught you before you ruined your appetite. Here, eat," he said as he pulled a fork from the silverware drawer and handed it to Eve. She slid onto the barstool next to Bo, and Luc leaned back against the counter in the corner with his arms crossed over his chest. He was looking just as sharp as everyone else in a tailored black suit and tie. His crisp, baby-blue shirt complemented his eyes. She noticed he was wearing different sunglasses, too. These frames were more rectangular, not round. Were these his "dressy" sunglasses?

Eoduun sauntered into the kitchen and opened the fridge. "You fuckers are making me hungry," he said as he scanned the contents. He then closed the fridge and opened the pantry, pulling out a bag of veggie straws. He ripped into it and grabbed a handful and shoved it into his mouth.

"The chicken nuggets will be done in just a few minutes," Zeke said as he squeezed past Eoduun to get at the paper plates in the cupboard. "You want any?" he asked Eoduun.

"Hey, give me some of those," Bo said to Eoduun, eyeing the bag of veggie straws and holding his hand out.

Eoduun dumped some straws into Bo's hand, several pieces falling onto the counter, and said, "Yeah, give me some nuggets," to Zeke.

Luc shook his head slowly. "It's a goddamn zoo in here," he said in annoyed awe.

"Welcome to the jungle," Eve jested. "Did you make this?" she asked as she took a bite of the chicken from the bento. "Mmm, damn that's good."

"I told you. The jerk can cook," Bo said.

On their way to the club in Luc's car, Luc asked, "Are they *always* there, hanging out in your apartment? I can talk to them, if you'd like, and tell them to give you some space."

"No, it's all right. It's a little annoying sometimes, but I don't hate it. It's actually kind of nice to know they choose to be around me like that. I'll take it while it lasts."

"Do you need me to restock your fridge? Your bounty for the last hunt should be hitting your account tomorrow, but the food allotment doesn't hit until the end of the month."

"It's fine. Speaking of, did you buy these?" She pointed at her shoes. "These are like fifteen-hundred-dollar shoes, Luc."

"Do you like them?"

"Does a bear shit in the woods?!" she replied emphatically.

He laughed. "Then they were worth every penny."

"It's going to take me forever to pay you back for these."

He shot her a startled look. "Who said anything about paying me back? They're a gift."

She looked down at her feet and admired the gorgeous shoes. She'd never received such an extravagant gift in all her life.

"Some people buy matching t-shirts. I prefer something a little more subtle," he added with a smirk.

That's right, he wore Louboutin's as well, didn't he? It was one of the first things she'd noticed about him. Not much time had passed since then, but so much had already changed. It hadn't taken her long to grow completely attached to this little band of lunatics she'd fallen in with.

Eve was surprised at the size of the club as they walked in. There were *so many people* there. She didn't even know that many people lived in Nebraska. And as they walked through the crowd, all eyes turned to Luc. Even if he wasn't the club owner, which most of these people probably didn't know anyway, he drew attention. He just had that commanding presence. He was tall and striking and confident and reeked of success and money.

She didn't belong on his arm. She looked out of place there. Someone tall, thin, and elegant would have suited him better. Someone cultured and beautiful and confident. Someone who looked like Mira. Eve looked like a street fighter in a dress and expensive shoes. Everyone had to be thinking the same thing behind those judgmental eyes: Lipstick on a pig.

She felt relief wash over her when Bo suddenly stepped into their path. Her reinforcements had arrived. Zeke and Eoduun weren't far behind him. They all made their way to the bar. Eve carefully perched herself on a barstool in her short dress, and Bo sat next to her. Luc slid up on her other side and remained standing, resting his elbow on the bar. Zeke and Eoduun took off together to check out the scene, but only after Eve promised Zeke she would join them on the dancefloor after she'd had a few drinks to build her confidence.

Eve turned to Bo while Luc was chatting with the bartender. "Shouldn't you be keeping an eye on those rowdy boys?"

"They can handle themselves," he said, lowering his mask to take a drink of something fruity with an umbrella in it. He tossed the umbrella onto the bar.

"Is that a sex on the beach?" Eve asked, holding back a snicker.

"Shut up."

"You really *are* a basic bitch, Bo," she teased.

"I never denied it."

Eve looked at the Long Island iced tea she'd ordered, then back at Bo's drink. "Actually, now I kind of wish I'd gotten one of those, too," she admitted.

Bo slid it over to her so she could take a drink. "You get *one* sip."

When Luc saw her take a drink from Bo's cocktail, he said, "I look away for five seconds and when I look back, you've got Bo's sex in your mouth."

Bo's face burned bright red.

Eve just about spit out her drink. "Luc!"

Luc threw his head back and laughed uproariously. "It's all right, I get it. You just wanted a taste." He lifted her chin with the side of his hooked finger and kissed her lightly. He then leaned into her ear. "As long as it's only a taste," he said, his lips grazing the ridge of her ear. "You have your own drink to focus on tonight, love."

Eve had a couple of drinks while Bo looked at manga on his phone and offered a little bit of conversation here and there, and Luc stood guard over her and schmoozed all the people that came by and recognized him. She bit her tongue when those people were of the feminine variety, but she made sure to reach out and touch his arm or hand as a signal to them that this particular man was not available.

As for Bo, he looked so unapproachable with his eyes on his phone and his mask over his face that there weren't any potential hussies she had to keep an eye on.

When Zeke and Eoduun came back for her, she was ready for some dancing. Luc informed her he had something he needed to take care of briefly, but he would be back momentarily. Bo remained at the bar, as he swore up and down that he did not dance. Before Eve went out with Zeke and Eoduun, however, she needed to take a quick trip to the little girls' room.

There was a line, of course, and as she took her place in it, she noticed a man watching her from the bar, some distance away. There wasn't anything outwardly wrong with him, as he was an average looking fellow of average build, but she felt an instant revulsion toward him. Every time she moved ahead in line, she checked her peripheral vision, and he was still watching her.

What a creep.

When she was washing her hands and checking herself in the mirror in the bathroom, an overly intoxicated and/or high young lady and her friend were trying to stumble to the sink, and one of them tripped over the garbage can. Paper towels and rubbish scattered all over the floor with a loud crash. Eve rushed to assist, helping the girl to her feet and righting the bin.

As she went to move the garbage can back to its original location, she saw something strange on the floor where it had been. It was some kind of sigil carved right into the tiles, about the size of a hockey puck, and stained reddish-brown with what looked to be dried blood.

That was weird. Noteworthy weird.

She put the trash can back over top of the sigil for now and walked out of the bathroom. Her eyes immediately glanced to the bar to see if the man was watching, but he had disappeared.

Then she felt someone standing too closely behind her. She whirled around.

There was the creep, smiling as though he'd never quite mastered the technique.

23
Well, That Was Dramatic

"Excuse me, ma'am," he said in an oily tone. "I couldn't help but notice what an amazing build you have, and I thought you might be interested in doing some modeling for Women's Fitness. I work for—"

"No thanks," Eve said as she turned to walk away.

He reached out to grab her arm, but she slid to the side. "Wait, I'm serious!" he exclaimed. "You would be perfect! And it pays—"

"Don't touch me, don't talk to me. Not interested. Go away. Last warning," she said firmly. She didn't want to start a fight in Luc's club on her first night here, but she wasn't afraid to subdue a dude if she had to.

"But…" he began, then she saw his eyes rise slightly, looking at something above her head, and he smiled apologetically and backed away. "Sorry, I didn't mean to bother you. I wasn't looking for trouble."

Eve turned around, and, as she suspected, the boys were standing behind her.

"Who the hell was that?" Zeke scowled after the man as he disappeared into the crowd.

"I don't know, some douche trying to feed me some bullshit. Why don't they take me seriously unless I have backup?" she asked in annoyance. "Do you have any idea how infuriating that is? I could've taken that guy down in seconds, but he wasn't even remotely afraid until you guys showed up."

"Something's not right about him," Bo said suspiciously. "He reeks of adrenaline."

"You want me to find him and read him?" Eoduun asked.

Bo considered it briefly. "How much have you had to drink tonight?" he asked Eoduun.

"Entirely too much. I mean, I'm not *sloppy*, but…not operating at peak performance."

"Then maybe not. But let's not let our guard down tonight, just in case."

"He's not the only thing that's weird," Eve said. She told them about the sigil on the floor under the trash bin.

"Show me," Luc demanded, suddenly becoming serious. He barged into the ladies' room with Eve close on his heels. He ignored the looks he garnered, and slid the garbage can aside.

"Hm. This can't be good."

"What is it?" Eve asked.

He pulled his phone out and snapped a photo of it. "I don't know for sure, but I suspect Ruth is involved. It looks like alchemy, but…not." He walked to the door and stuck his head out. "Zeke, come in here."

Zeke walked into the bathroom, his eyes darting around nervously at the women staring at them.

"Could you ladies please excuse us for just a few minutes?" Luc implored politely. "We won't be long."

One of the women came up to stand next to Eve, eyeballing Zeke and Luc. "Are you all right?" she whispered to Eve. "Do you want someone to stay with you?"

"What?" Eve then realized what this might look like. "Oh! No, everything is fine. Really!"

"You sure?"

"Yes. It's ok. I'm safe with them," she assured the woman. "I was just showing them some vandalism in here."

When the woman was satisfied that Eve wasn't in danger, she left the bathroom, throwing one last suspicious glance at Luc and Zeke.

When they were finally alone, Luc said to Zeke, "I need Dagon for a moment."

Zeke raised his eyebrows. "You want me to release Dagon *here*?"

"Just keep a hand on the reins."

Zeke shook his head uncertainly. "...Ok..."

His eyes surged red, and a wide, devious smile spread across his face. He immediately turned to Eve. "You look positively mouth-watering tonight, princess," he said lasciviously. "Maybe I should stab Zeke in the heart so you'll be forced to give me a taste."

Luc snapped his fingers impatiently in front of Dagon's face. "Focus, will you? What is this?" He pointed down at the sigil on the floor.

Dagon looked down. "Oh." There was a hint of surprise in his tone. "That, you hairless monkey, is a door."

"That's what I was afraid of."

"What does that mean? A door?" Eve wondered.

"Teleportation spell," Luc explained. He directed his attention back to Dagon. "Is it old?"

"Depends. Am I old?"

Luc rubbed the back of his neck. "We need to get everyone out of here. Goddamn it." He held his hand out, and a blinding bolt of lightning suddenly shot from his hand to the sigil, obliterating the tile with a thunderous crash. Eve threw her hands over her ears.

"Holy fuck!" she shrieked, cowering back. "What the shit?!"

"Sorry. Should've warned you," Luc apologized, somewhat insincerely. He wasn't himself. He turned to the door and, as he turned, he touched his index and middle finger to Dagon's forehead and said to him, "I'm done with you."

Dagon flinched, and his eyes flashed bright blue briefly before turning back to brown. "Ouch, Luc!" Zeke whined, rubbing his forehead. "I hate it when you do that! It's like getting stabbed in the brain."

"What was that?" Eve asked Zeke as they followed Luc out of the bathroom.

"Shock therapy, I guess? It knocks Dagon out of the driver's seat. But it was totally unnecessary. I was *right there*," Zeke complained.

Luc whispered something in Bo's ear. Bo glanced over at Eve, then nodded.

Luc turned to Eoduun. "Be prepared for a large-scale erasure. Something's afoot."

"I don't have the focus right now," Eoduun worried.

"I can give you a boost. Just be ready."

Eve was completely lost. She hated being out of the loop. She was just realizing how much she still didn't understand about her new life and her teammates.

She was, however, itching for a fight.

"What are you doing?" Zeke asked Luc.

"Evacuation," Luc said simply as he strode away, his face as cold as stone.

Bo began barking orders. "Z, go check the men's room for any other sigils, and then do a sweep of the club. If you find any, destroy them. Eoduun, hang out by the entrance and read everyone who leaves. If anything comes up strange, hold them. Eve, you're with me. We're going to watch the fire exit and monitor the room until Luc can get everyone out."

"I can help Zeke sweep," Eve offered. "I don't need a babysitter."

"You're still green, unarmed, and at a disadvantage." He pointed at her heels.

"These can come off at any time. I'm used to fighting barefoot. And who said I was unarmed?"

Bo's eyes scanned her body in that tight, skimpy black dress. "Are you *not?*"

She grabbed his hand and ran it up the inside of her thigh. Shocked, he tried to yank it back, but not before his fingers touched the sheath of the knife strapped to her leg.

"I stand corrected," he replied, mildly flustered. "However, that doesn't change my decision."

Zeke suddenly came charging through the crowd at them, holding something in his hand.

"We have a problem!" he shouted as he ran up to them. He held out a large, transparent flake or husk. The material reminded Eve of the shedding from a snake.

"Shapeshifter," Bo ascertained. "Fuck."

"It was in the men's room, in the trash can. I would put money on it that it was the guy from earlier," Zeke said. "The hair I found was the same color, and the clothes left behind looked like what he was wearing."

"But you didn't find any sigils?"

"Not that I could see."

"Ok. Go tell Eoduun what you found so he knows what he's looking out for."

The music in the club suddenly stopped, and Luc's voice boomed over the PA. "Good evening, ladies and gentlemen. We apologize for the sudden disruption in the evening's entertainment, but due to unforeseen circumstances, the club will now be closing for the night. Please leave your drinks and make your way to the exit. Again, we apologize for this inconvenience. On your way out, you will receive a voucher to waive the cover charge and two free drinks on your next visit. Thank you for choosing The Gutter, and we look forward to seeing you again soon."

The lights came on more brightly, and everyone started mumbling and complaining. Eve blinked against the light, and as people started to head toward the door, Eve saw Luc sauntering toward them against the flow of the crowd.

Then there was a shriek. Eve's eyes darted around the room, and she quickly found the reason. There was a woman standing on the bar, holding a knife to her own throat.

It was Ruth.

She began speaking in tongues, like she was chanting a spell in a language that didn't sound even remotely familiar to Eve. It sounded…primitive.

Ruth then sliced the knife deeply across her throat, blood pouring forth like water from an overflowing sink. She collapsed and fell backward off the bar.

"Well, that was dramatic," Luc said casually.

Everyone around them began to scream, and Luc disappeared.

"Close your eyes and think of Bob Ross with a squirrel in his shirt pocket," Bo instructed her urgently. Before she could question, he said, "Just do it!"

She clenched her eyes closed and imagined Bob Ross with a squirrel in his pocket, painting a big mountain with his palette knife. *A little roll of paint…happy little trees…give him a little friend, everybody needs a friend…*

"Ok, we're clear," Bo said. "Do you remember Ruthie on the bar?"

"How could I forget?"

"They did," Bo said, gesturing to the room. Everyone was back to complaining and shuffling toward the door. No panic, no screaming.

"How?"

"Eoduun. With a little help from Luc."

"Did Ruth really just kill herself? What the hell was that?!"

"That wasn't Ruthie. It was the man who approached you earlier. A shapeshifter, wearing Ruthie's visage."

"But how could you tell?"

Bo pointed at his nose. "I know my sister. And she's not here."

When everyone had finally vacated the building, the team stood around the dead body on the floor behind the bar. It no longer resembled Ruth. It was covered in a flaky, honey-colored, semi-transparent cocoon.

"What the fuck is that?!" Eve asked in disgust.

"Shapeshifter," Zeke said. "That's what they look like when they transform. Or, when they die when they're transformed. It's shedding its skin."

"Why didn't the guy at the convention look like this?"

"The convention monster wasn't your typical shapeshifter," Luc answered. "He was some kind of shapeshifter-hybrid. Some shapeshifting creatures, like cucuy, don't shed – they morph on a cellular level. But true shapeshifters are a lot more disgusting." He looked up at the team. "Don't tell Dizzy I said that." He then gestured to Eoduun. "See what you can get. This looks like a fresh one, not a zombie." He nudged the body with the toe of his shoe, and some of the shed skin flaked off.

As Eoduun kneeled down and peeled away the dead skin from the face so he could get to the eyes, Zeke stepped closer.

"Holy shit, isn't that the desk clerk from the shitty motel we stayed at in Texas?"

They all leaned in. "It could be," Bo said. "I only saw him briefly in passing, though."

"Well, let's find out," Eoduun said. He looked down at the face, using his thumbs to hold the eyelids open.

As he did, Eve had the most horrible thought. *Wouldn't it be terrible if Ruth had done something to the body to use it against us, knowing we would investigate it?* And as soon as she thought that, she felt an overpowering dread. It was going to happen. She thought it, now it would happen. She was certain of it.

"Eoduun, get back!" she screamed. She lunged for him and grabbed him around the chest, and as she yanked him back, there was a loud pop, like cheap fireworks, and Eve felt a strong force shove her and Eoduun across the floor. She and Eoduun landed in a heap ten feet away from where they started.

She groaned and sat up, then looked down at Eoduun. He seemed mostly unscathed.

She whipped her head around to assess the rest of the team. Luc was standing halfway between her and the dead shapeshifter; Bo was sitting on the ground, covered in razor blades; and Zeke was scrambling to join Eve at Eoduun's side, even though he had razor blades all up one arm.

"Are you ok?" Eve asked Eoduun.

"I'm all right. What about you?" he asked, his eyes searching her for injury as he rubbed the back of his head.

"I think I'm ok. What the hell was that?!" Eve inquired.

"She boobytrapped the body," Bo growled, blood streaming down his cheek as he pulled a razor blade from his face. He looked around at the candy that flew out of the body along with the razor blades. Caramel apple suckers. "Not funny, Ruthie," he said dryly.

Luc was at her side, his hands touching her everywhere, lifting her arms, turning her face, checking her back, and helping her to her feet so he could inspect her legs.

"Are you hurt?" he fretted. She saw him wince ever so slightly.

"No, but you are, aren't you?"

"It's nothing. We'll take care of it later. I'm afraid Bo got the worst of it, but I think everyone is ok."

When Zeke saw that Eve and Eoduun were ok, he rushed over to Bo's side.

"I would've gotten a face full of razor blades if you hadn't pulled me away," Eoduun said to Eve as Eve started to look Luc over.

Eve replied, "And we both would've gotten it if Luc hadn't used himself as a shield, wouldn't we, Luc?" His back was covered in razor blades. "I know you could've easily evaded those blades."

"This was my favorite suit," he complained light-heartedly.

"How did you know that was going to happen?" Eoduun asked Eve.

"I don't know. I just had a bad feeling."

Bo groaned as Zeke helped him to his feet. "Well," Bo rasped, "they might be deep, but at least they're clean cuts. They should heal well." He looked over at what was left of the shapeshifter's corpse. "Were you able to get a reading from the body?" he asked Eoduun.

"Ruth knows what Eve is. It was like a prerecorded message playing over and over and over, saying 'I'll get you, my pretty, and your little blood healer, too.'"

Luc smirked, then sighed. "Sensational."

Eve knew this was tremendously bad news, but first things came first. She carefully padded over to Bo in her bare feet (her shoes were strewn across the floor), being careful to avoid the razor blades and candy scattered everywhere.

"Here, let me heal you so we can get these razor blades out of you," Eve offered.

"No, take care of Luc and Zeke first. They're injured, too," Bo protested.

Eve frowned at him. "But you're in worse shape than them. Don't try to be tough."

He glanced around nervously at everyone watching them, then whispered to Eve, "Don't you remember what happened last time?"

Eve reached under her dress and withdrew the knife she had strapped to her leg. "Then I guess you'll just have to work a little harder to behave yourself," she replied. She sliced the knife across the side of her hand, then yanked Bo's mask down and shoved her hand over his mouth. As her blood trickled onto his lips, he inhaled deeply, and the dark charcoal color in his right eye was overtaken by that wolfish golden-yellow. He licked the blood on his lips, then his tongue caressed her hand, catching a drip of blood before it could fall.

"Fuck," he whispered against her hand. He opened his mouth and bit into her hand hungrily, drawing a sensual whimper from Eve's throat. The pain from his teeth only amplified the lustful need surging through her body.

While he sucked on her blood, she fought the desire burning in her belly, and used her free hand to pull the razor blades from his chest. Luc came to assist, but Bo suddenly glowered at him, a low growl rumbling in his throat.

Luc raised his eyebrows at Bo. "Really? What, are you going to bite me, big brother? Just try it."

Bo took Eve's hand from his mouth. "Sorry," he apologized to Luc half-heartedly. He ran his tongue slowly over the bite mark he'd left on Eve's flesh.

"That's enough," Luc said, snatching Eve's hand away from Bo. He glanced over at Zeke. "You have a handle on Dagon, right?"

Zeke nodded. "Of course."

Luc held Eve's hand out to him. He took her bleeding hand in his and looked down at it like he was a little afraid of it.

He looked up at Eve. "This is my first time with you," he said nervously.

That's right. It had been Dagon before, Eve realized.

"You're wasting it," Luc urged him impatiently, eyeing the blood that was running onto his hands.

Zeke brought her hand to his mouth and sucked from the cut, which now bore puncture wounds around it from Bo's bite. His eyes widened as the blood spread into his mouth, and he moaned ever so slightly. The sound sent pleasant shivers through Eve's core. It reminded her of the sounds he'd made when she had his cock in her mouth.

Luc quickly picked out the razors in Zeke's arm, and as soon as they were out, he yanked Eve's hand from Zeke's mouth.

Zeke wiped his mouth on the back of his hand. "Holy fuck." He looked at Bo. "Why is it so different?!"

Bo shook his head. He'd started pulling the razor blades from Luc's back, as Luc was next on the docket to be healed.

Eve looked between the two of them, then at Luc. He seemed just as confused as she was.

"What's different?" she asked.

"Your blood isn't like Shira's was. It's…" Zeke looked cautiously at Luc and Bo as he finished his thought anticlimactically. "…Different."

Luc lifted Eve's hand to his mouth and licked it. His eyebrows raised. "Goddamn." He put it in his mouth and sucked some blood from her. "What the fuck…" He took his sunglasses off and surveyed her with intrigued eyes, his brows drawn together.

"What?" she asked, growing concerned. "Is something wrong with me?"

"I got a little taste of your blood just a few days ago, and it was potent. More potent than usual. But now? It's laced with so much aphrodisiac that it's as potent as siren venom. Maybe more so," Luc revealed.

Fear gripped her throat like an icy hand. "What…what does that mean? Am I…a monster?!"

24
Give Me Another Taste

Luc took another pull from her hand. "No wonder Bo growled at me. You're lucky he hasn't devoured you," Luc mused.

When Eve shot a startled look at Bo, Bo held his hands up defensively.

"*I* want to devour you," Luc said lecherously. He looked seductively at Eve. "If I was as pent up as Bo, I would've been tearing at your clothes by now," he said in a low voice.

Bo grunted in embarrassed irritation.

"You didn't answer the question," Eve fretted. "Am I a monster?"

"Maybe. Aren't we all?" Luc replied lightly.

"Don't joke about this," Eve spat. "If I was a monster, wouldn't you know? Didn't you vet me already?"

"It's unheard of, Eve," Luc said dismissively. "A blood healer can't be a monster. It just doesn't happen."

"Then why is my blood siren venom?"

"I didn't say *that*. I only said it was *as potent* as siren venom." He licked her hand and groaned. "Fucking hell. I need to get you back to my apartment."

Eoduun suddenly came up behind her and snatched her hand from Luc, putting it straight to his lips.

"Eoduun!" Eve cried, whimpering the second syllable as he drank from her.

His dark eyes slid up to look into hers, like he was seeing her for the first time. "Well, shit," he said, swallowing hard. "Curiosity killed the cat."

"What the hell does that mean? Why did you do that?" Eve panted. She wrenched her hand away from Eoduun and held it to her chest so no one else could drink from her. She was getting sexual whiplash.

"I wanted to know what the fuss was about." His eyes lingered on her lips as he licked the remaining blood from his own. "Now I get it."

Everyone was gazing at her with that odd mix of desire and shame, like they were all fantasizing about her, but they knew the others knew it, too. The only one who didn't look ashamed was Luc, and that was likely because he was the only one of them that felt that he had some kind of *right* to those kinds of thoughts about her.

"I want to go home," she said quietly, trying to suppress the desire boiling up from deep within her. She was having the most depraved ideas about the four men who surrounded her, watching her with lustful eyes. She was uncomfortable with how much she liked being the focus of all those eyes. *Her boys.*

Luc grinned widely. "As you wish, love." He turned to the rest of the team. "Collect a sample for Mira – a finger or something, and burn the rest," he said with a dismissive wave of his hand. He retrieved Eve's shoes from the floor, then strode to her and handed them to her. "I'm taking Eve home. I'll see you all tomorrow."

They barely made it to the car before Luc attacked her. He shoved her up against the driver's side door and threaded his fingers into her hair, leaning down to crush his lips against hers. His other hand slid down her side and around behind her to cup her ass.

"How am I ever supposed to let you heal anyone knowing just how badly it makes them want to fuck you?" he complained between kisses. "Even Eoduun wants to fuck you now."

Eve pulled back. "It's not real. It's temporary," she said.

"Temporary doesn't mean it isn't real. This feeling is very, *very* real." He pressed the thick bulge in his pants against her belly. "You know you gave everyone a hard-on, don't you?"

Eve reached down and pressed the palm of her hand over the ridge in his pants, curling her fingers around it, sliding her hand up and down. Luc groaned.

"Watch yourself, love," Luc warned, "or I'll fuck you right here on the hood of this car. I'm barely clinging to the last shred of control I possess."

He reached up under her dress, his fingers tracing up her inner thigh, around her knife sheath, and up to the edge of her scanty thong underwear, leaving a trail of fire in their wake. He used his knee to spread her legs further apart, then slid her underwear to the side as he teased his finger along her slit. She simpered at his touch.

"Mmm, you're so wet," he whispered against her ear. He inserted a finger inside her folds. "So warm...and inviting..." He used her wetness as lubrication as he moved his finger to her clit and rubbed it in tight circles.

She twisted his suit jacket in her fist and leaned her weight into him. "Luc..." she moaned. At the sound of his name on her lips, his erection throbbed in her other hand through the fabric of his slacks. "Let's take this back to your place," she whispered breathlessly.

He chuckled low in his throat. "You're lucky I fucked you earlier today, or you'd be in so much trouble right now." He reluctantly dragged his hand from between her legs, then put his fingers straight into his mouth. He closed his eyes and moaned, then opened them slowly, looking down at her with hooded eyes. "You want to know a secret?" he asked as he licked her off of his fingers. "I think your arousal has the same effect as your blood."

Eve bit her lip. He had no right to be that damn sexy.

The ride back to the compound was tense and entirely too long, despite Luc's disregard for the speed limit.

Luc practically threw Eve into his apartment when they arrived, locking the door behind him and shucking off his shoes and jacket. When he saw her trying to shimmy out of her dress, he reached out and stopped her.

"Oh no, love. Leave it on." He eyed her hungrily. "The shoes too." He took her face in his big hands, and softly touched his lips to hers, kissing her lightly before whispering, "I want to fuck you in that outfit."

She inhaled his refined bourbon and cedar scent. He sat on the edge of the bed, pulling her up to him, his knees on either side of her thighs. His hands gripped her waist, and she was enraptured by how small she looked in his hands. She placed her hands over his, turned on by the size discrepancy. He was so big and powerful. It was intoxicating.

He slid his hands down to the hem of her dress, then he slowly lifted it just to the point that her underwear was peeking out. With his head tilted down, she could see his beautiful eyes gazing at her body from over his sunglasses. She reached out and slipped the sunglasses from his face, then tucked them into his breast pocket, as he sometimes did. She then got to work on his shirt buttons. She wanted to see and touch those hard ridges of his chest and stomach.

Luc unhooked the knife holster strapped to her leg and tossed it aside. His hands glided up her thighs, fingers curling into the string waistband of her thong, and he dragged her underwear down over her thighs. They dropped to the floor around her high heels, and she stepped out of them.

Once she had his shirt unbuttoned, her hands explored his firm flesh eagerly. God, the size of this man would never cease to amaze her. Her hands looked so small against his round, muscular pectorals.

Her fingers traced over his collarbone, rising and falling into all the delicious troughs and valleys around it. She moved her hands up to either side of his strong, sinewy neck. It was so thick, her hands probably wouldn't be able to fully encircle it.

She gazed into those crystal eyes, and for just the briefest moment, the L-word danced on the back of her tongue, threatening to slip out. She ran her fingers up the back of his head and twisted her fingers in his hair, leaning forward to bring her lips to his. Her other hand came up to the hard line of his jaw, running the pad of her thumb over his smoothly-shaven skin as her tongue slipped between his lips, seeking out his. He moaned into her mouth.

He loosened his belt and unfastened his pants while they kissed, lowering them far enough to free his aching erection. He reached out and grabbed Eve's hips, his hands sliding up under her dress and gripping her glutes firmly. He pulled her down onto his lap, her knees straddling him.

"I've waited long enough," he rasped. He flipped her over onto her back, keeping his hips between her legs. He ran his hand down her thigh and down her calf, urging her to hitch her legs around him. She did so carefully, trying not to stab him with her heels.

He positioned himself against her opening, using one hand to guide the head of his swollen manhood up and down through the dew along her slit before plunging inside of her. She inhaled sharply and bit her lip as her tight walls stretched around him. He looked down at her body in lewd fascination as he thrust into her with her dress scrunched up around her rolling hips. Her skin burned under that devious gaze.

"Fuck, Eve," he groaned. He tugged the straps of her dress down, pulling it down until her breasts slipped free. His mouth descended on one soft mound while his palm cupped the other. His tongue caressed her nipple in gentle circles that tingled all the way through to her core. She arched her back and whimpered.

He turned his attention to her neck, his tongue and lips lingering over her pulse-point. She knew he must be able to feel her pulse pumping against his tongue with the way her heart was pounding.

"Give me another taste," he murmured against her skin. "Just this once." He reached up and dragged her injured hand from his back, then brought it up in front of his face, holding it in anticipation between them. His eyes bored into hers imploringly.

She brought her hand to her own mouth and used her teeth to reopen the wound, wincing at the discomfort. But as soon as her hand went into his mouth, the sting melted into ecstasy. He closed his eyes and moaned, his cock swelling inside of her. Her core throbbed, her hips jerking involuntarily against his as her thighs clenched around his waist. She simpered beneath him, her whole body writhing with unbridled desire. Needing more. More of him. *All* of him. *Now*.

After just a short drink, he took her hand from his mouth, licked her wound, then interlaced his fingers with hers. He pressed her hand onto the bed next to her head while his lips descended savagely onto hers. His athletic, hard body melded against hers, her chest flattening against his. He rocked his hips with powerful thrusts into her, drawing muffled whimpers from her against his tongue.

Eve sobbed into Luc's mouth as her body was racked with the most powerful orgasm she'd ever experienced. Tears welled in her eyes. It was so intense, it was almost painful. Wave after wave, crash after crash, it felt like it was never going to end.

She tore her mouth from Luc's to gasp for air. "Oh, God, Luc," she gasped and sobbed as he pounded harder, chasing his own release.

"Fuck," he grunted as he slammed into her, spilling over inside of her, his cock throbbing and spasming against her walls as his hand squeezed hers tightly. She felt such an intense release of emotions that it mildly terrified her.

It was just sex. But in that moment, she wanted to keep him. Forever. Right here, wrapped up in each other like nothing else in the entire world mattered.

She buried the fingers of her free hand in his hair and hugged him to her desperately. *Don't say it. Don't say it.* She clamped her mouth firmly shut, afraid of what might roll from her tongue right now. *It's the endorphins. It isn't real.*

Luc squeezed her hand lightly, then released it so he could wrap both of his arms around her. She felt like a tiny little doll in those arms.

"I know you don't want to hear it," he whispered breathlessly, "but I love you."

She lay there silently, refusing to say anything, but she squeezed him just a little harder.

25

You Have All My Pieces, and I'm Still Trying to Set Up the Board

Eve didn't have a damn clue what she was *supposed* to be feeling right now, but she was fairly sure that what she *was* feeling wasn't…correct. And what Luc thought he was feeling was definitely not right.

It was her blood. She'd suspected it right from the beginning, but after what was revealed tonight, she was certain of it. Luc had brushed it off as ridiculous, but she had a deep sense that something else was going on to make her blood drive everyone so wild with passion. And whatever it was, it was affecting him.

It wasn't love. It couldn't be. She wasn't stupid. But as she lay beneath Luc, stroking her fingers over the hair at the nape of his neck, gazing into his incredible, striking eyes, her heart was completely fooled. Her mouth wanted to form those words so badly, and she had to fight the compulsion harder than she wished to admit.

I love you.

Nope. Not happening.

She tried to distract herself by thinking about something else. Anything else.

"Weird question," she blurted, "but what happens when a blood healer heals a minor or a family member? Because…ew."

Luc laughed, and the rumble reverberated from his chest through hers. "Is that really what you're thinking about at a moment like this?" He rolled to the side, but he kept his arms around her. "From what I understand, the aphrodisiacal component has no effect on prepubescents or closely related individuals."

"Even *my* blood?"

"What are you getting at? Do you have a family member you want to heal?"

"No. I haven't talked to any of them in years. I wouldn't even know if anyone was sick. I cut all ties a long time ago."

"I know. That's why I thought the question was odd."

"It bugs me that you seem to already know everything about me."

"Why? Is there a different version of yourself you wish you could present to me instead? Are there things you wish I didn't know?"

"No, but it puts me at a disadvantage. You have all my pieces, and I'm still trying to set up the board."

He chuckled. "This isn't a game of chess, love. It isn't a conflict. You don't need a strategy against me. Just be with me, and I'll give you any piece you want."

"Pretty words," she said cynically.

"Honest words."

She turned and looked at him without responding.

"I'll just keep trying to prove it to you until you believe it. We're on the same team, love."

It was always those closest to her that were the ones she needed to be the wariest of, especially those that made her feel like this. People like him didn't spare people like her a second glance, let alone fall in love. There was something else at play here. She couldn't resist playing his game, but she couldn't lose herself to him, or he would swallow her whole.

Luc's phone chimed. He seemed not to hear it. Then it chimed again. And again.

"Are you going to get that?" she asked.

"I wasn't planning to."

"It could be important."

"It could be."

"What if it's news about Ruth? What if something happened? What if Ruger is in jail again?"

"Cass can handle Ruger. And in my experience, most problems can't be fixed afterhours anyway. It can wait."

"For fuck's sake," she sighed. "Just check your phone."

He narrowed his eyes at her. "Are you trying to get rid of me?" he asked in mock suspicion.

"Someone might need you."

His amused grin faded. "Don't *you* need me?"

She hesitated. "I don't know how I'm supposed to answer that."

"How about honestly?"

"Do you want me to get your phone for you?" she deflected.

His brows drew together pensively. "No, I got it," he mumbled. He sat up and swung his legs over the side of the bed. Eve admired the way the muscles of his bare torso flexed and rippled beneath his skin as he walked across the room to retrieve his phone from his suit jacket. He looked down at the screen.

"Oh, that bitch," he hissed.

Eve sat up and situated her dress. "What is it?"

"We erased everyone's memory of the incident tonight, yet it was still leaked to the press. Video footage from someone's phone. Goddammit, I should've considered that."

"How the hell did that happen so fast?!"

"I'll give you one guess."

"Ruth?"

"I'm almost sure of it," he confirmed. He sighed. "My father is going to have a coronary. I need to take care of this before it spreads."

"Why would she even bother with something like that? It just seems petty."

"It is petty. But she also knows that only *I* can deal with it. She's trying to keep me otherwise engaged."

"To what end?"

"Only she knows that." Luc went to his closet and grabbed a fresh shirt. He shrugged into it and started buttoning it up.

"Are you leaving?" Eve asked.

"Do you care?" he shot back, taking her by surprise. His anger faded just as quickly as it arose. "Sorry. I didn't mean that."

"Since when do you say things you don't mean?" She found her underwear and slipped them back on. She tried to ignore the arrow he'd just shot through her heart.

"You're right. I don't say things I don't mean. But I'm usually more tactful than that."

"I don't understand why you seem mad at me."

"This is precisely the problem, love. You're lying to yourself and to me. You understand fully well."

"You expect me to be head over heels for you and declaring my love after a few romantic encounters? Is that it? I'm *not* your girlfriend, Luc."

Luc sighed, then smiled at her. He put a pair of his round sunglasses on, hiding his eyes. "No, Eve, that isn't it. I just want you to care that I care. Acknowledge that I have feelings. That's it."

He'd leveled her with just those few words. She felt like shit. Was he finally starting to see it – what a shitty person she was? The fact that he could say something heartfelt, and that she could still sit here and doubt his integrity? Doubt that his caring came from a place of sincerity?

She wanted to believe him. She desperately wanted to believe his feelings were true, were his own. But with this blood…could she ever trust anyone's feelings ever again?

"Please be safe out there," she said simply. Her brain had shut off her communication center for fear that she would only hurt herself more by saying something stupid. "When will you be back?"

Luc stopped buttoning the cuffs on his sleeves and dropped his hands to his sides. "Nothing? Not a 'fuck you, what do you want from me,' nothing? Just a full-on deflection?"

"I don't know what you want me to say, Luc."

"I want you to say something you mean, Eve!" he cried. "Not what you think I want to hear or what you think you should say, but *something real*! Please don't make me leave here tonight without *something*."

Her brain went blank. She didn't have any words. She had all kinds of feelings swirling around in her chest. The kind that ached and stung. But they didn't come with words or instructions, so she'd learned to just push them into the corner to be dealt with later. Unfortunately, later was usually too late.

"I...*I* don't know what I want to say," she confessed quietly. "But...I do care. That's real."

Luc finished buttoning his cuffs as he walked across the room to her. He smiled resignedly down at her as he took her face in his hands.

"I'll take it," he said, then leaned down and kissed her softly. He stood up straight again and ran his fingers through his hair, his signature, confident smile now gracing his features. "But you *will* love me someday. I *will* earn it. Mark my words, love."

Luc offered to let her stay at his apartment for the night, but she declined since her apartment was only a short walk away. Luc walked her to her door, just to have those last couple of minutes with her.

"Bo and the boys should be getting back any minute now," Luc informed her. "Please apprise Bo of the situation, and tell him I'll contact him later. And keep an eye and an ear out, ok? The compound is the safest place you can be, but Ruth could have something up her sleeve that even we couldn't have anticipated."

"How long will you be gone?"

"As long as it takes to douse this. Could be a day or two. I'll text you." He slid his arm around her waist and leaned down to kiss her. When their lips parted again, he said, "Miss me, will you?"

"I'll try," she said with a smirk.

Luc stepped back and disappeared.

She went into her apartment and started to close the door behind her, but decided not to. She wanted to know when the boys got back. She wanted them to barge into her apartment and invade her space and chase away this weird empty feeling Luc had left in her chest with his departure.

In the meantime, she traded her black dress and Louboutins for sweatpants, a tank top, and corpse feet.

She was making herself some popcorn when she heard a tentative, "Hello?" from her doorway.

She couldn't hear over the popping of the popcorn enough to tell who it was, so she peeked her head around the corner to see.

Cassie. "Oh, hi!" Eve called back. "How was the bar?" she asked as Cassie stepped inside.

Ruger came in behind her. "Fucking dumb."

"Well, it wouldn't have been if you had just left well enough alone," Cassie sighed.

"He grabbed your ass," Ruger grumbled.

"And I took care of it, didn't I? You didn't have to hit him with a pool stick."

"Eve. Tell me," Ruger said, "if someone grabbed your ass at a bar, would Luc just be like, 'Oh, that's nice dear'? Or would he kick some ass?" Before Eve could answer, he looked back at Cassie. "He'd kick some ass. It's the oldest rule in the book."

Eve couldn't imagine Luc in the middle of a barroom brawl. Or hitting someone with a pool stick. And she also didn't miss the fact that Ruger was assuming that she and Luc were an item, like everyone else. Luc did a thorough job of making it appear that way.

Remi stood in the doorway. "Not everyone is a caveman, Ruger. I'm pretty sure Luc would've found a more mature way to deal with it."

"Point is," Ruger said, raising his voice, "you stand up for your woman. It's just what you do."

"And you chose a pool stick?" Eve said.

"Goddamn right I did," he said proudly. He mimed swinging a baseball bat and made a crack sound with his tongue. "Right across his face."

Eve cringed. "Oh, not the face…"

"Oh yes. The face," Ruger grinned.

"The face," Cassie parroted, with much less amusement.

"Keep it up, and we won't be able to drink anywhere within a fifty-mile radius," Remi complained.

"It's not my fault people are dicks," Ruger said.

"Sure…*people*," Remi teased.

"I am *not* a dick!" Ruger argued.

"So, *anyway*," Cassie interjected. "I saw your door open, thought maybe we'd pop in and see what brought *you* home so early tonight. It's barely midnight."

"Oh. Yeah, we had a rather exciting night, too," Eve divulged. "Care to sit? I have popcorn and a story."

Ruger and Remi sat on the couch, and Cassie sat between them. Eve brought out popcorn and beers for everyone, then planted herself in the recliner to tell her tale.

As she was finishing up telling them about the club incident, she heard Zeke's voice in the hallway.

He popped his head in. "Hey, what's up?" Concern drew his brows together. "Where's Luc?"

Bo stepped in around Zeke, and Eoduun followed behind him, and Remi, Ruger, and Cassie saw their rather disheveled state. They all smelled smoky.

"Rough night?" Ruger teased. "I smell a burned body."

Eve informed Bo and the boys about Luc's sudden departure and the situation around it.

"Damn. Should've wiped the phones, too. Such a simple fucking mistake," Bo disparaged.

"How would you even do that? There were hundreds of phones there."

"Luc. An electromagnetic burst."

"Is he even human?" Eve asked in awe.

Bo gave her a sideways glance. "Quite."

"So, what's the plan, then?" Remi asked Bo. "Should we be doing something?"

Bo's phone chimed, and he pulled it from his pocket. "Ask, and you shall receive," he mused. He tapped his phone a few times, then Remi's phone chimed. "I just forwarded you the video that was taken from the club tonight. Luc wants you, Roy, and Zephlyn to work on deciphering what the shapeshifter is saying. I forwarded it to them too."

Both of their phones then chimed, and they looked down at their screens. Remi laughed, and Bo sighed.

"Roy's pissed, isn't he?" Cassie said knowingly.

"'Fuck off, I'll look at it in the morning. I don't look this fucking good by skipping my beauty sleep,'" Remi read Roy's response aloud.

Eve snorted.

"You should know better than to put him in a group chat," Ruger said. "He's going to get pissed about his phone going off every time someone messages in it and it isn't specifically for him."

"Why doesn't he just turn off the notifications for it?" Eve wondered.

"He doesn't know how. And he gets pissed off when you try to show him," Cassie said.

"He sounds like a delight," Eve observed.

"A real teddy bear," Ruger quipped, taking a drink of his beer.

Eve heard popcorn popping in the kitchen. She hadn't even noticed Eoduun disappear from the living room. Zeke heard it too, and he went to join Eoduun in his own quest for sustenance.

"*Mi casa es su casa,*" Eve mumbled.

Cassie caught Eve's comment, and while Ruger, Remi, and Bo all watched the video of the shapeshifter, she directed her attention to Eve.

"It's like living in a dorm, isn't it?" Cassie mused.

Eve laughed. "It is! I had the very same thought."

"What university?" she asked.

"Oh, not me. I didn't go, but I had a friend who did."

"USC for me. I didn't finish," Cassie disclosed. "Not because I failed out or anything. I was actually rocking a 4.0. But after watching my friends get torn apart by a coven of vampires one night on our way home from a party, everything changed for me. I felt like I had to do something, you know? I couldn't just turn a blind eye to it. Luc found me, and gave me a choice to either join or have it erased. I chose to join, and learned to hone my natural Jedi manipulation skills."

"And I suppose everybody jumped on you like fresh meat?" Eve said.

Cassie dipped her head to the side. "Well, maybe a little. But Ruger and I hit it off right off the bat and he put a claim on me fairly quickly," she chuckled. "I mean, of course Remi gets in on it, too, but Ruger..." she looked over at Ruger with clear admiration. "Ruger has my heart, you know?"

Eve was confused. She lowered her voice. "What do you mean by 'Remi gets in on it'?"

Cassie looked at her blankly. "Like, we fuck. Ruger is my husband, and Remi is my boyfriend."

Eve's eyebrows jumped to her hairline. "Oh!"

Cassie laughed. "You *are* still green, aren't you? The unwritten open-door policy around here applies to more than just our apartments, honey."

26
Struggle, Princess

"Ruger doesn't get angry about you and Remi?" Eve whispered.

"Oh, he gets a little jealous, I suppose. But them's the breaks. It's just how things are around here. Not a whole lot of choice of companions in this line of business. It's almost a necessity to have to share if you want to be part of a relationship that means anything more than a one-night stand. It's just impossible to have a life outside of all of this. And, in case you haven't noticed, there just aren't enough of *us* to go around," Cassie said, pointing a finger between herself and Eve.

"When I asked Z about women and the lack thereof here, he made it sound like it wasn't an issue," Eve countered. "I believe his words were, 'ain't nobody starving around here.'"

Cassie scoffed. "Yeah, ain't nobody starving. That's true enough. But if they want more than a snack, their options are limited. If they want an actual *meal*, they might have to sit down to the table and share it."

"Is that…is it *expected* of me? That kind of arrangement?" Eve wondered.

"Polyamory?" Cassie shrugged. "You'll figure out what works for you and what doesn't. Just…do yourself a favor and be open to it. I didn't think it was for me once upon a time, either, but here we are." Cassie narrowed her eyes thoughtfully, and added, "But then again, you're with Luc. Luc might play by different rules than the rest of us."

"I don't know if you could really say I'm *with* Luc. It's a little bit complicated at this point."

"Really?" Cassie was flabbergasted. "Could've fooled me. I've been here a long time, and I don't think he's ever let anyone sit in his chair at the head of the table. And I *know* I've never seen him treat anyone the way he treats you. To be honest, everybody's a little thrown off by it."

Eve sighed. "That's not likely to work out in my favor. Nobody likes the teacher's pet."

"Oh, I don't know about that. I think everybody's just wondering if the king has finally found his queen. He just never seemed the kind. Everyone is curious about you, but the way Luc hovers, they're also a little afraid of you. Nobody wants to step on Luc's toes."

"You guys aren't afraid to hang out with me," Eve pointed out.

"Because we won't be stepping on any toes, if you catch my drift."

"Oh. Yeah, I suppose not."

Cassie leaned closer to Eve and whispered conspiratorially, "If you don't mind me asking, is it true what they say about Dagon?"

"What do they say?"

"That he's completely obsessed with you."

"How the hell does anyone else know that?"

"So it is true?!"

"I think he's just fucking around."

"Power is just drawn to you, isn't it?" Cassie speculated.

Eve was surprised by that observation. "No, I don't think it's anything like that," she insisted. "I'm just the shiny new toy. The attention will pass."

"I don't know about that. It wasn't like this when I joined."

"Or maybe it's just the Panacea Blood."

Cassie shook her head. "It wasn't like this with Shira, either. Luc barely gave a her a second glance."

Shira. Eve had so many questions about Shira, but Shira felt like a taboo subject with her team, and she hardly talked to anyone other than her team. She wanted to pounce on the opportunity, but she saw Bo's head turn slightly in their direction when Shira's name was mentioned. Even though he was having a conversation with the guys, he was listening. Always listening.

"Then again," Cassie continued, "Shira was a nun, and I don't think she ever revoked or renounced her vows or whatever, so, maybe she's a bad example."

Eve was floored. "A *nun*?"

"Yeah. Knighco found her because she was performing miracle cures as part of her missionary work, some 'Blood of Christ' faith healer shit. When it got back to the Vatican, Sister Fiona sent Knighco after her, assuming she was some kind of vampire, witch, or jinn or something. But nope. Legit blood healer."

Cassie was a treasure trove of information and gossip, and, if Eve wasn't mistaken, she was itching for an ear to dump it all onto. Eve would gladly be that ear, but she needed to find an opportunity to get Cassie away from other prying ears. Namely, Bo.

But with Bo being her designated hoverer while Luc wasn't there to hover, that wasn't likely to happen anytime soon. It would have to wait.

Eve heard Bo telling Ruger and Remi that he needed to have a private team meeting with Eve and the boys, and Ruger and Remi collected Cassie and told Eve they would stop in again soon. And then it was just Eve and her team.

"We have a lot on our plates, guys," Bo said when everyone was gathered around the kitchen island. "Luc will probably be away for a couple of days, which leaves us in charge. We need to decipher the shapeshifter's message; we need to check the grounds for sigils like the one in the bathroom at the club; and we need to be watching for monster outbreaks. Ruthie is clever and unpredictable, but she leaves a calling card. She wants to be noticed, and she wants the credit. We'll have to keep our eyes on the news.

"On top of that, she's now not only after Dagon, but also Evie." He looked between Zeke and Eve. "I don't want either of you going out alone. She drew Luc away for a reason, and I can only imagine it's because she's planning an attack of some kind on our home turf. Ruger, Remi, and Cassie are spreading the word to the other hunters to be ready for anything. Sleep with one eye open tonight."

Before leaving, Zeke leaned down and whispered into Eve's ear, "Do you want me to come back later?"

The voice was unquestionably Zeke's, but her eyes darted to his neck to make sure there weren't gills. The way he said those words felt very much like Dagon.

"I think I'm just going to go to bed. I'll see you in the morning, Z."

"Ok. But if you get lonely, the offer stands. We don't have to do anything. We could just sleep."

As much as she liked the sound of that, she knew Dagon wouldn't leave it at that. As soon as Zeke fell asleep, he would pounce. She couldn't handle Dagon tonight.

When Zeke and Eoduun took off to their own apartments, Bo hung back. "You had a premonition tonight," he stated.

It took Eve a moment to understand what he was talking about. "Oh, with Eoduun. I guess so. Well…it was more of a 'what if this were to happen' thought that then turned into an 'oh shit, now it's going to happen' certainty. I didn't know *exactly* what was going to happen, but I had an overwhelming sense that Ruth had done something to the body and Eoduun was in danger."

"You dove in to save him." Bo watched her expression closely.

Eve raised a brow. "Of course I did."

"If Luc hadn't shoved you both out of the way and shielded you, that could've been really bad."

"It would've been worse if I'd done nothing. Eoduun could've been killed."

"You could've been killed. Were you willing to trade your life for his?" Bo's expression was inscrutable behind his mask. His mismatched eyes studied her intently. She had a feeling he wasn't as interested in what she said as he was in what her body language said.

"I was just trying to save him. I wasn't worried about myself," she replied. "I didn't really have time to stop and think about it." The thought hadn't even crossed her mind when she'd acted. It wasn't a conscious decision to trade her life for his.

"You have time to think about it now."

"And I'm not going to waste my time thinking about it, because it's over and done with. What's with these questions?" Eve asked irritably, crossing her arms on the counter.

"How are you going to heal your team if you're dead, Evie?"

Eve scowled. "Well, I'm not dead." She felt like she was being reprimanded for doing a good thing. She got up from her barstool in a huff, but Bo caught her arm, halting her retreat.

"Don't throw yourself in the line of fire ever again," he ordered in an uncharacteristically dangerous tone.

Eve turned and regarded him with surprise. "What's wrong with you? You act like you wish I'd let Eoduun eat razorblades."

Bo's temples flexed. "Obviously I don't wish that. But if I had to pick him or you for it to happen to, I would pick him. Do you know why?"

Eve just stared at him incredulously.

"Because it makes tactical sense, Evie. If he takes a face full of razors, there is a chance you can heal him, and everyone walks away. If you take a face full of razors, you're not healing anyone. Do you understand? A captain doesn't put their medic on the frontlines."

"Fine. If I have a premonition that something bad will happen to you, I'll just let it," she said spitefully. She hated the idea of essentially being benched. She was a fighter. Fighting was what she was good at. She refused to ride the pine.

Bo's eyes hardened, hiding something deeper. "If it means me or you? Good. Let it. I don't want you dying for me. I won't let that happen ever again."

"Again?"

He ignored her question. He stood up and released her arm, taking her face in his hands instead.

"You're more important than you realize," he whispered softly. "I can tell you think you're going to just do what you want to, regardless. But I'm your captain, and you'll do as I say. Understood?"

Eve nodded reluctantly, looking at anything but him.

"I fucking mean it, Evie."

"Yes, Daddy," she grumbled.

He narrowed his heterochrome eyes at her, the color rising to his cheeks from beneath his mask.

"Lock your door when I leave," he instructed gruffly. "Just call to me if you need me. I'm not far. Goodnight."

It didn't matter that Eve locked her door when he left, because her visitor came to her anyway. Dagon had an uncanny ability to get under her skin and into her head…and into her bedroom. He was like a mosquito bite on her back that she just couldn't stop trying to scratch.

She woke to find herself lying in bed on her back, in her t-shirt and underwear, the bedcovers torn off and cast to the floor. Dagon was standing at the foot of the bed in a loose white tank top and black athletic pants, his hands in his pockets, his eyes gleaming red, and a dangerous smile dancing across his lips.

"There's my princess," he purred.

Eve felt a tightness around her wrists, and when she looked down, she saw that her hands were bound tightly together with a black necktie.

"What is this?" Eve demanded. Fear rose in her chest, setting her heart in an erratic rhythm.

"A little light bondage. I think you'll like it if you give it a chance," Dagon sneered. He lifted the tank top off over his head, revealing the rest of Zeke's beautiful tattoos. Dagon ran his hand over his chest and abs. "You like this body, don't you? You're barely making any attempt to hide that lust in your eyes. I must say, I couldn't have asked for a better vessel. Zeke keeps everything in such peak condition."

He held his free hand out toward Eve, and her body began to slide across the bed toward him, as though an invisible cable were pulling her to him. When she got close enough, she flipped over onto her belly, tucked her knee up under her, and, using the momentum Dagon was already providing, thrust herself up. She torqued her body around like she was performing a hammer throw, using her bound hands as the hammer and Dagon's face as the target.

It should've been a powerful blow, but he saw it coming a mile away. He bobbed slightly and easily deflected her strike with the palm of his hand, sending her fists whistling over his head and spinning her around. He caught her with her back to him and seized her, slamming her back up against his hard chest. He gripped the necktie binding her wrists in one hand across her belly, and he clamped his other hand around her throat.

He hummed in her ear, his lips ghosting over the ridges. "Mmm, I like it when you fight me," he said in a low, sultry tone. "Struggle, princess. I fucking love it."

Eve was ashamed of the throb in her core and the flood of moisture between her legs.

He squeezed her neck lightly and ran the tip of his tongue along the shell of her ear. His other hand released her wrists and slid down to the waistband of her underwear. His fingers traced along the elastic, leaving a tingling trail of sparks in their wake.

"Should I?" he asked, tentatively nestling one finger beneath the edging.

"If I yell, Bo will come running," Eve warned.

"I don't think he'd be interested in joining. He wants you to himself."

"He'll put a stop to this."

"But you don't really want that, do you? If you did, you would've yelled for him already." Dagon's tongue swirled over the tender skin under her ear, finishing with a light kiss that then trailed further down her neck to her shoulder. His fingers slipped further into her panties.

He'd lit a fire deep in her core, and she was afraid that if she didn't let him douse it, it would consume her. She longed for those fingers to touch her, her pelvis involuntarily rolling up to try to meet them in their descent down her belly. She was disgusted with herself, but there was something else inside of her that craved this with an exigent intensity. Something broken inside of her was exhilarated by the sheer magnitude of his desire for her, aching for him to dominate her.

He smiled against her shoulder as his fingers nestled between her legs. "You're wet for me, princess," he purred. He massaged the palm of his hand against her mound as he fucked her with his fingers. She felt his hard cock throb against her ass from under his athletic pants. He pressed his hips forward.

"You want me to fuck you, don't you? If you ask nicely, maybe I will."

Eve wanted to respond with something snide and witty, but all that escaped her lips was a soft, pleading moan. "Dagon…"

"Yes, princess?"

His ministrations were pulling her closer and closer to that magic chord, and just as she was about to surge into it, moaning and breathless…he stopped.

And then he bit her, his teeth digging into the flesh of her trapezius. She cried out in an agonizing ecstasy.

He yanked her underwear down over her thighs, then ripped them completely off of her, throwing the tattered fabric aside. He pushed her forward onto the bed and climbed up behind her while she clambered to her knees and elbows. He put a heavy hand in the middle of her back, between her shoulder blades, and refused to let her rise any higher than her elbows.

"No, you stay right there. Get that ass in the air for me, princess."

She felt his hand on the back of her thighs, spreading her legs apart, and suddenly his mouth was on her slit, his tongue accessing her from behind. She gasped as his warm tongue wriggled over her sensitive petals, and within moments, she was near climax again. Sensing her imminent release, he devoured her with a brutal intensity, and she spasmed and cried out, her body rocking and jerking in wild paroxysms.

He spun her around as she was still recovering from the aftershocks, and he positioned her on her hands and knees in front of him. He lowered his pants, releasing his engorged, throbbing erection.

"My turn," he said in a low, husky tone. He tangled his fist in her hair and shoved his hips forward, pressing the head of his cock to her lips.

She parted her lips and pushed out a gush of saliva with her tongue, wetting both her mouth and his cock as it slid past her lips and over her tongue. He gripped her hair and rocked his hips with a deep groan. He pressed into her throat, and she gagged. He pulled out, then thrust it in again, making her gag again. She tried to bring her bound hands up to assist, but he stopped her.

"No. I only want to see those pretty lips wrapped around my cock. I want to fuck your mouth, not your hands."

She sucked and wiggled and pressed her tongue in all the places Zeke had liked, but there was a lot more gagging with Dagon. Then, he hardened and swelled so much that she was afraid her teeth were going to scrape him. With a grunt, he twisted his fist in her hair painfully and spilled down the back of her throat, and she gagged, then swallowed it, his cock spasming in her mouth.

He withdrew from her mouth, allowing her a few gulps of air, before snatching up her bound wrists and flipping her onto her back, slamming her hands onto the bed above her head. He pressed his body against her, and his hand settled between her thighs again.

His mouth descended upon hers with an animalistic brutality. His tongue pushed past her lips and dominated hers into submission while he slid his fingers into her like they were his cock.

He whispered against her lips, "Do you want me to fuck you?"

She nodded. She couldn't even pretend to deny it anymore.

"Yeah?" He kissed the underside of her jaw. "Too bad...I'm saving the real thing for when you're awake." He traced his lips lightly down her neck to the place he'd bitten her earlier. "For now, you'll get whatever I give you."

His tongue tasted the blood that the bite had drawn, and he clamped his mouth over it and drank from her. As he sucked and licked at her wound, it elicited a pleasure that was akin to the sensations his mouth had drawn from between her legs. He fucked her harder with his fingers, sensing that she was getting close to coming again.

She wanted to throw her arms around his shoulders as she hit that tipping point, but he held her wrists firmly into the mattress. The pain from his fingers digging into her skin strangely heightened the pleasure that swelled and surged in her core. The oversensitivity of her clit drew louder moans as she writhed beneath him and rocked against his hand.

As she shuddered and gasped through the aftershocks, Dagon grinned darkly down at her. "I love watching you unravel. But I have to tell you something before he wakes you up."

Eve looked up at him in confusion. What was he talking about?

"I know what the shapeshifter said. If they give me more time out, I'll tell them what the message was."

"But, wait, if you knew, why wouldn't you say anything?"

Dagon's face was mischievous. "I play my cards close to my chest, princess."

"If I tell them, can't they just get Eoduun to read your mind?"

"Eoduun can't read me. I'm more powerful than him. So, just tell them."

"Why don't you tell them?"

"Because it's more fun this way."

27

Be Wariest of the Men Who Say They Love You

Eve blinked her eyes open as Bo came rushing into her room, wearing only sweatpants. She almost didn't recognize him without his mask on. "What's going on?!" he shouted, his eyes scanning the room, two large knuckle knives in his hands, raised and at the ready.

She sat up, the bedcovers tangled up around her legs and arms, and whipped her head around. "What the fuck?! What are you doing?!" Eve shrieked. She tore her hands free from the bedding and held her fists up defensively.

When Bo realized the room was clear, he relaxed slightly. "You were yelling about Dagon. I thought he was…doing something to you."

Eve was grateful for the darkness as she felt her face flush. "…Oh. No, I was just having a…um…nightmare."

"Hm." He seemed dubious.

"Dagon told me something," Eve revealed slowly.

"Wait…he *was* here?" Bo's hands went back up.

"No…no, he told me something in my dream." She told him about Dagon's message. "Why would I dream that? Is it a premonition?"

Bo shook his head. "Maybe. Or it could really be Dagon."

"What?!"

"He has the powers of a god, and he is constantly pulling tricks from his sleeve. It's not such a leap to imagine he can dreamwalk, too."

"But…I don't get the point. Why would he want *me* to tell you instead of just telling you or Zeke directly?"

"Because he plays fucking games," Bo growled. "If this was really him, it means he can get to you, even locked away in Zeke's head." Bo gave her a knowing look. "He didn't just bring you a message, did he?" he stated rather than asked.

"…No…" The dampness in her underwear told her that Dagon's effect on her had been quite real, but as for the rest of the encounter, she seemed entirely unscathed. She looked down at her wrists. No evidence of being tied. She reached up and touched her shoulder where he had bitten her. No injury.

Bo stood there, looking helpless. "Shit."

"What?"

"I don't know what to do. I don't know how to keep him out of your head. I need to consult Luc."

"But he can't hurt me in dreams. Not for real," Eve pointed out.

Bo frowned. "I beg to differ."

"He bit me in my dream, but there's no mark. He can't hurt me."

"Did you feel it in the dream?"

Eve blushed again. "Well, yeah."

"If he had flayed you alive, do you think you would've felt it?"

Eve's stomach turned. Dagon wouldn't do that to her…would he?

"If you can hear his words and feel his touch, then it's real enough," Bo said. "And we need to stop it."

Bo was clearly upset. If he knew that Dagon could walk around in Zeke's skin when Zeke was sleeping, he would combust. It was a dangerous secret, and the longer she kept it, the worse it was going to be when it came to light.

But if she told Bo now, what would Dagon do? He'd promised he would hurt Zeke or someone close to her if she revealed his little trick. It didn't feel like an idle threat, either. She had to keep the secret. For now.

"Do you think he really knows what the shapeshifter was saying?" Eve asked.

"He very well may, but we can't trust what he tells us. That's the problem with Dagon. He's not part of our team. He's not on anyone's team but his own, and he only does what suits him. He's capricious and manipulative and selfish. He doesn't want to help us for the sake of helping us. He has a bargaining chip. But is it even one we can trust? Is the information worth the price? Doubtful."

"You really hate him."

"There's nothing to like about him. I wish you would be more cautious with him. He's not an admirer or lover. He's not in love with you. He's a dangerous evil that will only use you and hurt you."

Damn. That sounded like her usual type. Her poisoned apple.

Bo's fear and loathing of Dagon renewed Eve's. She was a fool to let him sweep her up in an erotic encounter, dream or not. She'd grown complacent with him, and she didn't fear him enough. She was going to end up like a lion tamer that forgot the lion was above her on the food chain.

It would be so much easier to remember that if he wasn't wearing Zeke's sweet face.

"I'll be more careful." Eve furrowed her brow thoughtfully as Bo put away his knuckle knives. "How did you get in here? I locked the door, as you asked."

Bo tapped his finger near the outside corner of his blue eye. "I walked through it."

That's right, he had the space warping powers, too. It was too easy to forget just how powerful the people around her were. She really didn't belong here. She reeked of mediocrity – a weed in a garden of splendor.

"Well, I'll let you get back to sleep," Bo said, turning toward the bedroom door.

Eve's hand shot out and caught the pocket of his sweatpants. He stopped and looked down at her fingers stretching the fabric, then raised his eyes to hers.

"Can you stay?" she asked. She was suddenly afraid that Dagon would show up in the flesh to finish what he'd started in her dream. She couldn't be alone with him. She couldn't trust herself around him. She would fly straight into his web.

Bo looked conflicted.

"Please?" she begged. She released his clothing and slid her hand into his beseechingly. His hand was so much rougher and more calloused than Luc's, she noticed. And not quite as gigantic.

Bo pursed his lips. "Fine, if it'll make you feel better. I'll sleep on the couch."

"Wait," she said, gripping his hand tighter when he tried to pull away. "Can you stay and talk to me for a while? I'm wide awake now."

"I'm tired, Evie."

She slid over and patted the bedcovers next to her. "Then lie down and let me talk."

"I'm not getting in bed with you," he asserted.

"I'm not asking you to get in bed with me. You can stay on top of the covers. Please? If you go out to the couch, I'll only follow you out there."

Bo sighed. It was so strange to be able to see his whole face and read all of his features, even if it was mostly in the dark. He really was a handsome man. He resembled Luc, but Bo looked like he'd seen a lot more of life than Luc had. If Luc was a brand-new Valentine teddy bear, Bo was the well-loved one that was missing an eye and had had its tattered arm sewn back on twice.

He was uncomfortable, but he caved. He slid onto the bed next to her, as close to the edge of the bed as he could get, and reclined back against the headboard with his hands folded behind his head, his ankles crossed.

Eve laid her head on his chest and tucked her hands between her chest and his side, and she felt him tense up.

"Relax. I'm not going to maul you," she said with a light laugh.

"What did you want to talk about?"

"Tell me about Shira."

"I'm pretty sure Cassie already told you about Shira."

"Tell me why she was special to you."

Bo was silent for a long time, then countered with, "Only if you tell me why you cowered away from Luc this morning."

Eve swallowed. "Too many men have unkind hands," she whispered. "Why do you think I learned to fight in the first place?"

"Tell me."

Eve inhaled deeply. "Ok…" After an indecisive pause, she started to explain. "I never knew who my real father was. The man who raised me, my stepfather, the only father figure I had ever known my entire life, never let me forget that I wasn't really his. That he didn't want me. He couldn't wait for me to leave home and not be his problem any longer. I became the focus of all of his anger and hatred, for everything that pissed him off. If I so much as glanced at him wrong, I paid for it.

"When I moved out as a teenager, I moved in with my boyfriend. He started off so sweet and loving and thoughtful. He was the *one,* I was certain of it. But things went sour so fast it made my head spin. Even so, I didn't leave him until the night he came after me with a knife. It still pisses me off that it took that much before I could bring myself to leave him. And then he stalked me for months, until I found a man who swore he wasn't afraid of my psycho ex." Eve gave a low, humorless chuff. "You want to know why he wasn't afraid of him?

Because he was worse. But he taught me to fight. He was the one who brought me into MMA, and he helped me secure my first paid fight.

"When I was with him, I had to be able to fight just to survive him. He would've killed me if I hadn't been able to defend myself. So, in my experience, the men who say they love you are the ones you need to be wariest of. The gentle hands that touch you so sweetly at night are the hard fists you need to dodge in the morning."

The room was silent until Bo said softly, "I'm so sorry, Evie." He brought one hand from behind his head and wrapped his arm loosely around her shoulders, gently cradling her head against his chest with his hand.

"I can't presume to understand what you went through, but I do know what it feels like to have a father-figure who loathes your very existence. It leaves a big hole. You try to find ways to fill it, but..." His voice trailed off.

"Sometimes you just end up punching more holes," Eve contributed.

Bo's fingers lightly caressed her hair. His voice was soft when he spoke. "Shira was special to me because I loved her like I'd never loved anyone. She was beautiful, but not in a sexual way, if that makes sense. She had these big brown doe eyes that I swear could look straight into the darkest soul and find even the faintest sliver of light. She could find the good in anything. There was an innocence about her that nothing could tarnish.

"It was what made her blood healing such an oddity. It's an unquestionably sexualized experience, but with her...there was such a strange purity about it. It was like losing your virginity. She and I were never lovers, but I accepted that she would never love me that way. She loved me the way she could, and it was enough. It was more than enough. And then Dagon took her from me."

The hatred that dripped from those words was like acid. She felt his whole body tense with rage.

He continued, "He was coming after me. *Me*. But he was in Zeke's body, and I couldn't bring myself to go full force at Zeke. How could

I kill my own teammate? There had to be another way, right? Well, he took me down pretty easily with my eye already fucked up from Ruth.

"Shira went after him. She was trying to protect me, and he ripped her throat out with his bare hands. While I was unconscious on the ground, she crawled over me, put her neck on me, and bled into my mouth, trying to save me. She died while I was healing. That's why this eye didn't heal properly. And every time I look at it, I'm reminded that I wasn't strong enough to protect her. I'm the reason she's dead. My weakness killed her."

"Oh, Bo..." A tear rolled out of Eve's eye and dropped onto Bo's bare chest. She reached up and touched Bo's cheek, then planted a small, chaste kiss on his other cheek. She nuzzled her face into his neck and squeezed her arm around his torso. Her heart broke for him.

She would never let Dagon touch her again. She was so disgusted with herself. Poor Bo. Poor Shira. It had happened almost a year ago, but the raw emotion in Bo's voice still felt like a fresh wound. She wondered if he ever talked about it. As far as she could tell, he did everything he possibly could to avoid it. She understood that tactic, because she used it, too. Box it up. Stack it in the corner. Deal with it later.

The problem is, those boxes just continue to pile up until the corner becomes an unmanageable mess, and then those boxes eventually topple and spill out all over the place in unpredictable and inconvenient ways.

When Eve awoke in the morning, she was alone in her bed. She rolled over and stretched, a loud groan croaking in her throat.

"*Ohayou*," Bo called from the kitchen.

"Oh, you're still here," she said in surprise. She threw some shorts on and joined him in the kitchen. He was dressed and had his mask on. "Oh, you went out this morning already," she amended, eyeing the coffee in his hand and the one sitting in her spot next to him. She slid onto the barstool and nudged his arm as he looked down at his phone. "*Arigatou*," she said with a grin.

"Don't strain yourself," he teased.

"Why do you know Japanese?"

"I don't, really. We lived in Tokyo for a year when we were teenagers. Our father's business ventures…" he explained vaguely. "*Ohayou* was one of the few greetings I picked up, so I said it a lot. It just stuck."

"Well, I like it." Eve took a sip of her coffee. "So, what's on the docket for today?"

"Training. I think after yesterday's premonition, you should spend a little time training with Zephlyn."

Eve's phone vibrated on the counter. She'd forgotten she left it out there overnight.

"Oh, and your phone has gone off three times since I've been sitting here," Bo said.

Eve picked it up. She had five text notifications from Luc, starting at 5:30AM.

Good morning, love. Are you up yet? I miss you.

Text me when you get up.

Are you training?

Bo said we have a Dagon issue. Please call me.

Blink twice if I'm annoying you.

Eve chuckled at the last text. She quickly replied.

Blink blink. I just woke up.

She turned to Bo. "What did you tell Luc about Dagon?"

"I told him what you told me. He has an idea for a temporary shield, but he's working on finding a permanent solution."

"What's the temporary shield?"

Bo hesitated, his eyes cast down at his phone. "Me."

"You? What about you? What do you have to do?"

"Sleep with you."

Eve's eyes widened, and when Bo glanced over at her, his eyes widened as well. "Oh, no, no, not *sleep with you* sleep with you," he laughed nervously. "Next to you. When I told him I stayed with you last night, it gave him an idea. I'm not as skilled as Luc in controlling it, but in close quarters, I act kind of like a Faraday cage. He thinks that maybe if I'm next to you, it'll keep Dagon from being able to get into your head. Like Magneto's helmet."

"Oh! Ok," Eve consented, then took a drink of her coffee. He watched her for some sign of distress, but she didn't show him any. She actually slept like a baby last night with him next to her. It was comforting having him there while she fell asleep.

Dagon wouldn't dare go into her room while Bo was there and blow his big secret, would he? She was betting not.

"That's it? 'Oh, ok'?" Bo asked.

Eve scrolled through the news on her phone while she drank her coffee. "Sorry. *Oh, no, that's terrible. Anything but that...*" she protested sarcastically. She looked up at him. "Better?"

"Ok, you talked me into it."

Eve chuckled. She went to the cupboard and grabbed two protein bars for breakfast. She tossed one to Bo as she returned to her seat.

She watched him lower his mask as he took a bite, and, to her surprise, he didn't raise it back up again. She reached her hand out and ran her finger along the white stubble on his sharp jawline.

"I didn't have an opportunity to shave," he remarked.

She was shocked that he was letting her do this. He wasn't hiding. He wasn't uncomfortable or fidgety.

"I wouldn't know any different. I don't normally see your jaw to know if you usually have stubble."

"It was catching in your hair this morning."

So he did sleep next to her all night. She wondered if he'd fallen asleep, too, or if he'd gone out to the couch after she passed out.

Her phone started ringing. It was Luc.

"Good morning, love. Playing hooky today?" he asked.

"I left my phone on the counter. I didn't hear my alarms."

"That's ok. I told Bo to let you sleep in. Do you miss me?"

"You haven't been gone long enough to miss you," she lied. She felt his absence. Acutely. But she wasn't going to tell him that.

He made a pained grunt. "That hurts, babe."

"When are you coming home?"

"Oh, so you *do* miss me," he said smoothly. "Two days. I can make one, *maybe* two big jumps every day, so that'll shorten the time I'm gone, but I do have a bit of traveling to do. Now, tell me about Dagon. Bo said he infiltrated your dream."

Eve relayed what Dagon told her in the dream, but she left out the details of the sexual encounter, saying only that he had her hands tied together and was his usual lewd self.

Luc told her not to agree to anything until he got back. No deals with Dagon. He also asked her about sleeping with Bo until he returned.

"I'm fine with it," she admitted. "I'm just a little surprised that *you* are."

"I trust Bo to keep you safe. And to keep his hands off of you, lest he wishes them rent from his wrists."

"No worries of that, I'm sure. He's a perfect gentleman," Eve replied. She turned and winked at Bo.

Luc laughed hysterically. "That, I assure you, he is not."

"I heard that," Bo said, unamused.

Eve heard Bo's phone vibrating, then she got a text notification shortly afterward while she was on the phone with Luc. She pulled the phone away from her ear momentarily to look. It was Zeke.

Where are you guys? We've been waiting 20 min.

"Oh, shit," Bo mumbled, looking at the watch on his wrist. "Tell Luc goodbye. We're late for field training."

As Eve and Bo approached the training grounds, they could see Zeke and Eoduun practicing 540 triple kicks with Mendal. Dizzy and Zephlyn were also with them, but they were sparring with each other. It was glaringly evident that Zephlyn was taking it easy on Dizzy. Dizzy looked like one of those tall flailing tube men they put out in front of car dealerships with his long, lanky limbs swinging about. It was comical – that is, until Dizzy landed punch to Zephlyn's shoulder and sent him spinning through the air like he'd just been clipped by a train.

"Oh, jeez, sorry Zephlyn!" Dizzy cried, covering his mouth with his hands and cringing his shoulders forward. Eve started to take off toward Zephlyn to see if he was ok, but Bo caught her arm firmly and stopped her.

"Zephlyn will be fine," Bo said in a low voice. "Stay away from Dizzy."

Eve regarded Bo skeptically. "What, you don't trust him?"

"I don't trust him around *you*." When Eve continued staring at him, Bo elaborated. "He's clumsy and doesn't know his own strength."

"Hey, there they are!" Zeke shouted, waving at Eve and Bo.

Eoduun was less animated. "What gives? Where the hell were you?" he demanded as they approached.

Bo stuck his hands in his pockets. "We had a phone conference with Luc. But we're here now. Did you find anything this morning?"

"Nothing. No sigils or any signs of infiltration that we could find," Eoduun answered. Bo must've had him and Zeke sweeping the grounds for Ruth's sigils before training.

"Good. All right. Let's get to it."

As Bo ran the team through conditioning drills, Eve found herself warily glancing over at Zephlyn's team, who were training nearby. Zephlyn was clearly favoring the shoulder that Dizzy had annihilated with that single hit earlier. She didn't need Bo's warnings to want to stay away from Dizzy. He was so awkward and strange, and that freakish strength seemed to surprise even himself. But shapeshifters were born that way, she'd read, so why did it seem like it was all still new to him?

After field practice, as they were gathering their things to walk back, Eve asked the team about it.

"I don't know why he's like that," Bo said. "He's always been like that. He's not a whole lot of use to us in a fight, but with someone like him, it's either bring him on or take him out. He can't function normally in society like that. He was hurting people unintentionally."

Eoduun spoke up, "I don't know why we don't have a separate organization for monsters like Dizzy."

"*People* like Dizzy," Zeke corrected.

"There aren't enough worth saving to warrant a separate organization," Bo answered. "Trust me, Luc looked into it."

"He's been useful to us," Zeke pointed out. "He's gotten us all kinds of intel with his transformations."

"Which is incredibly surprising, considering how fucking awkward he is," Eoduun said.

"Hey, guys, wait up," Zephlyn called from across the field. He jogged over to them, his black man-bun bobbing loosely after training. "Mind if I steal Eve for a bit?" He turned to Eve. "Bo agreed to let me work a little with you on honing your precognition skills. I have some training exercises I'd like to show you."

"I will bring her by after lunch," Bo interjected.

"I was thinking she could eat with us so I can get to know her a little before we start training," Zephlyn countered. "It makes it easier that way."

"Why don't you join us instead?" Bo offered.

Zephlyn fixed Bo with a knowing look. "He's not going to bother her. Your prejudices are unfounded."

Bo clapped Zephlyn on the shoulder Dizzy had punched, and Zephlyn winced. "Oh, I'm sorry, are you injured?" Bo asked in a sugary tone. "How did that happen?"

"We've all had training mishaps. You can't begrudge him any more than anyone else for that."

"I don't begrudge him for it. But I recognize a danger for what it is, and I act accordingly. I will bring Evie by to see *you* after lunch."

Bo nudged Eve along, and she looked back at Zephlyn apologetically. "I'll see you in a bit!" she called back, trying to seem cheerful.

Team Alpha all ate together at Eve's apartment. Eve found her eye stealing glances of Zeke as she ate her sandwich. He had no idea what Dagon was doing behind his back, did he? She looked over at Bo, but he was looking down at his phone. Should she say something to Zeke about the dream situation? Dagon would be listening, but did that matter? It wasn't like it was a secret to Dagon.

She ventured, "Hey, Z, has Dagon said anything interesting to you lately?"

Zeke stopped chewing and stared at her blankly. "Uh...no, not really. Why, did something happen?"

Eoduun snapped to attention. "Did he do something?"

Bo gave her a quick sideways glance, and it didn't take a genius to understand his sentiment. *Zip it.*

"Just curious."

"He's actually been really quiet lately," Zeke commented. "I don't know what's up with him. He's acting like a broody teenager, spending all his time closed up in his room."

"As long as he isn't doing what most of us did when we were teenagers closed up in our rooms," Eoduun commented.

Zeke scrunched his nose. "I don't think he can do that...in my head..." He shuddered.

"A little mental stimulation," Eoduun laughed.

"Stop," Zeke cried with disgusted laughter.

"Well, whatever is wrong with him, I hope he *comes* to his senses," Eoduun continued.

Zeke threw what was left of his sandwich back onto his plate. "Yep, I'm done," he complained.

After lunch, Bo took Eve across the grounds to the resource building, aka, the garage with the vast bunker beneath it. He brought her to a small room with odd, mesh-covered walls. Along one wall, there were shelves and cupboards, and in the middle of the room was a reclining chair with a drop-down dome attached to the headrest, like a hooded dryer chair at a salon. There was a small, round table in the corner, where Zephlyn was waiting for her, leaned back casually in his chair.

When Bo left and closed the door behind him, Zephlyn propped his elbows on the table and rested his lightly stubbled chin on his fists. He pinned her with an intrigued, obsidian gaze. "I've been dying to get you alone. You have secrets."

28
Johnny Cash Could Keep His Burning Ring of Fire

Eve was taken aback. "Secrets? Like what?"

Zephlyn narrowed his eyes at her. Then he held his hands out to her. "May I?" When Eve nodded, he placed his hands on either side of her head, his fingers splayed wide. He stared into her eyes for so long without blinking, she thought his eyelids were going to stick to his eyeballs when he finally did.

"That's weird." He withdrew his hands from her head and crossed his arms across his chest, chewing his lip contemplatively.

"That's never good," Eve laughed nervously.

"*You're* weird," he corrected.

"Thanks…"

"No, I don't mean it offensively. But you are. You're…fuzzy."

Eve blinked at him. "I don't understand."

"I don't either. I thought if I got a closer look at you, it would clear up. But you're surrounded by some kind of fog. And what I *can* get from you doesn't make sense. If I was *crazy*, I would be throwing the word lilim around, but…I'm not crazy. You can't be that. Blood healers can't be monsters. But I don't know how else to explain what I'm seeing."

"What the hell is a lilim?"

"Are you familiar with the lore around Lilith?"

"I'm aware of her, but I know nothing about her. It's Lilith's grimoire that Ruth claims to have."

"There are a lot of different origin stories about Lilith that go all the way back to Sumerian lore, which describes her as a demonic succubus, but the most accepted belief is that Lilith was the first wife of Adam, before Eve."

"Wait," Eve interrupted. "Are you telling me Adam and Eve were *real?*"

"They weren't the first *humans*, but they were the first humans with specialties, like us," Zephlyn explained. "Adam and Eve gave rise to the mutations that produce specialties. Lilith gave rise to monsters." Then he raised an eyebrow at Eve. "Actually, it's believed that Eve was the first blood healer, coincidentally."

Eve wondered if Zephlyn could see the smoke drifting from her ears.

Zephlyn returned to his story. "Anyway, Lilith. She refused to be subservient to Adam and submit to him, and left Eden. When she refused to return, the angels killed the children she and Adam had together, so some stories say she slept with an angel, Samael, and produced demonic offspring, called lilim, to replace the children that were taken from her. Other stories say she snuck back into Eden and took advantage of Adam in his sleep to produce the lilim. And other stories say she made the lilim without any male counterpart at all.

"The lilim, subsequently," Zephlyn continued, "were succubus types, often described as seducing and/or attacking men in their sleep, and in some lore, specifically men of power. But lilim have been extinct for millennia, according to sources at the Vatican."

Eve felt a burning, tingling sensation through her limbs. Cassie's words from last night rang through her memory: *Power is just drawn to you, isn't it?* Then Luc's comment about her blood: *It's laced with so much aphrodisiac that it's as potent as siren venom.*

Her heart threatened to rattle her ribs loose. No. She wasn't a monster. If she was a monster, she would know. Luc would know. *Someone* would fucking *know, right*?!

"So…what now?" Eve asked, trying to keep the tremble from her voice.

"I don't know. Which brings us to our first lesson in clairvoyance. When we don't know, Eve, we keep it under our hat until we do. Putting it out to others before we have a clear vision often only muddies it and causes confusion and misunderstandings. And sometimes simply voicing it can cement an outcome that was only a slight possibility before. It's best to know what you're looking at before you share it."

"What *can* you tell me, Zephlyn?"

"I can tell you that something is different about you. That I know for sure. But are you a monster? Part monster? Probably not. Like I said, blood healers can't be monsters."

"Luc said that too, but how do you know?"

"It's incompatible with monster genotypes. The only way it could ever happen is…"

Zephlyn suddenly fell silent, his focus drawing inward. He then gave Eve a tight smile. "Sorry, I'm not following my own advice, am I?" He mimed placing something under an imaginary hat on his head. "I'll just have to let it marinate for a while."

"That's not fair!" Eve protested. "How could it happen? You're saying it is *possible*, essentially, aren't you?"

"I don't know. I was just thinking out loud. It's probably nothing."

"You know what's wrong with me."

"I don't know that. And it's not necessarily anything *wrong*."

"But you suspect."

"I don't know, Eve."

Eve was terrified of what he wasn't telling her. He knew something. Something about her. He knew what was wrong with her, and he didn't want to tell her.

"Am I a monster?" she asked, point-blank.

"I can't tell you what I don't know. But I can tell you that Bo won't be quite so nice to you if it does turn out that you're a monster. He has a real prejudice."

Eve tilted her head. "I don't think that's true. He's part monster himself."

"And he would carve that part out with a dull knife, if he could."

The burning in Eve's limbs suddenly turned to ice. She couldn't bear the thought of Bo looking at her the way he looked at Dizzy. Or Dagon. Would he truly hate her if she was something like a lilim? Tears welled in her eyes.

She blinked quickly and changed the subject. "So what am I learning today? How can I turn 'Don't Think It, Don't Say It' into something useful?"

Zephlyn showed her some simple exercises to practice at home to help build her natural intuition. He gave her some tips on how to decipher a real premonition from simple invasive thoughts, as well.

As she was finishing up with Zephlyn, Bo walked in. He leaned against the door jamb and crossed his legs at the ankles, looking down at his phone while he silently waited for Eve to be ready.

Seeing him brought those fears from earlier rushing painfully back. She'd grown desperately attached to Bo. He was the first person she'd trusted when she was brought here, and he was still the one she trusted most. He was the person she felt safest with. It would crush her if those endearing mismatched eyes ever looked at her with even a hint of contempt.

Eve and Zephlyn joined him at the door, and Bo said, "We have a brief meeting in ten minutes. We'll meet you in the war room, Zephlyn."

Bo let Zephlyn go on ahead while he hung back. He looked down at Eve.

"How'd it go?" he asked.

Eve's chest grew tight. "It was ok. He thinks I have some latent skills, but it isn't very consistent. I'll have to practice."

"Hm." He stared at her. "You seem pensive. You weren't pensive when I left you. What happened?"

"Nothing happened." Eve started to move down the corridor.

"Hm," Bo grunted doubtfully as he followed along behind her.

When they walked into the war room, Eve looked around at the table. It looked like everyone was there, with one notable exception. Mira was missing. Maybe she was busy in the lab with the shapeshifter sample they collected last night. Zeke motioned for Eve to come sit next to him, and she gladly obliged. Bo went up to the head of the table, where Luc had been last time.

Bo briefed everyone on the club incident and Luc's subsequent trip away from the compound. He asked for any updates.

Celeste raised her hand. "I just want to point out that I have everyone set up on a secured, encrypted group chat, and if everyone would *use* it, we could all stay updated in real-time."

"Thank you, Celeste," Bo said. "I apologize, I forgot to download the app onto my phone. We will be sure to utilize it from now on. Any updates for me in the meantime?" Bo looked around at the table expectantly.

Remi spoke up. "So, Roy and I have been working on deciphering that video you sent us. Whatever language it is, it isn't anything in current use. All my translation apps basically told me to go fuck myself."

Roy added, "Near as we can tell, it's something ancient, like Sumerian. But I doubt there's any hope of us actually figuring out what the hell she's saying without Vatican resources and experts. If it was written, sure. But spoken word is a whole 'nother animal."

"Yeah, that's about what I figured," Bo sighed.

"When can we get back to hunting?" Mendal posed. "While we're all sitting here with our thumbs up our asses, chasing our tails, I could be out there killing monsters and saving people and chasing *other* tail."

"I second that," Kai agreed. "I'm basically useless here. Put me on a case until you have a need for me here."

"I'll talk to Luc," Bo deferred.

The meeting was adjourned before the restless hunters could bring up any more complaints that Bo didn't want to deal with.

Back at her apartment, Eve stared into her fridge at the produce Luc had stocked in there that was about to go bad if she didn't use it. She wished Luc were here to cook her something. She wasn't completely useless in the kitchen, but she was no master chef, either. If it took more than ten minutes of prep time or dirtied more than one or two pans, it was not likely to be found on her personal menu.

Zeke waltzed in as she was pulling out everything that needed to be used and placing it on the counter.

"What are you doing?"

"Putting this stuff all together so I can stare at it."

Zeke tapped his lips thoughtfully. "I think you're supposed to eat it."

"But how?"

"Hmm. With your mouth, I believe."

Eve rolled her eyes. "I mean how should I prepare it?"

They stood next to each other and stared at the pile of vegetables on the counter.

Eoduun's voice startled them. "Ramen." He'd walked in and was lurking silently behind them.

"I don't have any ramen noodles," Eve replied.

"I do. I'll bring them over if you make enough for us, too," Eoduun suggested.

"I can't promise it'll be any good," Eve warned. "I'm not the gourmet chef that Luc is."

"I wouldn't know. I've never had his cooking," Eoduun said. "I didn't even know he did cook until he brought you dinner yesterday."

"I'm sure it'll be amazing," Zeke said brightly.

"And if it isn't, there's a trash bin right under the sink," Eoduun added helpfully.

When the ingredients had all been acquired and compiled, Eoduun offered to help her in the kitchen. Zeke sat at the kitchen island with his chin in his hands, watching them.

"Is there anything I can do?" he asked forlornly.

"You can just sit there and look pretty," Eve teased as she got out the cutting board. Eoduun brought her the vegetables he'd just finished washing.

"Don't let him touch anything," Eoduun said, pointing accusingly at Zeke. "He tried to burn down my kitchen last time he 'helped' me."

"Oh, come on, one little kitchen fire and you're all, 'No, don't let Zeke near the stove!' You can't hold it against me forever."

"It was three weeks ago."

"Exactly. *Forever* ago," Zeke said.

"Who taught you how to cook, Eoduun?" Eve inquired curiously when the boys had ceased their spat.

"Me. My parents weren't around much. Hunters don't have a lot of time for their kids."

"Oh. I suppose I hadn't thought much about that."

"They didn't either," he mumbled spitefully.

"Where are they now?" Eve asked.

"Digested."

"Fuck, dude," Zeke said. "Going heavy on the dark tonight, man."

"I'm sorry," Eve consoled.

"Don't be. They kicked me out when I was thirteen because my mother read my thoughts and discovered I had more *open* preferences than they were comfortable with. Called me a disgusting abomination and told me they wished I was never born. So, yeah, fuck them. I hope that rougarou enjoyed her meal."

Eve didn't know what to say, so she asked, "Were they part of Knighco, too?"

"No. They were independent. My father's family had money, which helped fund their endeavors."

"Like Luc?"

"Nothing like Luc. Luc's family is on a completely different level. My parents were a two-person team."

"Did you at least get something out of it when they passed?"

"Not a dime. They made sure of that," he replied sourly. "But that's fine. I didn't want anything from them anyway."

Eve glanced over at Zeke. "So, what's your story, Z? How did you end up here?"

Zeke leaned back and rubbed the back of his neck. "Me? There's nothing special about me. Went to school, played football, had friends. Then I came here."

"We don't need to talk about all that right now," Eoduun said somewhat pointedly, giving Eve a meaningful glance as he handed her a knife from the butcher's block.

She began chopping up the spinach leaves, but as she did, she stole a glance at Zeke. His eyes were vacantly staring a thousand miles past the cupboards to her right, his shoulders slightly slumped.

Something terrible had happened to him, too.

Is this what Knighco was? A conglomeration of gifted but severely traumatized individuals who've been given new purpose by hunting the things that go bump in the night?

Her mind returned to her conversation with Zephlyn. She kept coming back to it every time there was a lull in her train of thought.

If I was crazy, I would be throwing the word lilim around...It's incompatible with monster genotypes. The only way it could ever happen is...Bo won't be quite so nice to you if it does turn out that you're a monster...

The more she thought about it, the more convinced she was that Zephlyn knew exactly what she was. But why wouldn't he tell her? What was he hiding? Who *was* he going to tell?

The way he described the lilim made Eve uneasy. It fit her situation too well for her comfort. Too well to completely dismiss it. Then again, that was only a recent development. A few weeks ago, she wouldn't have thought it fit well at all. She had no problem attracting men, sure, but it seemed that they always ended up wanting to destroy her, not the other way around. And they weren't falling all over themselves for her. She didn't turn every head in the room when she walked through the door. So what was different now? Why was it different here? Did it have to do with the fact that she had started using her blood healing? Was it connected?

As she moved on to dicing the carrots, she wasn't paying close enough attention to where her fingers were. The sharp kitchen knife sliced into the skin on her middle finger with little resistance.

"Fuck!" she hissed, and, stupidly, she dropped the knife. Even more stupidly, she then tried to use her leg to stop it from hitting the floor. It nicked the tender flesh on her bare inner thigh right below the hem of her cotton shorts before clattering to the tiles.

She reached down and picked up the knife, and when she stood up, Eoduun was standing close to her – as in, feel the heat from his body kind of close. He took her injured hand in his and brought it close to his face. His wet tongue flicked out and touched Eve's skin, tasting the blood from her middle finger in one long, slow lick. Eve inhaled sharply as he took her finger into his mouth and sucked on it. The sensation of his soft tongue and warm mouth around her finger heated and tightened her core.

"Eoduun!" Zeke barked.

Eoduun barely heard him. His eyes lowered to Eve's leg, where he spotted the gash on her inner thigh. A thin trickle of blood was making its way down toward the back of her knee. As Zeke jumped up from his barstool on the other side of the kitchen island, Eoduun released Eve's hand and dropped to his knees in front of her. His hands slowly slid up her legs, gripping her thighs. She closed her eyes as she felt his hot tongue dragging up the inside of her thigh, and his mouth covered the fresh cut, sucking up her blood like it was the most delectable thing he'd ever tasted. He moaned erotically as his tongue rolled in circles over the wound, and she reached down with her uninjured hand and twisted her fingers in to his long hair.

Zeke was behind her, watching helplessly, unsure what to do, until Eve turned her head and looked up at him from beneath hooded eyes. She held her bleeding finger out to him. He stared at it indecisively, glancing down over her shoulder at Eoduun sucking on her thigh, his mouth only inches from her core.

"Fuuuck," Zeke groaned, then took her finger into his mouth and sucked ravenously, like a thirsty man who'd been lost in the desert.

Eve's legs began to tremble as she was overcome with the need burning between her thighs. She pulled her finger from Zeke's mouth and brought it to her own. She licked blood from her finger, letting it linger on her tongue, and turned her head, pulling Zeke's mouth to hers. His tongue slipped into her mouth and lapped the blood from her tongue, and with a low groan, he deepened the kiss, pressing his erection into her backside. He snaked one hand up her shirt, cupping her breast, while the other hand cupped her jaw.

As Zeke kissed her mouth, Eoduun's tongue began to move up her inner thigh. She felt his fingers hooking into the edge of her panties and shorts, and he pulled them aside. It took every ounce of strength she had left to keep her knees from buckling when his warm, soft tongue invaded her folds. She moaned into Zeke's mouth and her fingers tightened in Eoduun's hair.

She already felt like she was about to burst apart at the seams, but she wanted more. *More.* She rolled her pelvis against Eoduun's mouth as she ran her cut finger down the side of her neck. Zeke's lips followed the trail of blood to the hollow between her neck and shoulder.

"I need to fuck you," he growled against her shoulder.

Her hand reached up and gripped the back of his neck as he leaned over her and kissed her shoulder, using him for support as Eoduun's tongue wriggled against her clit in just the right spot. Her other hand fisted in Eoduun's hair as he pushed her over the edge, and she spasmed and throbbed against his tongue.

Eoduun licked the wound on her thigh once more, then rose to his feet in front of her. He buried his hand into her hair and crushed his lips roughly against hers. There was nothing gentle about his kiss. It was like he was both furious *and* horny. And it was fucking hot.

Zeke tugged her shorts and underwear down from behind her, and both Zeke and Eoduun lowered their pants. Eoduun broke the kiss, and, as he gripped her hair tightly and Zeke pushed his hand against her back, they both urged her to bend over. Her face came down to Eoduun's awaiting erection. He held her hair with one hand, his hard length in the other, and he guided himself into her mouth. She put her hands on Eoduun's hips to help support herself as Zeke grabbed her hips and pressed into her slick opening from behind.

Eoduun thrust into her mouth while Zeke slammed into her from behind, making her eyes water as she was overwhelmed by the incinerating heat burning in her core. Eve arched her back and rocked back into Zeke, moaning around Eoduun's cock. When Zeke thrust into her, it pushed her to take Eoduun deeper into her mouth, and when he pulled back, her lips slipped back up Eoduun's thick shaft.

They ran that rhythm like a lewd rhyme until they were all teetering on the brink.

With one hand still in Eve's hair, Eoduun reached out with his other hand and gripped Zeke's hair, forcibly pulling his face to his. As Zeke and Eoduun's mouths met above her, she felt Eoduun's cock swell and spasm in her mouth. He grunted and moaned, his sounds muffled against Zeke's mouth, and the taste of hot seawater washed over her tongue and down the back of her throat.

Eoduun released her hair as she came up for air. She still gripped his hips for support as Zeke pounded into her. Eoduun reached under her, his fingers rubbing tight circles against her clit. Her encore release came quick and hard, and she gasped and whimpered as Zeke swelled inside of her and buried himself all the way to the hilt. He grunted and groaned as he spilled over, his thick fingers digging into her hips.

They all leaned and sagged into each other as they panted and tried to gather their wits, coming down from that spectacular high.

"Jesus fucking Christ," Eoduun breathed.

"Holy fuck," Zeke exhaled in agreement.

Eve looked at the temporarily forgotten vegetables on the counter and the water boiling away on the stovetop. "Well…who's hungry?" she panted, trying to make light of what had just happened.

Zeke zipped his jeans up and straightened his shirt. "I could eat."

Eve went to the bathroom to put a couple of bandages over her cuts, and then dinner prep was resumed.

What. The fuck. Was. That? It shouldn't have happened, but she couldn't deny that she loved every damn minute of it. She'd never been with two men at once, let alone two men drinking from her at once. It was an entirely new experience, and it soothed some hungry, insatiable beast inside of her…briefly. But it was strange. It was like scratching a mosquito bite – it feels so good for a few seconds, but then the itch comes back twofold. The satisfaction is brief and fleeting.

She was still longing for something. Something had been left unfulfilled.

As she sat next to Zeke and looked across the kitchen island at Eoduun, eating her mostly palatable ramen, she tried not to think about it. She should be spent. She shouldn't still be thinking about sex.

She shouldn't be yearning for Luc.

She kept checking her phone, wondering why he hadn't texted her all day. And, the hypocritical, selfish shitbag she was, she wondered if he was with another woman right now. Her blood boiled at the thought.

She was such a dumb bitch. He wasn't her boyfriend. He was dangerous. If she fell for him, he would break her. He would utterly *annihilate* her. She couldn't let him get under her skin. She couldn't let him worm his way into her heart, because he would only rend it asunder. That's what men like him did. They make you fall, and then they don't catch you.

And she was terrified that she was starting to slip.

After dinner, Eve found herself craving touch. Not a sexual touch, though. She just wanted to be close to another warm body that she felt safe with. She hated the word 'cuddle,' but it was what she needed. Zeke was rinsing the dishes and putting them in the dishwasher, so she walked up behind him and snaked her arms around his body, hugging him from behind. She pressed her face and body against his strong, bulky back.

"Oh, well, hello," he said sweetly, the smile clear in his voice. Her sunshine boy. She liked the way his back vibrated against her ear when he spoke. She squeezed him tightly.

"Want to stay and watch a movie?" she asked, her words warped by the way her cheek was smushed against his back. "I think Eoduun is already browsing."

"Sure," he said. He shut the water off, unable to finish his task with her clinging to him like that. "Is everything ok?" he asked. "You seemed a little preoccupied at dinner."

"I'm fine."

"Which means not fine, right?"

"It's nothing."

"Which means not nothing, right?"

"Stop doing that," she scowled, even though he couldn't see it. "'I'm fine' and 'it's nothing' mean that I don't want to talk about it."

"But you want to cuddle about it."

Stupid word. But... "Yes."

He turned around to face her and slipped his strong arms around her. "You miss Luc, don't you?"

That question jolted through her. "That's a weird question," she deflected.

"It's ok. He'll be back soon. Are you worried?"

"About what?"

"You tell me."

"I'm not worried. He's a big boy. He can take care of himself," Eve said impassively.

"Well, I'm here for you whenever and however you need me. I'm not *him,* and maybe I'm a poor substitute, but I wasn't kidding when I told you I was yours. I am."

"Guys!" Eoduun called from the living room. "*Boondock Saints* is on here. Want to watch it?" He then quoted a line from the movie, "'We could kill *everyone*!'"

Eve looked up at Zeke. "What do you think?"

Zeke raised an eyebrow. "'I'm strangely comfortable with it.'"

When they joined Eoduun in the living room, he was sitting on the floor in front of the couch with a pillow in his lap.

"If you'd just learn to behave yourself, we'd allow you on the furniture, Eoduun," Eve teased.

She and Zeke sat on the couch behind Eoduun. Eoduun pressed play on the movie, placed the remote on the coffee table in front of him, then leaned back against the front of the couch between Zeke's legs. Eve snuggled up in Zeke's lap, resting her head against his broad chest. Zeke wrapped his arms around her and sighed contentedly.

"Somebody play with my hair," Eoduun requested, leaning his head back so it bumped against Eve's leg.

Eve reached out and splayed her fingers into his hair, brushing her fingertips against his scalp as she slowly raked her fingers through his silky black locks. He hummed appreciatively as she repeated the motion.

As she reveled in all the decadent dopamine that was being released, watching the MacManus brothers brawling with Coach Beiste from *Glee* over the "rule of thumb," she wondered why this wasn't enough. It should be *more* than enough. She just needed to convince herself that it *was* enough.

She didn't need love. This was as close to the flame as she was willing to get. Johnny Cash could keep his burning ring of fire. That shit was dangerous.

29
Am I a Monster?

"Never say never, princess," Dagon remarked smugly. "I told you. And mmm...what a show."

Eve was in her living room, still sitting in Zeke's lap, but Eoduun was no longer there.

No, not Zeke's lap. There was something about the feel of his body against hers that was distinctly Dagon. Had Zeke fallen asleep and let Dagon out? Had Eoduun gone back to his apartment?

Dagon entrapped her in his steel arms before she could wriggle away. He held her cheek against his chest with an unyielding hand and stroked her hair softly with his thumb. Her mouth went dry as she understood she was completely at his mercy. Was that hand on her head the same one that ripped Shira's throat out? And if she *was* a monster, a lilim, or something of the sort, did that mean that he was free to kill her if he felt like it? Free to do with her what he pleased?

"As tired as I am of sharing you, I can't say I didn't enjoy watching you give in to your true nature," Dagon confessed. He buried his face in her hair and inhaled deeply. "It was glorious. You fucking loved it, too, didn't you, princess?"

What did he mean by her 'true nature'?

It was then that she came to the startling realization that, if she was a monster, Dagon would *know*. He could see monsters for what they were.

"Am I a monster?" she blurted.

Dagon's thumb paused mid-stroke in her hair, but only briefly. "What kind of a question is that?" he laughed derisively.

"A serious one."

"What, because you dipped your toes into a little depravity? That hardly makes one a monster."

"Zephlyn suggested there might be something wrong with me." She didn't know how much information was safe or smart to share with him.

"I assure you, there's nothing *wrong* with you. You're my perfect little princess."

"Yes or no, am I a monster?" she demanded boldly.

"It's such a vague term, isn't it? Am *I* a monster? I don't think so. Do you?"

"You are a monster. You aren't human."

Dagon laughed mockingly. "Is that the criteria? Humans can't be monsters? Monsters can't be human?" He put his mouth close to her ear. "I think you know better than that. Humans are the worst monsters to ever walk the Earth."

He wasn't wrong. "Fine. Am I something other than human?"

"Anyone with a specialty is something other than human. I guess you are all monsters, hm?"

"Am I a lilim?!" she hissed.

She felt his lips stretch into a smile against her ear. "Now where did you hear that?" he asked, his tone dripping with amusement.

"Am I or not?"

"You know, it occurs to me that I have something that *you* want now. I also have something that your entire organization *desperately* wants and will never get without me. Is it really in my best interest to hand everything over without getting something in return? What's my motivation?"

"Being a decent fucking person isn't motivation enough?"

"But you seem pretty damn sure that I'm a monster, not a person. Are you changing your stance, now?"

"You know what I mean."

"But do *you* know what you mean? You contradict yourself constantly."

"What the fuck do you want?"

"You. All to myself."

"Absolutely not happening."

"Your firstborn."

"Fuck off."

Dagon stopped stroking her hair and slid his hand under her jaw, tilting her head up to look at him. His vermilion eyes bore down into hers with a fiery intensity that incinerated every ounce of strength from her limbs.

"Let me plant my seed inside you."

Every inch of her skin broke out in goosebumps, and an icy heat spread its tendrils from her scalp to her toes. She was burning up and freezing all at once. Her voice vanished, but it was of no consequence. Her brain had ceased to function and it couldn't tell her voice what sounds to make anyway.

When she finally found her voice, it was weak. "Never."

How could he even ask for that?! It was preposterous. She had no plans of ever having children, let alone *his*. She'd never been more grateful for the IUD she'd had implanted last year. No babies for her for the next few years…and, as it turned out, no periods, either. She was one of the lucky ones who stopped having periods altogether.

But even if it *did* happen, how would that even work, anyway? Wouldn't it be Zeke's child?

No, maybe not. When he took over Zeke's body, it did physically change. Gill slits and red eyes. Did that mean that his gametes would be unique from Zeke's, as well? Would they make little evil god babies?

"Never say never, princess," he repeated in a low, arrogant tone, then kissed her neck lightly.

How could he so thoroughly disgust her, terrify her, and arouse her simultaneously?

"I'm not here to spit out babies for you," she seethed.

He chuckled with his lips against her skin. "That's true. You prefer to swallow them."

"You're fucking disgusting."

"And you fucking love it."

"I hate you."

Dagon paused, and his fingers tensed around her jaw. He raised his head and leveled a hard gaze down on her. "That's not very nice, princess. Be careful. You might hurt my feelings."

"You don't have feelings. You're a monster."

His eyes darkened. "You understand nothing of the depths of my emotions. If you did, you wouldn't dare to play these games with me. You haven't an inkling of the patience I've exercised with you," he simmered. He squeezed her jaw harder. "Don't *ever* tell me you hate me again."

Every fiber of Eve's being wanted to flee, but she was frozen under his gaze, captive in his arms. As a general rule, she was in no way weak or afraid to defend herself, but right now, she was a fawn, cowering in the tall grass, hoping to be passed over as his next meal.

His lips descended upon hers with ferocity. He bit her lip hard enough to make it bleed as he kissed her, and his tongue lapped it up before aggressively conquering her mouth. She whimpered against him.

"No struggle tonight?" he complained breathily. "Don't tell me I broke you already."

Those words sparked her anger. "Don't flatter yourself." But she still made no move to fight him. She was trapped in his arms, but in this curled up position, there wasn't much he could do to her other than hold her to him and kiss her. If he wanted to do anything else, he would have to reposition his arms and her body, and if he did that, she would have an opening.

She wouldn't waste her energy struggling away from a kiss that, if she was honest, wasn't entirely unpleasant anyway.

He gave an amused grunt, then licked the blood on her lip again. "This just doesn't have the same effect as the real thing," Dagon sighed. "Which brings us back full circle. I tell you what: I'll make a deal with you. I'll answer one question for you – *any* question – if you give yourself to me in the waking world. Just once. With blood."

"I won't let you put a goddamn baby in me, Dagon."

"I'm not asking for that. Just practice. Just one night while Zeke is sleeping."

"I'm not whoring myself out to you for a simple answer."

"Then just fuck me because you want to. You were begging me to fuck you last night in your dreams, so I *know* you want it. And, hey, the answer will be a happy perk. Or unhappy. I guess it depends on the question."

"No."

Dagon whistled. "Damn, you are a tough negotiator. Do you even *want* the answers? You don't actually want to know, do you?" He grinned. "Because if you did want to know, nothing would stop you from learning the truth. You have the perfect excuse to let yourself go with me like you did with Zeke and Eoduun, and you're still depriving yourself. And me."

"It's a matter of self-respect, all right? I'll fuck who I want to fuck *because* I want to fuck. Not because I want something else out of it."

"Oh, so you'll fuck for free, but you better not get anything in return," Dagon mocked.

"Don't twist it. You know that's not what I'm saying."

"Fine. Last offer," he sighed. "Blood. I want to drink from you." He sneered. "From whatever location on your body I choose."

"You just did. From my lip."

"No, this is a dream. It isn't the same in here. I want the real thing."

Blood. That wasn't impossible. But could she give him blood and *not* want anything more? Could *he* stop at just a drink if no one else was around to step in and stop him from taking it further? She shouldn't. It felt like a trick. She couldn't trust him.

But…she desperately needed to know if she was a monster.

"Ok. Fine. But how do I know you'll stick to your word?"

"Oh, that's easy. You don't. But we can shake on it if it makes you feel better."

"Cross your heart and hope to die."

Dagon scoffed, then laughed out loud. With his arm still around her, he moved his hand toward his chest and drew a cross over it. "Stick a needle in my eye."

"And you promise that you actually *have* the answer to my question? You *do* know whether I'm a monster or not?"

"I promise I have the answer to that."

"And you can't drink so much blood that it's dangerous for me."

"Wouldn't dream of it, princess." He smiled at her with an unusually earnest expression. His face almost could've been mistaken for Zeke's at that moment, if not for the red eyes and gill slits. He'd been absolutely terrifying a few moments ago. Now he looked like a soft puppy. Well…a homicidal puppy, maybe.

Eve woke up to the sound of Bo clearing his throat, and when she opened her eyes, he was surveying the sleeping trio from the doorway. She lifted her head from Zeke's chest and carefully withdrew her hand from Eoduun's shoulder, sliding it out from beneath his hand. She unwrapped her leg from across Eoduun's torso and rolled off of Zeke's lap. She stood up and stretched, raising her hands high into the air and groaning.

Judging by the progress of the movie, she'd been out for about forty-five minutes.

"Good to see everyone getting along so swimmingly," Bo remarked. "No corpse feet complaints tonight?"

"If there were, I wasn't awake for them."

Bo was uneasy. He glanced over at Zeke, who appeared to be out cold. "How long were you asleep? Any...visitors?" he asked cautiously.

Eve's raised brows and darting eyes gave the answer away before she had a chance to check herself.

Bo's lips tightened. "Hm. Bad?"

What was she supposed to say? She didn't want to tell him that Dagon had scared the ever-living hell out of her. She didn't want to tell him that Dagon wanted to be her baby daddy. And she *most certainly* couldn't tell him she'd just made a deal with Dagon. Hadn't she specifically been told *not* to make any deals with Dagon? Fuck, she had. But it was just a little blood. It had nothing to do with anyone else. Just her. So no one else needed to know.

She shook her head and tried to be casual. "Not really. No worse than usual."

Bo was scrutinizing her for what she wasn't saying, per usual. Sometimes she hated how perceptive he was, and then how he wouldn't say a damn thing about what he'd picked up. How he would look at her, and in an instant, she knew that he knew, and that he knew that she knew that he knew, but he would make no open comment about it one way or another. He spoke through his eyes and body language, and it was how he read others.

Maybe that was the real reason for his mask. It was his way of trying to hide the things he didn't want read on his face. Unfortunately for him, his eyes did more talking than his mouth ever could.

"Hm," he grunted simply. He looked down at the bandages on her finger and leg. "I smelled your blood earlier. What happened?"

"Oh, I dropped the knife making dinner. No biggie."

"Hm," he replied, saying no more about it. He walked up to Zeke and patted him firmly on the shoulder, then used his foot to nudge Eoduun. "Bedtime, children. Go brush your teeth and get in your jammies."

Zeke groaned and stirred, but Eoduun was dead to the world.

"Bo?" Zeke asked in confusion as he blinked up at his captain. "What are you doing here so late?" He looked at Bo's flannel pajama pants and white t-shirt. "And why are you here in your pajamas?"

"I needed to meet with Eve. You boys should head back to your apartments and get some rest. It's getting late."

Zeke stretched and nudged Eoduun with his leg. "Eoduun." He shook his shoulders. "Eoduuuuuuun…"

Eoduun grumbled and tried to lay down on the floor.

"Is he *always* such a pain to wake up?" Eve wondered.

Zeke replied, "If he falls asleep at night, yeah. But he's usually the first one up in the morning." He stood up and hoisted Eoduun over his shoulder like a sack of potatoes. Literally, like he weighed no more than a sack of potatoes. Eve often forgot how preternaturally strong Zeke was. He was always so careful and gentle that it was easy to forget that he could throw her couch through the wall if he so pleased.

"Goodnight! I'll see you guys in the morning," Zeke said on his way out. Bo closed and locked the door after him.

When Eve and Bo were alone, Bo said, "Luc said you weren't answering your phone."

Eve picked up her phone. Four missed messages, three missed calls, and one voicemail. She hated to admit that those notifications brought her immense satisfaction.

She opened the texts.

How was your day, love?

Are you busy?

Call me back when you can. I'd love to hear your voice.

She listened to the voicemail.

"You wouldn't be avoiding me, would you, love? I just wanted to call and tell you I miss you and let you know I'm going to be delayed a little longer. Call me back, please."

Delayed longer. Why did that piss her off so much? She tossed her phone onto the couch and brushed past Bo on her way to the kitchen.

"Something wrong?"

"I'm fine."

"Are you going to call him back?"

"No."

"He's not going to be able to sleep until you do."

"He's the one who doesn't want to come home."

"Evie."

She didn't have to look at him. The tone of his voice told her exactly what he thought. She was being petty and childish. Like she didn't know that already.

What the hell was wrong with her? Just call him.

This is why you will always end up alone.

She turned around, and Bo was standing behind her, holding her phone out to her. "Call the fool. Please."

She snatched the phone from him and sighed reluctantly. "Fine. If it'll make you feel better."

Bo grabbed a banana from the bowl on the counter and sat down at his usual spot at the bar at the kitchen island. Eve grabbed a bag of white cheddar rice chips from the cupboard and hit the call button on Luc's notifications. She sat down next to Bo and tore the bag open.

The phone barely rang once before Luc answered.

"Hello, love. I was beginning to think you were angry with me," he said.

His voice cascaded over her like a warm, calming blanket. Goddammit.

"Who says I'm not?" she retorted.

"Are you?" He sounded anything but upset about the prospect.

"I just think it would be better if you were here, with everything that's going on. But you keep delaying your return."

"Ready to admit you miss me?"

"I think everyone would be more comfortable with you here. I don't think Bo likes being in charge," she said, giving Bo a sideways glance. He dipped his head in absentminded agreement.

"Do you want me to come home?" Luc asked.

Yes. No. She wouldn't ask for that. "Just do whatever it is you need to do. What is it you're doing, anyway? Still dealing with the shapeshifter fallout?"

"No, that's been wrapped up. But something similar happened at another one of our establishments tonight. Ruth again. I feel like I'm chasing my tail. I'm following a possible lead, but this nonsense is taking longer than I expected."

"Is it dangerous?"

"For me?" He laughed uproariously.

"I know you're strong, but you aren't invincible."

"Are you worried about me?" he asked hopefully.

"Just don't hurt yourself while I'm not there to heal you."

"You miss me *and* you're worried about me. I could get used to this."

"I didn't say either of those things."

"Subtext, love."

"Just hurry up, ok? I'm going to go to bed with your brother now," she jabbed.

He gave a short laugh. "*And* you want to make me jealous. Is it my birthday or something?"

"Goodnight, Luc," she exhaled.

"Goodnight, love," he said sweetly. "Don't let my big brother bite."

She ended the call and set the phone on the counter in front of her.

"You didn't touch your chips," Bo pointed out.

Oh yeah. She'd forgotten about them the second she'd heard Luc's voice.

"I changed my mind. I'd rather have real chips, anyway. Would it have killed Luc to have stocked some normal food in the cupboards?"

She rolled the bag back up and put them away. She didn't know what she was complaining about. She liked rice chips just fine. "Are you ready for bed?"

"That is why I'm here," he replied.

Eve walked into the bedroom after brushing her teeth, and Bo was already in bed. He was again lying on his back, hands folded behind his head, as close to the edge of the bed as he could get without falling off. And his mask was off. He regarded her with those mismatched stone and ice eyes.

He was so ruggedly handsome.

She shut off the light. She approached the bed on his side and purposely climbed over him to get into bed, just for her own amusement.

"There are two other sides of this bed you could have used," he stated, indicating the foot of the bed and the opposite side of the bed.

"This was the shortest route," she said simply, snuggling up next to him. She rested her head on his chest and draped her arm over his stomach.

"You don't have to be touching me for the veil to block you from Dagon."

"But I want to. Does it bother you?"

"It doesn't *bother* me. I was just saying…"

"You don't like it?"

"I didn't say that, either."

"Not a snuggler?"

"Not as a general rule."

"Do you want me to stop?" she asked disappointedly, withdrawing her arm and lifting her head from his chest to pout at him.

He sighed. "Oh, for fuck's sake. Come here. Don't look at me like that," he grumbled as he reached out and snatched her wrist, pulling her hand back over his stomach. His other hand pressed her head back to his chest. He allowed his hands to linger for a few moments, but then he returned them to their interlaced position behind his head.

She grinned and closed her eyes. "Thanks, Daddy," she whispered.

"Don't even start," he said with exasperation.

She lay with her cheek against Bo's soft, clean white t-shirt, the steady beat of his heart drumming against her ear as his chest rose and fell gently with each even breath. His scent was light and woodsy, like being wrapped in fresh flannel sheets in a warm cabin. Everything about him comforted her.

Even so, Eve couldn't sleep. Her mind wouldn't rest. She worried about what Zephlyn had told her. She worried about making that deal with Dagon that she probably shouldn't have made. Definitely shouldn't have made. She worried about Luc being gone. She worried about Bo turning on her if she was something *other*.

Bo suddenly exhaled heavily. "I can't sleep until you do."

"How did you know I wasn't sleeping?"

"I can tell. Are you uncomfortable?"

"No. Not even remotely."

"Then what's on your mind?"

"Too much."

"Want to talk about it?"

"Yes and no," she answered ambiguously.

Instead of prying further, Bo just waited. If she wanted to talk, she would talk.

"Do you hate Dizzy?" she asked.

"What? *That's* keeping you awake? No, I don't hate Dizzy. I just don't trust Dizzy."

"Is it because he's a monster?"

"It's because he hurts people. You saw what he did to Zephlyn. He doesn't mean to, but he's clumsy. And last year, he tried to stop taking his meds without telling anyone, and he had a meltdown that took two teams to get him under control. He just...concerns me."

"Meds?"

"Dizzy has some emotional issues that are exacerbated by his...condition. It's usually fairly well-managed, but when he's doing especially well, he thinks he doesn't need his meds anymore. And then he lapses, and, as a shapeshifter with inhuman strength, he becomes incredibly dangerous to everyone, including himself."

"So it isn't that you hate monsters in general, then."

"Uh, well…I don't *love* them. It is our job to hunt and kill them when they threaten people's lives. I think a 'good' monster is the exception, not the rule. I would call Kai an exception. His curse line has been used to protect people from other monsters for generations."

"But not Dizzy."

"Why this sudden interest in Dizzy?" Bo asked.

"If I was a monster, would you hate me?"

"You can't be a monster," he replied simply.

"But what if it turned out that I was? Would you think differently of me?"

"You think I'm that shallow and narrow-minded? I like you for you, monster or not. That being said, if you started killing people and turned on us, it would break my heart to have to stop you. But I *would* stop you."

Well, that was dark and not at all comforting. Was he thinking about Ruth?

"But, like I said," he continued, "you *can't* be a monster. You're a blood healer. So, no need to worry. Now, go to sleep."

"Isn't it weird that I have other abilities, though? Like, the fact that my blood has a buttload of aphrodisiac in it? Or that I have premonitions? Or that Eoduun says I started to reach back into his mind when he was reading me once? Isn't it a little odd to you?"

"Having multiple specialties isn't unheard of. Being special doesn't make you a monster, Evie."

"Is Ruth a monster?"

Bo was thoughtful for a few moments before answering. "Ruthie wasn't born a monster. She's been made into a monster by circumstances."

"You and Luc seem to have very different feelings about her," Eve observed.

"Luc doesn't understand her."

"And you do?"

"You could say that. We were in the same shoes, in a sense. My father and Sharon – Ruthie and Luc's mother – couldn't be bothered to spend their limited free time with the wolf bastard and the little girl who hadn't inherited the *eyes*. They poured everything they had into Luc. Their golden boy. The heir. The one with the looks, the eyes, the powers, the brains. Ruthie and I were always an afterthought. It didn't bother me as much, especially considering I wasn't brought into the family until I was almost ten, when my mom died. I was used to being looked at as an outsider in my father's family. But Ruthie shouldn't have been raised like that. The nanny knew Ruthie better than Sharon did. Sharon would give her a pat on the head when she was around, and that was the extent of their relationship. Meanwhile, Sharon was attending all of Luc's school functions, getting him tutors, taking him shopping and out for lunch. He would go to work with our father quite often, too, to learn the ins and outs of the business.

"Luc isn't to blame, either. He didn't take particular advantage of the favoritism, but that's probably because he was so oblivious to it. It was just how everything was to him – all he'd ever known. He didn't know any differently. That was normal for him. It didn't help that he's so damn self-centered, it didn't occur to him to look at anyone else but himself. He had no idea what anyone around him was going through. He was too busy being perfect to care.

"And he had no idea that Ruthie idolized him. She was obsessed with him. She followed him around when he was home and waited by the window for him when he was gone. He would give her little trinkets sometimes when he could be bothered to take notice of her, and she treasured them as her most precious possessions. She had a special shelf in her room for them, like a shrine to Luc.

"But *I* was the one who was always watching out for her. I was the one who helped her when she was learning witchcraft from Sharon's old books, because, of course, Sharon couldn't be bothered to teach her the craft she was most skilled in. All of Sharon's training went to Luc. It was me who had to explain all those things moms are supposed to explain to their daughters when they come of age. It was me who had to warn her about boys and all the things fathers are supposed to explain to their daughters. It was me who held her hair when she came home drunk, and it was me who comforted her when yet another boy broke her heart.

"And it was me who assured her she was special and loved, because no one else could be bothered to. So, to say that Luc and I have very different feelings about Ruthie is an understatement. He doesn't *know* Ruthie. And he can never understand how growing up ignored, stepped on, and cast aside can make someone crave power and admiration, regardless of what it takes to get it. For someone who has always had power, that's an incomprehensible thing.

"She tried so hard to earn any kind of acknowledgement. Any kind of praise or admiration. But it didn't matter how hard she worked or how skilled she became with her witchcraft, no one noticed. No one cared. No one but me. But I wasn't enough. How could I be? I was the least important person in her life. She needed her parents to notice her. She needed Luc to notice her. She needed her family to care about her.

"She was made into this. She craves the attention she never got. She wants to be powerful, and to be *seen* as powerful, and admired. If she can't get love, she'll take fear. If she can't have the family she always wanted, she'll make one with monsters and play house with an ancient god. I couldn't stop her from becoming a monster, no matter how hard I tried. Love can fix a lot of things, but you can't love the hate out of someone. But it doesn't mean she can't be saved. She doesn't have to die. I think Luc could bring her back, I really do. But, if he can't, or won't…I'm fully prepared to be the one who has to put her down. If I can't save her, I can save everyone from her."

The air was heavy with Bo's story. Eve hated what Ruth had done, hated that she posed such a risk to Eve and her team and Luc, but it was a little harder to hate Ruthie, the little girl who hadn't inherited the *eyes*.

30

Does It Make Your Heart Go *Doki Doki?*

Bo said that it wasn't Luc's fault that he was raised the way he was, but it did make Eve wonder what kind of warped mentality that favoritism had created in Luc. He was charismatic, ambitious, and a natural leader, but he was also arrogant, narcissistic, and ostentatious. She could never tell if his feelings were genuine, or if they only seemed that way because he was so good at putting up a front. A façade. He was someone who got what he wanted, one way or another. Sometimes she wondered if he and Dagon were just two sides of the same coin.

Despite all of that, she couldn't shake him.

"I can't help but feel like that family dynamic had to have fucked up Luc, too," Eve opined. "Being spoiled rotten doesn't usually create a well-adjusted individual."

"Oh, he wasn't spoiled rotten," Bo said. "Yes, he got all the attention, but he also got all the pressure. Everything – the family fortune, Sharon and Father's hopes and dreams, the future of the company, the family name and reputation – it all fell on Luc's shoulders. He was permitted nothing less than perfection. He had to be better than Father's friends' kids. Better than everyone else. If he wasn't the best, he was a failure. 'Second place is just first place for losers' was our father's favorite saying. He got all their attention, sure, but they made him earn their love."

Oh. Well. That was fucked up.

"How did *you* come out of all that relatively normal?"

Bo grunted. "I had ten formative years with someone who loved me the way a parent is supposed to love their child, even though I wasn't actually hers."

"Wait, what?"

"My mom wasn't my biological mother."

"Jesus Christ, you're giving me whiplash, Bo."

"Too much excitement for a bedtime story?" he teased.

Eve threw her leg over his and adjusted her position slightly to get more comfortable, then mumbled, "Go on."

"Not much to tell, really. All I know is what my mom told me. Well, technically, she was my aunt. She said that my birth mother and my father were in love once. They were engaged to be married when she got pregnant with me. As my mom told it, there was a pack of werewolves that were out to get my father because of his association with hunters, and one night, they attacked my mother while he was away on business. They turned her rather than killing her. They knew that was worse. A turned werewolf has no hope of controlling their curse.

"Instead of killing her, my father had a special room made to contain her. He kept her there until I was born, because he thought he wanted to at least have the one thing they had created together. But when I was born, and he had to kill her, he couldn't stand to look at me. He just saw the monster inside me, the curse she'd passed on to me in the womb. I reminded him of what he'd had to do to the woman he loved. It made him hate me. So, he gave me to my mother's sister. She was the only mom I knew, and she was the best mom in the whole goddamn world. I still miss her, even now. I wish I could've saved her, but cancer is one monster I don't know how to kill.

"When she died, my father only took me in out of a sense of obligation. He still hated me. He will always hate me. But he let me live in his mansion and kept me clothed and fed and let me get to know my brother and sister. I'm grateful for that, at least. It could've been a lot worse for me."

Eve lay silently. Monsters were the reason his father hated him, essentially. Of course Bo hated them, even if he didn't want to say it as blatantly as that. But he didn't hate his father. He didn't hate Luc, or Ruth, or his birth mother. He hated the things that perpetuated the cycle of hate. He hated the things that tore families apart and broke hearts and stole lives they had no right to steal.

And Eve was fairly certain that Bo hated himself most of all, for all the people he felt he failed, for all the people he couldn't save, and for the monster inside him. He shouldered blame that didn't belong to him.

She rubbed her thumb back and forth over his upper obliques where her hand was resting on his side. She wondered if his self-hatred could be loved away. That kind of hate is the hardest to love away.

She knew a thing or two about that.

"Bo?" she whispered.

"Hm?"

"You're a good man," she said softly.

Bo said nothing in response, but he lowered his hands from behind his head and draped one arm over Eve's shoulders.

"Goodnight, Evie," he whispered.

Eve awoke alone in the morning. Her phone alarm was blaring at her bedside, plugged into the charger. She was pretty sure she'd forgotten it on the kitchen counter again last night. Bo must've brought it in and plugged it in for her when he got up. She shut off the 6AM alarm and wondered how early Bo had gotten up. She also saw that she had a text from Luc in the notifications on her lock screen. It had come in an hour earlier.

She never understood morning people. She'd rather stay up all night to do something at 5AM than to sleep for six hours and have to wake up at 5AM.

Good morning, beautiful. Text me when you get up.

She heard her apartment door open. She was starting to recognize the unique sound of Bo in her apartment. He opened the door, kicked off his shoes, shut the door, and walked to the kitchen island. Two cup bottoms and a phone clunked against the countertop, and the barstool slid out. A quiet creak of the stool as he sat in his usual spot, then silence as he read shojo manga on his phone and waited for her to get up.

She stretched and rolled out of bed. She padded out to the kitchen in her bare feet and pajamas, phone in hand.

"*Ohayou*," Bo greeted her kindly.

"Morning." She slid onto the barstool next to him and took a sip of the bitter black brew. "*Arigatou,*" she said with a little grin.

"How did you sleep?" he asked. "Any dreams?"

She had to stop and think for a moment. "No. Actually, *none* at all. Which is weird for me. And hey, if you're supposed to be protecting me from Dagon in my sleep, why did you leave while I was still sleeping?"

"Relax. I woke up Zeke on my way out. I don't think Dagon can do his little trick when Z is awake." Bo took a drink of his coffee, then asked, "Did you hear from Luc this morning? Apparently there was some buzz in the group chat last night that we missed. Luc is annoyed that I wasn't monitoring it. At 2AM." "I don't even know if I am part of it. I don't have any notifications."

"It's an app. I downloaded it this morning after Luc ripped me a new one. I dropped the ball. But still. 2AM. Come on."

"What's going on?"

Bo handed her his phone so she could read the group chat. From the conversation, Eve learned that Celeste had been using facial recognition to scour security footage around the country, looking for any signs of Ruth, and last night, she had a hit in Tulsa, Oklahoma. It was footage from a doorbell camera, and it showed someone who looked like Ruth coming and going a couple of times. Celeste got an address for the doorbell location, and tasked Levi with remotely scoping out the place.

While Levi was sweeping, Remi joined the chat to share what he'd found out about Lilith's grimoire. The good news for them was that the spells in it couldn't be photographed, transferred, or copied to anything else – according to the lore, any copied material would disappear or disintegrate within minutes – which meant that if Knighco got the grimoire, there was no chance that Ruthlys would still have copies of it. The bad news was that it was essentially a cookbook for every nasty creature out there, even the ones that had been extinct for millennia, and it purportedly contained powerful alchemy spells and formulas that were more powerful than anything in recent history. The only limitations were what ingredients Ruth could get her hands on. And, according to what Remi read, many of those spells called for, literally, the Blood of Eve. Panacea Blood.

Levi came back into the chat and said that it was definitely Ruth's hideout. Except it wasn't so much of a hideout as it was a mansion that she'd invaded and occupied. It looked to Levi as though she had turned all the domestic workers and the family who owned the house into her own indentured servants. He then informed the group that he thought he may have been had.

I thought she was sleeping, but she opened her eyes and looked right at me, like she could see me, and said, "Oh, we have company." I quickly returned after that. Guys, I think it's possible she knows we found her, Levi wrote.

Celeste replied, *Oh, ya fuckin think?! Somebody go get Bo. We need to send a team.*

Remi, a few minutes later, said, *He's not answering his door or his phone. I'll try Luc.*

They went back and forth about not being able to reach either of them. Then came the message that ruined Eve's day.

Celeste said, *I'll try Mira. She's with Luc right now.*

Eve couldn't concentrate on the rest of the messages. The gist of it was that nobody could get ahold of anyone until almost 5AM when Luc finally answered the phone and dispatched three teams.

Eve's chest was filled with bees. Buzzing, stinging, swarming. She remembered Luc ignoring his phone when the two of them were in bed together the other night, and couldn't help but wonder if that was the reason no one could get ahold of him or Mira last night. Because they were together. She swallowed the lump in her throat and slid Bo's phone back toward him.

"Huh," she grunted, staring blankly at her coffee cup.

"Yeah. If I'd seen this when it happened, I could've sent a team right then. It takes almost eight hours to get to Tulsa from here. We lost three hours because I had my phone silenced. The one fucking time."

"What about Luc? Why didn't he answer his phone?"

"He was sleeping. But it wasn't his responsibility anyway. I'm in charge of shit here while he's gone."

"Couldn't Luc just teleport over there and catch her?"

"Without backup? No. Besides, he's out of juice. He just made a big jump last night."

I fucking bet he did.

No. She had no right to be mad. Just look at what *she* was doing last night. And it only proved why she couldn't love him. She became completely unreasonable when it came to him. Well…more unreasonable than usual. He would just make her crazy. Well…more crazy than usual.

Bo continued, "So, Teams Beta, Delta and Flannel should be arriving at Ruthie's hideout at about 1PM. Although, with Ruger's driving, Team Flannel might get there before noon. If Luc didn't have the jet, they could've taken that, but not much we could do about that. Either way, we'll have to wait and see what happens. Luc will meet them there in the jet." Bo sighed regretfully. "I just wish I could've gone with them."

"Why couldn't you go?"

"Well, we couldn't exactly deliver you and Zeke right into her hands, now could we?"

"But you could've gone without us."

"I'm not leaving you to fend for yourself," he replied firmly.

"I'm sure I would be fine for a day or two."

"Your safety is my responsibility. I can't just leave you for a day or two. Especially right now, with Dagon and Ruthie both posing a danger to you. Not to mention, I need to run things here, as well."

"You have a lot on your plate, Bo."

"Mm-hm," he hummed. "So, let's get ready for the day and get to training while we wait for news."

Eve looked down at her phone while she drank her coffee, staring at Luc's text.

Good morning, beautiful. Text me when you get up.

He didn't call her "love." He always called her "love." Did it mean something? And there was only one single text. From an hour ago. Usually, he sent two or three if she didn't respond right away. It sounded so cold, too. Flat. Or maybe that's just how she was interpreting it...

No. She needed to stop over-analyzing a goddamn text. He wasn't her boyfriend. She wasn't in love with him. He was bad for her and she for him, and she was letting him get too close. She should just leave it alone. He could bide his time with *Mira*.

"What happened?" Bo asked Eve, looking down at his phone instead of her. She raised a questioning brow at him. He looked over at her and elaborated, "You've been out of sorts since you read the group chat. Why?"

"What is that app? I need to download it," Eve changed the subject.

Bo blinked at her, but decided to let it go. If she didn't want to talk, she didn't want to talk. "Here, I can find it for you and get you signed in." He took her phone, then when he saw it was opened to Luc's messages, he said, "Oh, did you want to respond to this first?"

"No."

He shook his head. "Ok…"

While he was messing around on her phone, she glanced over at his phone sitting face-up on the counter. She leaned slightly forward so she could see the screen better.

There was a scanned black and white manga page open on the screen, and the scene showed a young man with his hand aggressively pressed against the wall next to a young woman's head, his body close to hers as he looked down at her with scowling eyes. The girl looked up at him, her back against the wall, her innocent eyes wide and frightened and her hands clasped together against her chest, which was surrounded by *doki-doki-doki's*. Both characters had little hash marks on their cheeks under their eyes to indicate blushing.

Eve reached out to scroll to the next page, but Bo's hand shot out and snatched up the phone, covering the screen.

"Hey!" he cried, clearly embarrassed.

"Your face is doing what that guy's face was doing," Eve teased, drawing imaginary hash marks on her cheeks with her fingers.

"Here, you're in the chat," he grumbled, shoving her phone at her.

"What happens next?" she cajoled, trying to see his phone screen. "Do they fall in love? Does he kiss her? Does she cry and run away? The suspense is killing me!"

"Sometimes I get the feeling that you respect me far too little as your captain," he replied sternly.

"Says the man reading girly romance manga. Does it make your heart go *doki doki*?"

"Men are allowed to appreciate romance stories, too," he defended, his blush deepening. He took his coffee and stood up. "I'm going to go see what Zeke is doing. Get dressed and ready for the day and meet me across the hall." He went to the door and put his shoes on. Before he walked out, he turned and announced haughtily over his shoulder, "And for your information, yes, they do fall in love!"

As Team Alpha walked to the gym together, Eve's mind couldn't quit picking at what was revealed this morning about Ruth's hideout and the raid. She hoped everyone would come out of it all right. She was especially worried about Team Flannel. She was rather fond of them – Cassie in particular. She desperately wanted to be best friends with Cassie. She needed a girl friend who wouldn't be judgmental of her. One who wouldn't be interested in taking what was *hers*.

She wondered if Luc would come home after the raid. If all went well, and Ruth was caught, it was over, right? He could come home and quit chasing leads with *Mira*. He could get back to slowly but surely destroying Eve. Chipping away at her resolve and creeping under her skin; tearing bricks from her walls and digging holes under her barbed fences, just to get to her heart. Another conquest for his trophy wall, no doubt. And then he would throw her away.

Men like him don't fall in love.

And when he got back, he could do whatever he needed to do to keep Dagon out of her dreams, and Bo could go back to his own bed. And she could sleep alone again. All by herself. Cold.

She wondered if Bo's scent still lingered on her sheets. She could smell him on her pillow this morning when she woke up. It was such a comforting scent. He was such a comforting presence. *Such a handsome daddy,* she thought with a little grin.

She glanced over at him as he walked beside her. She wondered if he liked sleeping next to her, or if he was indifferent about it. She was pretty sure he didn't *hate* it. She liked it, probably more than she should have. When she was close to him, it was hard not to think about that night at the hotel when he came on to her and drank blood from her tongue. She wondered what kind of lover he would be. He was kind and thoughtful and careful, but when that scarred, dark eye flashed yellow, he became rough. Demanding. Primal. She could guarantee that his eye always turned yellow when he was aroused.

Stop that. She had no business thinking about that.

As they did some weight training and agility work in the gym, Eve noticed that Eoduun was in a surprisingly chipper mood today. She had a feeling yesterday's adventures may have had something to do with it. But she was surprised when, after training, he offered to take Eve to the library for crypto studies so Bo could work with Zeke on some defensive practice. Bo was reluctant to let Eve out of his sight, but Eoduun assured him Eve was safe with him as far as the library. He finally relented.

"It's unusual for you to want to spend time with me rather than Z," Eve said as they made their way to the library alone.

"I've been thinking about yesterday, when you were asking about Zeke's past. I wanted to try something, but I knew Bo and Zeke probably wouldn't be cool with it."

"If that's true, then what makes you think I'll be cool with it?"

"I want you to try to reach into my mind again, like you did when I read you. Are you cool with it?"

She hesitated. On one hand, she welcomed an opportunity to test any latent abilities she might have. On the other, she was harboring secrets that she didn't want Eoduun uncovering. What if he saw her memory with Zephlyn? Or her deal with Dagon?

"Why do you want me to do that?"

"Because I think you can. I've been curious about it ever since it happened. It makes sense that forging a link with someone else's mind could open myself up to a breach, but it had never happened before. If you can actually do this, I can help train you to use it, and you can help train me to figure out how to block it. Because if you can do it, there's a possibility others can, too, and I need to know how to protect myself from it."

"What does that have to do with Zeke's past?" Eve wondered.

"I have his memory. I want you to find it."

Eve was taken aback. "Why do you have his memory?"

"I erased him," Eoduun revealed. "But I only took the memories that hurt the most. He still knows what happened, because he made me promise to tell him about what he'd done after the memories were erased."

"Then why would he have you erase them at all?"

"He didn't want to lose the *knowledge* of what he'd done, but he wanted to be rid of the actual memories – the *reality* of what he'd done. It's the difference between reading about the horrors of war versus experiencing the horrors of war," Eoduun explained as they walked into the garage.

"Bo told me you didn't take people's traumatic memories."

"I make rare exceptions for the people I care about." He held the door open for her to the bunker. "So, are you in? Do you want to try to read my mind?"

"What if I don't want you to read mine?"

He raised a brow at her. "Keeping secrets?"

"No, I just don't necessarily want you peeping in on all my recent—" she cleared her throat, "— activities. It's personal."

Eoduun gave her a sly grin. "What if I just want to see one? A specific one. The only one I'll look at."

She narrowed her eyes at him and waited for him to elaborate.

"Yesterday. I want to see it from your POV."

Eve contemplated his proposal. "And you *swear* you won't look at anything else?"

"Nothing else. I don't want your secrets. Just put it at the forefront of your mind, and I won't have to rifle."

They walked into the library, and Eoduun shut the door behind him. He walked up to Eve and rested his hands on her shoulders. "Ready?"

"Wait. I don't know how I'm supposed to try to push into your mind. I didn't actually *do* anything last time. Your feelings and thoughts just started flooding in."

"On my end, it felt like you pushed back when I opened the memories you didn't want me to see, and like you wanted to know what I felt about it. So, just try to focus on what I'm thinking and feeling to help you get in. Then try to look for painful memories of

Zeke. See if you can find it. Look for him playing football. The rest will cascade from it."

Eve took a deep breath, and Eoduun smiled down at her, his eyes glinting with anticipation. "Ok. Hit me," she said, steeling herself.

Eoduun's irises shifted from almost black to that deep purple again, and began to spin, just as she remembered. As it happened, she saw the memory of yesterday in the kitchen, looking down at Eoduun as he sucked the blood from her inner thigh, and Zeke coming up behind her, sucking her finger. Tongues, lips, fingertips, sexual energy electrifying every inch of her skin.

She wanted to stay there, relive that moment. But she came to her senses enough to realize she had work to do. Eoduun. In her memory, when she looked down at Eoduun with his tongue between her legs, she tried to put herself in his mind. What he was thinking. Tasting. Feeling.

It all flooded in, just like last time. The arousal. Swelling. Aching. Need. Desire.

She was in. She was surrounded by thoughts and memories that didn't belong to her, floating images and fleeting feelings, words, sounds, tastes.

Zeke. She was looking for Zeke playing football. Something sad.

The memories all started to shuffle around and move away from her mind's eye, but one came pushing forward, and she fell into it.

She was seeing through Zeke's eyes. He was elated, heart rate high, evading the defense as he sought out an open receiver. There! Cassidy was open! In his heightened state and release of adrenaline, the ball left his hands with entirely too much power behind it. It felt strange. Where did all that power come from all of a sudden?

He watched the ball rocket toward Cassidy. Too fast. Too high. He was never going to be able to catch that. He'd fumble. Fuck.

But then something terrifying happened. The ball struck Cassidy in the front of his helmet, wedging itself between the guard and the top, and the force of it snapped Cassidy's head back. Too far. Too hard.

Cassidy crumpled to the ground. Zeke's heart stopped. His stomach flipped. What had he done?! The field erupted into mayhem. He ran to Cassidy, but he was afraid to see. He pushed through the other players surrounding his friend, and when he saw Cassidy lying on the ground, he wished he hadn't looked.

His head was twisted strangely, the football projecting from his helmet – but it had gone in too far. His face was covered in blood from the impact. Zeke's stomach suddenly lurched, and he spit out his mouth guard as vomit rose in his throat. He retched.

With horror, he knew. Cassidy was dead. He'd killed him. He'd killed his friend. He was a killer.

He wanted to take it back so badly it burned. Take it back. Take it back. No, this can't be happening. It can't. It isn't real. Wake up. It isn't real. It can't be. He isn't a killer. Take it back. Take it back. *Take it back*. Cassidy was his best friend.

He killed his best friend.

He couldn't breathe. The air was rushing in and out of his lungs, but he couldn't breathe. He was going to die, too. The world was fading out. Blackness overtook his vision.

Eve was thrust into another memory. She was looking at Zeke's parents and his older brother, Zander, through Zeke's eyes.

"I'm not a freak!" Zeke shouted, emotions high. He couldn't believe his own brother would say that to him. He couldn't believe they wanted him out of the house. Why were they so afraid of him? It pissed him off. They were his family. They were supposed to love him and help him, not abandon him. He just wanted to hit something!

He punched the fridge in his frustration. The door crushed under the weight of his fist, folding around his hand like tin foil.

What the fuck. Why did he do that?! He looked over at his family again, and the terror in their eyes tore his heart to pieces. They feared for their life. They thought he would hurt them. No! He didn't want to hurt anyone!

What was wrong with him? Where had this Superman strength come from?! Was he cursed?!

"Mom, please don't look at me like that. Dad, Zander. I'm still me! I'll get it under control. I promise!"

He walked toward them, and they took a step back. His mom even yelped. She *yelped*. Because he approached her.

It hurt like hell. His insides were going through a meat grinder. "Mom," he said softly, walking toward her with his hands held out invitingly. The tears were burning in his eyes as his voice cracked. "Mom, please."

"Stay the fuck away from her," Zander said with false bravado. He was just as terrified as everyone else.

"I'm not going to hurt anyone!" Zeke cried, the hot tears beginning to stream down his face. He looked to his mom with pleading eyes. "You're my family. I love you," he whispered as his voice left him.

"If you love us, you'll leave," his dad said quietly.

He was crushed, utterly and completely. Where was he supposed to go? His best friend was dead, and he wasn't even welcome to the funeral. His friends weren't talking to him. His girlfriend had left him. Everyone was giving him a wide berth and fearful glances.

His senior year wasn't supposed to be like this.

He was a monster. Everyone hated him, even the people who were supposed to love him unconditionally.

"Can I at least give you a hug before I go?" he asked his mom.

"Are you fucking serious?" Zander snapped, getting in Zeke's face. "You'll fucking crush her like an empty water bottle, you *freak*!"

A moment of rage was all it took, and Zander was in a heap across the room. All he'd done was push him away. He didn't want him in his face, that was all. A little shove, and Zander had broken ribs. His mom shrieked and ran past him toward Zander.

"Mom!" Zeke cried, and he reached out for her, catching her by the arm.

And broke her wrist. He felt the bones snap under his fingers. She screamed and slapped him, struggling frantically to get away from him.

"I'm sorry! I'm so sorry! I didn't mean to!"

"Get the fuck out!" his dad screamed. "And stay the fuck away from us! You're no longer welcome here!"

He ran from the house with the clothes on his back and nothing else, got in his car, and drove away with burning tears in his eyes, a shattered heart, and acid eating a hole in his stomach.

Eve was suddenly flung from the memory back to reality. She stood there, blinking back tears, staring into Eoduun's dark brown, startled eyes.

"Wow, that was weird," Eoduun said, his face pale. "Did you get it? Did you find it?"

Eve nodded and swiped the tears from her eyes, sniffling. She wanted to run to Zeke and hug the fuck out of him. "It was awful. I felt everything."

"Just be grateful you're only stuck with a memory of a memory of it. I have it with me all the time."

"You took that burden for him. That was an incredibly selfless thing to do."

"I couldn't stand to see it hurting him anymore."

"I can't imagine Zeke putting this on you. He asked you to do this?"

"He doesn't know it's like this. And you can't ever tell him. It would kill him if he knew he was just passing his hell on to me. I made him believe it wouldn't be a big deal."

Eve pulled Eoduun into a bear hug while he stood there with his hands at his sides. She had a whole new respect and admiration for him.

"I'll never tell him," she promised. Eoduun was right. It would kill Zeke to know someone else was suffering in his place.

She dropped her arms and wiped her eyes again. She asked, "Were you still in my head when I was in yours? Did you get the memory you wanted?"

"Only the beginning of it. And then something weird happened."

31
Don't Tempt Me

Eoduun scratched the back of his head, looking utterly perplexed. "I went blank. Completely blank. I couldn't see your memories, or what you were seeing in mine. It was like you firewalled me from both of our heads for a time, and I was just chilling in limbo. I don't even know how that's possible. It was unsettling."

"I'm pretty sure you kicked me out at the end, though," Eve remarked.

"I did. But it took everything I had to force you out. I don't want to do that again," he said uneasily. "It felt dangerous. There was a moment when I was legitimately afraid that I would never get back into my own head and would float in limbo forever."

"Is that even possible?"

"I don't know what's possible anymore. I didn't think any of *this* was possible."

"I feel like I've been hearing a lot of that lately."

Eoduun gave her a mildly suspicious glance. "You're weird."

She barked a humorless laugh. "I've been hearing a lot of that, too."

"We need to tell Luc about this. We'll probably get reamed for being reckless and trying this without permission or supervision, but he needs to know. He might have some insight. He might know what it means."

Eve was afraid of what it meant. "Is it really that big of a deal, though?" she downplayed. "I mean, it's not like I can get into someone's head unless they get into mine first. That's not all that useful."

"I'm not totally convinced you can't open the connection yourself, with a little training. I just don't want to be the one you practice on. I hated that." Eoduun shuddered.

What was up with her? She felt like she was...powering up, maybe? Like something was awakening within her. Ever since she'd arrived here, she'd been evolving into someone – or *something* – she wasn't entirely sure she recognized. She was still *her*, of course, but she was becoming aware of an *energy* inside of her that she couldn't quite put her finger on. Up until now, she'd just attributed it to the Panacea Blood. But maybe that wasn't the whole story.

"I'll talk to Luc about it whenever he comes home," Eve said. "Maybe you should do some studying, too. See if you can find anything about it," Eve suggested.

"I planned to."

Eve looked for any books on Adam and Eve, Lilith, and lilim. She was more convinced than ever that she was something other than a simple blood healer.

Eve found so many differing accounts of the story of Adam and Eve and Lilith that it made her mind reel. It was a story that had been told over and over and altered through millennia. Even the name for Lilith was different depending upon the texts.

Lilith was an interesting character. She'd been portrayed as this immoral, child-killing or child-stealing monster who was kicked out of Eden, gave birth to horrific creatures and spent her time engaged in depravity and evil. But that wasn't what Eve perceived when she read many of the stories.

The stories that portrayed her in such poor light came from religions that viewed anything outside of bland sex only done with the purpose of reproduction as a thing of immorality. Women's reproductive parts were the property of their husbands, essentially.

Lilith dared to challenge that. She dared to consider herself his equal and felt she shouldn't have to submit to him. That didn't sound evil to Eve. She sounded like any woman of today. Well, other than giving birth to monsters and wanting revenge on God and men. Or…well…other than the giving birth to monsters part.

Lilim. Some lore says they were from Adam's stolen seed, some say they were from Lilith's dalliance with an angel, but most say they were created by Lilith alone. But many of the texts indicated that there were several hordes of lilim from Lilith and her various powerful partners. And it was just as Zephlyn had said: they were basically the queens of succubi, consumed by the desire for sex and the ruin of man. And they were supposed to have all been erased from existence a long time ago. Or, perhaps, gone into hiding.

There was one piece of lore, from an old book that had no title on the cover, that further unsettled her. It stated that lilim were capable of mental manipulation, able to reach into the minds of their victims to pull out their deepest desires, to bend their victims to their will, and to make their victims see the lilim as whatever form is most pleasing to them.

Eve wondered if she was just reading too much into the lilim lead. Was she just falling into confirmation bias, looking for the traits that fit, ignoring any that didn't? She took a break from her reading to grab her phone to Google something, and her heart leapt when she saw new texts from Luc and two missed calls.

Are you sleeping in again today? I can't imagine Bo would allow that two days in a row.

Are you ignoring me? You wound me, love. I miss you.

Walking into battle soon. Would love to hear from you. I could die, you know.

Hello? Please? Something? Anything? You're killing me.

She realized she was smiling as she read through his texts, and she wiped it from her face. She looked at the time on her phone. It was almost noon. The raid would be going down soon. Luc was probably already in Tulsa.

She relented and texted him back.

Sorry. Don't you dare die, or I'll kill you.

She waited, but there was no reply. She decided to call him back, but it rang once and went straight to voicemail. Had he ignored her call?

Maybe she'd pushed him too far this time. Ignored him too long. She felt a hand squeeze around her heart, and it pissed her off. It was his hand, and it didn't belong there.

She noticed a notification dot on the group chat on the app Bo had downloaded onto her phone. She opened it and read through the updates posted throughout the morning.

Cassie had posted that they were in Tulsa, waiting for the other two teams to catch up. Levi had indicated that he could no longer see the mansion when he tried to remotely view it – it was like it had completely disappeared from existence. Zephlyn said that Ruth had likely cloaked it from him. There was no way she could teleport an entire mansion to another location. Luc popped into the chat to say that he had eyes on the mansion, confirming Zephlyn's conjecture. He went on to say that the grounds were quiet. Too quiet. The most recent message was from ten minutes prior, and it was Cassie, saying that Team Beta had arrived, and since Team Delta had been caught in a traffic jam and were way behind schedule, they were going in without them.

It had been silent ever since.

Eve couldn't concentrate on her studies anymore. She found Eoduun and told him about the updates in the group chat, and said she wanted to break for lunch. She had no appetite, but she was going to be useless until more news came in. Her anxiety was making her fingers numb and her scalp tingle.

As she and Eoduun walked back to the complex, she tried to conjure some kind of premonition. She desperately wanted to know what was happening, what was going to happen, but all she had was an ache in her chest from the anxiety.

When they walked up to the complex, Zeke and Bo were walking in from the training grounds.

Bo gave her a single glance and deduced, "You're uneasy."

"Have you seen the chat?" she asked.

He nodded. "I've been in contact with Luc, too. All we can do is wait and have confidence everything will go smoothly."

"Sorry, I'm a little short on confidence," she admitted.

Zeke drew near to her and put his heavy arm around her shoulder. "They have some of the strongest members of Knighco with them. They'll be fine," he assured her. "And they'll get Ruth, and then this will all be over. We can go back to hunting."

They all ended up back at Eve's apartment. "I need to go grocery shopping," Eve lamented as she looked in her fridge. "I hate shopping."

"I'll go with you," Zeke offered. "I need some things, too. We can go this evening."

"I need to go, too," Eoduun chimed in. "I'm out of eggs and pickles."

"What a coincidence, I'm out of pickles, too," Eve said sarcastically. "Which is funny, because I don't remember eating any."

"See? You didn't have to worry about me sticking my fingers in the jar after all."

Eve put together a hodgepodge lunch for herself while Bo ate an apple and Zeke and Eoduun scavenged the cupboards.

Bo's phone rang. He answered, then put it on speaker. It was Luc. Everyone leaned in around Bo's phone on the kitchen island.

"She's not here," Luc said in frustration. Even frustrated, Eve was warmed by his voice. The anxiety in her chest melted away. "She's been gone some time. She must've run as soon as she detected Levi. There was a sigil under a rug in one of the rooms, similar to the one in the bathroom at the club, and that's probably what she used to escape. We have no idea where it leads or even how to find out where it leads. She could be next door or in Timbuktu."

"What about her monster servants?" Zeke asked.

"She left them to ambush us. Ruger got bit and Cass broke her leg. I'm sending them home with Remi and Mira on the jet shortly, but Eve's going to have to be ready to heal Ruger as soon as he gets there. Mira gave him an antidote and a sedative, but he's not responding to it as well as he should be. These monsters were damn near alpha-grade."

"Any sign of the grimoire?" Bo asked.

"None. I'm waiting for Zephlyn to get here to see if he can work his mojo and get something for us. Something of her intentions or where she's going. Fuck, I'd take anything. I'm tired of this shit."

"Are you going to zap back home for a bit?" Bo inquired.

"Why, is Eve anxious to see me?" There was a smile in his voice.

"You wish," Eve replied.

"Well, hello, love," Luc crooned. His voice lost all of its frustration and became warm and sugary. "I'm sorry I missed your call earlier. I was a little occupied."

"Is there anything I need to know about healing Ruger? I've never had to deal with someone who is infected." She tried to keep it professional. She was embarrassed with everyone listening in like this.

"Straight to business, hm? Like an icepick, love." He sighed. "He was bitten by what seemed to be a vamp, but...not quite. It may have been a hybrid of some sort. But Bo knows the procedure. We have dental guards to protect you from being bitten by him when he's drinking. Even though you can't be infected, we still don't like to tempt the Fates. They'll fuck you right up the ass every chance they get."

"Poetic," she retorted.

"I'm going to finish up here, but I'm not sure how long it's going to take. I may be home tonight, or I may be home tomorrow morning. Either way, I'll be home soon, and we can regroup and strategize."

As soon as the call ended, Eve's phone rang. Luc. She answered and went to her bedroom to talk in private.

"You don't need to hide your admiration for me in front of your comrades," Luc teased.

"It certainly doesn't stop you."

"From showing my admiration for you? Or myself? Well…I suppose it's true, either way. And why should I hide it?"

"Everyone thinks I'm your girlfriend," she griped.

"I'm not seeing a downside."

"I'm not your girlfriend."

"You will be," he said confidently. "You can only resist me for so long."

"You're incorrigible."

"I'm a man of wealth and taste, love."

She paused. She recognized that line from a Rolling Stones song. "Are you saying you're the devil?"

"When it comes to you, absolutely. Have some sympathy for me."

"What do you want, Luc?" she asked in feigned exasperation.

"You."

"I mean what do you want right now?"

"You on my cock."

"Luc!" His lewd words painted a picture in her mind and made her core throb for him.

He laughed boisterously. "I'm sorry, did I offend your delicate sensibilities? My apologies, my lady. But it so happens to be true."

"Why are you *calling* me?" she clarified.

"You've been avoiding me today. Why?"

"I figured you'd be busy."

"I'm never too busy for you. You are my top priority."

"Then why did you take Mira with you and not me?" Oh fuck. Why did she say that? What the fuck, Eve? "No, wait, that's not…that came out wrong. That's not how I meant that. I was just wondering why Mira was allowed to help out but I wasn't."

"I needed her assistance. She's on the corporate board and handles a lot for me."

"Oh. Ok. Just wondered." Which meant she spent a lot of time with Luc. This wasn't a special circumstance. He relied on her. She would forever be glued to his side.

"I'm not fucking her anymore, if that's what you're worried about."

Anymore.

"It's none of my business who you fuck."

"I'd like for it to be your business. God, why are you fighting me so hard? I know you like me. I know you miss me, you want me home, you think about me, and you're jealous of other women around me. So why can't you just *be with me*?"

That was an easy one. "Because I don't trust you, Luc."

"I already told you, I'm not fucking Mira."

"That's not what I mean. I have no right to care about that. I mean, shit, I'm fucking other people, Luc."

"I'm well aware. But it doesn't mean that *I* am." His voice was stone cold. "And whether you have a *right* to care about it or not doesn't mean you *don't* care about it. I know you do. And you know what? I *like* that you're jealous. I *like* that you don't want me to be with anyone else. It means you want me for yourself, and that's a step in the right direction, love."

"You scare the hell out of me, Luc," she confessed softly. That was probably the most honest thing she'd ever said to him.

"Good," he said in a smiling voice. "Now you know how I feel."

"No. That's the problem. I have no idea how you feel. You can tell me you love me until you're blue in the face, but it all feels like a game with you. Like you're about to pull the rug out from under me at any moment. It doesn't feel like a safe place to be, standing on that rug. So, I won't."

"You will."

"Stop saying that," she complained.

"You already love me," he observed bluntly.

"Fuck you, I do not! Goodbye, Luc." She hung up the phone in a panic. She didn't love him. She didn't love him. She didn't love him.

She didn't love him.

What an arrogant jerk.

Oh, shit. She forgot the team was still there. But the kitchen was dead silent. Had they left?

She walked out of her bedroom, and Eoduun and Zeke started talking at the same time, like they were engaged in a fascinating conversation.

They'd heard everything. Fantastic.

Eve joined them in the kitchen to finish her lunch. She sat next to Bo in her usual spot while the boys leaned their elbows on the counter. She really needed two more barstools.

Bo's phone went off, and he looked down at it. He stared at it hard for several moments.

"Something wrong?" Eve asked him.

His head shot up. "Hm? No. Nothing's wrong. Luc says he is sending a…um," he glanced over at Zeke and Eoduun talking to each other, then continued quietly, "a *dreamcatcher* for you, with Team Flannel."

"Oh."

"Yep." He set his phone face-down on the counter and rested his chin in his hand. Did he look disappointed?

Eve glanced across the counter at Eoduun and remembered that she was going to talk to Luc about her newfound mind-reading power. She pulled out her phone and texted Luc.

Eoduun helped me find a weird new skill today. I will need to speak to you about it later.

The response was immediate: *Trying to make me jealous?*

She rolled her eyes internally. *It's a mind thing. But don't say anything to Bo about it. He didn't approve the method. I don't want him to yell at me.*

He was quick to respond again: *My lips are sealed. And don't worry, I'll gladly punish you myself. I wouldn't dream of leaving that to him.*

She pursed her lips and left the conversation at that.

When Ruger, Cassie, and Remi arrived later that afternoon to the bunker under the apartment complex, Mira wasn't with them. Eve took one look at Ruger and knew he wasn't himself. His eyes were hungry. Starving. Deranged. He was bound, muzzled, and half-sedated, but still seemed in full command of his senses. It reminded her of that scene in *Silence of the Lambs* when Hannibal is wheeled in on the dolly. Eve was on edge. She didn't want to get close to him, but she had to. If she didn't heal him before the change was complete, he'd be like this forever, and they would have to kill him.

She couldn't even imagine having to do that to a friend.

Then again, being Ruger, would he stay dead? She hoped they wouldn't have to find out.

Zeke and Eoduun flanked Eve while Remi and Kai muscled Ruger toward the chair he was to be strapped into. Bo stood alongside the chair, ready to tie him down as soon as he was seated.

As Ruger was led past Eve, his eyes flashed in her direction, and he growled menacingly. A wild look contorted his features, and he went completely rabid. He hulked out, snapping free of his restraints as though they were made of silly string, and in a flash of supernatural speed, he lunged at Eve.

In the blink of an eye, Ruger had crossed the room and was standing inches from Eve's face. But just as quickly, Zeke's hand flew out and caught Ruger by the neck, lifting his feet from the ground while Ruger clawed frantically at his hand.

Chaos ensued. There was a mad rush to contain Ruger and free him from the hand that gripped his throat.

"Don't kill him, Dagon!" Remi threatened, pulling at Zeke's arm.

Not Zeke. Dagon. Eve looked over at raging red eyes.

"He could've killed her, and you pathetic pissants almost let it happen! And you want me to let him *live*?!" Dagon roared.

"Zeke, get him under control!" Bo commanded.

"I will not be subdued!" Dagon snarled viciously. There was an obvious internal struggle happening, and finally, Zeke was able to take control enough to shove Ruger into the chair so he could be tied down. Once Ruger no longer posed a threat, Dagon calmed down, and Zeke was able to rein him in.

Mostly. His eyes flashed vermilion once more as he looked at Eve. "Don't heal him. Kill him," Dagon seethed. Then Zeke pushed him down and his eyes returned to brown.

She couldn't kill Ruger. It wasn't Ruger that had attacked her. It was the monster, and she had the power to eradicate it from his system. If she could save him, it was her duty to do so. She was shaken, but she was building her resolve.

Wearing the kind of Kevlar reinforced gloves that animal handlers use, Bo forced a protective guard into Ruger's mouth. He then gestured for Eve to come to him.

"It's ok. You're safe. It'll only take a minute," Bo assured her.

Eve nodded and stepped forward. As she extended her arm for Bo to make the cut, Ruger's wild eyes focused on her, rattling her composure. Then she felt a strong presence at her back, and a reassuring hand rested on her shoulder. Bo's eyes shifted to the man behind her.

"Dagon, we have this under control," Bo said levelly.

"Yeah, sure you do," Dagon doubted.

Bo made the cut, and guided Eve's arm to Ruger's mouth. Dagon stood over her and placed a hand on Ruger's forehead and one on his jaw as an extra measure to prevent him from biting down on Eve's arm. Bo kept his hands on her arm, ready to yank her away if he needed to.

Blood trickled into Ruger's mouth, and at first, he drank ravenously. But after a few moments, he started to calm down, and the next time his eyes rose to meet Eve's, it was all Ruger. No more monster. Well, aside from the surge of lust she saw.

But this was strange. She was mildly aroused as he drank, but it was nothing like when her team or Luc or Dagon drank from her. It was a difference in magnitude comparable to a banana pepper vs a Carolina Reaper. What did that mean?

She looked over at Bo as he pulled her arm from Ruger's mouth.

"That didn't feel right," she said to Bo as Remi was taking the guard from Ruger's teeth.

"Sure felt all right to me," Ruger said with a wink. Remi was quick to slap him upside the head.

Bo eyed her inquisitively. "Elaborate."

Before she could answer, Dagon snatched up her arm and put it to his lips, drinking deeply. He groaned, and a pulsing desire rushed through Eve's core. Her knees weakened, and she clung to Dagon for support.

That was more like it.

"Hey!" Bo barked, grabbing at Eve's arm.

Dagon released her, licking his lips appreciatively. "Felt all right to me, too," he purred.

His eyes quickly turned caramel brown. "Sorry!" Zeke apologized. "He's being a real fucking bugger!"

Bo looked down at Eve. "Are you good? You still have to heal Cassie. She's in the infirmary on a shit-ton of painkillers."

Eve nodded and followed him to the infirmary, a few doors down. She healed Cassie from the same open wound on her arm that healed Ruger, and this time, she felt next to nothing in terms of arousal. What was going on? Cassie was healing, so it wasn't that the blood wasn't working. Eve just wasn't producing the same levels of aphrodisiac for Team Flannel.

Not that she was complaining about that, as it could've made things rather awkward, but it was odd.

Once Cassie was healed, Eve took Bo aside. "Can you do me a favor?"

"What is it?"

She held her arm up in front of his mask. "Drink."

His dark eye shifted to a wolfish-yellow as the scent of her blood overwhelmed his senses. He shoved her arm away. "Don't tempt me like that, Evie," he warned.

"Please. I need to know."

"Need to know what?"

"Just a small drink. Please." She raised her arm to his face again.

"Don't do this to me," Bo pleaded. His eyes weren't on hers anymore, though. He couldn't stop staring at her bloody wound with that predatory gaze. "It's fucking cruel."

"I just want to see how it feels," she defended.

"You know how it feels!" he growled. His hands were now on her elbow and wrist, and he drew her arm closer to his face and inhaled deeply. He visibly trembled, like a thrill had run down his spine. "Oh, god. Please don't do this here. Get away from me while you still can. Please."

"…Bo…?" Eve asked, arousal and fear both rising.

His dramatically mismatched eyes slid slowly up from her arm to meet her eyes. "Now." There was something positively beastly in that expression, and it was mesmerizing. He'd never looked so goddamn hot and dangerous.

But he was saying no. He didn't want this, even if his body did. She reluctantly withdrew her arm from his grasp, and he exhaled with relief. His eyes followed her arm with regret, though.

"I think that answers my question anyway," Eve said.

"It's gotten even more potent," Bo remarked. "I can *smell* the aphrodisiac in it."

"Then why did it barely affect Ruger and Cassie? Or me? I was just wondering if the opposite was true."

"And how did it affect Dagon?"

"...Dagon was normal. Powerful response. But that's why I wanted to see what it felt like with you."

Bo looked over Eve's shoulder at the crew around the corner. "Just be glad you didn't try that when we were alone, and that I had my mask up to help dull my sense of smell. You have no idea the way just the *scent* of your blood affects me."

She looked at his eyes. The wolf-eye was still visible. "I have a sense of it."

He scoffed incredulously. "No, you don't. Not a fucking clue." He crossed his arms. "I don't know why it didn't affect Cassie and Ruger to the same extent. There's a lot I don't understand about your brand of Panacea Blood. You're a bit of an enigma."

"Are you saying I'm weird?"

He chuckled. "Yeah, I guess."

32

Crush Him Between Her Teeth

Before heading back to her apartment, Remi gave Eve a little burlap baggie tied with twine, bearing strange symbols on it. It was filled with what felt like potpourri and bird or rodent bones. He told her not to open the bag. He said Luc's instructions were to put a bowl of water under her bed, and place the bag in it, and leave it there. Refill the water as necessary, but never replace it. He then asked Eve what the witchcraft was for.

"Bad dreams," she replied simply.

That evening, Zeke was banned from hanging out with Eve. Bo didn't like how easily Dagon had overpowered him earlier, and he didn't want them left alone together. Zeke understood, but Eve was a little annoyed. Their grocery shopping plans had to be put on hold, and she was really looking forward to getting some more snacks. Eoduun of course chose to go hang out with Zeke, and Bo had to debrief Team Flannel, which left Eve alone for the evening. She hadn't been left to entertain herself in a while.

She pulled out her phone and stared at her last text exchange with Luc.

She typed: *Are you busy?*

Her phone rang a few minutes later.

"Good evening, love," Luc greeted her. "Did you get Ruger and Cassie all juiced up?"

"Yeah. They've been mended. But, damn, it's been a weird day," she said. She told him about what happened with Eoduun in the library, and then about the way her sexual response changed when healing Cassie and Ruger, but how it was still a strong response for Dagon, and how Bo reacted when she tried to get him to drink.

"Strange. But why the fuck was Dagon out?" he demanded.

"He stopped Ruger from attacking me. It happened so fast, I don't think anybody saw it coming but him."

"He saved you," Luc paraphrased. "So, it was kind of like the time Ruth attacked you, and he protected you."

"Yeah, I guess."

"And Zeke didn't have any control over him?"

"They were doing a lot of struggling, but after Ruger was healed and Dagon got his blood, Zeke took over again."

"Hm."

"You sound like your brother. 'Hm.'"

"Rude. Can I assume you've been separated from Zeke and Dagon for the night?" Before Eve could answer, he said, "Of course you have. Bo wouldn't risk it."

"Forget about Dagon. I'm more concerned with why my blood is changing and why I can read minds."

"The mind-reading could be related to your clairvoyance. Psychic abilities are all legs of the same animal. But it is rather unusual that you displaced Eoduun from his own mind. Even he can't do that, and he's one of the best erasers I've ever seen. That sounds more like a precursor for puppeteering and possession."

"That sounds a little scary," Eve said.

"In the enemy's hands, yeah. In ours? Fucking awesome. We've never had someone who could actually do that. We'll have to explore it some more."

"Eoduun won't let me do it again."

"I could work with you, and maybe Zephlyn, too. Eoduun can assist without participating. We'll figure something out. We can't waste it. Damn, love, you are so much more interesting than I ever could have hoped for," Luc said proudly.

"What about the blood?"

"What about it? It still healed everyone, didn't it?"

"Yeah, but…" She hesitated, and Luc waited for her to finish her thought. "…It just bothers me."

"Did you *want* to turn on Ruger and Cassie?" Luc asked.

"No!"

"Well, there you go. Maybe you're subconsciously controlling it."

"But that would mean that I *do* want to turn on you and Dagon and the whole team."

"Maybe, subconsciously, you do. Not such a stretch, is it?" Luc offered.

He was so flippant about all of it that she was left feeling a little foolish for being so worked up. Then again, he had no idea that Zephlyn had filled her head with doubts about her humanity. But she couldn't tell him. Not until she knew for sure. Even if she did try to tell him, he would just brush it off, anyway, like everyone else. *You can't be a monster.*

"So, let's get down to business," Luc said seriously. Then followed with, "What are you wearing?"

Eve rolled her eyes, then grinned. "Big ol' granny panties."

"Ooh, sexy. Are they all saggy and grungy?"

Eve laughed. "So saggy and grungy."

"What color are they?"

"I don't even remember. I think they were white once, but they're more of a dingy gray color now."

"Damn, love. You really know how to get my motor running. Rips?"

"So many rips and holes. There's a long strip of elastic at the top that's completely ripped from the fabric. I bet I can fit three fingers through it."

"Ooh, *three* fingers? You sure paint a picture. Such a seductress."

"It's an art."

Luc sighed. "I can't wait to see you. You'd better clear your schedule for tomorrow."

Eve talked to Luc for a long time, but she could hear people in the background trying to talk to him and get his attention. He was needed elsewhere, but he wouldn't let anyone pull him from his conversation with her. She was going to have to let him go first.

"I've monopolized enough of your time," Eve said. "I'll let you get back to business. The sooner you finish up, the sooner you can come home."

"You're anxious to see me," he perceived.

"I didn't say that."

"You don't need to. I already know."

"You're awfully full of yourself."

"And I can't wait until you're full of myself," he teased lewdly.

Butterfly wings tickled the inside of her belly as she pictured him on top of her, filling her with his hard length.

"Goodnight, Luc," she said with resignation.

"Goodnight, love," he replied cheerfully.

That night, Eve set up her little witchcraft bag as she was instructed, then climbed into her cold, lonely bed. She lay her head on the pillow and pulled her covers up around her. Bo's scent still faintly clung to her sheets and surrounded her, amplifying her loneliness. She wished he was here. She was used to being alone before she came here, so how had she already grown so dependent on the people around her for company and companionship? Why did she hate being alone so much now?

Or was it not necessarily that she hated being alone, but rather that she was lonesome *for* these people she'd grown attached to? Because the more she thought about it, not just anyone would do. She'd rather be alone right now than spend the evening with another team. Well, except for Team Flannel, but they'd had a long day and she didn't want to bother them.

Just as she was considering going out to the couch to watch tv until she fell asleep, she heard the deadbolt on the front door twist open, and someone entered. It couldn't be Bo. He would've just passed through the door without bothering with the lock.

"Oh, priiincessssss," Dagon sang quietly as his footsteps approached her bedroom. His shirtless shadow appeared in the doorway, dark and looming. He rested his forearm on the door frame. "I've come for what I'm due. A deal's a deal."

"This isn't a dream, is it? Is this real?" she asked. Maybe Luc's dreamcatcher wasn't working.

Dagon sauntered to her bedside and looked down at her, his vermilion eyes glimmering in the darkness. "You better fucking believe it." He reached one tattooed arm down and threw her bedcovers off her.

She sat up, but she didn't retreat from him. She had agreed to this, after all.

"I've been looking forward to this all day," Dagon said. He climbed onto the bed, his gym shorts exposing his muscular thighs and calves flexing appealingly with his movements. He sat back on his ankles in front of Eve and stared at her intensely, his head tilted slightly, a wide grin on his face. "I know exactly where I want to drink from."

Eve reached over to her bedside stand to retrieve the knife she stored there, but when she held it out to Dagon, he laughed.

"I don't need that." He crawled over top of her and grabbed the knife from her hand, returning it to the nightstand. "I have teeth."

"I didn't say you could bite me!"

"You didn't say I couldn't, either. That's how I want it."

"No. No way. I'm not letting you take a chunk out of me."

"I won't take a chunk. Just a little love bite."

"No! No. Knife, or deal's off."

Dagon narrowed his eyes at her. After a long deliberation, he relented. "Fine. Then take your underwear off."

She looked down at her underwear and t-shirt. "You never said I would have to get naked."

"I'm still not saying that. Just take your underwear off."

"Why?!"

Instead of answering, Dagon hooked his fingers in her panties and yanked them down.

"Hey!" She clawed for her underwear, but he was too quick. They were on the floor, and she was exposed. She pressed her knees together. "I didn't agree to this!"

"Shhh," he hushed her, a finger to his lips. "You wouldn't want to wake Bo up, would you? What would he think if he came in here and saw us?"

"You're changing all the rules!" she whispered angrily.

"You didn't put down any such rules. You agreed to let me drink from anywhere on your body. I want to drink…" Dagon ran a finger up her inner thigh and let it come to a stop in the dip between her pelvis and thigh, "…from there."

Eve flinched under his finger. She was horribly ticklish in that spot, and he was going to cut her there and have his mouth there? And all it would take was one slip of his tongue to unravel her. He'd planned it like this. She should've known he would. Maybe she did.

She clenched her teeth and squirmed away from his touch. "I'm ticklish there. I can't be held responsible if I hit you when you put your mouth there."

"Oh, I can take care of that." Dagon held his hand out, and without even touching her, Eve's body suddenly slid down into a supine position beneath him, and she felt an immense, invisible weight pushing her hands into the pillow over her head.

Adrenaline surged through her body. She didn't know he could do something like that. In dreams, maybe, but not for real. She was only just realizing how much he had been holding back with her – how entirely powerless she had been against him all this time.

She looked up at his dangerous eyes and muscular, tattooed torso looming over her. He was clearly pleased with the surprised expression on her face.

"You've underestimated me," he noted, smiling. "You really thought you could hold your own against me," he chuckled. "It was really quite adorable, and I couldn't help but play along. But I'm not playing anymore. I've waited long enough."

There was that familiar stirring of conflicting emotions that Dagon always aroused in her. Fear. Anticipation. Excitement. Disgust. Shame. Lust. Her body wanted him so badly, but her mind loathed him. He did awful things. He was manipulative. He was capricious. He was selfish. He was dangerous. Deadly.

And devastatingly, infuriatingly sexy.

"Don't," she protested weakly.

He raised a brow. "Don't what? I haven't done anything yet."

"Don't rape me."

He scoffed. "Princess, if I was going to do something like that, I would've done it the first night. Besides, I don't need to rape you. You'll be begging me for it before I've finished drinking from you. And if you're lucky, I just might oblige," he said arrogantly. He retrieved the knife from the bedside stand and held it in front of her face. "So, are you ready?"

"You swear you'll honestly answer one question after you get my blood?"

"We made a deal, didn't we? I crossed my heart and hoped to die, remember? I'd really rather not stick a needle in my eye."

"Fine. Just do it, then," she consented.

Dagon grinned eagerly. He touched the tip of the blade gently to the skin on her throat, then delicately traced a long, tingling trail from her neck to her bellybutton with it. He laid he blade flat against her belly and stared at it, watching it jump with each quick beat of her pulse.

"Nervous? Or turned on?" he wanted to know, his scarlet eyes looking up from the blade to meet hers.

"What the fuck do you think?" she spat.

"Both."

He continued teasing her skin with the tip of the blade as he dragged it down to the hollow between her pelvis and thigh. She twitched and bit her lip as she tried to fight the tickling sensation. He turned the blade vertically, only inches from her sex, and pressed the point into her skin. She hissed at the stinging pain.

The sting was dulled as Dagon's tongue lapped fervently over the skin he'd just sliced. Her stomach clenched against the overstimulation of her nerves in the spot he'd chosen, and she didn't know whether to laugh, cry, or moan. The sound that came from her throat was a strange hybrid of the three.

Dagon gripped each of her thighs with his hands as he sucked and licked the wound erotically, like he was pleasuring her injury with his tongue. As he drank, Eve was aware of a desperate, growing heat inside of her. If her hands were free, it was possible they might have found their way to Dagon's hair. It was possible she might have urged him to venture just a little to the right with those undulations of his tongue. Very, very possible.

Oh, god, she wanted that tongue between her legs so damn badly. She *needed* it. Her body *screamed* for it. Her back arched off the bed as her hips swiveled, trying to encourage his tongue to wander into her aching heat. She began to whimper pleadingly.

"Dagon..."

He moaned at the sound of his name on her lips, and his teeth sank into her flesh as he drank. She gasped and cried out at the acute sensation of oddly sweet torture, but Dagon's hand flew up and clamped over her mouth, muffling her cries.

Her frustration grew the longer he drank. Her hands were still being held down by whatever invisible force he commanded, but she

340

was aching to get her fingers in his hair. She wanted to touch him, to dig her fingers into his flesh, to *feel* him. As soon as his hand slid down to grip around her neck, freeing her mouth to speak, she begged, "Fuck me with your tongue."

Dagon finally lifted his head from her cut, gazing at her from under his brows. He tightened his fingers around her neck.

"And if I say no?" he inquired.

"You don't want to say no," she stated boldly. "So just do it."

His deep laugh shook his whole frame. With his hand still around her neck, he leaned forward, his body shifting over hers, and he brought his lips close to her ear. His scent surrounded her, eliminating any lingering echoes of Bo's. He smelled differently than Zeke did, but only the undertones. He still had that clean, pine-citrus scent, but there was a deeper trace of something that reminded her of a cool, salty ocean breeze.

The tip of his tongue traced the outer ridge of her ear, and he whispered, "Make me."

She wrapped her powerful legs around his waist and clenched her thighs. She'd intended to pull him down to her, but he didn't budge. Instead, she ended up lifting her lower body off the bed, pressing her bare heat up against the hard cock straining behind his shorts. She fought the pressure on her wrists, but it was still unrelenting. God, she wanted to touch him. She wanted to feel his power. And she wanted to conquer it.

"I thought you weren't playing anymore," Eve taunted. "Or maybe you're all talk?"

Dagon chuckled behind closed lips near her ear, then lifted his head to look down at her. Embers flared in his eyes as he grinned at her. "A whole different animal," he mused. "You were begging me not to rape you just a few minutes ago. Now you're threatening to rape me."

She was growing impatient. "All talk, then?"

His hand squeezed her neck threateningly, and he thrust his hips against her. He leaned down, his face close to hers again. "Or maybe

I'm just not sure how much power you should have just yet," he answered.

She didn't understand what he meant. "Are you insinuating that I can't handle you?"

"Oh, I have no doubt you can handle me, princess. That's not what I'm talking about."

Eve rolled her hips, grinding herself against Dagon's rock-hard erection. "God, just fuck me already," she begged.

His cock throbbed against her, and a low groan rumbled in his throat. "I think I like you begging. Do it some more."

"Fuck me, Dagon."

He grinned.

Eve lifted her head off the pillow to kiss those full lips that were so tantalizingly close to hers. The hand on her throat loosened its grip, and Dagon's thumb traced lightly over her jawline as he deepened the kiss, pressing her head back down against the pillow. He lowered his hips down so that her back was pressing into the mattress again, and he began to slowly grind his hardness against her.

His lips left hers so he could pull her shirt off over her head. He trailed hot kisses down her neck to the hollow between her collarbones. He licked the little dip, then skimmed the tip of his tongue down to her breast. He took her breasts in his hands and laved one nipple with his soft, hot tongue, then took it into his mouth and sucked on it. He shifted his attention to the other peak, and as he licked at sucked at it, he paused. His eyes slid up to meet hers, and a wicked grin spread across his lips. His eyes still capturing hers, he took the soft peak into his mouth and clamped his teeth down.

She gasped and arched her back, and for a brief moment, her hands lifted from the pillow above her head.

Dagon's eyes widened when he saw it happen, and her hands were again forced back down onto the pillow. He lifted his head and looked at her with a strange mix of amusement and uncertainty.

"Interesting," he said vaguely before dipping his head back down. He returned his mouth to the cut that was still bleeding lightly in the juncture of her thigh and pelvis, his tongue swirling over the blood that had collected there. This time, however, he didn't linger there. When Eve whimpered and rolled her hips impatiently, he allowed her to shift herself into his mouth.

When his hot tongue finally touched her eager, awaiting petals, she gasped and mewled. He thrust his tongue inside of her, the heat of his mouth only fueling the fire growing in her belly. He moved his attention up to the sensitive nub at the apex of her sex, his fingers teasing her petals open, and her legs trembled with every undulation of his tongue. She began to gasp for air as the coil in her core wound tighter and tighter, and just as it was about to snap, Dagon stopped, grinning mischievously at her. He knew how close she was.

"Dagon!" she cried, and her hands suddenly broke free from their invisible restraints. She plunged her fingers into his hair and pushed his face back down to her core.

Dagon's fingers dug into her thighs as he moaned against her mound, vocally appreciative of the power of her desire for him. She rocked her hips against his tongue, and within seconds, she found the release she sought. Her body exploded in a surge of euphoric bliss, and she came hard. Dagon groaned and sucked at her juices as she crested and rode the wave of ecstasy.

He didn't wait for her to finish coming down before he lowered his shorts and mounted her. She was so slick with his saliva and her own juices that the only resistance he was met with was the tightness of her swollen, aroused core as he slid his hard length inside of her. She moaned as he filled her, his hips pressing into hers.

She clung to him, molding her body to his large, solid frame. His chest rubbed against hers as he thrust into her repeatedly, one hand gripping her thigh, the other fisted painfully in her hair. The way he was fucking her felt desperate. Insatiable. Urgent. Animalistic. She responded in kind, her nails clawing into his back as she held onto him and met him thrust for thrust.

The more he gave her, the more she wanted to take. She wanted to own him. To conquer him. To ruin him. She'd never felt like this with anyone else, and it was both empowering and troubling. Her passion wasn't fueled by love; it was fueled by rage. Hatred. She wanted to destroy him, to take everything he had, to wring him dry. She wanted to crush him between her teeth.

She thrust her hip up and rolled him onto his back, rolling with him and coming to a stop on top of him, his cock still inside of her. He looked up at her in surprise, but the shocked expression was quickly replaced with burning desire. He grabbed her by the hair at the nape of her neck and dragged her down to him, their lips crushing together in a fiery kiss. She moaned into his mouth as her hands snaked around his throat and her hips gyrated against his.

The ache in her core was growing again, tightening, and Dagon's cock was hitting all the right places in her position on top of him. She could tell by the way he swelled and throbbed inside of her that he was close to spilling over.

"Not just yet," he panted against her lips. "Wait." He tried to slow her pace with a hand on her hip.

"No," she refused. She slid her hands from his neck and ran them down his arms. She interlaced her fingers in his and slammed them down onto the mattress with surprising ease. Was he letting her do this?

She was overcome by a surge of violent energy, like he'd just injected her with adrenaline. She squeezed his hands and brought her mouth to the side of his neck. She could feel his pulse against her tongue as she licked the salty sweat on the tender skin below his gill slits. The roots of her teeth suddenly itched, and before she realized what she was doing, she bit him. Hard.

It took everything in her willpower to stop herself from ripping his throat out.

He grunted and thrust his hips up into her, and she felt him throb and spasm inside of her as he came. Feeling him lose himself in his pleasure gave her the last little push she needed to nudge her over the edge into a wild, rage-filled orgasm, and she rolled her hips with his as they finished and came down together.

She panted against his neck, her head resting on his chest and shoulder. Now that the moment was over, her strange desire for violence and dominance dissipated. She wondered what had come over her. "I didn't mean to bite you," she whispered.

"It's quite all right, princess," he replied breathlessly. "I bit you first."

Eve rolled off of Dagon, and he pulled his shorts back up. They lay next to each other, still catching their breath, and stared at each other.

"I feel like I licked a battery," Eve mused. She felt like she could take on an entire defensive line right then. Energized. Powerful.

"You did," Dagon said. He sat up, leaning his shoulders back against the headboard. "And you earned yourself an answer. Or did you already forget?"

Jesus, she almost had forgotten. And now that the moment was finally here, she hesitated. All she had to do was ask, and he would tell her. And whatever came out of his mouth could upend everything she thought was true.

Or nothing would change. He could just as easily say there was nothing special about her. That was equally possible, right?

She took a deep, calming breath, then looked him in the eyes. "Am I a monster? And I don't mean someone with a specialty, I mean something that the rest of the team would hunt."

Dagon raised an eyebrow and gave her a crooked, satisfied smile. "Yes."

Her stomach twisted, and her fingers and toes went numb. "What?!"

"Yes, you're a monster." His eyes gleamed with intrigue. "And I, for one, am fully supportive. Big fan."

She sat up and leaned toward him aggressively. "What the hell?! What kind of monster am I?!"

Dagon clicked his tongue. "Unh-unh. I said I'd answer *one* question, princess. I answered it."

Eve was frantic. "Are you fucking kidding me?!" she growled.

"Hey, you made the deal with me."

"You fucker. I'm not sorry I bit you," she hissed.

Dagon laughed. "I'm not sorry either. I liked it. I hope you do it again. Maybe I'll answer another question for you if you do."

Her hand shot out and gripped Dagon by the throat. "I wish I could squeeze the life out of you right now, you fucking asshole."

Dagon grabbed her hand, but as he tried to pull it from his throat, she squeezed tighter. The intrigue in his eyes grew. "What the fuck," he choked out.

Startled, she dropped her hand. Was she...*overpowering* him?

He laughed with surprised amusement. "Well, that's fun."

"I...I can *hurt* you right now?" she ventured.

"It would appear so."

Her hand returned to his throat. "Then tell me what I want to fucking know," she demanded as she squeezed.

"Or what, you'll kill Zeke?"

Fuck. She loosened her grip, but didn't drop her hand.

"Besides," he continued. "You don't want me dead. I'm the reason you're so strong right now."

Eve changed tactics. She softened her expression, and she cupped his face instead of trying to choke him. She climbed onto his lap and straddled him.

She leveled with him. "Do you even know what I am?"

His smug expression faltered. When he still didn't answer, Eve touched her lips to his and kissed him sweetly.

He kissed her back, his arms wrapping around her possessively.

She leaned back and searched his eyes. "Please, Dagon," she pleaded.

He narrowed his eyes, then sighed. "Not exactly. All I'll give you for free is this: you're *different*. Something both ancient *and* new. Familiar, yet foreign. But if you want more than that, you have to meet with me like this again."

"Do I get to keep this new power over you?"

"I guess we'll just have to see, won't we?"

Eve rolled off his lap and climbed off the bed. She got dressed back into her underwear and t-shirt, throwing on a pair of shorts this time. She stood next to the bed with her arms crossed as he swung his legs over the side and rose to his feet. He suddenly reached out and fisted his hand into the front of her oversized t-shirt, pulling her roughly against his chest, and kissed her.

"You and I were made for each other," he said softly, tucking her hair behind her ear. "Are you finally starting to realize that?"

"I think nothing of the sort," she denied, then pushed away from him.

"I'm the one who awakened you," he revealed.

She paused. "What does that mean?"

He grinned. "If you want to know, you know what you have to do." He turned and walked from the room. "I'll see you soon, princess. We'll chat then."

Goddamn him. *Goddamn him.* She stood there, alone, her head spinning. There was too much to sort through.

But one persistent thought kept throbbing in her brain, like a stubbed toe.

She was a monster.

TO BE CONTINUED

If you enjoyed *Eve's Monsters*, look for the next book in the
Abomination series:

Eve's Curse

Read on for a preview of the first chapter of *Eve's Curse*.

1
You're the Worst

She was a monster.

What did that even mean? And what had just happened with Dagon? That wasn't a casual romp in the sack - some kind of switch in her had been flipped. One minute, she feared him, and the next she was dominating him. Taunting him. Tempting him. Using him. She'd received more from him than simple carnal pleasure, but what was *it*, exactly? Power? Energy? Had he given it, or had she taken it? Was she stronger, or was he weaker? Or both? She *felt* stronger.

She had so many questions. How many could he even answer? Who else could she go to for answers? Everyone else assumed that she couldn't be a monster because she was a blood healer.

Everyone but Zephlyn.

Zephlyn knew something. Or suspected something. He was likely her best bet, other than Dagon. If she tried to get help from anyone else, there would be questions about how she'd gotten her information in the first place. Questions she didn't want to answer.

Or...*or*...she could put it under her hat and pretend everything was fine. She *could* do that. Right? Nothing was really *stopping* her from doing that, was it? Just a few days ago, she had no idea that the possibility that she could be a monster even existed. She could just go back to that. Besides, Dagon could be *lying*, couldn't he, just to keep her coming back to him? That was absolutely something he would do.

She wasn't a monster. Dagon was a liar. And Zephlyn never said she was a monster either, not definitively. He just said she was weird, and couldn't be a monster *unless*...

She wasn't a monster. She was Evrys Alarie, the girl with the rare Panacea Blood, which meant she couldn't be a monster.

Momentarily deluding herself into believing that nothing was wrong, Eve went to the bathroom. She grabbed a bandage for her cut, but when she pulled her shorts down to apply it, there was no wound to apply it to. Just a hint of a red line and two faint crescent marks from Dagon's teeth. That was the fastest she'd ever healed.

Luc had told her that the more she healed people, the faster she would heal, and she had given a lot of blood today.

After she used the toilet and washed her hands, she reached for the towel hanging on the wall. When she tried to yank it from the metal ring, the entire unit ripped from the wall.

"What the..." She stood there, holding the towel, the ring hanger lying on the countertop. The screws were still affixed through it, and there were two gaping holes in the wall where she'd ripped them out, anchors and all. She hadn't even pulled that hard, had she?

She pushed it to the corner of the counter. She'd have to fix it tomorrow. These things happen.

She went out to the kitchen for a midnight snack to settle her nerves. Her cupboards were growing bare, but she had enough cereal left for one bowl. As she reached in the fridge for the milk, she grabbed a bottle of unopened juice to move it out of the way, but stopped as she lifted it. It felt light.

Too light.

She pulled it from the fridge and looked at it. Did someone drink it all and put it back empty? She squeezed the container slightly, and immediately regretted it. The plastic crumpled and cracked, and juice splashed everywhere.

"Fuck!" She rushed the container to the sink as it continued to spill its contents. "What the fuck?! Cheap-ass plastic…" she complained, rinsing the juice from her hands.

She wiped up the juice all over the floor and countertops. As she stood over the sink, wringing juice out of the kitchen rag and rinsing it out, she glanced over at the juice bottle in the other well of the sink, and a silly thought flitted through her head. She held her hand out toward the bottle and imagined she could move it with an invisible force, like Dagon had done to her.

The crushed bottle rattled in the sink.

Eve dropped the rag in the sink and leapt back, fear coursing through her veins with icy prickles. Had Dagon done something to her? Or was this just some weird side-effect of sleeping with him, like her sudden power over him in bed? She was beginning to feel like a stranger in her own body.

She slowly returned to the sink and stared down at the crumpled jug. She held her hand out again, but this time, she clenched her fist and imagined she was Force-choking the juice bottle.

It crinkled. Only a little, but it crinkled. Her heart was in her throat.

"Holy shit. I'm a Jedi," she whispered.

But she didn't want to be a Jedi. She wanted to be Eve. This new power scared the hell out of her.

She grabbed the jug and threw it in the trash can, then rinsed out the rag in the sink and finished wiping down the counter and floor. She needed sleep. In the morning, maybe everything would be back to normal. If not, she could tackle this new problem with a fresh perspective and possibly go talk with Zephlyn when he returned.

…But did she trust Zephlyn with this? She barely knew the guy.

Eve climbed back into bed and cocooned herself in the covers. She buried her face in her pillow, inhaling the comforting scent of Bo that somehow managed to survive her and Dagon's horizontal antics. She could still smell sex and Dagon in her bedding, too, but she focused on Bo's warm flannel scent.

And thought of Luc.

Her insides warmed when she pictured him. Her belly tingled when she imagined being wrapped up in his big arms. She'd been aware of a dull, hollow ache behind her sternum since he left, and now that she knew he would be home soon, it had turned to a knot.

She hated how she longed for him.

Eve growled in frustration and rubbed her sternum. Why did emotions have to be so physical? The longer she tried to fall asleep, the more she tossed and turned. It was futile.

She climbed out of bed and went to her apartment door. She peeked her head out into the hallway. All was quiet. She quietly closed the door behind her and slipped down the hallway to the apartment two doors down. Eve knocked softly on the door.

She heard the latch flip and the knob turned.

"Evie," Bo greeted her with a questioning expression on his maskless face. He was shirtless, wearing only plaid boxers. His hair was tousled, and he had a pillow line on the side of his face. Her heart melted a little.

"I can't sleep," she confessed pathetically.

He scratched his head and stepped aside so she could enter his apartment. When she was inside and he'd closed the door, he asked, "Something you wanted to talk about?"

"No."

He stared at her uncomprehendingly.

"I don't want to sleep alone," she clarified.

"Ah. Ok," he replied simply. He gestured toward the bedroom, which was in the same location in his apartment as it was in hers.

As she followed him through the living room and past the kitchen in the dark, she wondered why his apartment had such an empty feeling. Their footsteps even echoed strangely. It was the exact same setup as hers, but it wasn't filled like hers.

"Why is your apartment so empty?"

"We don't normally spend much time here. And it's just me. I don't need a lot."

When she walked into his room, however, she saw a huge bookshelf that spanned an entire wall from floor to ceiling. The shelves were overflowing, but it didn't look like they were filled with normal books.

"Are those *all* manga?!" she gaped.

"Yeah, yeah, I have a problem, I know. Get in bed." He held the covers back and gestured for her to get in.

"Okie *doki-doki*," she punned, then giggled uncontrollably at her own joke as she climbed under the covers. She was already feeling more at ease.

"You're the worst," he complained as he slid into bed next to her.

She plopped her head onto his chest and threw her arm and leg over him. "Shut up, you love me," she chirped flippantly.

He grunted indifferently.

Curled up next to his solid, warm body, Eve melted into him with a contented sigh. Ah, that was the stuff.

Eve awoke in the morning as Bo was working to extract himself from the tangle of her limbs. She purposely gripped harder.

"Nooo," she grumbled.

"God, you're like a fucking octopus," he griped as he lifted her arm from his torso, only to have her snake her wrist free from his grip and cling to him again.

"I'm a kraken," she corrected.

"Whatever. Release me, kraken. I need to shower and go get coffee."

"Just make some," Eve suggested.

"It is made. At the coffee shop. I just need to go get it."

Eve groaned cantankerously and released Bo from her tentacles. She looked over at the clock after he climbed out of bed. It was only a little after 5AM. No wonder she was still so tired.

She rolled over and sat on the edge of the bed, dangling her legs over the side as she ran her hand through her messy pink locks. She watched Bo standing in front of his closet in his boxers, sorting through it for the typical tactical cargo pants and plain t-shirt or long-sleeved shirt he tended to favor.

With most of his body exposed to her, she was again struck by just how many scars he had. He was covered in them.

"Why are you so much more scarred up than everyone else?" Eve inquired.

"I've had a lot of injuries," he replied obtusely.

"Well, duh. I know why Luc isn't scarred like that, but Zeke and Eoduun aren't, either."

"By the time they're my age, they will be," Bo pointed out.

"And what age is that, exactly?" Eve wondered.

"Thirty-four," he answered. "I'm four years older than Luc." He then added, "And Zeke has more scars than you've probably noticed. Those binding tattoos hide a lot."

"Binding tattoos?" Eve echoed.

Bo turned and looked at her with his clothes draped over his arm. "Yeah. All that tribal-looking shit is Luc's handiwork. It's what keeps Dagon from completely obliterating Zeke as his vessel, like keeping a nuclear reactor encased in steel and concrete." He started toward the door, then looked back at her. "Are you going to hang out for a bit?"

Eve shook her head. "I'll scurry on back to my apartment," she said, making her fingers look like a running spider.

"I'll stop by when I get back," Bo said over his shoulder as he went into the bathroom. As he closed the door behind him, Eve's eye shifted to the bookshelf full of manga on the far wall. There were hundreds of them. She pushed to her feet and crossed the room. She selected a book at random and pulled it from the shelf, making note of where she took it from.

An austere man with dark hair and bright blue eyes looked contemptuously up from the cover, while a cute, pink-haired girl hung from his neck and grinned cheerfully with one oddly sharp tooth, holding a two-fingered peace-sign sideways over one eye while the other eye was squinted into a wink. Two little devil horns poked up through her hair.

She flipped it open, and immediately realized that these were not just comics. Definitely NSFW, and completely uncensored. Explicit. Smut. But it was kind of hot.

"Dirty boy, Bo," she said under her breath.

She wondered if they were all like that, but just as she was returning that one to the shelf, Bo opened the bathroom door and yelled out, "Stay out of my manga!"

"I think you mean *porn*," she called back.

"Evie!"

She grinned to herself. She may have to talk him into letting her borrow one. She could totally get into that.

On her way out of the apartment, she knocked on the bathroom door. "I'm heading out. See you in a while, Daddy. Doki-doki!"

She heard an exasperated sigh on the other side of the door, and it brought her deep satisfaction.

As Eve stepped out of Bo's apartment, she glanced up and saw Eoduun coming out of his apartment. Their eyes met, and they both froze.

Shit, this looks scandalous.

Eoduun gave her a once-over, and Eve knew that it was obvious she'd just climbed out of bed.

"Morning," she said cordially. "You're up early."

"I'm always up early. But you aren't."

She laughed uneasily. "Yeah, no, not usually."

"Is Bo up?" he asked.

"Uh, yeah. But he's in the shower. So..."

"Did you tell him about our brain swap?"

"No, I didn't want to piss him off. But I did tell Luc. He wants to explore it more," Eve said.

"Is Luc back yet?"

"I haven't heard from him yet." Shit. She left her phone in her apartment all night.

"So, uh, is this something I need to, like, pretend I didn't see?" Eoduun asked, pointing between Eve and Bo's apartment door.

"It's not like that," Eve insisted.

Eoduun nodded and raised a dubious brow. "Ok."

"It isn't!"

"I said ok!" He definitely didn't believe her.

She probably wouldn't either, if she were him.

Eve returned to her apartment and hopped in the shower. She wasn't sure why she was so defensive about being caught leaving Bo's apartment. It wasn't her honor or reputation she was afraid of being tarnished. Oddly enough, it was Bo's. Just because she was enjoying some sexual freedom didn't mean that he wanted to be part of it. In fact, he seemed to want to avoid it. She didn't want Eoduun or anyone else to think that Bo was just another casual fuck.

Bo was special. He wasn't the casual fuck kind, and she would fight to the death anyone who dared question his honor.

She giggled in amusement to herself as she rinsed the shampoo from her hair. She was imagining herself in a suit of armor, jousting Eoduun on horseback to defend Bo's honor. Bo was, of course, in a pretty white gown, cheering her on from the stands. She was sure she would earn his favor. Maybe he would give her his embroidered kerchief.

Yeah, she was fucking weird.